WHAT YOU CAN'T LOSE

MIKAYLA ROBBINS

Published by The Kayla Journal Press

ISBN 979-8-9987-7140-8

Book Cover Design by Carpe Librum Book Design

Edited and Proofread by Leah Taylor

Formatted by Mikayla Robbins

EARLY PRAISE

"*What You Can't Lose* is a story with grit and tenderness. Mikayla blends heavy topics and themes with a blossoming hope and love into a beautiful, seat-gripping tale."
    — HANNAH BETH, author of *The Groom Advertisement*

"This is one of those stories that stays with you for days and weeks after reading it. It's the kind of story that keeps you up at night as you ache to see the broken characters find healing in each other and find out what happens. *What You Can't Lose* is a masterpiece of tender love found in the worst of circumstances, melting prose and a touch of thrill. It's everything you want it to be and nothing like you expect!"
    — EVA CEDARLAND, author of *The Final Bloom*

"*What You Can't Lose* has a beautiful setting, a small-town charm, and a cast of characters that are unique, fearfully and wonderfully made, and filled with the kind of integrity one needs in a story like this one. Robbins always writes with care and grace, but she just keeps getting better and better. This book is my new favorite of hers and I am grateful for her decision to pursue the gift of writing

that the Lord has given her. Whether you're a lover of historical fiction, a Christian wanting to read a solid romance, or someone walking through any kind of fertility battle, this story is one you won't regret picking up."
— CHELSEY GORDON, author of *Echoes of Absence*

"Saddle up for an incredible journey to the Montana frontier! *What You Can't Lose* is a profound story of having faith even when it's hardest. Full of loss and love, impactful truths, nail-biting twists, and heart-warming romance, Robbins' latest work is sure to leave you turning pages late into the night."
— S.L. KLEIN, author of *Waves of Redemption*

"I've read all of Robbins' novels, and I can confidently say that it is the strongest one yet. This story is next to impossible to put down, and you'll be skipping your lunch breaks to read it. Every twist and turn will have you on the edge of your seat. Oh, and Travis is mighty handsome."
— E.P. KLOPP, author of the *Hope in Heartland* series

"Raw and heartfelt, What You Can't Lose draws you in from the very first page. With relatable characters, faith, and a deeply riveting plot, Robbins will have you on the edge of your seat until the very last page."
— FAITH R. MATHEWSON, author of *All the King's Horses*

"*What You Can't Lose* is a tender and honest delve into themes that are as harsh as the Montana winters: betrayal, loss, faith, and healing. This story will tug on your heart strings with its lovable and relatable cast of characters, and features a plot that will keep you eagerly turning the pages!"

— CAITLIN MILLER, award-winning author of *Our Yellow Tape Letters*

"From the Blue Ridge Mountains of North Carolina to the Rocky Mountains of Montana Territory, *What You Can't Lose* reflects the reality of life in the 1870s. I particularly enjoyed Robbins's careful attention to lay healing on the frontier, from injury and childbirth to the treatment of disease. Set amidst the upheaval brought by the Civil War and shifting cultural norms of the Reconstruction era, this novel does not shy away from hard truths but instead honors a woman's courage to protect her child in the face of domestic abuse and offers an alternative, Biblical example of what marriage should be: a covenant built on respect, honesty, and love."
— JEWEL CARRIE PARKER, Historian

"I couldn't imagine Mikayla Robbins could write a more compelling novel than her *Abide With Me*, but I was mistaken. An uplifting story, *What You Can't Lose* will leave readers feeling closer to God and pleading for the sequel."
— COURTNEY RANGER, author of *In Thy Tender Care*

"Oh my. Mikayla has outdone herself again. *What You Can't Lose* will have you on the edge of your seat, heartbroken one moment and giggling the next. Sweet and tender, yet raw and vulnerable, it's a perfect balance of hope and healing amid the grit and trials of the west. Once I started, I couldn't put it down until I was finished. I just had to know, 'How will it all end?'"
— LEXI T. WALKER, author of *Preserved by a Promise*

For my uncle, Stacy Walker. We miss you every day.

BOOKS BY MIKAYLA ROBBINS

Abide with Me
The Coal Miner's Niece

Advantageous Marriages series:
The Chosen
The Favored

Montana Brides series:
What You Can't Lose
There's Only Been You

PREFACE

Dear Reader,

I believe there is a time and place for everything in Christian fiction. This book explores more mature themes than my previous works. With that in mind, I encourage you to read the following content warnings before deciding to continue. The last thing I want is to cause offense or distress.

Before writing this novel, I asked the Lord to place the themes He wanted me to share on my heart. This story includes portrayals of the aftermath of abuse and trauma within an unwanted marriage, as well as profound grief following the loss of a spouse. This book is a Western romance with elements of suspense, rather than a lighthearted, upbeat romance.

Within these pages, you may encounter violence, post-traumatic stress disorder and brief flashbacks related to spousal abuse and miscarriage, a sociopathic antagonist, prejudiced remarks stemming from racism and misogyny, childbirth, infant and spousal loss, one fade-to-black intimate scene, and discussion of abortion from a pro-life perspective.

If any of these themes may affect you negatively, I encourage you to read with care.

At its heart, this is a story about finding light at the end of a dark tunnel. In order to reach peace, the characters must confront the darkness in their lives and ultimately turn to the Father for healing and redemption.

If you enjoy a meaningful redemption story, I hope this one speaks to you.

With love,
Mikayla Robbins

"He is no fool who gives what he cannot keep, to gain what he cannot lose." – Jim Elliot

WHAT YOU CAN'T LOSE

PART I

PROLOGUE

Charlotte, North Carolina; April 1872

SHE COULD STILL FEEL the sensation of his hands gripping her throat as if it were happening all over again. His thumbs pressing in harder, forming two deep holes in her neck. Him pushing until her air supply was completely blocked; her lungs screaming like they were on fire, pleading for one more gulp of air, just one more breath.

Josie shook the haunting memory away, clutching her dark velvet cloak as she scurried through the dark, deserted streets of Charlotte. Her limbs ached, her feet throbbed, but she refused to slow down—just like she hadn't hesitated when Mammy called for a carriage. Every moment counted; her time was dwindling. If they caught her, she would be shown no mercy. Surely she'd be locked away forever, or worse, swung from the gallows.

But in her mind, what she did wasn't a crime.

She had wrestled with two choices—life and death, and she chose to live.

Keeping her gaze fixed on the cemented cobblestones, Josie drew deep breaths, steadying her racing heart despite the raw sting in her throat. Her brown eyes keenly gazed over her shoulder. No one was there—only the ghost of her beast, permanently trapped in her mind. Dawn was breaking, the sky gradually lightening, yet darkness still remained. Just like Josie wanted it to.

She was safe.

She was invisible.

Josie kept her head lowered as she approached the iron gate, encircling the brick mansion before her, hidden behind a row of maple trees. Shielding her from the world, their large trunks would protect her from harm. Josie had asked her driver to take her three-quarters of the way so she wouldn't draw attention. Her arrival had to go unnoticed. She paid him in gold, offering more than he could earn in an entire year.

She trusted him.

She had no choice.

For years, Josie dreamed of this freedom but never anticipated it would come with a target on her back. *Leave before first light*, she kept telling herself, and she arrived in time.

Just barely.

Josie observed the massive lock on the gate. *Act invisible. He can't find you now.* She pushed back her hood and retrieved a hairpin from her bun. She inserted it carefully inside the keyhole until she heard the click. She closed her eyes and sighed, her heavy limbs at ease. After pulling the hood over her head again, she slowly opened the gate, holding her breath when it creaked softly.

Gritting her teeth, Josie stepped inside the courtyard. She looked upward at the outstretched maple limbs, which reminded her she was safe, as though they were speaking aloud. Reaching the home's front steps, she paused. Her throat still burned with every inhalation, but she pushed the discomfort aside, just like she did with all the other pains she tried to suppress.

She was strong.

Stronger now than ever.

Josie knocked on the door and stepped back, waiting patiently, or so she told herself while the hair on her neck stood. She had expected a butler to answer the door, but to her surprise and comfort, it was the one person in the world she was overjoyed to see—Great Aunt Tia.

"Josephine?" The elderly woman's tired, saggy eyes opened wide like her mouth.

After studying Josie with keen eyes, she pulled her into a firm embrace. Josie held her breath, but she couldn't hold back the tears as they fell onto her aunt's shoulder. Aunt Tia softly stroked the back of Josie's head.

"I didn't know you were coming tonight."

Josie swallowed hard, her sore throat burning as a sob escaped, sending trembles through her body.

"You're safe now," Aunt Tia whispered. "You're safe now."

However, it would take more than words to bring Josie ease. Even though she escaped seven years of torment, how could she ever be safe again? Those memories would never go away. She'd remember that nightmare, and as many times as she'd hear, "all is well" or "you're safe," the gruesome memories would never fade. His face would be in her mind forever, torturing her for what she did.

"Come inside quickly," Aunt Tia instructed, gripping Josie's sore arm—bruised from an earlier touch that held no affection, only cruelty.

Josie pressed her lips together, fighting back a whimper. Aunt Tia tapped her cane softly against the mahogany floor, the sound muffled as they moved onto the damask-printed rug lining the hallway. Passing through the foyer, Josie could barely make out the wall art, but moonlight streamed through the tall Gothic windows in the corner, allowing a faint glow through the cracked curtains, allowing her to see without tripping.

Aunt Tia retrieved an oil lamp from the wall shelf beside a clock and pressed a cool hand to Josie's cheek. She smiled. As she lowered her gaze, the lamp's glow illuminated Josie's skin. Aunt Tia's eyes widened, her mouth parted, and a gasp of horror escaped her lips.

"Good heavens, child. Are you all right?"

Josie lightly touched her neck with her fingertips. "I will be," she said hoarsely.

Aunt Tia motioned for her to follow and opened a door, leading Josie into another dim room. A whiff of citrus and nutmeg mingled with the faint scent of kerosene. Aunt Tia set down the lamp and lit another, casting a soft, orange glow around them.

Josie blinked, adjusting to the light as she took in the parlor's interior. Deep burgundy damask wallpaper adorned the walls, thick brown velvet curtains framed the windows, and mauve settees complemented the delicate pink and blue china with floral patterns displayed around the room within the clear glass cabinet.

"Sit down, and I'll fetch you some tea."

Josie eased onto the soft settee, listening while her aunt hobbled away, the tap of her cane fading down the hallway. Hands in her lap, Josie peered around her aunt's parlor again, observing the paintings above the tiny fireplace's mantle and a large photo of Josie's great-grandmother, Helena Callahan. The woman's golden ringlets framed her pale, round face, and her features matched Josie's late younger sister, Susannah. The nose was the same, sharp along the edges yet narrow at the bridge. Josie sighed inwardly and leaned back, realizing how long it had been since she sat in this parlor.

Before the war, of course.

Everyone was high on hope when it finally ended, but the danger and violence never quite concluded for Josie. She had fought hard against the war within the walls of her home, but it had never been a home she could truly call her own. Josie and her family lived in Asheville on their plantation, *Belle Vallée*, the most beautiful place in the world until the Yankees destroyed everything in her life.

Then the real monster took everything from her.

Aunt Tia hobbled back into the parlor, carrying a tea tray. Josie quickly stood and took it from her. "Here, let me." She balanced the tray with one hand while guiding Aunt Tia to her seat with the other.

Her great-aunt eased onto the settee. "Thank you, dear."

Josie set the tray on the table beside her aunt. Before she could pour the tea, Aunt Tia patted her hand. "Sit down. Let me handle this. You need your rest."

Josie obeyed, though she found it ironic that she was the one told to rest. Aunt Tia was just as she remembered—stubborn. She poured Josie a cup of tea and twirled her spoon around in it for a moment.

"Here." The cup rattled atop the saucer from the elderly woman's shaking hands. "This will make you better in no time."

Josie sat in silence, sipping the hot beverage as it soothed her bruised throat. From the corner of her eye, she noticed Aunt Tia's prying gaze. Even her stare raised goosebumps on Josie's arms, but she understood her aunt's concern. Aunt Tia would undoubtedly have countless questions, and Josie would find herself burdened with answers that were too painful to explain.

"Is he looking for you?"

Josie shook her head, placing her teacup on its saucer. She shut her eyes, remembering the terrifying event hours ago. Her husband, Marcus, had been more violent than usual. Drunk, yes, but other concerns set him off. Aunt Tia and Josie had been secretly corresponding for months due to his dislike of the woman. When he found one of Aunt Tia's letters, begging Josie to move in with her, he had been heated with rage. He wanted to beat sense into her, as he had done hundreds of times before. That was until Josie took action and made her escape.

"He won't be hurting me again . . . or coming here." She placed her hand on her abdomen as her stomach churned. Josie pushed her tea away on the table beside her, unable to take another sip. She wanted to deny the truth—accept it all as a dream—but it had been real.

Mammy's scream.

Josie's grip on the stair rail, trying not to faint.

Aunt Tia's eyes widened. "Did you?"

Josie looked into her aunt's aging brown eyes. She didn't have to say the words aloud. The truth was too hard for her to admit herself. Josie nodded slowly, acknowledging her actions for the first time.

"My goodness," Aunt Tia gasped, her palm covering her mouth. "How?"

Josie looked away, biting her nails. "He wanted to kill me. He was determined this time . . . He said I'd been no use to him." Josie closed her eyes, drawing in a breath. "Last night was his final straw."

Aunt Tia leaned forward and removed her hand from her mouth. "But . . . the baby? Did he know? Surely that would have changed his mind."

Josie's eyes stung. She rubbed her stomach with her thumb. That innocent child seemed safe within her, but in truth, it wasn't. Nothing inside her could be safe. She wasn't a safe vessel that offered protection. She was a broken one. Her womb hadn't saved the other three pregnancies, even when Marcus hit her with knowledge of what it might do.

"You're not strong enough!" he screamed. Josie was always doing something wrong. She tried to obey him, but it wasn't enough. A man like him could never be pleased, making survival impossible, not without consequences.

"No, and he wasn't going to. Seeking refuge with you was my first step, but now . . . I don't know what to do."

Aunt Tia wrapped her arm around Josie. Josie sank into her embrace, resting her head on her aunt's shoulder. Aunt Tia sighed, rubbing the back of Josie's head. "I'm going to write to Mammy and tell her to keep this matter quiet until we have your problems solved."

Mammy. Josie's tears fell faster. Poor Mammy had not been part of this, yet she was caught in the middle, having discovered Josie over Marcus's lifeless body. No one else knew the truth—only the two of them.

"Send me word when yuh're safe," Mammy had whispered before Josie boarded the carriage. There was no telling what would unfold once the sheriff knew of the death. Someone who killed a man as important as Marcus wouldn't be let off too easily. And with Josie's immediate disappearance, she would be the prime suspect.

"What do you mean?" Josie asked, wiping her tears. "How can we solve this? I *killed* my husband."

"You were defending yourself, Josephine. Think about your child. What would have happened, hm?"

Josie pressed her lips together and shook her head. "The law won't see it that way, and you know it. I need to get out of here." Salty tears blurred her vision. "I can't stay here. Help me, Aunt Tia."

Aunt Tia's head moved from side to side, scanning the dimmed room. Her brows rose, setting her sight ahead. She turned to Josie and gripped her hand. "Do you trust me?"

Josie nodded. "Yes."

Aunt Tia balanced herself on her cane and pulled herself up. "Wait here." She wobbled across the room and stopped at the chair beside a corner window. She turned, holding a folded newspaper. After settling herself on the settee, she opened a section and handed it to Josie. Then Josie's stomach dropped.

Mail-Order Brides Wanted

Josie nearly choked upon reading the headline. Aunt Tia was up in age, but she wasn't crazy—at least from what Josie knew of. However, this was the first sign of her mental decline. The old woman couldn't be serious.

"Aunt Tia? What are you trying to say?"

Aunt Tia bit her lip. "I think you know."

Josie's jaw tightened, throwing the newspaper down. "I cannot marry a stranger. You already know what happened last time. Marcus was handpicked by my father. A stranger! I won't go through that again."

"Josephine, look at me," Aunt Tia commanded, scooting closer.

Josie turned her head away, clenching her fists in her lap.

"Josephine, you're a stubborn girl. Look at your aunt when she's speaking to you."

Josie huffed and faced her aunt.

Aunt Tia's brows furrowed as she pointed to Josie's flat abdomen. "Now, that baby of yours is in real danger. If you stay here, he or she will be without a mother and thrown into an orphanage with shame cast upon them. If you marry again and move to the wild country, you will have security and protection. You can't make it on your own, and you can't stay here. Make your choice."

Josie's gut nearly convulsed.

"You said you trusted me, now keep your word," Aunt Tia rebuked. "My heart goes out to you, dear, truly. I love you, but you have no other options, none that will keep you and your child together and safe."

Josie hugged herself, her fingers and arms quivering. *You can't be seriously considering this idea, Josie. Are you going to listen to your crazy aunt? You can't be that foolish.* Josie was finally free, and now she was thrown back in time. Seven years ago, she had been a foolish girl of sixteen, marrying a man because her father told her to. Josie couldn't fight back then, but she could fight now. But at what cost? She wanted this baby more than anything, and she'd give her life to protect it.

She swallowed a lump in her throat, nodding slightly. "Fine. I'll listen. Tell me your plan."

Aunt Tia picked up the discarded paper. "Mail-order brides are common, always have been. There's a man's name I stumbled upon the other morning, and his story has stuck with me for some strange reason." Aunt Tia placed a hand on her heart, her bottom lip quivering. "I truly believe God had a hand in leading me to it."

Straightening her posture, she cleared her throat and lifted the paper closer to her face. "Willow Grove, Montana. Travis Blythe, widower and father of four. He writes, 'I'm searching for a woman willing to love and raise my children as her own.'"

Josie's heart sank, leaning back against the sofa. *Those poor dears.* She pressed her fingers against her lips, stifling a gasp. What was happening to her? They were just words on a page—nothing more. Yet they tugged at something deep inside her. She couldn't let the heartfelt advertisement manipulate her emotions. What if this was just a cruel trick, a way to get a woman to feel sorry for him and then take control of her? Since the war, she understood men better than before—control and greed were the essence of who they were.

"He's just a desperate man trying to make a woman feel sorry enough for him to marry him," Josie spat firmly. "I won't do it. Find someone else."

Aunt Tia groaned, lowering the newspaper into her lap. "Josephine, you are just like your grandmother, judgmental and picky," she muttered, shaking her head. With a sigh, she placed a hand over her chest. "However, I understand you. Your father was foolish to marry you off to that monster of a man, but you must learn to trust, not for your sake but for your child's. Think about those four children without a mama. Think of your child being fatherless."

"And would this man want another baby? One from another man?"

Aunt Tia carefully folded the newspaper, her gaze low. "We'll meet that difficulty when the time comes."

"Aunt Tia," Josie chided. "I never said I would."

Aunt Tia smiled and patted Josie's hand, unmoved by her skepticism. "Let's not argue. Sleep on it, my dear. It's been a long night. Let me escort you to your room."

Josie stood as her aunt gestured for her to follow. She held her breath, just like she had earlier when sneaking into the train station and crossing town. They climbed the stairs in silence, their footsteps light against the worn steps. On the fourth floor, Aunt Tia unlocked a door and pressed an oil lamp into Josie's hands. The sharp scent of kerosene filled her nostrils as the flame flickered in the darkened hallway.

"Stay in here," Aunt Tia whispered, her voice dropping an octave from its usual feminine tone. "I can't let my staff see you. The fourth floor has been closed for years due to repairs."

Josie nodded, her grip tight around the lamp, her other hand wrapped around her forearm. Aunt Tia rose onto her toes and pressed a soft kiss to Josie's cheek. "I love you, my darling niece."

Josie blinked back a tear, quickly swiping at her cheek with her hand to wipe away the salty residue. "I love you too, Aunt Tia."

She stepped inside the room and glanced back at her aunt before closing the door with a soft click. The small orange flame from the lamp flickered across the walls of the drafty room, enough for Josie to make out the shadowed outlines of furniture. She surveyed the space, realizing it was less than a fourth the size of her former bedroom. Still, anywhere felt better than that prison, a place lavishly decorated as if fit for a queen. A captive queen, at that.

In the corner stood a small twin bed beside a modest desk. On the far wall, a window was boarded up with only a narrow crack allowing a sliver of dawn light to seep through—just enough for her to catch a glimpse of the dark outside world.

Josie sighed, setting the lamp on the desk before lying down on the cool bed, letting her tears come. She gripped the thin sheets in her hands. Her tears soaked through the fabric and into her skin. Josie wanted her baby more than anything, and the mere thought of abandoning it nearly shattered her heart. How could she deny her child a mother—when the only part of herself left behind would be the mark of a murderess who had swung from the gallows?

Perhaps marrying this stranger could be a new beginning, the answer to everything. Montana was thousands of miles away and secluded. She could hide out with a new identity. Whoever this man was, his children didn't deserve to be motherless, just like her child didn't deserve to be fatherless. Josie cupped her flat abdomen. She wasn't too far along, no more than a month if her calculations were correct. She sighed. Her baby was in danger, and she'd never forgive herself if her stubbornness ruined its chance of a better life.

Josie moved to the small desk, opened the drawer, and found pen and paper. She shifted the oil lamp closer and stared at the blank paper. What could she say to a man she didn't know? What was his middle name? What color eyes did he have?

She needed to push back the awkwardness. If he didn't write back, maybe it was the Lord's will. But Josie had to try—for her baby's sake. *Think about those poor children. Think about your baby.* She dipped the pen in ink and began writing.

Dear Sir, she began. Josie thought it would be appreciated to address him in a proper manner rather than Mr. Blythe or whatever his name was. *My name is Josephine . . .* Josie paused, letting the ink drop on the empty space. She shivered, nearly writing her last name. She was a widow now, but she couldn't return to that name. If she was going to leave and marry a stranger, she needed a new identity. She would choose her maiden name, Callahan.

Josie exhaled and rubbed the crease between her eyes. She would give anything to go back to her sixteen-year-old self, so innocent and naive of the troubles lying ahead, especially in a marriage to a war hero. Josie shook away the thought. She crumbled the paper and began again.

Dear Sir,

WHAT YOU CAN'T LOSE

My name is Josephine Callahan . . .

CHAPTER ONE

Willow Grove, Montana; May 1872

TRAVIS BLYTHE AWOKE WITH a small, warm body pressed against him. Turning over, he noticed four-year-old Lillian nestled beside him, her eyes closed in peaceful slumber. His lips curled slightly, but not enough to be a happy smile. Lillian had often crawled into bed with him and Sophie when she was alive. Travis closed his eyes and exhaled softly, rubbing his face. He missed those days. It was no longer the same with one body missing from the bed.

Sophie weighed on Travis's mind night and day, never leaving him, as if she were a ghost, haunting him, with reminders lingering everywhere he turned—the smell of coffee she'd brew each morning, the taste of huckleberries fresh from the vine which was her favorite treat, and the way the wind whispered, sweeping his hair across his ear and tickling him like she used to. And how could he forget those emerald-green eyes? They were like the trees viewed from the height of a mountain peak—so deep they could drown a person, beautiful enough to lure one in, yet impossible to escape.

Travis had never wanted to be free of her; if she wanted to haunt him, he'd let her. Forever, her ghost would remain in this cabin, built by his own two hands for the girl who had become his whole world. From the moment he was a young boy, falling in love with the new girl who came to the valley to farm alongside her father, she had been his everything.

At seventeen, Sophie finally said yes to courting him, three years her senior, and from that moment on, Travis's world revolved around her. Within six months, they were married, and, after two years, their first daughter, Ivy, was born, followed by Jonas and Lillian. Each of their children inherited their mother's copper-brown hair—all except the last addition, who had Travis's coal-black hair.

Gideon. Travis's breath caught, instantly removing the covers from his body, careful not to disturb Lillian's rest. Tiptoeing across the rickety floorboards that desperately needed replacing after a decade of wear, Travis hurried to the corner of the room to check on the sleeping seven-month-old. The child still slept, sucking his thumb in his crib. Staring down at the perfect little angel, Travis couldn't smile. Every time he looked at Gideon, the smile faded before it could reach his lips.

Travis reeled away, his stomach churning with the familiar nausea. He prayed that one day he could see the child without the burden of this anguish, but how could he ever forget? One day, his son would learn the truth about his existence, and when he did, he would surely lay the blame at Travis's feet. Keeping emotional distance, Travis often told himself, would make it easier. The less he knew Gideon, the less it would hurt when the truth finally came to light.

Travis opened his tiny closet that still smelled like the honeysuckle perfume he'd bought Sophie four years ago during a trip to Bozeman. He quickly retrieved his work clothes and shut the door, covering his nose. His pants were ripped in many places, but time did not allow for them to be mended. That was Sophie's job. She could have them mended within an hour. But it didn't matter anymore anyway; they were for work only, not Sunday best.

After changing behind the dressing screen, Travis snuck out the room and closed the door behind him. However, his quiet attempts hardly mattered once he heard rummaging in the kitchen. Aunt Polly always rose early to help with the children and household, but she had a homestead of her own to run and a bed of herbs to care for. As the town's healer, she had long lists of patients whose cures required long hours of brewing and drying herbs. But now, she hardly had the time. Travis never asked his father's sister-in-law to devote so much time to his family, but he didn't know how he'd manage without her. Maybe that was why he never asked her to stop.

The strong smell of bacon consumed the air, making Travis's stomach grumble. He peered around the corner, seeing his aunt flip long strips of bacon on a cast iron skillet atop their iron stove. Like always, her silver hair was pulled back into a long braid that extended down her back. She looked up, giving Travis a warm smile.

"Good morning, Travis."

"Good morning," Travis said, giving his aunt a kiss on the cheek.

"There's coffee on the table for ya."

Travis retrieved a tin cup hanging above the stove and paused, the familiar scent hitting his nostrils. *Don't do this to me now, Sophie.* To distract himself, he held his breath, filling the cup to the brim. He blew gently over the top, the steam swirling as he sat down at the table, trying to focus on anything but the memories that had flooded back.

Aunt Polly handed Travis a plate with two fried eggs and three sticks of bacon that glistened with grease. Travis licked his lips.

"Thank you," Travis said.

Aunt Polly smiled. "You're welcome."

After Travis's first bite of bacon, Aunt Polly sat in front of him, drawing his attention. He paused, his brows arched high.

"Is everything all right?" he asked, reaching for his coffee. This was unusual; Aunt Polly rarely paused in her morning routine, always eager to get the children up and ready.

Travis forced hot liquid down his throat. He winced for a moment, the burn spreading across his tongue, then pushed the cup away. *That should be enough to get through the day.* A burnt tongue was better than slacking off from exhaustion. He couldn't let grief—or even coffee—stop him from providing for his family. He looked up at Aunt Polly, her fingers tapping on the table

"Travis, we need to talk . . . There is news."

"What is it?"

Aunt Polly dug into her apron pocket and pulled out a letter. She handed it to Travis. He carefully examined it, quickly noticing the return address. It came from as far as Charlotte, North Carolina—a place he never dreamed to go near.

A southern state.

"After all these months, we finally get a reply, hm," Travis said flatly, taking a large gulp of coffee, only to regret it immediately as the scorching liquid burned his tongue again. He broke the wax seal, shaking his head with a grunt.

Travis leaned back, ready to be entertained by a prank. No one in town knew Aunt Polly had talked him into placing an advertisement in a newspaper, one that went far east, up north, and apparently down South. A woman had penned the letter—he could tell by the careful, neat script.

Dear Sir,

My name is Josephine Callahan, and I am replying to your post regarding a mail-order bride. I confess, I am just as uncomfortable writing this as you probably are reading. However, I felt compelled to answer anyway, given your current situation and my desire to help in your time of need. Since I have never tried this before, I thought it would be wise to introduce myself.

I grew up in Asheville, North Carolina, and I am temporarily residing with my great aunt in Charlotte. I'm afraid I do not have much experience caring for children except growing up with my younger sister, Susannah, who was three years younger than me.

Despite my experience being low, I must add that I know what it is like to lose a mother. If you do not want to consider me as the answer to your posting, I understand. Your family will remain in my prayers.

Sincerely,

Josephine Callahan

Travis read the letter twice. He rubbed his chin, processing the information. He wasn't keen on marrying again, but Aunt Polly convinced him to put away his selfishness and think about the children. After four months of waiting, there hadn't been a response. Travis personally didn't blame the women. Who would want to move out to the wild country and marry a man with four children?

Travis specifically requested to mention only a mother instead of a wife. Having a wife was his last priority; he experienced enough love to last him a lifetime, and if he married again, it would be nothing more than a professional arrangement. The only woman who would ever have a chokehold on his heart was Sophie, whether she was dead or alive.

"What does it say?" Aunt Polly asked.

Travis tossed her the letter then leaned back in his chair. "Read it for yourself."

Aunt Polly held the letter closer, her eyes narrowing. It didn't take her long to finish. "She sounds like a wonderful woman, humble to respond and respectful to mention her intentions. Will you propose?"

Travis huffed, folding his arms over his chest. "This doesn't feel right. How can I bring a stranger into my own home to raise *my* children?"

Aunt Polly put down the letter. "And how many women are in the valley, lining up to marry you with those four children to raise?"

"Miss Callahan doesn't have experience raising children."

Aunt Polly smiled and shrugged. "At least she's honest. If it makes you comfortable, I can stay around until she has the hang of things."

Think about your children, Travis kept telling himself. His face flushed with heat, shame washing over him. The very thought seemed like a betrayal towards Sophie, as if pondering the potential marriage somehow tarnished her memory.

"I just..." Travis stuttered, raking his hand through his hair. "It was one thing sending out an advertisement, but now the day has come... It's even harder thinking about another woman running this house... Sophie's house."

"I know it's hard. I often think about what I would have done if I were in your shoes twenty years ago. It makes me realize how lucky the twins were..."

Travis's stomach sank. "I'm sorry, Aunt Polly, I didn't think about—"

She patted Travis's hand. "Don't ya worry about silly 'ole me. The past is in the past now. It's those children's future you should worry about." She stood slowly, letting out a soft sigh. "Now let me get them young'uns ready. They'll get lazier if they sleep an extra minute."

Travis winced as he took another sip of coffee, his eyes landing on the letter in front of him. Would he write back? His fingers gripped around his cup. How could he? He stared at the words, trying to imagine Josephine stepping into this house and caring for his children. Except he couldn't picture her in his mind. How old was she? Her writing was legible, displaying her education, but did she know anything about homesteading? Could she cook? Clean? What about tending to livestock and harvesting wheat? Miss Callahan might become a wonderful homemaker and mother, but what about a farmer's wife?

Travis stared at the name, written in elegant cursive penmanship. He chewed his bottom lip. This was driving him crazy! This woman was a mystery. Why would she give up everything to come out west and marry him of all people? And she didn't even know him! Travis could be an evil brute or a drunkard, yet she was willing to sacrifice everything to stand by his side, in sickness and in health. It didn't make sense.

"Who are you, Josephine Callahan?"

CHAPTER TWO

Charlotte, North Carolina; June 1872

JOSIE SAT ON HER bed, nervously fidgeting with her cameo brooch. It had been over a month since the accident, and no warrant had yet been issued for her arrest or a death announcement mentioned in the newspapers. Nothing felt right. Mammy told her she wouldn't announce the death until Josie was safe, but how long could a body be kept secret?

Even if there was a search warrant, would they be able to find her in this confined space? She had gone unnoticed when she arrived, cloaked and discreet. None of Aunt Tia's servants had seen her. Marcus forced Josie to cut ties with her aunt, so why would Aunt Tia be suspected?

Josie never left the attic, not even for fresh air. Aunt Tia encouraged her to roam the grounds at nightfall, but Josie wouldn't budge. She spent her nights and mornings in this confined space, safe and secure. The room wasn't a prison cell; she was only a prisoner to herself and the threats that lurked outside.

Aunt Tia had brought Josie tea earlier that morning, along with some preserves and biscuits, but Josie could hardly stomach anything but the tea. Anything that looked like food nauseated her. She rose, poured herself a cup of tea, and peered through the small crack in the window, observing the city of Charlotte from the attic's height.

Her aunt's home was larger than Josie's childhood home, *Belle Vallée*, and the horrid mansion in the city of Statesville, where she had been forced to play the role of a frightened and fragile wife. From the attic window, Josie quickly took notice of the police roaming the streets in their navy blue uniforms and hats. She turned away from the crack, her back pressed firm against the wall. Though they couldn't see her, their presence made her shudder.

The door squeaked open, and Josie jumped. To her relief, it was Aunt Tia again. She exhaled, her hand resting on her chest.

"Josephine, I have news," Aunt Tia announced softly, stumbling in while balancing herself on a cane. She held up a letter. "Mr. Blythe has replied."

Josie's mouth fell open. After waiting nearly two months, the response she both dreaded and hoped for had arrived. One thing in that letter was for certain—an answer. Josie didn't know which response to fear more. Rejection stung like a bee, but a proposal filled her with dread.

Aunt Tia settled herself at the corner desk, and Josie took the letter into her possession. Her teacup rattled on its saucer from her trembling hands. Josie set the cup down, sucking in a steadying breath. She stared at the return address and name, hardly able to make out the penmanship because of her quivering limbs. *Travis Blythe. Willow Grove, Montana.*

"Well, open it for goodness' sake," Aunt Tia instructed impatiently.

Exhaling, Josie broke the seal, her pulse racing. Carefully, she pulled the letter from its envelope and scanned the handwriting. The penmanship was unlike the neat script of the upper-class men she knew, but what could she expect from a man out West? However, the mystery drew her in. What words would a man shaped by the untamed frontier say? Would he speak proper and educated, or would he be a disastrous, uneducated buffoon?

Dear Miss Callahan,

I'd like to express how pleased I am to have received your reply. My name is Travis Blythe. I'm thirty years old and from Willow Grove, Montana, a small wheat farming town twenty miles east of Bozeman. Of course, you already gathered where I live from the advertisement. I just didn't know how else to introduce myself. I will admit, this is strange for me, too. I confess I never wrote to a stranger either, let alone anyone in North Carolina.

My children and I live in a modest cabin in a valley, surrounded by a background of snow-capped mountains and a blooming meadow where my children like to play. We have a two-decade old farm that hasn't failed our family thus far. I grew up in a dugout with my parents, and ten years ago I built my own place. My mother passed on six years ago, so now it's just us.

I hope this doesn't frighten you away, knowing we don't have much. Our life includes hard labor, but it is worth it when we have each other. My aunt has pitched in since my wife's passing and volunteered to stay a little longer to help you settle in if you accept my proposal.

If you choose to decline, I understand, but I wanted to be honest with you as you have with me. If you choose to marry me, my children will be very glad to have a mother again. I have enclosed the money to fund your journey. It is long and expensive, but I trust you'll use it wisely.

Sincerely,

Travis Blythe

Josie dug deeper into the envelope, finding the money Travis set. Her face burned hot as a rush of shock overcame her.

"Money? Why would this man send you money?" Aunt Tia asked.

"It's to pay for my fare," Josie explained, her throat dry. She swallowed. "He wants me to come."

Aunt Tia poured herself a cup of tea. "Hmm, you must have left quite an impression for him to trust you with his money."

Josie folded the letter and returned both it and the money to the envelope. "I'm sending it back."

Aunt Tia's brows arched and lips pursed. "You are not! You're going to Montana to marry this man."

Josie sat at her desk and took out a blank sheet of paper. "I won't," she said firmly, shaking her head. "Him choosing me is a mistake. I was honest with him, saying I lack experience with mothering, and he wants to marry me."

"The man is smart in choosing you," Aunt Tia remarked, taking a sip of tea. "What girl, in her right mind, would willingly apply to mother children and be a wife in a godforsaken land? He admires that and respects you."

Josie huffed, rolling her eyes. "He's crazy then. I'm not going." Josie rose from the desk and peered through the window crack.

"You don't walk away from me, Josephine Eleanor! You may be a grown, widowed woman, but I am still your great aunt."

Josie folded her arms "It's been two months, Aunt Tia. Police aren't looking for me. I'm cleared." That was a big lie. Just one glimpse at her, and Marcus's connections would take her down in an instant, escorting her to the gallows without mercy.

Aunt Tia stayed silent. Josie shifted her gaze, seeing the woman looking down at her teacup, her fingers nervously tracing the rim.

"Aunt Tia? What is it?"

Aunt Tia rubbed her forehead. "Mammy covered for you, saying you were with cousins in Wilmington, but there's only a matter of time before the truth gets out. You must go. It's too dangerous."

Josie pressed her hand against her abdomen. Aunt Tia was right. She only had so much time, and it wasn't just her life she should be concerned about.

"What about the baby?" Josie squeaked, her breaths coming in rapid gasps. "What man would want to take on another man's child?"

"You won't tell him."

Josie's eyes widened. "What? I can't do that. There's only so much time until I'm showing. I'm *three* months along."

Aunt Tia patted the desk chair beside her. "Sit down, child."

Josie obeyed and settled beside her aunt. Aunt Tia looked her in the eyes with a seriousness that cut through Josie's inner turmoil. "I am going to give you a piece of advice that your mama never gave you. Men don't believe women, nor do they trust them. You have no voice and no power."

Josie peered down at her lap. If anyone knew that pain personally, it was her. It didn't matter that her plantation home doubled Marcus's shareholdings; she was no more than his wife—no voice, no control. The wealth meant nothing when it was her freedom that had been stripped away, her choices discarded like worthless scraps.

Aunt Tia's eyes saddened. "What man is going to believe a woman who is so desperate to go west and marry a stranger with four children? You may be a widow, but he won't believe it. Not one bit. You're too young and attractive."

Josie bit the inside of her cheek. She believed her aunt. How could this Travis trust her when she didn't trust him? This marriage would be her only chance, but what could she do with the baby? How could she trust Travis to father a child that wasn't his? He was too honest in his letter, enough to send his life savings. What Josie counted would take years for a wheat farmer to save. How could she show up and deceive him?

The words in that shaky penmanship now echoed in her ears, as though it were mocking her conscience. *I wanted to be honest with you as you have with me.* Josie clenched her teeth. He trusted her.

"So . . . What do I do about the baby?"

"You make him think it's his," Aunt Tia explained before taking a sip of tea.

"What?" Josie's chest pinched. "Surely you're not suggesting . . ."

Aunt Tia nodded, retrieving the sugar pot from the tea tray. "Yes, I am."

Josie clung to the desktop as her stomach convulsed. She pushed her tea away and turned her head towards the peeling gray wallpaper. Bile rose in her throat again. She sucked in a breath, then exhaled slowly, her hands pressing against her unsettled belly.

"But the baby will be early . . . Earlier because it will take a while before my acceptance letter reaches him, maybe longer."

Aunt Tia stirred her tea. "You won't be writing. You'll send him a wire and get on that train first thing tomorrow morning."

So soon. Josie closed her eyes tight, fighting the urge to vomit. She'd be a wife again. She had only just tasted freedom, and already she'd be tied down once more. She couldn't go through with it; the mere idea made her heart race with fear and dread.

She wouldn't.

She couldn't.

Josie hugged herself, trying to catch her breath. "I can't . . . I can't . . ."

Aunt Tia placed her hand over Josie's. "You must. This isn't the ideal picture I had for you—marrying an uneducated farmer—but this is the only way."

Josie pressed her lips together. After a few moments, she nodded. "I understand."

"Good. I'll arrange for your departure, send a telegram, then you'll take a train first thing tomorrow morning." Aunt Tia arose from the table and made her way out the door.

Turning back to the desk, Josie picked up the letter again and held it in her hands. The money was too much—too much for a farmer. The savings she had set aside would be enough for two trips. She'd return Travis's money because it wasn't hers to take. After all, he would need it when a tiny, unexpected member joined his family in six months.

CHAPTER THREE

SWEAT TRICKLED DOWN TRAVIS'S forehead as he stood under the hot sun, rereading the yellowed paper in his grasp. Ronan Walsh, his neighbor and friend, had brought the telegram from town. Like Travis, the man had a steady number of chores to tackle on his farm before harvest, so whenever they went to town, they checked each other's mail to avoid extra trips.

Travis's chest tightened, processing the message. Never did he expect his world would change in a single day. Miss Callahan was coming soon. He had anticipated waiting another month for a reply, but her swift response showed she was eager—eager to marry him. Travis exhaled and wiped his forehead. He admired the woman's determination, yet his doubts taunted him. Did he truly want her in their family, with all the complexities her arrival would bring?

A part of him found her decision relieving, that way, he couldn't back out of the marriage. Miss Callahan could be already on her way, boarding a train, full of hope she'd come home to a husband and children, and it would be wrong for Travis to send her back. When Travis went out of his way to place an advertisement, he had no idea how costly a mail-order bride would be. He hoped a woman would respond close by, but it had to be North Carolina.

The state lay thousands of miles away and would take her at least six months to reach by wagon train. But to arrive faster and safer, she'd have to take several train passages to Cheyenne then a stagecoach that was more than four hundred miles.

The money Travis had sent amounted to nearly half of his earnings from the last two harvests. Sending money to a stranger was a risk, but Josephine Callahan left a promising impression on him with her honesty and willingness to come out west.

Miss Callahan would need to be strong to endure the journey and life on the homestead. But in those long weeks of travel, she might begin to acclimate. Or Travis prayed so. The woman constantly occupied his mind, the mystery torturing him. Travis overheard rumors once mail-order brides were usually old maids seeking out husbands, but how old was *too old*? Travis turned thirty only three months ago. What if he was too old for *her*?

When Travis and Sophie married, she had been eighteen, but Travis was close to her age, being twenty. Now, being a decade older, a sour pit formed in his stomach. Travis crumbled the telegram. How could a young girl mother three children and a baby? Let alone, how could he marry a mere child? He wasn't like those bawdy old men seeking a young, pretty thing to warm their beds. He needed a woman of strength and resilience, someone with a humble mind and a heart big enough to love the children he already had. He didn't need more, and he certainly didn't need a blushing bride.

Even now, the telegram itched at his curiosity more intensely than ever. Not even meeting her yet, Travis didn't know how their arrangement could work. All he knew was Josephine would be his wife, but in name only. Nothing in the advertisement promised romance. Maybe that was why he hadn't received a reply at first. But what was different about this Josephine Callahan? Was she desperate? Or did she pity him? What if Travis couldn't take his vows seriously with Josephine, given his heart was loyal to another?

Travis wiped his face with a bandana before stepping inside the cabin. Upon entering, his senses were met by the strong smell of venison stew. Travis scrunched the yellow paper into his pocket.

Now that Miss Callahan was on her way, he'd have to break the news he pained to admit to himself. How would he tell the children? How would they feel about having a new mother, only eight months after Sophie's death? Betrayed of course. And confused. How could Lillian comprehend this at four years old? Ivy and Jonas could protest all they wanted, but they needed a mother, one who could be there for them beyond the grave.

Travis removed his hat and hung it on the hook beside the door.

"Pa!" his three children shrieked, running towards him. They gathered around him, hugging his legs tightly. Seeing his children after a long day of weeding and fertilizing the wheat fields made Travis smile. After Sophie's passing, he found little to smile about—except when his children came near. He kissed each of their heads, holding them close.

He looked up to see Aunt Polly holding Gideon on her hip. Travis swallowed a lump in his throat. Gideon smiled, revealing his two bottom teeth, and held his arms out to Travis. Each time Travis stomached to look at the boy, he seemed to double in size.

Six-year-old Jonas took Travis's hand, tugging it in the opposite direction. "Pa, come to the table. See what I drew."

Ivy pushed Travis towards the table. "Come see, Pa."

Travis looked at the picture Jonas held, and he couldn't resist grinning. Jonas appeared so proud of his drawing, his head held high and chest out. Lillian held hers up next, which was just squiggly lines, and Ivy held up her picture of a tree. She had improved so much over the years.

"Nice job, children. I'm very proud."

Jonas pointed at his picture. "It's your horse, Pa. Can't ya tell?"

"I thought so." Travis knew nothing about art. He couldn't tell Jonas's drawing from a clump of random shapes, but he patted the boy's head with pride.

Aunt Polly clapped, interrupting the moment. "All right, you three, clear this table for supper."

The children swiftly removed their pencils and paper and headed down the tiny hallway into their bedroom. Adjusting Gideon on her hip, Aunt Polly pulled down the bowls and spoons from their usual spots on the shelf above the stove.

Travis set Jonas's drawing down on the table "Let me help with that."

His aunt shook her head in protest. "Sit down, Travis. Relax while I set the table."

Gideon's green eyes met Travis's, and he quickly looked away, his heart sinking. "I hate that you work so hard for us, Auntie."

"Nonsense!" Aunt Polly declared, setting the last bowl down. "It's always a joy to care for a family again."

Before Travis could open his mouth to speak again, the children rushed back. Travis pulled out the chair for little Lillian, who was too small to do it herself.

"What did you young'uns do today?" Travis asked as Aunt Polly scooped the stew into their bowls.

"I got the eggs!" Lillian exclaimed.

"No, *I* got the eggs," Ivy corrected, pointing to herself.

Lillian slouched and lowered her head. "I put them in the basket."

Travis nodded, lowering himself into his seat beside Lillian. "Well, I am proud of you gals. Gathering eggs is a very important job. We wouldn't have breakfast in the morning without you two."

"Aunt Polly said she'll give me a nickel when she sells them at Mr. Lynde's store," Ivy announced.

Travis looked up at Aunt Polly, raising his brow.

"They earned it," she said, bouncing Gideon on her lap.

Travis cleared his throat and patted the table. "So long as you work hard, you'll keep earning your nickels."

"What 'bout me?" Jonas asked. "Can I have a nickel, too?"

"It's not your job," Ivy scolded with thinned eyes. "You gotta keep muckin' the stalls."

Jonas folded his arms and wrinkled his nose. "I hate muckin' the stalls. Pa, can I please do somethin' else?"

"Mucking out the stalls is important too, Jonas. Without you, the barn would smell worse than it does."

The children let out loud, collective giggles.

"But can I get paid?" Jonas asked, his eyes bright.

Travis sighed. Jonas was a good kid and hardly ever got into too much trouble. Travis wished he could pay the boy or spoil him with an award, but with Josephine's arrival, money would be tight until harvest.

"I bet your sisters would be glad to share their nickels with you."

Ivy and Lillian groaned.

"But Pa—" Ivy whined.

"I won't hear it," Travis said sharply, rubbing his face. As much as he loved his children, their bickering caused his temples to beat. Oh, what he'd give sometimes for peace and quiet after a long day's work. But he'd rather have his children at the table instead of sitting alone, grieving over the empty spaces. "Your brother works hard, too, and he needs a little reward."

Ivy's bottom lip quivered. "But my paint. I was saving for paint."

Travis frowned. Travis's heart cracked as Ivy's disappointment spilled across her face, her eyes glistening. Ivy had always dreamed of the day she'd have paint, but that day had never come, slipping through her fingers like sand.

"We'll get you paint soon, Ivy. I promise."

Her lips curved into a small smile.

"I'm sorry to interrupt, but our supper is going to get cold," Aunt Polly warned, folding her hands into prayer position.

Travis nodded. "I agree. Lillian, would you like to say the blessing?"

The child smiled and bowed her head. "Dear God, thank you for our food, thank you for the water from the well, and the chickens that give us eggs, our horses, because without them we'd have to walk a long way to town, and please let our wheat grow big and tall so we can make lots of money and Ivy can get her paint. Amen."

"Amen," Aunt Polly said with a slight chuckle in her voice.

The children and Aunt Polly dug into their food immediately, but Travis barely touched his plate, the heaviness in his stomach making it hard to eat. Gideon squirmed in Aunt Polly's lap, letting out a squeal as he patted the table. Travis sucked in a breath then exhaled. Gideon needed a mother. He observed the rest of his children. All of them did. Aunt Polly was an excellent help, but the children didn't need just help—they needed maternal guidance, a light into the home that would fill their empty hearts.

Travis pushed his stew aside and decided to let loose of the secret that was nearly eating him alive. "Children, I have something I need to speak with you about. It's very important."

The room went silent as little eyes were upon him. Travis tugged the collar of his shirt and cleared his throat. "Earlier this year, I put an advertisement in the newspaper about finding a new wife." He stopped, studying their confused faces. Heat crawled up his neck. "A month ago, I received a reply. Her name is Josephine Callahan, and she will be coming here in a few weeks." Travis could barely form the words from his mouth. His stomach twisted while he prepared himself to say them. "She will marry me and be your new ma."

The children stayed silent. Jonas and Lillian were too young to understand, their innocent faces reflecting confusion. But Ivy was old enough; her face turned as white as a sheet, fear dawning in her eyes. Aunt Polly shot Travis a look that urged him to continue.

Travis leaned forward, folding his hands in front of him. "Do any of you have any . . . questions?"

"Will she replace Ma?" Lillian asked, her posture leaning forward and her blue eyes and brows displaying evident confusion.

Travis fought to hold back the tears welling in his eyes, the weight of Lillian's words shattering his soul. "Of course not. Your ma was a special woman who loved all of you very much, and no one will ever replace her."

"Will I have to call her Ma?" Jonas asked.

Travis shook his head. "No, Miss Callahan would be fine. After we're married, you can call her Josephine."

"That's a long name," Lillian said, leaning against Travis.

Travis chuckled for a brief moment, yet he couldn't find anything funny about the situation. "It is." Travis looked over at Ivy. "Is there anything you want to ask, Ivy?"

Ivy looked down at her barely eaten food. "May I be excused?"

Travis nodded. "Yes, you may."

Ivy stood from her seat and pushed the chair under. Aunt Polly took her bowl. "I'll put this on the stove and keep it warm."

Ivy nodded and walked away. Travis's chest ached for her. Peering up, he shifted his focus to Gideon, who looked at him with a bright smile that lit up his face. The boy didn't know what was happening. Josephine Callahan would be the only mother he'd ever know. This sacrifice would change everything—for better or worse.

Chapter Four

Willow Grove, Montana; Early July 1872

A DULL THROBBING PULSED in Josie's temples and chest when the stagecoach arrived in Willow Grove. She sighed in relief, but as she looked down at her shortened nails, her fears resurfaced. It had been a long, tiring journey—six grueling days by train to St. Louis, then on to Kansas City, Denver, and finally Cheyenne. After that, Josie endured an excruciating fourteen-day stagecoach journey, jolting and rumbling across the plains.

The relentless motions had left Josie feeling sicker than she did cooped up in Aunt Tia's attic. Vomiting and headaches had been her loyal traveling companions, refusing to leave even as passengers came and went at every stop. Each day had seemed like an eternity, and the weariness clung to her bones, aching in every attempt to stretch. Now all she wanted was a soft bed. Maybe a hot meal. Or just possibly a warm bath. Anything but more traveling.

Josie poked her head out the window, letting the gentle mountain breeze wash over her face. When would this nausea go away? But every wave of sickness, every cramp and tightness in her muscles, she reminded herself why she had embarked on this journey. She loved the baby in her womb more than anything, and her sacrifices proved how much she did. She wouldn't be marrying a stranger if it weren't true.

The stagecoach finally came to a halt, and the driver opened the door, extending his hand. Fatigue wore Josie down, but a tinge of excitement pushed her forward. What would a small wheat-farming town look like? This would be her home now, the place where her child would grow up. In the past weeks, Josie had grown restless, wanting to know everything about Willow Grove.

She stepped onto the soft, muddied ground, her boots sinking slightly as she took in her surroundings. Worn buildings lined the streets, and wooden planks created a boardwalk in front of them. For a moment, the town resembled Cheyenne, only smaller and more weathered. The buildings lacked paint, and only two wagons rolled by instead of the usual bustling traffic.

The second driver removed her bag from the top of the coach and dropped it down to her. The brown carpet bag was light, containing only what Aunt Tia could spare without suspicion. After taking her belongings, Josie brushed the dust from her linen burgundy skirt and button-down bodice, taking a moment to collect herself. The wind whistled and whipped her hair free from its pins. She sucked in yet another breath, closing her eyes as she tucked the loose strands beneath her bonnet. *This is it, Josie. You're home now. You're safe. No one will find you here.*

When she opened her eyes and lifted her chin, her heart paused. Squinting and shielding her face from the hot sun with her hand, she made out the figure of a man, standing under a sign that read "Post Office." His gaze locked with hers, making Josie nearly forget to breathe. She remained frozen in the street, perhaps staring too long, but he kept his eyes locked on hers.

When he moved in her direction, Josie's throat tightened, rendering her mute. She clutched her carpet bag handles, her grip increasing as the seconds ticked by. *If this is Travis, I hope he is pleased.*

A brown suit coat, with sleeves rolled to his elbows, fit snugly over a matching vest. A white shirt peeked out at the collar, along with an uneven tie. If this wasn't Travis, then some poor wheat farmer had dressed foolishly for July.

The man paused in front of her and removed his hat, revealing his dark slick-back hair that stopped just below his ears. Sweat visibly glistened from his forehead.

"You must be Miss Callahan," he said, extending his arm towards her. His low baritone voice carried a crisp edge.

Josie hesitated for a moment before shaking his hand. *Goodness, Josie, don't appear a fool.* "And I gather you must be Mr. Blythe," she said, taking his hand.

His grip was loose—too loose. His palm was clammy, but Josie forced a smile, determined to hide her discomfort.

"I hope your trip went well," Travis remarked, pulling his hand away. He hid it behind his back, wiping his palm on his trousers.

"Tiring—but the sights were worth seeing."

Travis opened his mouth to speak again but closed. He bit his lip and looked down at Josie's bag. "Let me take that for you," he offered, reaching forward.

"Oh, there's no need." She gripped the handle tight. "I can carry it."

"I don't mind. My wagon is just over there."

Josie followed his gaze and spotted a wagon parked and hitched by two horses in front of a gray building. She forced a soft smile. "Very well then."

Travis took her bag, his sleeves tightening around his forearms, outlining his muscular build. Josie's eyes widened upon studying them. Travis wasn't as broad as Marcus had been, but his muscles were large and powerful. One hand latched around her throat and it wouldn't take long to—

"Just this way." Travis's warm voice removed Josie from her thoughts. She nodded, lifting up her dragging petticoat.

Josie trailed behind him as he made his way down the muddy road. The recent rain had deepened the mud, making every step a challenge. *At least you didn't wear your good shoes.* She carefully proceeded and focused on keeping her balance. The last thing she wanted was for Travis to see her as a clumsy woman. She needed this marriage to happen. If he found her unfit, he'd send her home. Josie pressed a hand to her stomach while it twisted in knots. *We won't go back. We won't.*

The gray building boasted a sign reading "Lynde General Store." Its painted exterior stood out against the surrounding unpainted buildings of raw lumber and mortar. Josie looked upward, studying the merchandise through the large windows—fabrics, jars of preserves, shelves of canned goods, and a display case of carved wooden toys. A boy and a girl stood beside their mother as she conversed with the man at the counter. The children giggled, pointing at the candy jar. The mother's eyes narrowed at the children and she snapped at them. Josie laughed softly. *Oh, how mischievous children are at that age.*

Travis loaded Josie's bag, then brushed his hands together. "Sorry about the street. We were recently blessed with a downpour."

Josie dropped her arms at her sides. *Blessed* was an understatement for a farmer, dependent on rain to make a decent living. "I'm all right."

Travis climbed up the wagon and extended his hand towards Josie. His strong arm led her upward, and she situated herself on the driver's seat. Travis didn't seem like a horrid man, but Josie knew better than to judge too quickly. He wasn't what she had expected—clean-shaven, well-mannered, lacking the ruggedness she imagined. Those striking blue eyes of his caught her off guard—they were inviting yet mysterious, and she couldn't help but think he was rather handsome.

But looks didn't matter in the grand scheme of things. What truly mattered was if she could trust him with her life—and her baby's

A wave of relief came over Travis as his curious questions about his bride were finally answered. Miss Josephine Callahan wasn't at all what he had expected—she wasn't a woman of spinster age or a girl too young to be considered a woman. Instead, she embodied the perfect image of a mature woman—well-mannered, modest, and dressed in fashionable yet proper attire. Her bonnet, with its ridiculous flowers at the brim and silk ribbon tied under her chin, might be too gaudy for a humble farmer's wife, but her high-neck bodice and matching petticoat were simple enough for Sunday best.

Not only was Miss Callahan of proper marrying age, but she was also easy on the eyes. Her blonde hair, the exact shade of wheat, peeked out from under that gaudy bonnet, shimmering like gold beneath sunlight as the wagon rolled down the main road. Travis did notice her a mite too skinny, her cheekbones sharp beneath her skin and her waist too narrow. But after weeks on the trail, he could sympathize with her.

While Travis didn't mind her petite frame or youth, one concern consumed him: how would she adjust to the rugged realities of frontier life? He had witnessed the challenges it posed to even the strongest individuals—his father and uncle, both of whom passed before turning forty. He could envision the tragic day like it was yesterday, his father dropping dead from a heart attack because of the laborious work. Travis pushed the memory away, like many times before.

No matter if Miss Callahan lacked experience, her delicate demeanor might not be suited for the hardships they would face. When shaking her hand, he was shocked by how soft her hands were—smooth like a baby's skin. She'd need calloused hands, strong stamina, and determination to survive. Yet who was he to say she lacked those skills?

"So . . . um . . . Was it difficult saying goodbye to your family?" Travis asked.

Miss Callahan opened her mouth to answer but then hesitated. Her face turned a deep shade of red. Had Travis said something wrong? He couldn't tell if the heat caused her to flush or if he had somehow upset her. *You fool,* Travis scolded himself, clutching the reins tighter. *What a stupid question to ask. Of course it was upsetting. You can see it on her face.* The last thing he wanted was to make her more uncomfortable than she already seemed.

"I don't have much family," Miss Callahan answered softly, timid like a skittish mouse. She dropped her gaze. "I only have my great-aunt."

Travis chewed his lower lip and looked ahead. "I'm sorry."

He averted his eyes back to Miss Callahan just in time to catch her sneaking a brief glance at him. Her gaze quickly shifted away. Sensing her hesitation, Travis remained silent, allowing her the space to speak when she was ready.

"Don't be," she finally said. "My family had a plantation before the war. I had three brothers who perished in the war, leaving my parents and my younger sister, Susannah. They passed from fever seven years ago."

As Travis caught another glimpse of her, he quickly took notice of the pain in her expressions. Her bottom lip slipped under her teeth and her arms wrapped around her body, as though she were hugging herself.

Travis swallowed hard, her painful loss reminding him of his own. "I . . . I am so sorry."

Miss Callahan looked ahead, dropping her hands into her lap. "A lot has happened since the war, but I've learned to manage."

"I heard it was bad." Travis cleared his throat, rubbing the back of his neck. "My family has lived here all my life, so we didn't feel the need to enlist."

"You have a beautiful country here from what I've seen," Miss Callahan said quickly, her voice a bit perkier than before. Her chin lifted. "The mountain peaks are remarkable. Our mountains in North Carolina look nothing like this."

Her words brought a lop-sided smile to Travis's face. "I hope you grow to love it."

Silence stretched between them again like the rolling prairie, but the stillness soon broke when Travis pulled up to the homestead. Miss Callahan fidgeted with her skirt and sat straighter when his children bolted out of the cabin with Aunt Polly behind them, holding Gideon on her hip. Travis gently pulled back the reins, slowing the wagon to a halt. Lillian and Jonas both beamed, their smiles wide and welcoming as they caught sight of the woman who would become their new mother.

Ivy, however, stood back, her expression reserved as she watched beside Aunt Polly. Travis couldn't help but feel a pang of concern. He knew Ivy wasn't one to easily warm up to new people. Still, he hoped she would at least be welcoming and polite to his soon-to-be-bride. After all, this was a fresh start for all of them, and he wanted it to go as smoothly as possible.

"Pa!" Lillian and Jonas shrieked, jumping up and down beside Travis's side of the wagon. Travis dismounted, and the children immediately embraced him. Their hugs tightened as though they hadn't seen him in weeks. Travis squatted to their level and kissed the tops of their heads.

"Be polite," Travis whispered in their ears before turning to help Miss Callahan from the wagon.

Her hand quivered in his as she took careful steps, her fingers cold. When Miss Callahan's muddied shoes hit the ground, Travis's pulse raced. Her eyes intensely studied the homestead and children with a cautious look on her face. There wasn't much to see if she grew up on a plantation. The farm consisted of a modest-sized cabin, a two-story barn with rusting hinges on its doors, and a fenced area behind the barn that held their horses and dairy cow. Beside the cabin stood a chicken coop large enough for twenty chickens, while twenty acres of sprouted wheat stretched beyond it.

Travis removed his hat and raked a hand through his hair. He blew out a breath, saying a fervent prayer. In truth, a part of him longed to see Miss Callahan beg to go home. But looking down at his children, guilt panged at his heart. After everything he put them through, he owed them a new mother.

Travis stood awkwardly by Miss Callahan's side and cleared his throat, ready to introduce her. "Aunt Polly, children, this is Miss Josephine Callahan."

Aunt Polly put out her free hand, offering a friendly smile. "It's so nice to finally meet you, my dear."

Miss Callahan smiled lightly, shaking her hand. "It's nice to meet you Mrs . . ."

Aunt Polly chuckled, adjusting the squealing Gideon on her hip. "Polly Blythe, but you may call me Aunt Polly. That's who the town refers to me as."

Travis moved Miss Callahan's attention to the children. He pointed to Ivy first. "Miss Callahan, this is Ivy. She is my eldest of eight years."

Miss Callahan smiled, putting out her hand. "It's nice to meet you."

Ivy deliberately avoided Miss Callahan's gaze and hand by staring at the ground, kicking stones with her boots. Normally, if Ivy had been meeting a relative or welcoming a new settler, Travis would have reprimanded her for such behavior, but he understood his daughter well. She was cautious, her heart guarded after everything she had been through.

Travis pointed to Jonas, who stared up at them with a grin. "This is my eldest son, Jonas. He is six."

Josie put out her hand. "Nice to meet you, Jonas."

While shaking her hand, Jonas used the other to pull a piece of paper from his pocket and hand it to her. Travis looked over Miss Callahan's shoulder out of curiosity, his brows high. The picture was a square with lines and circles, presumably doors and windows.

Miss Callahan gasped, her grin widening. "Thank you, Jonas. This is beautiful."

Jonas's eyes lit up. "It is?"

"I would love another one if you don't mind."

Jonas looked up at Travis. "Can I, Pa?"

"If you ask your sister first," Travis answered. "You know how picky she is about her pencils."

Jonas turned to Ivy. "Can I, Ivy? Please?"

A long pause lingered between the children. Travis hoped Ivy would be considerate of her brother drawing for Josephine.

Ivy shrugged. "Sure."

Travis exhaled. The tense moment had caused his shoulders to stiffen. He stood behind Lillian and patted her head. "This is Lillian."

Miss Callahan squatted to her level. "And how old are you, Lillian?"

Lillian held up four fingers, making Travis swell with pride. Aunt Polly's schooling was paying off.

Miss Callahan gasped. "You are so smart."

Lillian grinned, bouncing on her toes. "How old are you?"

The group grew quiet. Travis would have told Lillian to hold her tongue, but like Aunt Polly, he remained silent, eager to hear the answer.

"Twenty-three," she answered.

The words were like a lightning bolt of shock. *Twenty-three?* His eyes rounded. Travis had thought her to be twenty-six or slightly older, but twenty-three? His palms grew clammy as the reality of it settled in. How could someone so young be ready for the responsibilities that awaited her? He had hoped for a homemaker, someone with a bit more life experience, someone who could stand strong beside him and his children in the challenges they'd face out west. But now, the image he had built in his mind crumbled. Could Josephine Callahan handle this life? Could she handle *him*?

Miss Callahan stood and turned to Gideon, her expression softening as she took in the sight of the little boy. A gentle glow spread across her face. For a moment, the worries that had weighed so heavily on Travis's mind began to lift. Her eyes beheld something tender and genuine in the way she gazed at Gideon—a way Travis longed to do. The woman knew nothing about the family nor about Gideon's existence until now, and she gave him more affection than Travis ever had.

Gideon's first interaction with his new mother was almost too perfect, as though the match had been sealed. The boy, curious and innocent, reached out towards her with a small, chubby hand.

"Who is this little man?" Miss Callahan asked, tickling his belly. Her eyes squinted as another laugh belted out of her like a lyrical melody.

With slow, dreaded steps, Travis reached Josie's side. "This is my youngest, Gideon," he answered, his gaze low.

"Gideon," Miss Callahan repeated. "What a lovely name."

Travis cleared his throat, the sound cutting through the moment and drawing Miss Callahan's attention away from the child. He didn't mean to disrupt the moment, but so much needed to be addressed—so much still had to be said and done.

"We've changed sleeping arrangements for the night. Our cabin only has two bedrooms. I'm moving Jonas to my room so you can sleep with the girls."

Miss Callahan nodded, her hands clasped in front of her. "That is fine."

"I would ask you to stay with me, my dear," Aunt Polly said, patting Miss Callahan's forearm. "But my cabin is almost half this size. I wouldn't want you overwhelmed and crammed on your first night."

Miss Callahan turned to the girls. "I would love to spend more time with the girls, anyway."

Lillian clapped and bounced on her toes in excitement while Ivy kicked another rock. Travis faced Aunt Polly. "If you don't mind getting Miss Callahan's bed ready and bringing the children inside, I'd like to discuss something with her."

Aunt Polly smiled, adjusting the babbling Gideon on her hip. "Will do." She whistled sharply, getting the children's attention. "Come along, children. Let's give Miss Callahan and your pa some privacy."

Travis's pulse moved to his throat after the door closed behind them all. Miss Callahan's gaze locked with his, eagerly waiting for him to speak. He studied her eyes—dark brown, rich like a glass of brandy, yet impossible to see through. What lay hidden behind them? Would he ever truly know her?

"Miss Callahan," Travis began, scratching the back of his neck. "I've been thinking about the day we marry . . ." He paused for a moment. Despite every urge to delay the wedding, he couldn't ask her to stay under his roof for more than a few days. The last thing he wanted was to bring shame upon her. "Would you be willing to get married this Saturday? I know you'd like to have a day or two to settle in and get to know the children beforehand."

Miss Callahan nodded, then slowly wrapped her arms around herself, her gaze dropping to the ground. "I think . . . that'd be best."

"Good. I'll meet with the pastor tomorrow to get it all set up and complete some errands in town. Would you like to watch the children for a few hours then . . . Aunt Polly is close by if you need her."

Miss Callahan smiled, her timid eyes meeting his. "All right."

Before Travis could say anything else, Lillian's squealing voice interrupted him. She peeked her head out the door.

"Miss Callahan! Your bed is next to mine. Come and see!"

Miss Callahan softly chuckled as they heard Aunt Polly getting onto the child. "I guess that's my cue."

She turned around to follow Lillian, but Travis felt obligated to offer his gratitude. For a woman with no prior experience and fresh off a long journey, Josephine Callahan was doing remarkably well bonding with his children. No woman would travel thousands of miles, wade through ankle-deep mud, and still have patience for a four-year-old unless she had a profoundly good heart.

"Joseph—I mean . . . Miss Callahan," Travis stuttered. His ears and face burned. *Get yourself together, Travis.*

Miss Callahan turned around. "Yes, Mr. Blythe?"

"Thank you."

She nodded before taking Lillian's hand. As the door closed behind them, Travis placed his hands behind his head, drawing in a deep breath before exhaling slowly. This was actually happening. In two days, he would be a married man again. His eyes burned as he stared up at the vast blue sky. *Forgive me, Sophie.*

CHAPTER FIVE

BRUSHING HER HAIR WHILE seated on Jonas's bed, Josie reflected on how supper went hours ago. Travis had sat quietly while Aunt Polly did most of the talking. Josie had been nervous they'd have so many questions to ask about her, but thankfully Aunt Polly mostly spoke about the town and the projects the church ladies were working on.

Carrying too many secrets was a treacherous burden, especially when previous secrets had once put her life in jeopardy with Marcus—and now, her child's life rested in the hands of a stranger who could just as well be cruel. One wrong word could blow her cover and expose her deception. So she found it safer to remain quiet, speaking only to the children. After all, they were one of the reasons she was here.

When Travis asked about her family in the wagon, Josie told the truth, only leaving out her husband and baby. She didn't have much time left now that she was four months along. Soon, she would be showing. Josie placed her hand over her small bump. *Only two more days,* she told herself. But reminding herself of her true intentions made her stomach sour again. Travis was a polite man from what she had seen in the short time she'd known him.

Josie touched her throat and swallowed hard. *Until he has you in his grasp.*

"Hello, Miss Callahan," Lillian said cheerfully, entering dressed in her nightgown. Ivy followed behind her, her hair tucked inside her nightcap.

"Hello, girls."

From what Josie observed, Lillian was a chatterbox and Jonas was very passionate about drawing and animals. However, Ivy wasn't very talkative. Josie didn't blame the girl. After losing her own mother, Josie could imagine the child's pain in getting a new one.

Ivy pulled back her bed sheets while Lillian pounced onto Josie's bed. Lillian reached out to touch Josie's hair. "Your hair is pretty."

"Lillian!" Ivy snapped, her lips pursed in a scowl. "Don't touch Miss Callahan's hair."

Lillian jumped back and lowered her head. "I'm sorry."

Josie smiled, rubbing Lillian's shoulder. "It's all right. I don't mind."

Lillian's frown curved into one of her signature smiles—her mouth widening enough to expose the top of her gums. Lillian began rubbing the ends of her brown hair. "Miss Callahan, Pa says when you're married, I have to call you by your first name, but I forgot."

"It's Josephine," Josie answered.

The child's eyes widened. "That's a *long* name."

Josie chuckled. "It is, but you may call me Josie."

"Josie," Lillian repeated with her blue eyes bulging. "I like it!"

Ivy huffed, falling back onto her mattress. "Lillian, come to bed. Let Miss Callahan rest."

"All right, all right!" Lillian grumbled, rolling her eyes. She reached out, giving Josie a hug. "Goodnight, Miss Callahan."

"Goodnight, Lillian," Josie said in a soothing whisper, rubbing the child's back. When Lillian pulled away, Josie turned her head towards Ivy, who was already tucked under the covers. "Goodnight, Ivy."

Ivy didn't respond. The covers rustled as they settled into their beds. Josie peeled back her quilt and went underneath. She closed her eyes, taking a deep breath that filled her lungs with the comforting scent of fresh linen. It was the first time she had laid down all day, and as her body sank into the mattress, she let out a soft sigh. The tension in her back eased as it straightened against the supportive surface, and for a moment, she allowed herself to forget the day's events, surrendering to rest.

Her eyes practically closed on their own, and she placed her hands on her midsection, bidding her little one sweet dreams. Within minutes, Josie's mind settled enough for her to sleep.

However, her rest was interrupted by a small cry. Josie opened her eyes and sat up. The crying carried through the thin walls. She grabbed her shawl from the chair where she had laid it and pulled it around her.

Josie crept down the hallway until she opened the door to Travis's bedroom, except Travis wasn't there. He mentioned earlier he would be sleeping in the barn loft. She made her way to the crib, her heart softening at the sight of the tiny, wailing figure. She pulled Gideon up and sat in a rocking chair in the corner of the room.

"Shh," Josie whispered, rubbing his soft head. "It's all right."

The baby quieted within moments as Josie cradled him against her shoulder, gently rocking him back and forth. Soon enough, his cries faded into soft breaths, and he fell asleep again. As Josie glanced up, she spotted Jonas fast asleep in his father's bed, the covers tucked snugly around him. *The boy sleeps like a rock.*

Josie sighed as Gideon's small, gentle breaths echoed through the silence. The moment was so peaceful, she didn't want to leave the chair. She wanted to stay in that rocker forever, holding her soon-to-be son. What would it be like to hold the baby growing inside her? She had been so consumed with running away, she rarely thought about holding it in her arms.

Looking down at Gideon, she thought of Travis. Would her unborn child have a father to hold him or her too? However, that depended on how she acted Saturday night. Josie buried her face in Gideon's shoulder. In this room, she'd deceive Gideon's father. Her thoughts were sickening, but her concern for her unborn child outweighed her morals.

Aunt Tia's voice echoed in her mind. *What man is going to believe a woman who is so desperate to go west and marry a stranger with kids? . . . You're too young and attractive.* Josie had nowhere else to go, no one to turn to.

Josie kissed the sleeping baby's head. "I'll try my best with you, but I can't promise, little one," she whispered. "I'll try to be your ma."

CHAPTER SIX

Travis's pulse raced while he sat on the church's front pew, waiting for Reverend Levingston. He didn't know who to talk to about the situation, other than Aunt Polly, but she was a woman. What about a husband's perspective? The reverend had children. Would he remarry for the sake of his children if his wife died? And what about the townsfolk? What would everyone think Sunday morning when he entered the church house with a new wife on his arm? Would they accept Miss Callahan?

Reverend Caleb Levingston entered through the church doors with his black leather Bible in hand, his chocolate-brown hair slicked behind his ears. He wasn't much older than Travis, so Travis was confident he could ask for advice. The reverend, of all people, would know what to say.

Travis stood and shook the man's hand. "I strongly appreciate you meeting with me."

"No place I'd rather be," Reverend Levingston said, patting his Bible. "Do sit down."

Travis nervously fidgeted with the patch on his thigh, looking down as the reverend sat next to him. Travis curled his fists, trying to calm himself, but the throbbing in his mind continued. It seemed his head would explode from his thoughts. Not every day a man had to ask his pastor to officiate a wedding to a woman he barely knew.

"What brings you here today, Travis? You seem nervous."

Travis scratched behind his ear. "Is it that obvious?"

Reverend Levingston raised an eyebrow and pointed to Travis's fidgeting leg.

Travis stopped twitching. His cheeks burned. "Oh. Sorry."

"Whenever you're ready to speak, I'm here."

Travis folded his hands in his lap, leaning forward. "I can't stop thinking about Sophie. It's been ten months, you know?"

"The congregation isn't the same without her. She was a special woman."

"Yes, there is no one like her." Travis tried to bring up the advertisement, the reply, and having a woman he didn't know watching his children, but the words caught in his throat. The words were too hard to salvage, just like they were too difficult to admit.

"I've been worried for my children. They need a motherly figure . . . especially Gideon. Aunt Polly asked me . . . well . . . to consider putting an advertisement out for a wife . . ." Travis paused, looking up at Reverend Levingston, who was nodding along. He seemed not to be as disgusted as Travis thought he'd be. Travis cleared his throat, adjusting his collar. "I received a reply from a young woman . . . Miss Callahan from North Carolina. She arrived yesterday, and . . . I was wondering . . . if it's not any trouble for you . . ."

"To officiate your wedding?" Reverend Levingston finished.

Travis nodded, relaxing his shoulders in relief. "Yes, if it is not a problem. But if it is . . . I'd like to ask for the church's forgiveness."

Reverend Levingston laid a hand on Travis's shoulder. "Travis, there's nothing wrong with wanting your children to have a mother, or you desiring a companion. The Bible clearly states a man shouldn't be alone. That's why God made Eve for Adam. There was something missing in His creation, so God made a woman."

Travis's throat tightened. "I'm just . . . I'm worried. W-What if I make the same mistake. You know what happened to Sophie . . . I can't bear putting another woman and my children through that again."

"Travis," Reverend Levingston said calmly. "I know you are still grieving Sophie, but you must stop blaming yourself. What happened to her was terrible, but you must move on. Take Miss Callahan as a blessing. Love her. Care for her. Knowing Sophie, she'd want you to find love again."

Travis looked up at the reverend. "Do you think Sophie would approve of this?"

Reverend Levingston nodded. "Very much. She wouldn't want you and the children to remain unhappy."

Travis sat quietly, his gaze fixed on the pulpit, the polished wood gleaming in the soft stream of sunlight. For the first time in his life, he was utterly confused. He would be a married man again in a day's time, but he didn't know what to think. Could he truly give Josephine Callahan a life of contentment when she'd never be more than his children's mother?

He thought of Sophie and the love they had shared, a love he felt he was about to trade for a stranger. How was any of this fair? How could he vow to love and honor Miss Callahan if he could never promise her anything more than companionship he wasn't sure he wanted? He closed his eyes. *Lord, please help me find a piece of my heart to be a kind and considerate husband. Help me learn to care for her. Help soften my hardened heart to welcome her into our home—for the sake of my children.*

"When would you like the ceremony to be?" Reverend Levingston asked.

"How about tomorrow morning? I would like it to be as small as possible. Just your wife and sons, Aunt Polly, and the children. I'm just not ready for a big celebration."

"You have my word," Reverend Levingston promised with a smile.

Travis grabbed his hat from the pew and stood. "Thank you, Reverend."

Reverend Levingston arose from his seat and shook Travis's hand again. "Your family will be in our prayers."

"I appreciate that," Travis said. "It means a lot."

Travis stepped inside his cabin, only to be met with a thick, foreign silence. Aunt Polly sat at the table, mending Jonas's clothes—torn during a church picnic when he caught them on a fence.

"You're home early."

Travis hung his hat on the hook behind the door. "I went to see the reverend and decided to get supplies another day."

"Oh? What did our dear reverend have to say?"

"He will officiate the wedding tomorrow, and he is praying for us."

"How kind of him," Aunt Polly said with a smile. "I can't wait for Miss Callahan to meet his sweet wife."

Travis crossed his arms. "I hope they will get along well. She needs some female companionship other than the girls and you ole' grump."

Aunt Polly chuckled and threw Jonas's shirt at him. "You crazy fool."

Travis snickered then peered out the window. "Where are the children and Miss Callahan?"

"They're out having a picnic in the meadow."

Travis picked up Jonas's shirt and sat at the table. Aunt Polly stared at him, her eyes narrowed and forehead wrinkled.

"What?" he asked sharply.

"Why don't you go join them?"

Travis shook his head and swatted the air. "Nah, they need some bonding time with her. I don't want to interrupt."

"What about *your* bonding time with Miss Callahan?"

"We have the rest of our lives to get to know each other."

"Don't you want to know more about the woman you're marrying?"

"I already know her," Travis claimed, but it wasn't true. The more he thought about Miss Callahan, the more of a mystery she was to him.

Aunt Polly snorted, pulling a thread through Jonas's trousers. "And what do you know?"

Travis slumped forward. "Well, she's from North Carolina, her brothers died in the war, her parents and sister are dead, she has one great aunt, and she—"

"What about *her*?" Aunt Polly pushed. "What makes her laugh? What does she do during her leisure time? What is her favorite childhood memory?"

Travis sighed, leaning back in his chair. "What's the point? It's not going to be a real marriage."

"It's a real marriage if you say vows before God." Aunt Polly's gaze softened. "I know Miss Callahan isn't Sophie, but can you at least try for the children? What example are you setting, hiding away from her like she's a disease? Why would Ivy want to warm up to her if she notices her father isn't making an effort?"

Aunt Polly did have a point. *Blasted woman!* Why did Aunt Polly have to be right all the time? The day before, Travis had noticed how distant Ivy acted with Miss Callahan whenever the woman tried to engage with her. What if Ivy never accepted Miss Callahan as a mother? The little girl could carry the loss of her real mother as a barrier between them forever.

However, here Travis was, doing the same thing in his own way. The realization hit him like a punch to the gut. Perhaps if he interacted with her today, he could set an example. He didn't have to carry a deep conversation, just act as though he was making an effort.

Travis stood. "I guess I'll go. You made your point."

Aunt Polly laughed. "What can I say? I'm always right."

Travis grumbled under his breath and grabbed his hat. "Sure you are." He turned to walk out the door, but Aunt Polly's voice interrupted him.

"Wait." She approached him, cleaning an object with her apron. She finished then handed it to Travis. He stared at the golden ring in his palm, clearly too small for him to wear.

"That was mine when I married your uncle. I want you to have it—to give to Miss Callahan."

Travis blinked, shifting his weight. "What? A-Are you sure about this?" He held up the shiny piece of jewelry. "This is *your* ring."

Aunt Polly placed her hand over his, closing the ring into his fist. "More than anything. You've been through a lot, Travis, and I know how you are feeling, but this is a new beginning—a brand new start."

A lump swelled in Travis's throat. "She deserves more, Aunt Polly. How could I let her settle for a dirt-poor farmer?"

"That's her decision, Travis. She came all this way for *you.*"

His grip tightened around the ring. "She can't have me. She's here for the children."

Aunt Polly kissed his stubbly cheek. "I love you. You're like a son to me, and I just want you to be happy."

"Love you too," he croaked. Travis shoved the ring into his pocket, fighting back tears. He pressed his lips together and walked out the door.

The tall prairie grass swayed in the wind as he made his way to the far side of the property where a wild meadow was in full bloom. Shades of lavender, yellow, green, pink, and blue danced before his eyes. Meadows were all over the place it seemed, and Sophie adored them. She always had their house filled with different arrangements. There was always a new arrangement on the table with a variety of colors.

How he missed that. Travis hadn't known how much he wanted it back—until she was taken from him. Now that Sophie was gone, he wished he could have told her how much he loved that, even when he complained about the strong, odd smells some of them had. Oh, the things he would do to see those arrangements again—just the way she did them.

Travis stood behind the trunk of a large pine tree, his hands resting on the rough bark as he watched Miss Callahan and his children in the distance. Jonas sat on the picnic blanket, playing with Gideon while the girls picked flowers with their soon-to-be stepmother. Lillian stuck close to Miss Callahan, her tiny hand never far from the woman's skirt. It warmed Travis's chest to see Lillian getting along so well.

His gaze shifted to Ivy, who lingered on the edge of the group as she plucked flowers at a distance. Though she wasn't entirely withdrawn, she had a lingering hesitation that Travis recognized in himself. Ivy seemed caught between wanting to join in and holding herself back.

Miss Callahan's hair was styled differently than the day before. Her long blonde hair fell freely down her back, the color nearly blending with the wheat fields in the distance. The sight took Travis's breath away, stirring something deep within him that he hadn't expected. His gaze followed her across the field, her voice carrying through the valley. Yesterday he could barely get a word out of her, and when he had, it had been so soft.

Miss Callahan's hand fit in Lillian's as if she had already molded into their lives. Travis wished they could continue the arrangement without matrimony, but that wasn't an option. Though he admired how easily the children bonded with Miss Callahan, he could hardly stand to watch any longer. A knot tightened in his stomach. The thought of her fully taking Sophie's place was more than he could bear.

Travis decided to leave. He didn't want to see any more. He pivoted on the ball of his foot and set off to the homestead.

"Pa!" Lillian shrieked, interrupting him in his path.

Travis wiped his face and exhaled before facing his family. Attempting a slow turn, he noticed his daughter running towards him, her pigtails flying behind her. A smile tugged at the corners of his mouth as he bent down and scooped her effortlessly into his arms. She giggled, wrapping her arms around his neck as he lifted her. Travis kissed her cheek and forgot all his worries and anxieties from moments ago.

"I love you," he whispered against her cheek.

"I love you, too, Pa," Lillian said back, her hands cupping his face.

Travis carried the lightweight girl back to the picnic area where Ivy and Jonas greeted him. Ivy reached out for his hand while Jonas tugged at his shirt. Miss Callahan, who had been quietly watching from a distance, didn't say a word. Instead, she leaned over and picked up Gideon, who squirmed on the blanket. Gideon giggled and squealed as she nuzzled his face.

"Pa, look what I found!" Ivy exclaimed, showing him her wild-flower bouquet.

"It's beautiful," Travis said. The bouquet nearly brought tears to his eyes. Not only did Ivy have her mother's features, but she also had her mother's gift.

"Josie helped us pick them," Lillian said.

The name caught Travis by surprise. He raised a brow. "Josie?"

Lillian gasped and covered her mouth. "Oops. I meant Miss Callahan."

"I told her she may call me that," Miss Callahan quickly explained with her face blushing. Her gaze remained fixed on his chest. "It was difficult for her to say Josephine."

Travis smiled politely. "No harm done. It suits you."

Miss Callahan turned to Gideon and planted a kiss on the side of his head. Gideon clapped his hands and looked at Travis, flashing him a wide-mouthed grin. Nausea swirled in Travis's stomach. He glanced down at Ivy, desperate to escape what should have been a happy family moment.

"Ivy, would you mind taking Gideon from Miss Callahan?" Travis asked.

Ivy nodded and obeyed without question, stepping forward to take Gideon into her arms. The little boy went willingly, his small hands clutching his sister's dress. Travis rubbed his hands together.

"Children, I need to speak with Miss Callahan alone," he explained. "Go join Aunt Polly at the cabin, please."

Travis set Lillian down. Just as her feet hit the ground, she pushed Jonas. "Race ya!"

"Hey!" Jonas shouted, scrambling to his feet before he bolted after her.

Finally alone with his bride-to-be, Travis threaded his fingers through his hair. He hesitated for a moment, searching for the right words. "I spoke with the reverend today . . . He said he doesn't mind officiating . . . if you still want to get married."

Miss Callahan nodded, her gaze flickering toward him briefly before dropping back to the ground. "That is fine with me."

Travis noticed the way she avoided his eyes, the subtle change in her posture. She wrapped her arms around herself and shifted up and down on her feet. Was this timid behavior simply her acting shy? Or maybe it was the awkwardness he felt, a part of the distance he desired to create between them.

"Miss Callahan, I was hoping . . . if you don't mind telling me why you wanted to marry me?" Travis wiped his forehead, his palm damp with sweat. "I hope I don't offend you, but you're very young and . . . surely you must have plenty of suitors at home. Why would you tie yourself down to me and four children in the middle of nowhere?"

Her eyes widened, clearly caught off guard by his question. She blinked a few times. "I-I just wanted a family," she said slightly above a whisper. "It has been a long time since I had anything like this. Today was a dream come true, being with your children. They're wonderful, and . . . I felt like I belonged."

Travis's lips curled at her response. It made him somewhat happy to know that Miss Callahan was genuinely committed. She wasn't as desperate as he had initially perceived her to be; she had a real intent behind her decision. But still, the question lingered in his mind. Why wasn't she married already? She was beautiful by all means, with her qualities and gentle demeanor. Wouldn't North Carolina be full of eligible men? She was only twenty-three, hardly old enough to be labeled an old maid.

Travis hesitated, choosing his words carefully. "It will be hard, Miss Callahan," he said, his tone firm and serious. His arms fell stiff to his sides. "I'll be honest with you—money is tight until the harvest comes in. Being a farmer's wife and a mother isn't the easiest profession. It's demanding, not glamorous. I don't want to mislead you into thinking it's anything other than what it is."

"I know," Miss Callahan answered sharply. "I understand, and I won't abandon these children because of the promise of hardship." She raised her chin high, her shoulders rolled back. "I'm tougher than you think, Mr. Blythe. I've known war, loss, pain, and hunger. *I* was the one running my father's plantation while the men were away at war. I know what hardships are. I've *lived* them."

Travis stepped back, startled by the intensity of her words. "I . . . I didn't mean to offend . . ." he stammered. "I just—"

Miss Callahan held up a hand, her voice softening a touch. "I understand your concerns, truly. I know I don't look like much, but I am *far* from delicate."

"Josie! Come play tag!" Lillian called from the cabin.

Miss Callahan curtsied, surprising Travis with her sudden display of formality. "Until later, Mr. Blythe," she said faintly before turning away.

Travis watched as Miss Callahan ran through the tall grass, her laughter mingling with that of the children. She seemed to embody a blend of grace and resilience that he couldn't quite reconcile. Despite her upbringing as a Southern belle, she didn't fit the mold in the slightest. Even after weeks of wondering—and getting his answers about her looks and age—the itch remained, stronger than ever. This woman was complex, full of surprises.

Who are you, Josephine Callahan?

CHAPTER SEVEN

JOSIE ADJUSTED HER COLLAR and straightened her mother's cameo brooch pinned against her bosom before meeting Travis's eyes. She took his hand, her bare palm fitting against his as he assisted her down from the wagon. The wooden church building stood before them, the small steeple reaching towards the heavens. The exterior that seemed to have once been painted white had mostly faded, leaving the natural wood exposed and weathered, as if no one had touched it with a brush in ages. A parsonage stood beside it, the exterior painted gray and the shutters a robin-egg blue. Rose and hydrangea bushes sprouted around the outside and potted ferns hung from the porch's ceiling.

As Josie stepped onto the ground, her insides churned and breath hitched softly. Her limbs trembled as each moment passed. In a matter of minutes, she'd be a married woman again—and to another stranger.

Would this time be different?

Could she truly find contentment with Travis and his children?

Josie looked down at her plain button-down sage-green dress. It didn't hold a candle to her first wedding gown, an ivory gown of English lace that once belonged to her mother. The sage green dress would have to do; she wasn't expecting anything fancy for a ceremony, anyway.

She recalled her first wedding day, the dress—though breath-takingly beautiful—itching her skin like it were yesterday. After mourning her losses for months, looking in the mirror had given her a new feeling of confidence and beauty. Growing up, Josie always felt slightly awkward with her long legs, flat chest, and fair complexion, but seeing herself as a bride, she had never felt more beautiful.

Holding onto her father's arm, she had been terrified with all the eyes on her. However, those eyes should have been the least of her worries. Nothing had been more frightening than the man standing before her. But what could one expect from an innocent sixteen-year-old? Her past self had been a sweet, naive girl, hardly knowing what to expect in a marriage, other than carrying on a man's last name.

Josie closed her eyes and shook away the memory, exhaling softly. This marriage would be different—being only for the children's benefits—but she couldn't help but remember Aunt Tia's advice when it came down to her own child. Just the thought sent a shiver crawling up her spine. *Worry about it tonight. This moment is about these four children. Think of those poor, motherless dears.*

"Josie!"

Josie opened her eyes, seeing the smiling Lillian holding a bouquet of pink, purple, and blue wildflowers.

"I made this for you."

Josie grinned as she took the child's precious gift. She brought the flowers close to her face, smelling the sweet fragrance. "Thank you, Lillian."

Aunt Polly smiled and extended her free hand that wasn't holding Gideon. "Come along, Lillian. Let's go inside and get situated."

Lillian started to follow her aunt but swiftly turned, wrapping her arms around Josie's legs. Josie stiffened for a moment, caught off guard, before gently returning the embrace.

"I can't wait for you to be my new ma."

The words from Lillian's mouth made Josie's heart flutter. Knowing how excited the child was soothed her jittery nerves. Yet as Josie glanced up and met the eyes of her soon-to-be husband, a lump formed in her throat. She forced a smile, hoping Travis wouldn't see through her facade. He couldn't know how anxious she truly was; if he did, he might delay the wedding—or worse, send her back. Going back wasn't an option. Her child's future depended on this man.

"Are you ready?" Travis asked. The man's hair was slicked back like it had been when they first met. Josie had noticed the day before how fast his dark stubble grew back, and his face was now smooth again.

Josie nodded, forcing herself to suppress the screams in her mind, begging her to run. As she walked beside Travis, she kept a careful distance, her grip tightening around the trembling bouquet in her hands. Each step seemed heavy, and she forced herself to breathe calmer as Travis opened the door. Inside, the children and Aunt Polly sat in the front pew, along with two boys around Ivy's age. In the center aisle stood a man in a suit alongside a woman in a blue cotton dress.

The woman's caramel-brown hair was pulled up with winglets framing her face, making Josie self-conscious about her hair that hung loose past her waist. Her hands couldn't keep steady that morning, making it impossible to pull her hair back into a proper updo.

Travis pointed ahead. "Miss Callahan, meet Reverend Levingston and his wife."

The woman smiled and embraced Josie. "It's so nice to meet you, Miss Callahan."

"Please, call me Josie." She pressed her lips together, forming a smile.

Mrs. Levingston pulled away. "Then you must call me Rose."

Their moment was cut short when Reverend Levingston cleared his throat, patting his Bible. "Shall we begin?"

Rose planted a kiss on Josie's cheek and squeezed her hands. "May God bless you both."

Josie's legs shook as she took the steps towards Travis and Reverend Levingston. However, when she glanced into Travis' face, she realized she wasn't alone in her feelings. Sweat glistened on Travis's forehead, just like that day on a hot afternoon, except this time they were indoors. The thick walls blocked a cool breeze that Josie longed to flow through the closed windows.

Josie held her bouquet instead of taking Travis's hands. Just the thought of touching him at the altar reminded her of holding the hands of a man twenty-five years her senior, his face marked by a deep scar that ran from his right eye down to his cheek. Before she met Marcus, she imagined him having a soft and gentle demeanor beneath that rugged facade. But she had been so wrong. Her head had been poisoned by romantic poetry nonsense.

She knew nothing of the world nor the true evil that happened during war. Josie remained at home, sheltered by her mother, who instructed her never to read those dirty newspapers. That innocence ended when she fought in a war of her own every day in what was supposed to be her safe place, her home with a man who vowed to be her loving husband.

Josie kept her eyes downcast as Reverend Levingston began with a few Scriptures, unable to meet Travis's gaze any longer. Shame fell over her like a heavy quilt, reminding her she was unworthy to stand there before Travis and God. Travis had no idea who he was really marrying. He believed he was marrying a young, untouched woman from North Carolina who longed for a family of her own.

That was a lie.

The truth would be impossible to hide when the baby arrived, healthy and full-term. Then he would know. And when he did, he'd lose all respect for her.

Josie bit her bottom lip. Maybe times were different. She didn't like what she was doing, but she'd do it all for his convenience and her own. She'd hold up her end of the bargain, becoming a mother to Travis's children while he provided for her and the child she carried. Bumps rose on her arms. *But it's still deception.*

"You may join hands while you say your vows," Reverend Levingston said.

Josie's breath caught in her throat, exiting her thoughts. She had no idea what the reverend said beforehand, but those words—words about touch—brought her out of her little world and into reality. *What are you doing, Josie? You're making the same mistake. You hypocrite.*

She closed her eyes. Her lungs contracted, her heart punching her ribcage. *You must do this, Josie. Forget about your fears. Think of your child.* Josie tried her best to soothe her nerves, but a small hand touched hers. Startled, she looked down to see Ivy gently reaching for her bouquet. Josie managed a smile, her tension easing slightly.

"Thank you," Josie whispered. Ivy returned the smile, a faint version.

Josie lifted her chin, meeting Travis's gaze. Slowly, his arms rose from his sides then extended towards Josie's. His touch sent a shiver through her, but she forced herself to endure it, aware of the little ones watching from the front pew. She couldn't let Travis see how broken she truly was. As his damp fingers curled around hers, she noticed the slight flush of embarrassment on his face. He was nervous too.

Despite her fright, Josie forced out the words, "I do." She didn't want to say them, but she had no choice. When Travis spoke, she noticed a slight stutter in his voice, a small tremor that assured her he was just as uncertain. This wasn't about them—it was about their duty to the children, born and unborn.

Travis pulled out a gold ring from his pocket. Josie's eyes widened. *Gold?* Travis was full of surprises. He slipped it around her cold, trembling finger. As Josie watched him, his lips pressed thinly together, as though he was fighting back tears.

"I now pronounce you husband and wife. Travis, you may kiss the bride."

The thought of the kiss made Josie's stomach churn. Holding his hands had already been too much, and now this? She could sense Travis's discomfort as well; he hesitated, clearly unsure. Instead of forcing a kiss on her lips, he leaned in and placed a quick kiss on her cheek. At her first wedding, Josie hadn't been given a choice—neither with the kiss nor with what came after. Now, letting out a steady breath, she realized that this time, maybe things could be different.

The children ran towards them, and Lillian hugged Josie at her feet. "I love you so much, Josie."

Rose appeared at Josie's side, separating her from Travis. "It was a beautiful ceremony."

"Thank you," Josie said, her cheeks warm.

Rose beckoned to the two boys sitting with the children, and they dashed over to her side without hesitation. She shook her head with a soft sigh.

"Boys, you know you're not supposed to run in God's house," she scolded, pulling them close. Their wild brown curls bounced around their faces, clearly untouched by a brush that morning. Turning to Josie, Rose smiled. "Josie, I'd like you to meet my two boys, Paul and Andy."

Josie's lips curved. "Nice to meet you boys."

"Travis's children were very welcoming to them when we settled here two years ago."

"Where were you from?"

"Missouri," Rose answered. "My husband attended a seminary in Liberty. We settled in New Madrid, where he first pastored before here."

"I spent a brief time in Missouri, and from what I've seen, it's a beautiful state."

Rose patted Paul's shoulder. "We hated to leave, but coming here has been a great blessing for church settlements out west." Rose crouched down. "Boys, you are excused. Go play with the children."

They bolted out the door. Josie turned her attention to Travis speaking with Reverend Levingston. A warm, tingling sensation settled over Josie. *So, this is my family now.* Her new reality almost didn't seem real. Not only was she carrying a child in her womb, she had children outside it. Blood didn't matter. She was a mother now, like she had always dreamed of being.

"I hope you don't mind, but I have spent the morning preparing refreshments at my home," Rose said with a friendly smile. "The parsonage is just next door."

Josie gasped, her palm to her mouth. "Oh, Rose, you didn't have to do that."

"I wanted to," Rose replied cheerfully. "I wanted you both to have a proper ceremony."

Proper. There was hardly anything proper about her life anymore. Josie looked down at the golden ring on her left hand. Could she do this? Would her life ever feel proper again?

Travis stiffly settled onto the Levingstons' sofa while Gideon slept peacefully on his chest. It had been months since he'd been this close to the child. When Aunt Polly went outside to monitor the children, Travis had no choice but to step up and be a father. The child nuzzled against him, making Travis long for these moments more, but with every breath, every tiny snore, he was reminded of why Miss Callahan—Josephine, to him now—was here in the first place. Today was her wedding day, and he wouldn't burden her with caring for Gideon.

He pressed his lips together, swallowing down the sorrow as he looked over at Josephine, seated at the parlor table in the corner, sipping tea with Rose. Sophie and Rose had never been particularly close; Sophie was always busy running the homestead and caring for three children, leaving little time for socializing. But here was Josephine, taking advantage of female companionship. Travis knew this would be Josephine's last chance to connect with a woman her age until after the harvest, yet the sight of her laughing softly with Rose eased him.

Travis glanced down at his left hand, where a simple metal band now rested around his ring finger. That hand once wore a gold band that Sophie bought him after selling ten dresses she had sewn one summer. He had grown accustomed to the bare finger over the past few months, but now he would have to adjust to wearing a ring again. Except this wasn't his usual one. This one came from the mercantile and cost less than a third of the price Sophie had paid for his gold band.

During the ceremony, Travis expected Josephine to be somewhat cheerful because it was her wedding day, but she acted skittish as a mouse. Knowing this wasn't a dream wedding every woman hoped for made Travis sick to his stomach. He wanted to look into Josephine's eyes during the ceremony and admire her like a star-struck groom should, but each time he tried, she looked away.

When he took her hands in his, she quivered beneath his touch. Perhaps Josephine was nervous about what she believed would come next—the wedding night. The thought made him cringe. He remembered Sophie's own nerves on their wedding day, her every attempt to avoid coming home with him. But after a long talk, she had come to realize she had nothing to fear. They were husband and wife—two people who loved each other and would never harm one another. The thought of comforting Josephine in the same way made his gut twist. Travis wished he could reassure her that she was safe, but their circumstances were different.

He considered talking to Josephine about her expectations, wanting her to know she didn't have to feel obligated to be a traditional wife. But the idea was too awkward; how could he look that beautiful woman in the eyes and reject her? He gulped, closing his eyes. Why would he think about rejecting her at all. He wouldn't dare put himself in that position. Travis would avoid her at all cost—including even thoughts of the marital bed—so she wouldn't expect anything from him.

"Mr. and Mrs. Blythe."

Travis looked up to see Reverend Levingston peeking through the door that led into the kitchen and dining area.

"Would you two like to cut your cake?"

Travis looked at Josephine the same time she looked at him. Travis shrugged. "Why not?"

He stood slowly, careful not to disturb the sleeping baby in his arms. Even though an ounce of him liked the fact he was holding his son, he was anxious to hand him over to his aunt. He made his way into the dining room, where Aunt Polly was gathering the children. The cake before him wasn't as grand as the one he and Sophie had shared ten years ago, but the guest list was nearly the entire town. This cake was simple and white, adorned with delicate pink roses from the Levingstons' garden, beautifully arranged at the top.

Travis held Gideon securely against him as he glanced at Josephine, who gazed at the cake with wide eyes, admiration etched on her face.

"This is beautiful, Rose," she said.

Rose pressed her hand to her reddening cheek. "Thank you, dear. You are too kind."

Reverend Levingston wrapped his arm around his wife, wearing a playful smile on his face. "I keep telling my wife she needs to open up a bakery here. Don't you think?"

"Darling, don't embarrass me," Rose giggled, her cheeks flushing even more as she playfully swatted at him.

Soon enough, Aunt Polly returned with a trail of excited children following closely behind her. Travis gently handed Gideon over to her, and she cradled the hefty baby in her arms with surprising ease, despite him weighing at least twenty-five pounds.

As Josephine picked up the cake knife, Travis hesitated, unsure if he should help her like he had with Sophie. Before he could ask, Josephine cut into the cake. The Levingstons and Aunt Polly clapped while the children cheered and licked their lips, eager for the sweet treat. Josephine picked up a plate and put the piece on top. Travis's eyes rounded in surprise as she handed him the slice with her warm, curved smile.

"Thank you," he said, but she barely acknowledged him, turning to face the crowd gathered in front of them.

"Who else wants a piece?" Josephine called out, her voice light and cheerful as she lifted the knife again. The children erupted with excitement, raising their hands and shouting eagerly as they surrounded her.

Travis stepped away and joined Aunt Polly in a corner. He dug his fork into the cake and watched as his new wife interacted with the children. *I don't know why she said she didn't have experience. She's a natural.* Yet as much as it delighted him, it hurt just as much. He dipped his head, chewing the inside of his cheek. *You should be here, Sophie. You should be holding your son and visiting with the Levingstons in their kitchen.*

There was no doubt that Josephine would make a wonderful mother. Perhaps he had made the right choice for his children. Despite her youth and lack of experience, Josephine seemed perfectly suited for the role. Travis managed to gaze in her direction, watching while Lillian and Jonas wrapped their arms around her legs, hugging her tightly, their smiles bright and full of affection.

Aunt Polly rocked Gideon from side to side and elbowed Travis. "She's a beauty."

Travis nodded, taking a bite of cake. "That is so."

"I spoke with the children while they were outside. I'm going to let them stay the night with me."

Travis nearly dropped his fork, a sudden shock running through him, almost choking on his food. "What? Why?"

Aunt Polly sighed as she lightly patted Gideon's back. "It is your wedding night, and I thought I'd give you two some privacy."

The thought disgusted Travis. After a long day of gaining a new wife to replace Sophie, the one thing he wanted was having the comfort of his own children. How could Aunt Polly not consult him first?

"That is unnecessary. There will be *no* proper wedding night."

"That is none of my business," Aunt Polly whispered. "And since it isn't, I will assume this is a normal marriage and give you privacy. Don't spoil the children's excitement. They've never stayed the night anywhere."

Travis rubbed his forehead as he held back a heated groan. "You will pay for this."

Aunt Polly giggled. "If you say so."

A knot formed in Travis's stomach. Josephine was beautiful in every way—her wavy golden hair cascading down her back, her small, delicate frame, and those doe-like eyes that were so gentle and sweet. Each feature only deepened his turmoil. He glanced down at his feet, unable to bear the sight of her any longer.

Man shouldn't be alone, Reverend Levingston had told him. A man finding comfort in his own wife wasn't a sin, but Travis couldn't bring himself to consummate. He didn't need comfort of any kind—only knowing his children were cared for.

Most importantly, he wouldn't subject his own heart to the trouble such a choice might bring. Everything attractive about Josephine was a curse to him. He vowed he wouldn't touch her or dare come closer than five feet. She was a great temptation, one that could easily destroy him and the arrangement they made.

CHAPTER EIGHT

JOSIE CALLAHAN, NOW JOSIE Blythe, felt her stomach tighten with each passing second, desperately trying to suppress the urge to vomit. Bile rose in her throat and her hands and neck grew clammy when nightfall came. She sat alone in the children's room, her eyes fixed on the nightgown packed in her suitcase that Aunt Tia gave her for this very moment. Deep down, she wanted to deny that the day had come, but it was happening now—there was no escaping it.

She had fulfilled the first step of marrying Travis, but the next step was far too daunting to bear. With the children at Aunt Polly's for the night, it was the perfect opportunity to execute her plan. *Think about the baby. Do you want him or her to grow up fatherless? Do you want to disgrace Travis's sweet family with a baby everybody knows isn't his?* There wasn't much time. She could save herself with an early delivery as an excuse, but waiting too long would make the lie even harder to believe. Would Travis believe it? Knowing him for three days, she observed him to be smarter than that.

The front cabin door closed. Travis had returned from checking on the wheat. His footsteps echoed down the hallway, and she heard the soft creak of his bedroom door opening. Placing her hand on her stomach, she took steady breaths, inhaling and exhaling to calm herself. Her heart pounded like the clip-clop of hooves, carrying her back to a stagecoach ride. But this was her last stop to seal her child's destiny—and her security. *Now or never, Josephine.*

Was Travis expecting her to come to *his* room? They hadn't discussed this part of their arrangement. Would they share the same room? Would she stay with the children and he in the master bedroom? Josie glanced at the ticking clock on the children's nightstand. She chewed on her short nails. Was Travis waiting for her to join him? Travis seemed shy, so maybe he was waiting for her to make the first move. Josie didn't want to make the first move, but it was a matter of *having* to.

Another minute ticked by, and Josie's nerves twisted, tapping her fingers on the oak bed rail. It was getting late, and church would be early. There wouldn't be much time for intimacy if they waited any longer.

Josie changed into her nightdress, her hands quivering with every movement. Glancing in the mirror, she blushed at her reflection. The light pink chemise clung to her, and the neckline dipped much lower than she was comfortable with. She took a deep breath, trying to calm the fluttering in her stomach. *At least the cabin is dark*, she thought, but that thought quickly faded. She'd be bare soon anyway—what was the point of hiding?

Josie combed her fingers through her curls, trying to appear more presentable. She adjusted her hair carefully, draping it over her chest in an attempt to add a layer of modesty. Her pulse calmed slightly. She placed a hand against her abdomen. "This is for you," she whispered.

She considered grabbing a shawl to ease her discomfort, but a voice in her head urged her on. *He's your husband. Toughen up.* At last, she opened her bedroom door and tiptoed across the weakening floorboards. Gritting her teeth, she reached for the doorknob, her heart thundering in her chest. It seemed as if it were pulsing loudly enough to drown out all other sounds. But she survived worse. Seducing the husband she hardly knew was nothing compared to the horrid things she had already endured.

Josie swallowed her pride and cracked open the door, peeking into the dimly lit room. Travis stood with his back to her, rummaging through the drawers. The moment he turned around, a feverish heat flooded Josie's cheeks, coursing through every fiber of her being. Travis's mouth hung open in surprise, his face paling as their eyes met.

Silence stood between them—a silence that was not pleasant. Travis broke the stillness, glancing down at the floor as he cleared his throat, running his fingers through his hair.

"I apologize. I . . . I just—" he stammered, his voice trailing off for a moment. "I came to gather my things . . ."

Josie's breath hitched and looked down. She moved the rest of her hair in front of her chest for privacy. "I'm sorry I . . . I didn't—"

"No, I'm sorry," Travis said as he stepped forward, his eyes still downcast. With a shaking hand, he handed her a coat that was folded on the bed. Josie took it quickly, immediately wrapping it around her. It practically swallowed her form.

What are you doing, Josie? You must fight for this. This is your child you're talking about. Josie could almost hear Aunt Tia's voice in her head, begging her to try harder. Travis sat on the bed and folded his hands. Before she could speak, or at least say something she hoped might lead to a conversation, Travis interrupted her.

"I apologize. Strongly. It's my fault I avoided the conversation of our . . . marital arrangements." Travis cleared his throat and coughed again. "I decided to move into the loft while you and the children stay in the cabin. I am sorry if this confused you with Aunt Polly taking the children. I-I didn't know she would do that."

Josie considered more to say, but she was rendered speechless, her mouth lacking moisture, barely allowing her to form a single word. The air grew thick and the room hot, just like her face and neck. How could she think that doing this would save her child? Seducing Travis was a lost hope. Aunt Tia was wrong—this wouldn't save her; this would be the end of her and the man she married. She was no better than Marcus, conniving and manipulative.

Tell him. Tell him before it's too late. But how could she tell him now? They had been wedded hours ago. He would put her out on the streets and seek an annulment. Josie would be alone and vulnerable. How could she offer her child safety then?

"I'm sorry for . . . being confused."

Travis shook his head. "No, don't be. I am the one who should be blamed, blamed for everything. You deserved a proper wedding like girls dream. You also deserve a proper wedding night, but I . . . I cannot give it to you."

Josie looked down, pulling a strand of hair behind her ear. "It doesn't matter to me." *But it does, Josie. Think of your baby. Its life depends on this night.*

"It does matter," Travis said sharply. "A family isn't enough for you."

Josie took a step forward, gripping the coat more tightly around her body. "A family *is* enough for me." She bit back the half-lie. She wanted to say what her heart screamed. *I just need your cooperation, Travis. To save me—to save us all.* Instead, she continued what she could say. "This family has welcomed me with open arms, and I don't deserve it. I feel like . . . I feel like I've known your children forever."

Travis sniffed and rubbed his nose. "Don't give up on them, please. Ivy she . . . she is having a tough time, but she'll come around."

"I understand. I would have felt the same way if my father had remarried."

Travis patted his thighs and stood. "I must go."

He didn't hesitate, swiftly gathering his clothes with an urgency that left no room for second thoughts. Before Josie could even muster a protest, he was out the door, closing it firmly behind him. Josie clutched the coat tightly around her petite frame, the warmth doing little to soothe the chill creeping through her bones. For the first time in what felt like ages, she let her tears flow freely.

She had one option now, knowing Travis couldn't be seduced. She'd have to tell him the truth and be at his mercy. Even so, how could she—knowing there was a possibility her child would be at risk?

Tomorrow would be a new day, and she'd try again. She'd fight for this baby, even if it meant more humility and shame.

Chapter Nine

Josie hugged herself nervously after the church service concluded, and curious eyes turned from the pulpit to face her direction. It was her second day as Mrs. Blythe, yet nothing felt different. The newness of the title didn't fit, like a dress tailored for someone else. The looks she received in the church made her feel like a guest, as people tried to uncover who she was and why she sat with a widower, holding his son.

Hours ago, she had woken alone in the medium-sized bed, the sheets cold beside her. Travis had indeed kept his word, avoiding her with his choice to sleep in the barn. The house was quiet, almost too quiet, without the usual chaos of getting the children ready and Aunt Polly cooking breakfast. It should have been relieving, but Josie had never felt more alone, waking up in her new bed that was big enough for two. But she didn't want Travis there, only to use him as the cover for her child's father. She didn't even see Travis until he drove her to church. He had risen early, left out a pot of coffee, and gone to feed the livestock.

Gideon squirmed in Josie's arms as the church service concluded, and she instinctively pulled him closer to her chest while older women approached with bright, warm smiles. Josie's pulse raced, each of their steps making her cheeks grow hot and her head feel lighter. For the first time, Josie wanted to be close to Travis now. Not romantically, but as her shield from the three elderly ladies who walked towards them.

As the women, dressed in her bonnets and Sunday best, reached Josie and Gideon, Travis gently nudged Lillian forward, positioning himself closer to Josie. His elbow brushed against Josie's, and the unexpected contact nearly made her gasp.

"Good afternoon," one of the ladies greeted.

All three had graying hair pulled back into tight buns. However, what caught Josie's eye was the neatly curled bangs of the woman who first approached her. The style was familiar, reminiscent of the fashions she had seen down South. Her mother wore the same updo, which helped settle Josie's nerves.

"How is Mr. Gideon doing?" the one on the left asked, tickling the baby's feet. He let out a loud squeal, lightening the mood with follow-up laughs.

"He's doing well," Travis answered stiffly. "He's still trying to get the hang of crawling."

The woman's eyes widened with surprise. "Crawling *now*? What is he, ten months? My eldest was crawling by six, walking by ten."

"Now, now," the lady in the middle with curly bangs gently interjected, her smile warm as she gazed at Gideon. "Every baby is different. I'm certain Gideon will be walking soon enough." Then she turned her attention back to Josie. "My name is Rebecca Scott. My husband, Harland, and I live half a mile from the Blythes. These two are Mrs. Wilma McHenry and Mrs. Geraldine Kent."

Josie shook each of their hands in turn. "I'm Josie Blythe." Months ago, she would have introduced herself as Josephine, but having the children call her by her family's nickname made her feel as though Josephine was dead. She was now Josie Blythe, taking on a brand-new beginning—mother of five and wife of a humble wheat farmer.

"Blythe?" the three women all said in unison, their eyes widening and jaws dropping.

"You mean you're his *wife*?" Mrs. McHenry asked, her forehead creased in disbelief.

Josie's face turned hot, bouncing Gideon on her hip. "Yes, ma'am. We were married yesterday."

"Yesterday?" they repeated in harmony once more, their shock only growing.

"Travis, I had no idea you were courting, you silly goose," Mrs. Scott teased, her curly bangs bouncing as she playfully elbowed his shoulder. "How'd you two meet? And how come I never knew about this sweet girl? Is she from Bozeman?"

Josie opened her mouth to answer the truth that she was ashamed of—being a mail-order bride from down South—but Travis interrupted her.

"I met my wife through some relatives. We corresponded by letters for a good while and extended a courtship. I proposed over a month ago, and we married yesterday."

The three women sighed in unison, their expressions softening with the romanticized version of their story.

"That is so romantic," Mrs. Kent said, clapping her hands together. "I had no idea you had other family connections so nearby."

"Distant," Travis quickly corrected. He glanced down at Lillian, Ivy, and Jonas, who stood awkwardly by their sides. "You're excused to go play," he told them, and they didn't hesitate, darting out the door to join the other children already outside.

Josie stood in stunned silence, shocked by Travis's lie. She couldn't understand why he would choose to make up a false, romanticized story about their relationship. Mail-order brides were common enough, so why did he feel the need to pretend they had fallen in love through letters? Was he ashamed of her? Did he suspect her as a fraud? Her pulse quickened. How much did he know?

"And to think she's gonna raise your four young'uns. She's a keeper all right. Not every pretty young thing wants to raise another woman's children," Mrs. Scott remarked, leaning in towards Josie with a smile. "He's a quiet man. No wonder it's so easy for him to keep secrets."

Josie looked down, seeing Travis's fists curl. Did these women think he tricked her into marrying him? She was the deceiver. Not him. If they suspected anything, she was the liar.

Gideon let out another delighted squeal, babbling in his baby language as he pointed toward a family on the other side of the church. Josie could hardly keep him in her arms. Each time he reached out and squirmed, she was afraid she'd drop him. Travis quickly noticed her distress and scooped Gideon into his arms.

"Sounds like he saw his buddy. Josephine, would you follow me? I have someone for you to meet."

"Nice to meet you three," Josie said swiftly before following her husband. Thank goodness for Gideon's behavior and Travis's excuse.

Travis led her towards a family of seven, gathering their belongings on a pew. The woman at the center of the group had bright red hair, the same shade shared by the two older girls standing beside her. The taller girl carried a boy just slightly older than Gideon, and the woman held a girl of similar size. Two toddlers—twins perhaps. A boy around Jonas's age pulled on his father's sleeve, asking to go outside. The man nodded, and the boy took off out the door.

The man smiled when he made eye contact with Travis. "Aye, Travis. How good it is t'see ye." He tickled the squealing Gideon's belly. "And ye too, wee lad."

They shook hands, and for the first time Josie saw her husband smile—truly smile. Travis wasn't trying to break an awkward moment or trying to fake his emotions. Here with his friend, he appeared genuinely happy.

Travis balanced Gideon on his hip and shook the woman's hand. "Good day, Caroline." Travis nodded towards the two older girls who looked as though they were between the ages nine and thirteen. "How are you, girls?"

The taller one fought against the toddler's grip on her red hair. "Doing fine, sir." The other one smiled, looking down and avoiding his gaze. The girl's demeanor made Josie smile. Despite her red hair and freckled complexion, the girl's demeanor was almost identical to Susannah's. Susannah had a quiet manner and hardly looked anyone in the eyes, even her acquaintances.

Travis extended his free hand towards Josie, and she joined his side. His arm wrapped around her shoulders, nearly making her jump. She'd have to learn to get used to his sudden, innocent touches. She faked a smile, eager to perform as the newlywed bride.

"I'd like you to meet our neighbors, Ronan Walsh, his wife Caroline, and their children. Or as you see now, the leftover bunch. There's one missing." Travis's lips curved at his joke. "The eldest is Alice, the other is Nan, the little boy is Brendon, and the girl is Molly."

Caroline chuckled. "My eldest boy, Liam, just ran outside to play. He enjoys playing with Jonas.

Josie smiled. "That's all right. He seemed like a lovely boy when I saw a blur of him."

"A handful too," Caroline added.

Caroline's voice caught Josie off guard. It was precise and proper, just like the women of her class, except the woman didn't have a southern charm. It seemed as though she was a Northerner, but from where? The woman was indeed educated and well-mannered with her posture.

"'Tis a pleasure to meet ye, Mrs. Blythe," Ronan said in a thick accent, almost Celtic like the neighbors Josie's family had from Ireland. "Ye've married well, no doubt about it."

Josie's cheeks warmed again, clasping her hands in front of her. "Yes, I believe I did."

Caroline handed her small daughter to the shy one called Nan. Caroline stepped closer to Josie, her shoulders rolled back and chin held high.

"I confess, I was excited when Ronan told me Travis wed. Since then, I have been wanting to ask you something, but I did not want to disturb you while you were settling in. Would you like to contribute to our Founder's Day celebration? It's this Saturday, and I'm in desperate need of volunteers to make pies and cobblers. Rose is baking a cake."

"I would be honored." The thrill of baking seemed almost too good to be true. Josie had adored baking at her home in Asheville. Mammy had been the best teacher, and when Josie married Marcus, he forbade her from such activities. He said her duty was to him, not the kitchen.

"Lovely," Caroline said. She turned towards her daughters. "Did you hear that, girls? It seems like you have some competition."

Josie chuckled, placing her hand on the pew siding. "I'm a little rusty, so I definitely won't outshine y'all."

"My Alice likes to cook," Caroline said. "And Nan here is still learning. I hope to introduce her to our family special recipes."

"Special?" Josie repeated. "That sounds like something I can't compete with."

Caroline placed her hand over Josie's which still rested on the pew. "We are delighted to have you here. I have been longing for a companion close by."

"Well, you have one now," Josie said gently, her grin growing. Caroline seemed too good to be true, and so did Rose. In seven years, Josie hadn't had this, a connection between women near her age.

Travis turned to Josie. "Are you ready to go? I think Gideon needs to be changed."

Josie nodded. "Yes, I believe that would be best." She turned back to Caroline. "Come by and visit any time."

"You won't be seeing the last of me," Caroline said through giggles.

Josie turned towards the doorway, noticing most of the church members had left, leaving her nerves behind.

Travis sat in silence next to Josephine on the way home. The children giggled in the back, playing with Gideon. Travis glanced at Josephine, who was looking straight ahead, her expression unreadable with her hands resting in her lap.

He chewed his inner cheek. After last night, he wasn't sure what to say or how to act. The image of her standing in his doorway, dressed in something far more revealing than he ever imagined she would wear, had been seared into his memory. Nearly torture to admit, but in that moment, Josephine had been breathtaking. Her beauty had caught him off guard, stirring feelings he had buried deep within himself.

But he couldn't let that moment, or those feelings, take control of him. He had to remember Sophie and the promise he had made to himself. His relationship with Josephine was meant to be practical, a partnership for the sake of the children. He had never intended it to be anything more, no matter how his body and mind betrayed him. He tightened his grip on the reins, forcing himself to focus on the road ahead, even as the memory of Josephine lingered, making the silence between them seem even heavier.

Travis wasn't entirely surprised that Josephine came to his room. In hindsight, he realized he should have set clear boundaries, no matter how awkward it might have been. That choice could have spared Josephine the embarrassment.

Poor girl, he thought to himself, his soul heavy with guilt. He rubbed his face with a sigh. Each time he tried to push the night away, flashes kept returning. Those eyes of hers, wide with humiliation, her perfectly shaped lips parted and trembling, a bright shade of red rising across her pale skin, blooming in uneven splotches that crept up her neck and over her cheeks.

"Why did you do that?" Josephine asked.

A sharp pang shot through Travis's chest, nearly stealing his breath. His mind raced, just like his heart. Did Josie know what he had been thinking? How could she? Was it written all over his face? He rubbed the back of his sweat-coated neck. *Take me now, Lord.*

"What?" he asked quickly. *Surely she's not bringing this up with the children in the back.*

"You lied to those women. Why couldn't you have told them the truth?"

Travis drew in a breath, relieved that the subject of last night had been dropped, though the guilt about his lies remained. He hadn't planned to lie in God's house when he woke that morning. The falsehood had come over him suddenly. He had panicked, longing to save Josephine's reputation. Josephine was already embarrassed enough for not being a proper wife like she probably hoped.

Did she hope? Had Travis accidentally led her to believe she and him would be properly wed? Had it been those looks he snuck? Perhaps the golden ring Aunt Polly gave him? As for her reputation, surely she wouldn't want the world to know about their arrangement. Josephine, the mail-order bride—that was who she'd be before the town knew her personally. Yet Travis didn't know her either. Josephine the mail-order bride was who she was to him. A stranger brought into his life by necessity, not love. That was the role she would continue to play in his mind, no matter how much time they spent together.

"It was to protect your reputation," Travis said hoarsely, his mouth dry. "No woman wants to be known as a mail-order bride for the rest of her days."

"But it was a lie."

Travis stiffened. "I know." He turned to her. "I'm sorry. If you'd like, I can correct myself and explain—"

"No," Josephine interrupted. She lowered her head and wrapped her arms around herself. "You were just trying to do your best. Forget what I said."

Travis's wife grew silent again, but there was something peculiar about her. Why did she cower away from him so quickly, right when he wanted to set things right? Josephine slumped forward and tucked a strand of hair behind her ear. Travis turned away and snapped the reins. His muscles eased when the sight of his farm came into view, burying his odd observation.

CHAPTER TEN

JOSIE SAT IN THE rocking chair beside the unlit fireplace, bouncing little Gideon on her lap. Lillian and Jonas sat cross-legged at her feet, their small hands making wooden farm animals gallop across the floorboards. Seated at the table, Ivy hunched over her sketch pad, her pencil moving in quick, deliberate strokes, lost in her own world, avoiding the family gathering. Josie enjoyed spending time with the children, but she wished Travis was more involved. She could almost feel the space he put between them, as if her presence was something he had to escape.

She didn't mind the distance when the children weren't around, but why be distant again when she was watching the children? If they were all supposed to be one big family, didn't the father need to be in the picture? They had gone to church together that morning, so why couldn't they continue the act at home? Why couldn't they be one happy family, even just for a little while longer?

"Josie, look!" Jonas exclaimed, his voice bubbling with excitement.

Josie lifted her eyes from the squirming baby in her lap, watching as Jonas made his wooden horse soar through the air with enthusiastic whooshes. A warm smile fell across her face. "He is one fast horse."

"His name's Flash," Jonas declared proudly. "It's the name of Pa's horse."

"I wanna ride Pa's horse," Lillian chimed in, still guiding a wooden pig across the floor.

"You're too little to ride Pa's horse," Ivy snapped.

Josie's gaze drifted to Ivy. "What are you drawing?"

For a moment, Ivy remained silent, her pencil pausing mid-stroke. Josie held her breath, waiting, wishing for something more than the quiet distance between them. Finally, Ivy sighed, her voice flat as she muttered, "Mountains."

Josie set the wiggling Gideon on the ground. "What kind of mountains?"

Ivy stared at her, her facial expressions not changing. "Mountains."

Josie smiled as the visions of home entered her mind. "Where I'm from, the mountains look very different than the ones here."

"What ya mean?" Jonas asked, his eyebrows raising. "How different?"

"They're called the Blue Ridge Mountains. The ones here are called the Rocky Mountains."

Lillian's eyes widened in wonder. "Are they blue?"

"Indeed, they are. They're blue and green. The mountains here are much pointier, while the Blue Ridge ones are flatter."

"I wish I could see them," Jonas said, lying on the ground with his elbows propped up. Gideon crawled to him and squealed.

"I could draw them for you," Josie offered, a gentle hope in her voice.

Jonas gasped, his mouth growing wider. He sat up and turned to Ivy. "Ivy! Ivy! Let Josie draw them! Let her please!"

Ivy closed her notebook and hugged it against her chest. "Josie can't draw."

"I can, Ivy. I'd like to show you if you'd let me."

Ivy huffed and walked over to Josie, her jaw clenched. Josie took the pencil and opened Ivy's book to a blank page. Then she pointed the pencil's end downward and began sketching the familiar outlines of the Blue Ridge Mountains. Her pencil glided across the paper, curving out the gentle slopes and filling in the blank spaces with texture to make up for the lack of color. After ten minutes, she finished. She held the sketchbook up, showing the children.

Jonas gasped. "Woah! That does look different."

"It just needs some color," Lillian added, tilting her head as she examined the drawing.

Ivy yanked the notepad back, letting out a frustrated sigh. "If only Pa had the money to buy me paints."

"Pa says we gotta wait 'til the harvest," Jonas explained.

"He said that last year," Ivy scoffed. "And the year before that. I'll never get my paints."

Josie's stomach sank at Ivy's disappointment. The girl's posture slouched and her bottom lip puckered. Josie still had the money Travis had sent before their marriage—nearly four hundred dollars. If she returned it, Ivy could have her paints, and Travis wouldn't have to stress out about the harvest so much. Maybe that was why he was avoiding her. He sacrificed everything to give these children a mother, and he could never love her as a husband should. Josie would be a burden to him for the rest of her life. Just like how she was to Papa after the war and then to Marcus. Josie shuddered.

No, this was different.

"When you get some, Ivy, I'll give you a lesson," Josie offered gently.

Ivy's eyes widened. "You paint?"

Josie nodded, a smile curving on her lips. "I do. It's one of my favorite things to do."

For the first time, Ivy truly smiled in Josie's presence. *Perhaps that was all Ivy needed. Something in common with me.*

Josie looked at the time from the wall clock. It was almost eight—time for the children to be put to bed. Through the large living room window, a faint glow of a lantern shone from the barn loft. Travis was still out there. She knew she needed to return the money he had given her, and maybe this was also a chance to talk. Maybe one last try.

Then she'd never disappoint anyone again.

Travis sat on his tiny cot, the pages of his Bible spread open in his lap while the faint light of his lantern flickered against the wooden walls of the barn. He read the words, searching for guidance, for some kind of comfort in the midst of his pain. Never had he needed it more than now—and answers that would help guide him make the right choices.

He was a new husband to a woman he felt compelled to keep at arm's length, a woman who deserved far better than him. The guilt grew with each passing moment in her presence and set up quarters in his mind and gut, eating him from the inside out. Josephine would only find herself disappointed once he opened up to her. She'd see him for who he truly was—a selfish monster.

Sophie was his wife—the only woman he had ever genuinely loved, and the one person he had betrayed. That betrayal hung over him like a storm cloud, darkening every thought, every interaction with Josephine. How could he ever move on? How could he let go of the past when it clung to him so fiercely? Josephine wasn't really here because of the advertisement. She wouldn't be here if it wasn't for Sophie's last day on earth—the real reason she passed.

He closed the Bible, his hands trembling slightly as he let out a shaky breath. The words Travis read seemed distant, almost meaningless against the weight of his regret—both for Sophie and Josephine. How could he find peace when his heart was still tied to that one memory?

He closed his eyes as he shuddered. Blood. Those wide eyes. Dr. Gordon pulling him aside, telling him he had a choice to make. Travis gripped the Bible in his hands. *Be smart about this,* the doctor had said a year before Gideon was born. *You two have much to lose. Be careful.* Travis's teeth sank into his lip. He could almost hear Sophie's voice audibly clear. *I'm expecting, Travis. We're having another baby.* The joy on Sophie's face had been immeasurable. Travis knew at that moment they would have a miracle. How could God take the life of a woman so happy?

He remembered Dr. Gordon's frightened face when they told him the news. *I told you two to be smart about this,* he scolded. Travis argued with him, telling him he was wrong. Then Dr. Gordon shattered his excitement, saying Sophie wouldn't survive the birth, perhaps the pregnancy. *I can perform a procedure, one that will terminate the pregnancy. Sophie can live.* Travis threw a punch in the doctor's face after that disgusting and foul comment. Travis threatened to kill the man if he ever brought that up again, or anything to do with Sophie's condition.

Even if Josephine learned about the past and still wanted to be with him, he'd be betraying another woman. He could try to care for Josephine, to be the husband she deserved, but he knew, deep down, that she would always be second in his heart. Every moment they spent together, every touch, every glance, would be tainted by the memory of Sophie. He couldn't help it; every time he saw

Josephine with the children, he thought of Sophie—the life they could have had if only he had listened to the doctor.

What if Josephine became pregnant? How could Travis bring a child into this mess, into a marriage built on a foundation of lies and half-truths? How could he look his own child in the face and admit that its parents' marriage was a sham? The thought of it made his gut churn with dread. And what if it all went wrong? How could he put his children through losing a mother again?

A soft knock on the barn door pulled him from his thoughts. He looked down from the loft, and there she was—Josephine, standing in the dim light, her yellow hair catching the glow from the lantern. *Oh, blast.* She was still wearing the black checkered dress she had worn to the church service, the one that clung to her hips, highlighting the outline of the form he had seen the night before. *Why are you doing this to me, God?*

"Mr. Blythe?"

Travis cringed hearing 'Mr. Blythe' from the mouth of the woman he married. "Yes?"

"I must speak with you," she said with her whiskey-brown eyes peering up at him.

"All right," Travis said, turning away to swallow the burn in his throat.

Josephine moved toward the ladder, and before Travis could stop her, she started climbing.

"No, no, you don't have to do that. I'll come down," Travis said quickly.

He could no longer protest. Josephine reached the top, her hands brushing together as she steadied herself. A lump swelled in Travis's throat, the sight of her standing there, so close, making his heart throb against his ribs. *Alone with Josephine.* He wasn't ready for this conversation—whatever it might be—but there was no turning back now. Josephine glanced around, her head shifting from side to side as she took in his living arrangements.

Heat crept at Travis's skin. He hoped it wouldn't hurt her feelings to see how desperate he was to be away from her at night. What man in his right mind would reject sharing a warm bed with an attractive woman and instead live in a barn?

Travis pointed to his cot. It was the only place to sit down that wasn't dirty. "Would you like to sit?"

Josephine nodded. She settled herself with her hands resting in her lap. Travis sat beside her, leaving a great gap between them.

"Mr. Blythe—"

Travis held his hand up. "Please call me Travis. I'm a little too young to be referred to as that."

Josephine's cheeks reddened, and she lowered her head. "Oh, sorry."

"It's all right," he reassured her, his voice softening. "May I call you Josie? I mean . . . since the children are calling you that."

Josephine nodded, pulling a lock of hair behind her ear. "Please. It's what I'd rather be called, anyway."

"Then why did you write to me as Josephine? I feel rather foolish introducing you as such."

Josie half-smiled. "I haven't been called Josie in a long while. It's what my family used to call me. No one has referred to me as Josie in seven years. It feels good to be called that again."

"It suits you," Travis said. His breath seized. *What did you mean by that, Travis?*

Josie lowered her head again. Each time Travis attempted to be social, it seemed as if she cut him off with her wary looks. He looked at her lap, where her hands rested, and his stomach sank. Her fingers were trembling, and her nails dug into her skin. Was he really that terrifying to her? The thought struck him hard. He had never intended to make her feel this way.

"Travis, I have something for you." She reached into her pocket and pulled out an opened envelope.

Travis took it from her, surprised by its weight. He opened it cautiously, and the breath nearly left his lungs. Inside was the money he had sent her—the cash that remained untouched. His eyes widened, gaping at her.

"You didn't use it?"

Josie shook her head. "No, it didn't feel right. I had plenty of money saved."

Travis stared at the envelope, then back at Josie, running his hand through his hair as disbelief washed over him. The money he had fought so hard to scrape together to bring her here and keep his family from hunger was back in his hands.

"Josie, I-I don't know what to say. You shouldn't have used your savings."

"I didn't want to spend what should be yours. I just put the children to bed and promised Ivy I'd give her painting lessons once you had the money for paint. I'm in no position to tell you what to spend or not, but I think it should go to Ivy's paint."

Travis stuffed the money into his back pocket. "It means the world to hear you say that. It really does." Then it hit him. He blinked and turned towards her. "You paint?"

Josie laughed softly. "You sound just like Ivy. I can't believe it's *that* hard to believe."

Travis enjoyed seeing Josie laugh, especially when directed at him. There was something infectious about her joy, a brightness that made their tension feel lighter. The brilliance of her smile calmed Travis's pulse in a way he hadn't expected. Those lips of hers were the color of wild pink clover, and those sweet doe eyes made his chest swim with warmth. But the thought sent a chill through him.

"Travis, are you all right?"

Travis stood up abruptly. "I think it's time for you to go," he said, his tone sharper than he intended.

Josie gasped and jerked her head to the side, her shoulder slumped down. Travis's brows raised. Why had she cowered at him once again? He crouched beside her. "Josie, are you all right? I didn't mean to—"

Her wide eyes met his. The color drained from her face, leaving her pale and stricken. "I-Is it something I said? D-Did I push too far with promising painting lessons?"

Travis shook his head, trying to soften his words. He put his hand out but stopped himself. This wasn't the time or place to touch her. "You didn't offend me. It was a wonderful gesture that I am grateful for. It's just I—" Travis scratched behind his ear and stood. "I can't have you in here."

Josie hung her head, twisting a strand of her hair. "I'm sorry again. I'm sorry for last night, too."

Her voice was small, but it cut through him like a knife. He could see the weight of his tone bearing on her, and a pang of regret tugged him.

"It's not your fault," Travis said gently. "I want to give you the world, but . . . I can't. Your duty must remain with the children."

Josie stood slowly, her eyes finally meeting his. "I don't want to know my husband. I want to know the children's father. Why didn't you come inside when the children and I were playing all afternoon and evening? You only stayed when Aunt Polly was here."

Travis turned away, folding his arms over his body. She had noticed. However, he couldn't explain himself. He wasn't ready

to talk about Sophie. He could share his life with Josie, but she wouldn't share his past or grief. "I am not distant. I see my children every day. I wanted to give you time with them."

"You are a good father, but when I'm there, you avoid me like a disease. How am I supposed to be a part of this family if you keep me at a distance? Why do that to your children?"

Despite her soft and timid tone, her words pierced him. Sleeping in the barn was a testament to that distance. He couldn't play the happy married couple—not even with the children in their presence.

"Go, please," Travis said stiffly. "Tell the children goodnight for me."

Josie didn't say a word as the sound of her footsteps echoed down the ladder. Travis sat in the silence that followed, unsure how he'd face her now. He was a coward. Such a coward that he couldn't go inside his own house to say goodnight to his children.

CHAPTER ELEVEN

"WHAT IS THIS?" MARCUS sneered. His eyes glared with fury as he held up Josie's secret letter from Aunt Tia.

Josie gulped, thinking quickly and carefully about how to answer. With one slip up, history would repeat itself like the last three times. She had to be smart if she wanted this baby to live. Marcus may have taken her virtue and inheritance, but he wouldn't take another unborn child's life.

"Aunt Tia was asking me to visit," Josie said in her meekly calm voice. "I thought you and I could go."

Marcus stepped closer. The reek of alcohol still clung to his fetid breath. "I told you to cut ties with the old woman. Her mind isn't sane enough to be in anyone's company. She is an embarrassment, and I won't have her ruin us."

"Darling," Josie said calmly, touching his forearm. "She's my only relative. Shouldn't we pay her a visit? I haven't seen her since our wedding day. We wouldn't want to offend my dear great aunt."

Marcus jerked away and pointed in her face. "You're a disgrace to this family to be writing to such a woman! You disobedient little wench! I should have an heir by now but you're weak and pathetic!"

Josie tried to stay poised and calm her husband, but it was hard to help the man during his violent rages.

"I am sorry, sir," she answered shakily, her eyes downcast. "I have tried my best."

Marcus grabbed her hair and yanked it hard. His scarred eye bore into hers with a glaring intensity that sent a shiver crawling down her spine. "What shall I do with you, hm? You have disappointed me time and time again. I was promised four sons by now and you've given me weak ones, just like their mother."

He yanked harder. Josie cried out as pain seared across her scalp—like her hair was being torn from the roots. His other hand moved to her throat; his fingers pinched her skin. "If I kill you now, no one would care. You have no one. I can tell everyone it was an accident." His smile grew more sinister. "Or that you took your own life. Wouldn't that be more believable?"

"Please," Josie croaked. "I'll do better. Please . . . Let me go. You don't mean that."

Tears welled in Josie's eyes. For seven years, she had never felt so low and breakable. She was too feeble, and Marcus was right. She failed him. Those beatings were to shape her into a more obedient wife, but she couldn't survive his blows. She couldn't protect her babies in the past, but she'd try everything in her power to protect this one.

Josie struggled for air as Marcus's grip tightened. His thumbs pressed hard and harder, forming two deep holes in her neck, blocking off her air supply. Her lungs stung, and she begged for air.

"Marcus, stop," she wheezed, pushing against his chest.

Josie could stop it all by telling him the news, but she wouldn't risk it. She wouldn't dare let the beast know. He wouldn't lay a finger on her child. It may have his blood, but it would never be his. She'd make sure of it.

With a sudden burst of determination, she reached for the vase of flowers sitting on the decorative table beside her. She swung it as hard as she could against Marcus's head. The vase shattered, the sound of breaking glass echoed through the home. Marcus let out a low growl, staggering backward. He shifted from side to side, struggling to regain his balance. For a brief moment, his eyes rolled back, and it seemed like time slowed as he lost his footing. Josie screamed in horror as her husband fell helplessly down the staircase.

She couldn't breathe. Fear jellied her legs. Gripping the staircase rail, she looked down as Marcus's body laid still in a puddle of blood, spreading across the polished floor.

"What have I done?"

Josie sat up in her bed, gasping for air. The sight of her lonely bedroom had never felt as relieving as it did in this moment. Her bleary eyes wandered over to the cedar dresser, the vanity with its dusty mirror, and the crib in the corner. Each modest piece of furniture was a stark contrast to the nightmarish master bedroom she once shared with Marcus. Josie drew steady breaths in and exhaled steadily, clenching her fists in her lap.

Marcus was dead.

North Carolina was thousands of miles away.

Orange light leaked through the sheer green curtains, and the birds engaged in a chorus of summer songs. Josie's heart steadied as she stood from her bed, making her way to the window. The sunrise reflected over the wheat stalks and the towering mountain peaks in the distance stood firm over them. Opening the window, a gentle breeze whooshed in and kissed her face. She closed her eyes, but images of Marcus and his grip around her throat entered her mind. The hair at the back of her neck stood straight up as though he were watching her from behind.

She shut the windows and stepped away, her hand resting on her neck. He wouldn't bother her again. No one knew where she was. She wouldn't be hanged or imprisoned. Her child was safe.

Marcus was beyond wicked, but Josie never planned to kill him. Maybe she dreamed it when he caused her pain, but never would she pursue it. She planned to leave him and find sanctuary with Aunt Tia. Marcus wasn't supposed to find that letter. He wasn't supposed to be drinking that early in the evening.

Josie chewed her pale knuckles as the memory of his body falling helplessly down the staircase replayed in her mind, the thud of him hitting the hard ground echoing like a closing of steel doors, sealing off her consciousness. Josie leaned over her empty washbasin and heaved. She was free from Marcus but not from her past. It wouldn't be long until a marshal came looking for her and shamed Travis's sweet family.

Josie stared into the dusty mirror. She must keep her identity hidden. She didn't trust Travis quite yet. He seemed like an honorable man—especially covering up her being a mail-order bride—but he could still turn her in. Josie shuddered at the thought, wrapping her arms around her form. Would Travis really betray her? It would be a good way to get rid of her once he found out she was pregnant with another man's child.

The perfect excuse to annul a marriage he obviously didn't want.

Josie pulled a shawl over her nightdress and moved towards the doorway. She needed coffee and fast. The day would be long but productive as a mother and wife now that the Lord's Day was over. Laundry needed to be washed and mended, the floors needed to be swept and scrubbed, and lunch and supper needed to be prepared. When Josie made her way into the kitchen, she paused, noticing Aunt Polly standing over the stove.

"Good morning, Josie," she said with a welcoming smile.

"Good morning," Josie repeated, tightening the shawl around her.

Josie's stomach rumbled at the scent of pancakes and bacon. Her body was strangely fickle—nauseous one moment, ravenous the next. Since she was eating for two, she'd have to be smart about her nutrition. Food needed to be rationed in appropriate portions for the children and Travis, but Josie would need at least two helpings. Lord forbid if she ate so much the children starved.

"Want some breakfast?"

Josie smiled, pulling her braid over her shoulder. "Yes, please. I'm famished."

Aunt Polly giggled. "Well, good because I made a lot."

Josie sat as Aunt Polly handed her a plate of three pancakes and two strips of bacon.

"Coffee?" Aunt Polly asked, holding up the pot.

"If you don't mind."

Aunt Polly poured a cup and handed it to Josie.

"Has Travis come by?" Josie asked, blowing over her coffee.

"About an hour ago."

Josie thought over the night before. She didn't expect to open her mouth and speak her mind—mostly because she had been trained not to—but Travis's distant behavior pushed her too far. Was Josie so bad that he had to sleep with the animals? She understood his grief, but asking for a wife yet avoiding her and the children was too much. Josie's role was to mother them, but it was driving Travis away. He needed an equal amount of time with his children. However, wasn't that his problem?

"What time do the children head to school?" Josie asked.

Aunt Polly returned to the stove and stacked the extra pancakes onto an empty plate. "We don't have a teacher nor a school."

Josie's eyes widened, setting her cup down on the table. "What?" It almost didn't seem possible. With the number of children Josie saw in church, she figured there had to be one.

"We used the church house when Travis was younger, but it's been hard to keep a teacher. It's a difficult life in these parts, so the pay gets pretty steep. None of us can pull enough pennies for that. Our children don't have time for studying, especially us farm folk. Too many chores to be done."

Josie set her coffee down again after taking a sip. "That's terrible. The children deserve the right to an education."

Aunt Polly pulled out a chair in front of Josie and settled herself in the seat. "You can say that again. I've been teaching Jonas and Ivy basic arithmetic and spelling, but it has been too much with caring for Gideon and Lillian. They need a steady hand and full attention from a true teacher, one who'll give them the time and patience they deserve."

Josie's heart quickened. She sat up straighter, her chin high. "I'm confident I can do that. I was studying for a certificate years ago, but the war took a toll on all of us. I was taking care of my mother and sister when they were ill, and after they died—" Josie paused, digging her fingernails into her palm. She was getting too personal. Aunt Polly couldn't know what happened next. Marcus was taking control of Josie's mind again. Seeing his glaring eyes and scar down the right side of his face made her shudder.

She needed to finish her sentence. She needed to say something vague, something that couldn't be traced back to her husband. "I began managing the estate."

Half-truth. She managed the estate by doing as her father asked—agreeing to marry Marcus. He restored *Belle Vallée* in exchange for an heir, but that promise was never fulfilled. Josie's blood rumbled with rage, her fists clenching. As a punishment,

Marcus sold her precious home to Yankees, Yankees who were a part of the army that killed her brothers.

"That must have been hard, my dear," Aunt Polly said gently.

"Very," Josie managed through gritted teeth. *Harder than you think.*

"I am sure the children would appreciate you teaching them."

Aunt Polly stood and opened the jars situated on the shelf above the stove. She returned with a stone bowl and a large rock. Josie's eyes squinted as she focused on Aunt Polly's hands. The woman poured a dried green substance into the bowl and began grinding it.

"What are you doing?" Josie asked.

Aunt Polly's forehead creased in deep concentration as she continued to grind the substances. "Making a healing liniment for a lady at church. She's been having terrible headaches all summer."

Josie's brows raised. *A healing liniment?*

Aunt Polly paused and looked her in the face. "I know what you're thinking."

"What do you mean?"

Aunt Polly chuckled. "I promise you I'm no witch."

Josie's eyes widened. She blinked twice. "What? I never said you were a witch."

"I'm the town's healer. Some say I'm more resourceful than our dear Dr. Gordon."

Healers. Josie had heard whispers about such things before but had never encountered them herself. She knew of witches, magic, and potions from stories, yet it had never crossed her mind that Travis's aunt might be one of them.

"How does it work?" Josie asked. "Do you have a healing gift?"

Aunt Polly snorted. "Goodness no. I wish." She opened an empty jar and scooped the crushed herbs into it. "Many years ago, I suffered a great loss. I was out of my mind with grief, and I wanted to get as far away as possible from here. It was then I suffered fever in the wilderness and nearly died."

Josie covered her mouth. "My goodness. That's terrible."

Aunt Polly tightened the jar's lid. "I was rescued by a tribe of Blackfeet Indians. I lived with them for almost a month, and while I was there, they taught me their medicine. You see, their cures are far different from ours. They don't have medical knowledge, only nature. It is so fascinating how God's creation can cure us."

Aunt Polly sprinkled more herbs into the bowl as she chuckled again. "You would have found out from town gossip soon enough. I'd rather you hear it from me. After I returned and planted my herb garden, rumors started that I turned into a witch. I've had people threaten me, and some come for potions that aren't even possible."

Josie chewed her bottom lip and peered downward. If only there was a potion that could take her pain away, to make her forget everything she endured the past seven years. "What kind of potions?"

"Love potions mostly." Aunt Polly let out a little snort. "When Travis was in school, three girls came out here asking for it because they were infatuated with a boy who didn't seem to know they existed."

"What did you do?"

Aunt Polly chuckled, grinding the herbs. "I mixed some rose water and sugar and told them to rub it on their necks every day. It was nothing but plain ole' perfume."

"I wonder who the boy was."

Aunt Polly paused and smirked up at Josie. "I think we both know who *he* was."

A flame soared up Josie's cheeks. Travis must have been a handsome fellow during the days of his youth. She couldn't doubt it, given his looks now, but the thought of him getting attention from other women raised questions. How could he not find a wife in Montana?

Aunt Polly brushed her hands together then wiped them on her apron. "If you don't mind waking Gideon and changing him, I'll get the girls and Jonas up and going."

Josie took the last few bites of her pancakes. "Of course." She proceeded to her bedroom where Gideon was sound asleep in his crib. She picked him up in her arms, and his eyes drifted open. A small yawn escaped his lips, making Josie's heart overflow.

"Good morning, my sweet boy," she whispered. She held him close to her chest. "I love you."

Those eyes of his were green, unlike Travis's and the rest of the children's, which were blue. Perhaps the mother's eyes were green. However, she wouldn't ask. If it was important, Travis would have brought it up—including the late Mrs. Blythe's name.

Gideon's mouth parted, giving her a grin that displayed his two bottom teeth. Her heart nearly melted. This baby was hers now, just as much as Travis's. But for how long? Her chest ached looking at her covered window.

The law couldn't find her. No one would search this far.

Travis spent the day preparing for the harvest. He checked each stalk of wheat from every acre, searched for pests, and spent the remainder of the day in town, searching for supplies. Since Josie was in the picture, they needed an extra scythe. Even though Josie claimed to have suffered and endured hard labor after the war, he could hardly picture it. Her delicate appearance, with a slender waist and thin arms, suggested she hadn't touched anything but a needle and thread in years.

How had she looked during the war? Strong, perhaps? The only image he saw was her sitting with her elderly aunt, sipping tea in a great parlor with pristine white walls, heavy drapery made of silk over the great windows so high eagles could see through from their soaring heights. Maybe she would surprise him come harvest time.

Pulling up to his homestead, Travis' heart beat in excitement. Next to him sat a brown bag of paints he bought from Mr. Lynde's mercantile. Travis couldn't help but smile, imagining Ivy's face when she'd receive the paint she begged for. He kept his promise, and now Ivy could depend on his word again. When Mr. Lynde brought out his paint inventory, Travis picked every color—blue, orange, green, yellow, pink, and purple. The price at the counter was outrageous, but at least his debts were paid.

Travis's immediate thought went to Josie. This could be it—painting would bring them together. Ivy would have a mother again, and Josie would feel accepted into their family. Josie was a blessing, an answer to prayer, and a woman like that needed more than he could give her.

Sophie had been easy to read since he met her—an open book. But he couldn't read Josie. Travis let out a breath and shook his head. As her long yellow hair and whiskey eyes entered his mind, he couldn't shake away his curiosity of why she hadn't married. Perhaps she was running from a broken heart. That would explain why she was crazy enough to come to Montana. However, she was too attractive and nice to be rejected.

Yet there Travis was, rejecting her since the day she arrived. So, it wasn't nearly impossible.

Travis halted the wagon in front of the cabin and unhitched the horses, leading them to the fenced area behind the barn. He had moved them outside the stables days ago, mostly because they were too disruptive, skittish from every sound.

When Travis entered the cabin, his heart sank and his strong posture slumped. A sharp sting pierced his core—more painful than the one he had felt upon seeing the picnic days ago. Instead of his copper-brown-haired Sophie, there was a blonde at his stove, carrying Gideon on her hip. She bent, pulling a pan of biscuits out of the oven. A pot of gravy simmered on the stove. Jonas's eyes lit up while seated at the dining table, holding a slate.

"Pa come here and see!" he exclaimed. "Josie's teachin' me 'bout numbers!"

Travis smiled faintly, clutching Ivy's paints in a paper bag. He stepped closer to observe the children's work. Lillian showed him what he thought to be the alphabet. Her handwriting still needed improvement.

"I know my ABCs, Pa!"

Travis kissed his daughter's head. "I'm so proud of you."

"Just A through D," Josie explained, fanning the biscuits with a rag. "It's her first day, and school keeps her occupied as I work with Jonas and Ivy."

Travis stood behind Ivy who was writing simple words like "bat," "rat," and "cat."

"You are doing very well, Ivy. Your handwriting is more legible than mine."

"Thanks, Pa," she said quietly.

Ivy sighed, propping her right cheek against her palm, her elbow resting on the table. Travis pressed his lips together. Ivy's melancholy had slightly improved months ago, but it seemed she was down again. Travis knew exactly how she felt since he lost his father at a young age. Except he couldn't relate to her feelings towards Josie, given that his mother never remarried.

Travis forced a smile and reached into the paper bag, hoping the paints might lift her spirits, even if only for a moment. "I think you need something better to write with," Travis said with a wink.

"A pencil?" Ivy asked, craning her neck to see him.

Travis's heart skipped as her eyes brightened at the sight of him pulling out her paints.

"Oh, Pa!" she screeched, leaping into his arms. He scooped her up, her embrace tightening around his neck. Travis's heart swelled with joy—it had been far too long since he'd seen his daughter this happy. Ivy reached down, eagerly grabbing the bag, her small hands rummaging through the colors, examining each one with delight.

"Pa, there's a rainbow!" Lillian shouted from the ground, looking upward with star-glazed eyes.

He placed Ivy on the ground. When he looked up, his breath caught as his gaze tangled with Josie's. She was grinning, bouncing Gideon in her arms. *Thank you,* she mouthed to him. Gideon reached out a chubby hand toward Travis and Ivy, babbling in his baby language. Josie stepped closer, and Gideon squealed, the baby patting Travis's arm.

"You can't have these, Giddy," Ivy giggled. "They are mine. You should ask for your own." She looked towards Josie, and her smile didn't waver. "Can you help me paint later, Josie?"

Josie nodded. "Of course."

Travis sat at the table, watching as Josie and Jonas worked together, setting the plates. It took him a moment to realize they were alone; Aunt Polly was nowhere in sight. Travis pushed the thought away and smiled, enjoying sitting with his family—the whole family.

Under the table, he gripped his pant fabric in his fists, fighting back his pain. *Try just this once. For the children.* Josie brought out the biscuits and gravy, placing them in the center of the table. She settled into the seat at the end, where Sophie once sat. It hit Travis like a blow to the gut. He chewed the inside of his cheek, desperate not to scream. Travis turned quickly to Ivy, who was smiling brightly. Was that smile of hers real, full of genuine gratitude for the paints, or was she like him, trying hard to appear strong for the sake of the family?

Josie reached out her hand to Lillian and the other to Jonas. "Would you like to say the prayer, Jonas?"

Jonas nodded eagerly, bobbing his head five times. As they all bowed their heads, Travis couldn't help but squint, his eyes lingering on Josie. Gideon squirmed in her lap, his tiny fingers reaching for her hair. *How long until this feels natural?*

After the prayer ended, he stiffened in his chair. Travis desired for this marriage to work, but sitting together as one family, it felt like the utmost betrayal to Sophie. And not only that, his new wife was already sitting in Sophie's seat.

CHAPTER TWELVE

AT THE FOUNDER'S DAY celebration, melodic music from string instruments drifted down from the mercantile's two-story balcony. The atmosphere reminded Josie of the good ole days, full of romantic balls complete with hoop-skirt gowns, suitors, and strawberry punch. Before the war, she attended them every weekend, sometimes visiting the same home twice in a row. Her family often traveled over twenty miles and stayed nearly a week with hosts.

Papa adored balls probably more than Mama did. He liked to socialize and play cards in the hosts' parlor until the last dance. Then he'd join Mama for a waltz to her favorite tune. Josie would watch from the corner, refusing to entertain a suitor for the last song. She wanted to watch her parents and feel the warmth of their love from afar. That had been the life she envisioned when she learned she was betrothed to a handsome, older war hero.

Bumps prickled across her skin, despite the crisp, summer sunlight glowing on her back. The day before her first wedding, she learned Marcus's name and put the pieces together. That man may have been a hero, but rumors circulated the county that he killed his own wife just two months earlier. However, it was never proven, and one of his former slaves was hanged for the murder.

Marcus claimed that the girl poisoned his wife, but why would a sweet, young thing want to poison anyone, especially when Lincoln granted her freedom? Papa assured Josie it was all rumors, but on the wedding night . . . she was convinced it was true.

Josie closed her eyes, taking in deep breaths. *Those days are behind you. Move forward.*

"Josie?"

Josie opened her eyes, realizing she had frozen in the middle of the street with her pie in hand. Her cheeks flushed, seeing Caroline and Rose motioning her to the dessert table covered by a blue checkered tablecloth beside the mercantile. Josie straightened her posture and walked in their direction, moving through the sea of people. She adjusted the ringlets that fell loosely from beneath the flower crown Lillian and Ivy had made.

"Oh, how lovely it is to see you," Rose said, embracing her. "For a moment I thought you were lost out there."

Josie scratched the back of her neck. "Sorry. I'm just not used to crowds."

Caroline chuckled, taking her pie. "We might not have as many people as Virginia City does, but we are close-knit." She uncovered the pie and smiled. "This looks delicious, Josie."

"Thank you."

She observed the goods on the table—plates of cookies, cakes, pies, and cobblers. The aroma of vanilla, chocolate, cinnamon, cloves, and nutmeg flowed through the warm Montana breeze. The icing on the cakes seemed a little runny from the heat, but the rest of the items appeared to be made with artistic care and pride.

Josie didn't care much for the competition. She had never before entered a contest that required a servant's skill, but she hoped to establish a good reputation that eliminated her proper upbringing. But what if the pie's taste proved she wasn't a baker like the women of Willow Grove? Had she measured the sugar correctly? What if the huckleberries were over-ripe? What if they were too sour? Her pulse raced as Caroline placed it next to other pies with lattice crusts and braided edges. Since Josie hadn't baked in so long, she had forgotten how to make a pie crust that was dependable. This one flaked and the edges were slightly browner than the rest. She was hardly an expert at anything baking related.

"What did Alice make?" Josie asked.

"An apple turnover," Caroline answered, arranging the desserts.

"Maybe it will stand up to your huckleberry cobbler," Rose told Caroline. "I don't think anyone can beat it—even if Alice has your talent."

Caroline chuckled. "Oh, Rose, you flatter me so."

Rose grinned. "What are friends for?"

The orchestra changed to an upbeat tune, and Reverend Levingston appeared out of the crowd, making his way to Rose. He bowed and extended his hand. "May I have this dance, Mrs. Levingston?"

Josie blinked twice. Reverend Levingston was a romantic?

Rose took his hand and kissed his cheek. "Of course, my dear husband." He wrapped his arm around her waist, and Rose waved. "See you ladies later. Good luck!" They disappeared into the crowd, joining the dancers in the street.

Caroline sighed and stood beside Josie. "They're a different couple, aren't they?"

Josie turned her gaze to Caroline, who was watching the dancers. "What do you mean?"

"Their affection," Caroline explained. "I highly assume you've never seen a minister and his wife behave that way in public. There's no denying their marriage is legitimate."

Josie folded her arms over her pink cotton dress. "I'm not following. Are you implying they aren't married?"

Caroline gasped with her hand over her mouth. "No, dear. I meant none of that at all. I meant how their marriage isn't based on convenience—it's based on love."

The word *convenience* made Josie's core tighten. She swallowed hard and adjusted her lace collar. Could Caroline see through Josie's facade?

"Ladies believe ministers are perfect and will never break their hearts, but a heartbreak from them is the worst kind. They have a habit of seeking out women for their own benefit. In order for a minister to be respected, he has to be married. The woman must master such etiquette and skills that will benefit her husband in the church."

"How do you know about this?" Josie asked sharply, but she recovered with a soft voice, hoping Caroline wouldn't take offense. "I mean, if you don't mind my asking."

"I grew up in Boston," Caroline explained. "I hope you don't hold it against me because I'm a Yankee. I can tell by your accent you're originally from Dixie."

Josie shuddered. She didn't mind Caroline being a Northerner, but the term "Yankee" had another connotation in Josie's book. Yankees were her enemies—killing her brothers and causing her family to crumble.

"The war is over, Caroline. I haven't judged anyone because of their location. Here I am out west. I guess you can say I left it all behind." *Left it all behind?* The lie left a bitter taste on her tongue.

Caroline's lips curved. "Well, I assume you can say that. This *is* neutral ground." Caroline sucked in a breath then exhaled. She turned her body towards Josie, leaning in closer. "I was engaged to a minister once, Reverend David Fortenberry. More intellectual than he was handsome. My mother and he said it was God's will for me to be his wife. I knew nothing of love, but I believe I loved him because it was God's will we were to wed." Caroline lowered her head, clasping her hands in front of her. "Then one day I realized the reverend was using me. He needed a piano player, and I was the perfect choice."

Josie gasped. "I'm sorry. I had no idea."

"No one expects this behavior from ministers. That's why you should watch Ivy and Lillian when a preacher comes calling on them romantically." She straightened her shoulders. "I have nothing against the man of the cloth, God forbid, but they can be just as terrible as any man, especially one who uses God's name to manipulate you to do what he wants." Caroline sighed as another song began. "You're lucky to have Travis, though. He fell in love with you over letters. That's once in a lifetime."

Knots coiled in Josie's stomach again, but this time she was afraid she'd faint or vomit. She looked at her shoes, breathing in and out steadily. Her marriage was as much a sham as it could have been for Caroline and Reverend Fortenberry. She was using Travis. She was the "reverend" in this story, seeking out a man who could father her child. Her cheeks heated, and the world around her became cloudy.

Caroline turned around, handing Josie a cup of water. She smiled warmly. "You look like you need it. Your face is turning red."

Josie's skin prickled, placing her hand on her cheeks. "Oh, it is a little warm out." She took the water. "Thank you," she said before taking a sip. The cool beverage soothed her mind, and she turned about from the dancing romance before her. "How did you meet Ronan?"

Caroline chuckled, her hand on her chest. "Oh my, where do I begin? He was *not* the man my parents wanted me to marry. He was an Irish boxer and fought weekly at the saloon across from the church."

Josie nearly choked on her water. "Really? Ronan was a boxer?"

"Yes! He tried to find work, but no one would hire an Irishman, so he became a star." Caroline smiled, looking towards Ronan near the dunking booth, carrying the twins in both arms. No doubt he had the strength of a boxer.

"Ronan wanted me because he loved me. He never tried to change me, and I never tried to change him. That's the kind of man I want my daughters to marry."

Josie smiled. "No doubt he's a wonderful man from what I've heard and seen."

When Ronan turned, Josie noticed Travis beside him, laughing as the children jumped up and down, pointing at the man in the dunking booth who had just been knocked down by six-year-old Liam Walsh. Travis met her gaze with a smile for a sharp moment, then turned his attention to Jonas who patted Liam's back.

A lump of sorrow formed in Josie's throat. Travis deserved more. The children deserved an honest mother. Josie would never forget Caroline's story. How could she be friends with this woman and be a deceiver in her heart? Caroline had once been hurt by the same type of person Josie was.

As the sun set over the snow-caped peaks, Travis watched Josie dancing with Jonas. The sight of Josie in messy curls and a colorful flower crown made her stand out, like a fairy from the children's storybooks. Her ringlets bounced and her light pink petticoat twirled around her as she danced. Travis wiped the sweat on his forehead. *What are you doing to me, Josie?*

Josie was young, but so lively as she spun in circles with Jonas. Travis had never possessed the confidence to dance openly in front of the town or behave so playfully. Josie was fitting right in, just like the couples and children having the time of their lives, letting the music move them.

Who could exclude such a lovely woman as she? Her soul was sweet as a honeycomb and her heart was bigger than any woman he met since Sophie. Josie cared for the children like her very own, and she treated Travis respectfully. Travis peered at the ground. He didn't deserve her at all.

The music stopped, and Travis felt a tap on his shoulder. He looked behind him. Aunt Polly held Gideon on her hip.

"She's a lovely thing, ain't she?"

Travis nodded, his gaze painfully following Josie as she clapped and laughed, her joy as bright as the lanterns swaying above. She curtsied to the couples beside her, graceful and poised, like a princess acknowledging her court.

"Why don't you ask your wife to dance?"

He hesitated, his hand reaching up to scratch the back of his neck. "I'm not much of a dancer, Auntie. You know that better than anyone."

Aunt Polly chuckled. "Pfft! Hogwash! You and Sophie used to dance until your shoes wore out."

Travis chewed his bottom lip, the familiar ache tightening in his chest. He could still see Sophie's smile, hear her laughter as they spun together under the stars. She had loved to dance, and he had loved her—loved her so much that he would have danced until the sun rose, just to see her happy. But that was their thing. Their special bond. To dance with another woman was a betrayal, like erasing what he had shared with Sophie. He had already replaced her in so many ways. He couldn't take dancing from her, too.

"I can't do it," he murmured, more to himself than to Aunt Polly.

His aunt sighed. "I understand your grief, Travis. I lost my husband and boys on the same day. It took years to heal that hole, but you have a wife and four children to think about. I won't have you spoil their lives because you're too frightened to love again."

The thought of moving on made the ache in his heart more painful. Each thought was like a piece of skin being ripped off, making it impossible to scab over. Travis had known Sophie since childhood. Losing her made him lose a piece of himself. He was half the man he used to be without her. He closed his eyes. *Don't do this to me, Josie. I can't fall for you.*

"Please, Travis. Think about them," Aunt Polly begged. "Don't let people think you're one of those old couples who just get by and grow sick of one another. You're young. Take a leap."

Travis's gaze rested on Jonas chasing after Paul and Andy. Behind them, Josie stood awkwardly, peering around with her hands at her sides. He could tell she enjoyed the dancing, and he couldn't take that away from her, not when every married couple was out there. Would he really leave her without a partner, only to watch the rest of the couples act as happy as she once was with Jonas?

The sorrowful view of her, her arms pinned across her chest and gaze downcast, pricked at Travis. He rubbed his chin, letting out a sigh. *Just one dance.* He owed her that much, given he couldn't be the husband she would need.

Travis footed towards her, his heart beating against him like a jackhammer. When she turned, her gaze rested on him and her eyes rounded for a brief moment.

"You seem to be enjoying yourself," Travis said, his fists pressed to his hips.

Josie's eyes crinkled into slits as her mouth curved. "I am. I love dancing. It reminds me of my home before the war. I loved going to balls."

Travis extended his hand when the music started again. "Would you care to dance with me, Mrs. Blythe?"

Josie's eyes gaped, her lips parted. "Are you sure? Is this too much for you?"

Yes, Travis wanted to say, but he couldn't spoil the day for Josie. "No, I want to dance with you."

Josie reached out, her fingers softly wrapping around his hand. Her bare hand fit perfectly in his, her warm touch sparking something within him—a feeling he couldn't quite identify as shock or something deeper he didn't dare to admit. With a gentle nudge, he led her to the dancefloor, his pulse thrumming like a drum. As her hand rested on his shoulder, he instinctively pulled her closer, his arm settling around her slender waist, feeling her form press against him. Her hand met his, and he tried everything in his power to remain calm. Travis remembered the steps he took with Sophie the year before—slow and rhythmic.

As he let Josie sway in his arms, he noticed how she kept her gaze down, as she often did, avoiding his eyes. Despite her shyness, there was a softness in her movements that made the moment feel intimate, even fragile. She was so small in his arms, his hands practically swallowing hers.

"You don't have to look away," Travis said.

Josie lifted her chin, her innocent eyes meeting his. "I apologize."

"There's no need to be shy around me, Josie."

"I'm not shy," Josie denied sharply.

He raised an eyebrow, a teasing grin tugging at his lips. "You've been acting like I'm going to strangle you each time I'm near."

Her hands tensed in his, shock flickering across her face. She shriveled from his gaze, her breath hitching, as if his comment had struck a nerve. The sudden change in her demeanor puzzled him. *What is wrong with this woman?*

Josie tore away from him mid-song. "I'm sorry, Travis. This is wrong—"

Travis stepped closer, his hand extended. "It's not wrong, Josie. I know you like to dance. I owe you this much."

Josie's cheeks blazed as she scratched her forearms. "Forgive me. I'm just not used to you . . . being so close to me."

Travis thrust out a breath. He never thought the day would come when he'd be in such close proximity with another woman. But Josie wasn't just a woman—she was his wife.

"I know our situation is . . . odd, but I'm your husband, Josie. Whatever you need, you can come to me. You have helped me so much this past week, and I wanted to help you in return."

Josie's pale face pinked, and her forehead glistened. What was she afraid of? Travis had forgotten all about his discomfort while they danced. He became so lost in the moment that he rather enjoyed it, despite his inner protests.

"Thank you for the dance, Travis," Josie said with a curtsy, and she took off into the crowd, leaving Travis standing still as a statue among the sea of dancers.

Josie gently tucked Jonas into his bed, smoothing the covers up to his chin. He smiled up at her, his blue eyes sparkling.

"Thank you for teachin' me how to dance, Josie."

"I'm glad you enjoyed it, sweetheart," Josie replied, brushing his hair from his forehead.

"I want to be a good dancer like you when I grow up."

"You will, Jonas. Just keep practicing, and I promise you'll be the best dancer around."

"Can you teach me next?" Ivy asked, rolling over with her hand under her pillow.

Ivy's voice made Josie's heart skip a beat. "I would be delighted to."

Josie kissed the top of Jonas's head. "Goodnight, Jonas." She walked over to the girls' beds and kissed them too. "Good night, my lovely girls."

"Goodnight, Josie," Lillian said with a grin on her face. "I love you."

Josie's lips parted. Those words nearly knocked the breath out of her. "I love you, too." She glanced over at Jonas and then down at Ivy. "I love all of you."

Josie closed the door behind her, and when she turned, she nearly screamed. Travis stood behind her, holding his hat against his chest.

"Travis," she whispered, tightening her shawl around her shoulders. "What are you doing here?"

Travis cleared his throat. "I hope I didn't offend you earlier."

"What do you mean?"

Josie thought back to earlier, her hand rested on her hammering chest. *You've been acting like I'm going to strangle you each time I'm near.* To him, it seemed like a harmless joke, but the fact was true. It was the nightmare she had lived for seven years and was finally free from.

"Dancing with you. I haven't . . . danced in a while. I hope I didn't . . . embarrass you with my rustiness."

Josie covered her mouth as she laughed quietly. "I haven't danced in ages. I thought *I* was the rusty one."

A smile formed from Travis's corners, lightening the tension. "I'd like to thank you again for being such a good mother and . . . wife."

Josie's pulse quickened. Travis stepped closer, and her mind raced. *Now or never.* Was this the moment she desperately hoped for? Would this night save her child? Caroline's story still lingered in the back of her mind. Could she really go through with deceiving him? *But if it's this easy, then why not do it?*

Travis leaned down, his breath brushing against Josie's cheek, sending shivers down her spine. She closed her eyes, her temples throbbing like a frantic drum. She hadn't much experience with kissing, let alone a lover. Marcus had always felt like an obligation—an attempt to calm him, a desperate measure to shield herself from his wrath.

However, this could be different. As Travis drew closer, a warmth cascaded from her chest to her toes. Now, she would taste the realness of what a kiss was supposed to be. *Whatever you need, you can come to me,* echoed in her ears from the dancefloor. But those words were limited. If he only knew what she needed . . .

To her surprise, the kiss didn't land on her mouth but her cheek. Josie opened her eyes and watched Travis put his hat back on. He tipped it in her direction, stepping back.

"Goodnight, Josie." He turned and walked away, leaving Josie standing there, too shocked to respond. The door clicked shut behind him, and tears pricked in her eyes. Her heart slowed as sorrow consumed her. She needed to accept the truth.

It's too late now. You're doomed, Josie.

PART II

CHAPTER THIRTEEN

Statesville, North Carolina; Mid-July 1872

GENERAL MARCUS WELLINGTON GROANED as his heavy eyelids lifted. His temples pulsed like two bass drums during a march to battle. He raised his hand, touching his tender forehead, only to discover a bandage and a sharp, zapping pang. Biting back a moan, he blinked twice until the blurry room became clearer. A canopy draped above his bed like a veil, and darkness clouded his vision.

He slowly craned his neck, making out what appeared to be his mahogany nightstand and the full wash basin. Then a strong pulsation reverberated against his skull, as though it were splitting it open. A scream of agony tore through his throat, despite his attempt to fight against it. The pain pierced, as if bullets were ripping through his flesh again.

"Josephine!" he called out, but the resonance of his voice was met with silence. "Josephine!"

General held his throbbing head in his hands, his breathing rapid. *That ungrateful, useless girl. Where is she?*

"Josephine!"

His scream cut through his parched throat like a bayonet through soft flesh as he tried to sit up, but each time his palms dug into the mattress and he balanced his weight, another jolt of pressure squeezed his brain, stronger than before.

Rapid footsteps pounded up the staircase and down the hallway before the door burst open, sending another spike of pain through the general's skull. The outline of Josephine's overweight Mammy stumbled in, breathless and heaving.

"General Wellington! Oh, General, yuh're awake!"

General growled softly, his palm resting on his banded head. "Mammy, where is my wife? You know good and well she's supposed to come when I call." His teeth clenched hard, his words hissing through his teeth. *Idiotic women.*

Mammy caught her breath. "Don't yuh remember?"

"Remember what?" General huffed. "Where is my wife and why does my head feel worse than a bottle ache?"

General squinted his eyes, studying Mammy's nervous complexion. She had one hand over the other, trying to steady it. Her lips quivered and her forehead creased. Marcus couldn't remember anything since lunch hour in Raleigh on April 10th. He remembered the brandy being poured, the rich brown liquid sliding down his throat. The shuffle of cards. The weight of money chips stacked in his hand. A full house lying in his grasp.

"Suh," Mammy began calmly. "Missus Wellington is away on a family emergency in Wilmington. Do yuh remember anythin'? Yuh'r accident?"

"Accident?" General spat, peering through his fingers. "Why is my wife in Wilmington without my permission? She doesn't have any family except that old wheezer in Charlotte."

Mammy scratched behind her head. "Distant cousins, suh. One'a the girls had a baby and has been feelin' mighty poorly. Missus Wellington went to help."

General scowled his lips. "That stupid woman. She should think about supplying me with an heir before tending to others' children," he muttered under his breath. "When will she return?"

"She don't rightly know, suh. I didn't want the missus to worry. Yuh accident happened hours after she left. I couldn't let her turn her back on that poor, ailing mother."

General's fist curled. *She'll be horsewhipped for that. How many beatings does it take for her to learn?* A sharp ringing pierced his ear, and he smacked the side of his head, only to grimace as the pain flared worse.

Mammy patted General's leg. "Suh, let me get ya some laudanum. I'll call the doctor immediately." She rummaged through a drawer beneath the nightstand, the clatter of metal and rustling of cloth making the general groan.

"Stop that ruckus!" he barked, his fist slamming against the mattress. "How long ago was my accident? I demand answers!"

Mammy hesitated and peered down at her empty hands. "Nearly three months, suh." Her fearful gaze met his. "The doctor—he didn't rekon yuh'd make it. He didn't think yuh'd ever wake up either."

"Three months?" General growled, his jaw hardening. His nostrils flared, heated breaths exhaling like puffs of smoke. "How did this happen? Who did this to me?" This was all impossible. He was in perfect health. Those scars on his body were the testament to his invincibility. Whatever this was couldn't be an accident.

"Yuh fell down the stairs, suh. Yuh had a little too much to drink and—"

General's anger bubbled, and his ear grew hot enough that he believed steam would burst through. "Shut your mouth! This isn't my folly. It's those stupid housemaids' fault. They did this to me! I'll hang them for it!"

"Please, suh," Mammy whimpered, her head lowered. "I'm sorry. Forgive me for sayin' all that."

His whiskey didn't cause this. Someone was to blame for his accident. He couldn't remember anything, but he'd get to the bottom of it soon enough. He ran his fingers along the side of his face, tracing the beginning of his long scar, then up to his scalp, where another jagged mark met his touch.

"What is this?"

Mammy gulped, pressing her lips together.

"Answer me!" General demanded, punching his mattress. He leaned his back against the headboard, fighting back another groan. Mammy jumped, and her breath hitched. She looked at her feet, folding her hands in front of her.

"After yuh fell, yuh weren't breathin'. We had the butler check yuh pulse, and there weren't nothin'. We proceeded with the burial, and before Dr. Colson put yuh in that box, yuh flinched. Nearly jumped outta my skin, me and the maids. I screamed 'He's alive, Doctor! He's alive!' Dr. Colson told me to calm myself, and I did. I stood there watchin' as he put that instrument in his ears and pressed the other part to yuh heart. Then he looked at me with the widest eyes, full of fear. I ain't never seen the man look like that, even when . . . yuh know what I mean.

"Then he said yuh was alive. I couldn't believe it! But yuh wouldn't wake. So, the doctor took yuh to the finest surgeons in Raleigh. They decided to do an experimental surgery, one they believed could bring yuh back to us. They ain't never tried it on anyone."

General gripped the sheets. How could Dr. Colson do such a thing? Just the thought of those doctors doing an experiment on him like he was a piece of science made his nostrils flare.

"Then when we took yuh home, yuh stirred and woke a few times, but never like this. Yuh wouldn't speak and would hardly move. We had to put ya back to sleep. It's a miracle, it is!"

General growled inwardly and gritted his teeth. Some miracle, they say.

"Go fetch Dr. Colson. I need him now! Bring a glass of brandy while you're at it."

How could he be asleep for three months? How could he fall down the stairs? Whoever did this would surely get a piece of his mind. He'd ensure they endured a torment that surpassed the very definition of suffering.

CHAPTER FOURTEEN

Willow Grove, Montana; Mid-July 1872

SLIPPING INTO A SIMPLE brown dress for the first day of harvest reaping, Josie noticed in the mirror how her body had changed—the once-loose fabric now clung to her hips. After two weeks with the Blythes, a small bump appeared through her tight waistline. Panic gripped her as her heart pounded in her chest. *Too late. You must face your consequences.*

Travis may not notice the weight gain now—let alone anything about her—but Aunt Polly's observant eyes were another matter entirely. Josie couldn't let the woman know her secret, not until after she confessed to Travis.

Josie grabbed her gray shawl and pulled it around her, desperate to hide her form. For now, it would help distract any curious eyes, especially with Aunt Polly's medical knowledge. Josie had always been slim, and her bump took time to appear in past pregnancies. She glanced down at her round belly, pressing her palm underneath. At just over four months along, she was nearly as far as she had been in her second pregnancy. The longest she had carried was five months, and she had been slightly larger than this.

Josie turned away from the mirror, clenching her shawl. She needed to stop dwelling in the past and focus on her future. Her future depended on her honesty, and she clung to it as her only chance now. She might lose Travis's respect, but could she win it back by confessing? Josie sucked in a breath. *Lord, please give me strength.*

She minced towards the window and peered out again, observing Travis and Aunt Polly cutting the stalks. With each swish of their blades, the wheat tumbled. Travis set down his scythe, gathered the cut stalks, and loaded them into the wheelbarrow. Anxious to prove herself as a hard-working and capable farmer's wife, Josie pulled her waist-length hair over her shoulder and began braiding.

That morning, Josie had woken at the crack of dawn to make breakfast and get the children ready, leaving no time to ready herself. She could have woken earlier with her dress on and hair brushed, but she had grown tired, hardly getting a wink of sleep with her body aches and Gideon's crying.

Josie braided faster, her heart sinking at the sight of Ivy greeting Travis with the barrow. *So much for a farmer's wife.* Why did she have to be so late? Josie closed her eyes for a moment, envisioning her younger self, picking cotton, weeding gardens, chopping down trees, and cooking whatever she could to feed what was left of her household. Those days were about survival. Josie opened her eyes and rolled her shoulders back, tossing her braid behind her. She would remember and put herself in that sixteen-year-old girl's shoes again.

Josie paced out the back door and headed to the fields, where she spotted Lillian running towards her. Jonas and Ivy chased each other around the wheat piles while Gideon sat, playing with a rattle.

"Josie!" she called before taking her hand. "Come on!"

Travis set down his scythe, wiped his face with his sleeve, and strode toward Josie. She had barely seen him that morning, exchanging only a quick hello and goodbye when he grabbed a biscuit from the pan before heading to the fields. Josie quickly untied her shawl to cover her midsection.

"Sorry I'm late," she said, heat crawling up her neck.

"Don't apologize," Travis insisted. "You have the children and a home to care for. I can't ask you to put everything aside and join me out here as soon as possible."

Josie folded her arms over her chest. "What will you have me do?"

Travis removed his hat, dabbing his face with a white handkerchief. "If you don't mind looking after the children, I will be very grateful. In a little while, you and them can bind the sheaves."

Josie's lips parted in disbelief. How degrading of him! Despite her exhaustion and the urge to stay in bed and rest, the last thing she wanted was to be reduced to a mere babysitter. Despite being sleep-deprived, she had woken up early, rushed to clean the kitchen as fast as her hands allowed, and stepped outside, ready to put in a full day's labor as a farmer's wife. Yes, she had married Travis for the children, but she also wanted to contribute. What kind of wife would she be if she sat idle, watching the children play? With over twenty acres to harvest, she refused to stand by while Travis and Aunt Polly labored.

"I want to help," Josie stated firmly, her chin high.

Travis gestured towards Aunt Polly, who was cutting through a section with her scythe. "Have you scythed before?"

Josie wanted to roll her eyes. "You must not have listened when I said I don't shy away from hard labor. I've plowed fields and picked cotton in weather hotter than this."

Travis's forehead creased. "This is harder than you think. I don't even let my children get near those blades, and I know they could do it. Just wait for the threshing. There will be plenty of time for you to work."

Josie chewed the inside of her cheek. Looking into Travis's blue eyes, shadowed by dark circles beneath them, she couldn't bear it any longer. "Please, Travis. I want to help. I can't have you and Aunt Polly doing all the work."

Travis sighed and put his hat back on his head. "All right, come over here, and I'll show you what you have to do."

Josie looked down at Lillian who was still at her side. "Go tell Ivy she's in charge and to look after Gideon."

Lillian nodded. "Yes, ma'am."

Josie followed after Travis, grateful for the stalks' height, which helped conceal her midsection. The crop was breathtaking—golden and swaying with the breeze, reminding Josie of the Book of Ruth. Travis grabbed his scythe, its long wooden handle curved into a sharp blade. He lifted it with ease like it weighed nothing at all.

"You'll want to hold it with your left hand below your right. Aim to cut low, right at the stem."

Josie nodded. She understood the concept but wasn't sure how she'd manage to lift the scythe and cut for hours without her arms aching. She watched as Travis swung the blade in a smooth arc, cutting through the stalks with ease. He moved steadily down the row, leaving a clean path behind him, as if he put in little effort.

"Wanna take a turn?" he asked.

Josie nodded, straightening her posture and pulling her shoulders back. She was eager to please him, determined to show her husband that she was more than just a Southern belle meant to sit in a parlor, sip tea, and knit all day long. "Yes, please."

She took hold of the scythe and nearly jumped when she felt Travis standing behind her. The hair on her arms stood tall like the stalks before her. The scythe was heavier than she had anticipated. Travis gently lifted it from the bottom to help guide her hands. His hand rested over hers, positioning them correctly, and his strength made the tool feel lighter and more manageable.

"Take a swing," he said close to her ear, making the skin behind her neck tingle.

Josie swung the scythe as hard as she could at the wheat stems, the curved blade slicing through the air with a satisfying swish. She focused on the motion, trying to remember Travis's instructions about the angle and the grip. With each swing, she grew more confident, but the weight of the scythe began to wear on her arms as Travis's grip loosened.

"I'm going to step away and get my spare. Can you take this from here?" Travis asked, setting the scythe down.

Josie pulled her braid over her shoulder, catching her breath. "I can try."

Travis ambled off, and Josie was alone with the chore she volunteered for. Her braid started to unravel, loose strands of hair plastering to her face from sweat. She imagined her skin reddening under the sun, but she was thankful for the high-neckline of her dress, which offered some protection. Still, she wondered if it would be enough as the temperature continued to climb. With the relentless sunlight beating down on her, she realized she had made the wrong choice in her attire—shawl and all.

Josie glanced ahead as Travis used his scythe to slash through the stalks, his muscles flexing with each swing. His sweat-coated white shirt clung to his body, highlighting the muscles of his back. Travis wasn't as muscular as Marcus, but that didn't mean he lacked strength. She turned away, focusing on the scythe in her pale, soft hands. Josie couldn't look at Travis that way—not when there was no telling what he'd do once the truth came out.

She swung the scythe back and forth like Travis had instructed, refusing to let fatigue stop her. If Josie was going to be a farmer's wife, she needed to learn the work that came with it. Yet, a nagging worry crept into her mind—what if he wouldn't want her after she revealed the truth? She pushed the thought aside, focusing instead on the rhythm of the scythe cutting through the golden wheat, determined to prove her worth in this new life.

Josie, Travis, and Polly stopped for a break during the mid-afternoon. They had finished half a section, but they'd have to separate the stalks into piles to dry out then bind them together—meaning Josie and the children had work to do on their own. Josie looked out into the seemingly endless field and exhaled, her muscles already sore and fatigued. Few clouds dotted the sky, making the weather hotter than ever.

They would work from sun-up to sundown every day until this field was cleared. The harvest season was going to be grueling, but they had to finish before they could turn the wheat into grain and receive payment.

Josie sat on a log while she watched the children play in the distance. Travis and Polly stood in the fields, drinking water from their canteens. Josie used her shawl to wipe the sweat from her neck. Hiding her pregnancy was more exhausting than the physical labor itself. She was burning up in her shawl and dark-colored dress, the fabric clinging to her skin as sweat trickled down her back.

She closed her eyes, savoring the cool breeze while it washed over her, like an answer to her prayers. When she opened them moments later, she was surprised to see Travis strolling toward her, his canteen in hand. His thin lips held a hint of smile, eyes glinting in the sunlight as he held it out to her.

"I figured you'd want some water. Fresh from the well."

Josie mustered a smile of gratitude. "Thank you." She took hold of the canteen, desperate to soothe her parched mouth. The cool water slid down her throat, instantly relieving her. When Travis sat beside her, Josie's breath caught, and she nearly dropped the canteen. Though her throat had just been soothed, it grew dry once more. They were alone. The oppressive heat only added to her misery. Perhaps now was the time—to face her confession head-on and finally endure the inevitable consequences.

Travis's gaze focused on the children for a moment, then he looked down at his feet with a sigh. His posture slumped, folding his hands in his lap. Lillian held Gideon's hands as the little boy took wobbly steps. Josie's heart skipped, both solemn and delighted at Gideon's effort. It wouldn't be long before he was running all over the place, and Josie would be even more worn out.

The thought brought a faint smile to her lips, but it quickly faded as the weight of her secret pressed down on her. What if, by the time Gideon could walk on his own, she was no longer in his life? That motherly bond she developed would be gone, and the boy would never remember her. Worse yet, the older ones would see her as nothing more than a liar who tried to deceive their pa.

Josie set the canteen down and wiped her mouth with her sleeve. "It won't be long until he's full grown. He's almost a year old now, right?"

Travis stiffened. "Yeah." His hand gripped around his knee, and he swallowed hard, his Adam's apple bobbing. Josie's brows rose at his behavior. He pressed his lips together, as though something bothered him. A bad memory perhaps? Worse yet . . . the baby? Could he tell?

"What's wrong?" Josie asked, her stomach tightening.

Travis shook his head, rubbing his nose. "Nothing."

"You look like something's bothering you. What is it? You can tell me."

Travis looked up at Gideon, who squealed as Lillian tried to take his hand. He folded his lips under his teeth and closed his eyes. "I don't know how . . . I'm ever going to celebrate any of his birthdays."

"Why is that?"

Travis picked up a stray stick and dug it into the ground. "Because that was the day his mother died."

Josie's mouth fell open. "Oh, Travis. I'm so, so sorry. I shouldn't have pressed—"

"It's fine," Travis muttered. He removed his hat, holding the brim in his lap. "I just don't know how a day can be joyful when it's my fault he doesn't have a mother."

Josie could sense the heartbreak in his voice. The poor man. Here she was, living in freedom, while Travis was still trapped in his own nightmare. Her heart ached for him, and without thinking, she softly whispered, "It's not your fault."

"Yes, it is," Travis said sharply, turning to her. "The doctor said she shouldn't have any more children, but I didn't listen." His voice broke, looking up at the sky. "Sophie wanted another—I could sense it. That is why I talked her into trying again. She was fine and healthy during her pregnancy, and I believed the doctor was wrong. But . . . he was right," Travis hesitated, his features tightening. "She was in so much pain, and it was all my fault."

Josie reached out, her hand close to his but not touching. Her mind immediately drifted to the many babies she lost. However, those had been one person's fault—Marcus's. Travis seemed nothing like him; therefore, Mrs. Blythe's death wasn't his fault.

"We can't understand why these horrible things happen, but we have to trust God has a plan."

Travis looked down as he fidgeted with his hat again. "Whatever it is, I can't fathom why He'd take four children's mother away." He aligned his gaze with hers. "I hope you understand why I cannot give you a proper marriage. I-I can't go through that again. I can't risk these children losing another mother."

Josie's lips parted in shock, and she fought back a gasp. Guilt flooded through her, making her chest tighten. *You heartless fool.* It was wrong—so terribly wrong—to be married to Travis. She hadn't considered how having a baby would affect his family, how it might tear apart the fragile life they were trying to build together.

She couldn't tell him. Not now. Maybe not ever. Yet she couldn't make time freeze nor go back. The only way was forward and to tell the truth.

Travis stood, exhaling a breath. He didn't bother to look at Josie, not since he confessed his inner struggles. "We need to get back to work."

Josie watched as Travis walked towards the field. She buried her face in her hands. "Dear God, what have I done?"

Fatigued after a long day, Travis swallowed his third cup of coffee, watching the sun set. Josie was inside with the children; the clanging of dishes echoed through the thin pine walls while she cleaned the kitchen. Ivy whined, begging Josie to let her paint instead. Travis snickered to himself. That girl had a bite of her own, just like he did as a child. He'd give anything to get out of field work, but his pa had put his foot down, giving him no other choice but to work.

Yet, Travis managed to sneak off, resulting in his father taking on labors that were too much for one man. Travis closed his eyes and rubbed between his eyes. *So many lives gone. So many because of your foolishness.*

He wiped his forehead with his hand and sighed deeply into the stifling air. He had exposed himself to Josie. All the shards of his most secret regrets were now in Josie's hands, too, clear as day and utterly unveiled. Travis had killed his wife. Maybe not with his bare hands, but he had cost Sophie her life. That look on Josie's face said it all—wide eyes and a pale face. She had been terrified of him at that moment. Never once had he seen her so frightened—that look surpassed their wedding night.

How could he tell her about Sophie? Yet it felt good to get it off his chest. Having someone who had been honest from the start sitting close to him made it easier to go on, allowing him to share every detail that had haunted him for nearly a year. Josie hadn't said much to him since his confession. Perhaps his confession would be the savior of their arrangement. She would remain distant from him, disgusted by what he had done to that poor wife of his, so young and vibrant, taken so soon.

Travis squinted, looking out towards the road where he saw a man riding on horseback. Travis's inner pain melted away as his heart beat with joy—his friend, Ronan Walsh, was coming for a visit. Oh, how he longed for company right now. Travis stood and waved as Ronan's horse charged toward him. With a firm "whoa," Ronan pulled back the reins, bringing the horse to a halt. He gave the animal an approving pat on the neck. Travis clapped, and Ronan bowed, seated upon his panting horse. It leaned down to the water trough, taking large gulps.

"That horse getting too confident for ya?" Travis asked, chuckling with his hands on his hips.

"Ye know me, he's perfect." Ronan grinned. He dismounted and rubbed his hand together. He pointed at Travis's empty coffee cup and full kettle, sitting next to the porch's rocking chair. "Got another cup?"

Travis patted Ronan's back. "Right this way."

Travis handed Ronan his empty cup and poured the coffee. Steam rose from the drink, curling into the air. The smell eased Travis—as though Sophie were in their presence. He could see her as though it was yesterday, ambling down the road with a basket of flowers in hand.

Ronan smiled, taking the cup. "Atta boy. Ye know just how to treat an ole pal."

Travis sat next to Ronan in the next rocking chair—Sophie's chair. Ronan rubbed the back of his neck, shaking his head.

"How's it all goin'? New wife and all."

Travis leaned forward, folding his hand over his knees. "What you can expect from two strangers."

"Ye haven't made her yer wife, huh?"

Heat rushed up Travis's neck, his face burning as his heart hammered in his chest. "What? She's my wife. You can ask the reverend yourself."

Ronan chuckled before taking a sip of coffee. "I ain't talkin' 'bout no weddin'."

Travis ran his fingers through his sweat-soaked hair. Of course, Ronan would be the one to ask such nonsense. They were close enough to talk about personal situations, and it was part of Ronan's culture to speak openly about private matters. Travis was just thankful Ronan didn't have any lewd tavern talking.

"I told her about Sophie today."

Ronan's eyes widened. "Aye? What did the lass have'ta say?"

Travis looked towards the kitchen window. He leaned in closer to Ronan, hoping neither Josie nor the children would hear. "She says what happened wasn't my fault. Then again, her expression said something different."

"What ye mean?"

"She looked terrified. Josie has displayed discomforting looks since we met, but this was something new entirely."

Ronan leaned back. "Well, it ain't none o' me business, but I'm here to tell ye—be patient and honest with her. She's yer wife, ye know. She might've come from that advertisement, but yer partners for life now. Me and the missus, we've had our fair share o' troubles, but we got through 'em together. Ye need to let her in." A smirk curled up half of his face. "Now, ye don't have to let her into yer bed just yet but at least give her the time to adjust to ye."

Travis threw his hat at his friend. "You're really gonna give me a hard time about this wife thing, aren't you?" Ronan and the reverend were the only two people outside the family that knew about Josie and his arrangement. Ronan promised he wouldn't tell a soul—not even Caroline.

Ronan chuckled, pointing the hat in Travis's direction. "Ye're sure right. Yer friend's an Irishman—it don't get no better than that. The lass is a lovely one. Don't let 'er go, ye lucky man."

He threw the hat back, and Travis couldn't help but laugh. "Just don't go staring at my wife. I'll have to get Caroline on ya."

Ronan puffed out a breath and shook his head. "Don't ye be threaten' me about me wife. That red hair o' hers is some kinda warnin', and I should'a listened. Fiery temper." He stood, placing the empty cup on Travis's armrest. "I gotta be goin'. Wheat ain't gonna harvest itself early tomorrow."

Travis stood and shook his friend's hand, followed by a clap on the back. "Thanks for coming out. I appreciate it, even if it's to tease me."

"Anytime," Ronan said, putting his hat over his shaggy blond hair. "Take care."

As Ronan climbed up on his horse and took off, Travis leaned against the porch's wooden pillar. Was he a fool to push Josie away? Travis glanced through the kitchen window, seeing Josie wiping a dish. His heart skipped a beat. *A lovely lass, she is.*

CHAPTER FIFTEEN

IT HAD BEEN FOUR days since the harvest began. The first half of the fifth acre had been cleared, leaving behind organized piles of wheat, waiting to be bound into sheaves. For the first time, Josie could see the Montana soil beneath her, clear as day. Her arms ached with each swing of the scythe, and while she had learned to endure the weight, her mind hazed with exhaustion. By the time evenings came, she could barely muster the energy to put the children to bed. When she'd settle herself for bed, it took her a while to sleep, especially when Gideon had cried more than usual the past two nights.

Finding a comfortable position became increasingly difficult for Josie, her body sore and her stomach stretched to its limits. Josie couldn't stop thinking about what Travis said. Days went by, and those words still made her sick. *I can't risk these children losing another mother.* He didn't deserve the nightmare of possibly losing his wife again. He'd worry himself to death, just watching a baby grow inside her. She couldn't bear to place that burden on him, yet here she was. She was his wife now, in sickness and in health, until death parted them.

Josie set down the scythe and wiped her neck with her shawl. The heat beat down on her, while fatigue gnawed on her muscles.

Her legs and arms ached as if they might give way at any moment. Glancing over her shoulder, Travis and Aunt Polly worked tirelessly, slashing the stalks back and forth. *You're weak. Just like Marcus said. You're no good to Travis or anyone else.* Josie grasped her scythe, ready to resume her work, but was halted by a sudden, sharp pinch in her abdomen that almost knocked the wind out of her. She leaned forward, resting her hands on her knees, hoping the discomfort would pass, but it didn't. Her abdominal muscles tightened, and a wave of nausea washed over her. Pressure clasped her airways as the pain returned more intensely than the last. Her world blurred before her eyes as a cold sweat broke out above her brow.

She cried out softly, hoping no one could hear her. *Breathe in, breathe out.* She tried to steady herself, but the ache sharpened, and the familiar dizziness returned. She had experienced this three times before. Tears brimmed in her eyes, stinging as she held them back.

"Please, God, I beg you. Not again. I'll do better. I promise," she prayed through her whimpers, her voice barely above a whisper.

You are good for nothing! You are too weak to give me what you promised! You worthless woman! Josie could hear it as though Marcus was standing before her, just like when she had these same pains. Perhaps she was weak. Marcus didn't have to beat her to prove it this time. Why couldn't Marcus leave her alone? He was still in her mind, torturing her.

Josie closed her eyes, clenching her teeth as she cried louder—no longer caring if Polly or Travis could hear her. All she wanted was someone to hold her, promising the baby was fine and it would live.

"Josie! Josie!"

Jonas appeared behind her, pulling at her skirt as she hunched over. She tried to smile and brush off her ailing, for no child should see a woman act this way, especially one who was supposed to be their strong, maternal figure. She opened her mouth to speak, but the pain increased like a punch to her stomach, making her groan.

"Are you all right, Josie?"

Josie cried louder, bending over and clutching her abdomen as the ache intensified—it was too late, just like those three times before. She would pay the price for being an evil trickster to a kind man, and no one would love her. She was better off swinging from the gallows, and no one would care because she had no one. This family wasn't hers; she knew that now.

Jonas ran off. "Pa! Pa! Come quick! It's Josie!"

Josie closed her eyes, pressing her lips together, muffling a cry. *Not now. Please, God. Send him away. I want to be alone. He mustn't see me like this.*

Before Josie could protest, Travis was at her side, concern etched on his face. His hands wrapped around her shoulders, steadying her.

"Josie, what's wrong? What happened?" he asked through rapid breaths.

Josie was too weak to respond, her body shuddering in his arms. Aunt Polly knelt beside her and gently lifted her chin, her eyes filled with concern. "Honey, what's the matter? Are you hurt?"

Josie shook her head, but the pain made her vision blur. Her legs wobbled, threatening to give way, and just as she began to collapse, Travis caught her in time. Her mind spun as she found herself cradled in his arms. Resting her head against Travis's muscular chest, she let her grief wash over her. Deep down, she knew she didn't need a diagnosis; the baby was gone.

Travis's legs devoured the field as he sprinted to the cabin with Josie cradled in his arms. He didn't slow, didn't pause for breath—only the desperate need to get her to safety drove him forward. Seeing her hunched over in pain made something snap within him. She seemed fine earlier that morning. How could one's health slip so fast? She was exhausted like everyone else; however, exhaustion didn't leave one crying, bent over, and limp with extreme pain. Only his father had suffered like this—pushed too hard because of Travis's irresponsibility. A lump formed in Travis's throat.

Bursting through the cabin door, he glanced down at Josie's pale face. She stirred, clinging to his shirt with her fists as she cried out. *How could you do this again, Travis? Why must you hurt everyone you care for?*

The children ran after him, demanding to know if Josie was all right. Aunt Polly was already hitching up the wagon, ready to fetch the doctor. What worried Travis the most was that the town's healer went for medical help. Dr. Gordon and Aunt Polly had always butted heads about their patients' well-being—whether they needed natural substances or science. What could be so wrong with Josie that even herbs couldn't help?

Travis kicked Josie's bedroom open, darting towards the bed. But when he laid her down, he felt a wet sensation on his hand. He looked down, seeing blood, bright red blood on his palm. His heart seemed to stop, and his stomach clenched so violently he thought he might be sick.

"No. No. No. It can't be," he whispered.

His mind spun all over the place, but his one focus was keeping his wife alive. He watched helplessly as she writhed on the bed, her body trembling with pain. Josie's eyes remained tightly shut, teeth clenched, while she gripped the blankets as if holding on for dear life. Tears streamed down her pale cheeks, and her damp hair clung to her face, slick with sweat. Seeing the once-determined Josie reduced to this state tore him apart, dragging him back to a dark place he swore he'd never revisit. He was here again—in the same room, covered in his wife's blood, waiting on the doctor. Travis stumbled backward, his hands clutching the back of his head as he fought to hold back tears, threatening to break free.

Sophie's labor had been excruciating and drawn out—her body too fragile to fight, fidgeting and moaning in bed, tears of agony streaming down her face.

"You're a doctor, do something!" Travis had screamed, grabbing Dr. Gordon by the collar and shaking him in desperation. Dr. Gordon then gulped, placing his hand on Travis's shoulder. They hadn't seen eye-to-eye, especially when the doctor suggested a vile procedure to take away Gideon's chance at life. That disagreement had only deepened the rift between Dr. Gordon and Aunt Polly. Yet even Aunt Polly had admitted that Sophie needed a doctor that day.

Travis's heart stopped beating when Dr. Gordon explained Sophie wasn't going to make it—but there was a way his son could. He could let both of them die or save Gideon. Travis remembered looking into Sophie's eyes, seeing how much life was drained from her. He didn't want to admit it, but his wife was dying. Travis should have listened to the doctor when he said another pregnancy would kill her.

"Save him," Sophie whispered in a voice one could hardly call a whisper. *"Save our baby."*

Travis's eyes filled with tears. He couldn't bear to let Sophie go, but he knew she'd never forgive him if he didn't try to save Gideon. After agreeing to her wishes, he watched in horror as Dr. Gordon performed the deep incision to deliver their son. Travis clung to Sophie's hand, his heart shattering with each of her screams. By the time Gideon cried, Sophie managed a weak smile, and then she was gone. Lying motionless on the pillow, she didn't look like herself anymore—this wasn't the vibrant girl Travis had fallen in love with. He had, in his own way, killed her.

"Pa? What's wrong with Josie?"

Travis glanced over his shoulder, seeing Ivy and the other children peeking through the crack in the door. His heart sank—this was not something they should see. Without hesitation, he stretched his foot out, bracing it against the door to stop it from opening any farther.

"Stay back," he said, his voice tight, trying to keep the panic from spilling. Their eyes gaped, brimming with tears.

"Ivy, I need you to take your siblings to your room and stay there until I come for you. None of you need to be here."

"But Pa," she wailed. "Will Josie die like Ma?"

"Josie gonna die?" Lillian asked, her bottom lip quivering.

"Please don't let her die, Pa," Jonas cried, his face red from tears.

Travis swallowed hard and squatted to their level, wiping his hands on his pants. "Don't think like that. Just pray for her, all right?"

He stepped through the door and pulled Ivy and the others into a tight embrace, kissing the tops of their heads as he held them close. He had to save Josie. The thought of putting his children through another loss was unbearable, a weight he couldn't imagine forcing them to carry again.

"Go to your room," Travis whispered hoarsely. As the children dashed off, Travis rubbed his face, trying to erase any trace of his tears. When he returned to the room, his heart ached as he saw Josie moving her head from side to side, moaning softly in pain.

Travis sat next to her, taking her hand in his. Her palms were clammy, and her pulse raced beneath his fingers. "They need you, Josie. Whatever this is, you have to fight it. Fight it for us." He looked up to the ceiling, swallowing back his tears. "Dear God, don't take her. Think about my children, please. You can have me any day. Just don't take their new mother away."

Travis sat at the dining table, tapping his fingers on the surface while he waited to hear the doctor's report. Aunt Polly settled next to him, rubbing his back. Josie was strong; Travis knew that when she first met the children, taking on the role of a mother despite her youth and inexperience. Over the past two weeks, she had proved herself capable and resilient. Whatever this affliction was, she could fight it. His mind raced through possible reasons for her illness—exhaustion, a virus, some unknown disease? Was it contagious? And why was she bleeding?

Perhaps it was just her monthly courses. He remembered how Sophie had sometimes complained about cramping and nausea, but after taking Aunt Polly's homemade remedies, she always felt better. Maybe that was what Josie needed. Yet Aunt Polly had gone for the doctor—why would she seek help from a man she loathed when it came to something as personal as a woman's cycle? Surely Dr. Gordon had patients suffering from far worse conditions. However, when the doctor arrived, he wasted no time, kicking Travis out of the room and instructing him to wait.

Aunt Polly patted Travis's back. "Be calm. She's going to be fine."

"How do you know that?" Travis asked sharply. "I've never seen her act like that." Aunt Polly didn't answer him. He turned to her, his pulse racing in his ear. "What do you think is wrong with her?"

Aunt Polly stiffened. "I don't know. That's why the doctor is here."

"But you don't trust him. The only time you brought him here was when Sophie was giving birth."

Aunt Polly bit her lip and folded her hands in her lap. "Truth is, Travis, I'm worried about Josie. I can give her different variations of herbs, but I want a second opinion before I jump to conclusions. Josie is the mother of your children now, and like you, I don't want to risk any more loss."

Travis's nails dug into his palm. "And what do you believe is the cause of her affliction?"

The bedroom door closed, interrupting them. Dr. Gordon entered the main room, his expression notably less grave than it had been during Sophie's ordeal. Travis shot up from his chair, tension coiling in his muscles.

"How is she, Doc? Is she going to be all right?"

"She should be fine," the doctor answered, drying his hands with a rag. "Bleeding and cramping are quite common for a woman at this stage of her condition. With some rest, she should recover smoothly. Just make sure she doesn't overexert herself—no working in the fields this year."

Travis shriveled his gaze to Aunt Polly then back to the doctor. His heart punched his ribcage, cutting off his air. "Condition?"

The doctor raised his eyebrows. "She didn't tell you?"

"Tell me what?" Travis demanded. What could be wrong with Josie that he didn't know? She had seemed perfectly healthy, a hard worker dedicated to the harvest. He couldn't imagine stopping her from contributing. Whatever this was, it had to be fatigue; it couldn't be anything more serious. If it were, Josie would have told him.

Dr. Gordon stepped closer and grinned—a grin Travis hadn't seen on the man in months. He placed his hand on Travis's shoulder. "Congratulations, Mr. Blythe. You're going to be a father again."

Travis's eyes widened in disbelief. His breath hitched in his throat, nearly choking him as he took a step back, bracing his hand against the table to steady himself. He had to have heard the doctor wrong. He should have insisted that Aunt Polly stay and prepare a healing element instead of relying on Dr. Gordon, a man he couldn't trust. This was the same doctor who had failed to save Sophie, and now he was making vile accusations against Josie.

"What do you mean? My wife isn't *expecting*. She can't be."

"If my calculations are correct, you should have a Christmas baby." The doctor retrieved a bottle from his leather bag and handed it to Aunt Polly. "Here's some laudanum. I know you won't give it to her, but just in case. It will help with the discomfort she's been feeling."

Aunt Polly slid it into her pocket. "I'll brew some yarrow from my garden. If she asks for the laudanum specifically, I'll give it to her."

The doctor patted her shoulder. "If you need any more assistance, let me know."

Travis gripped the table, staring into nothingness. He wanted to demand another examination, but he stood, frozen in place, unable to speak. Suddenly, everything came together.

A beautiful woman came out west to marry a vulnerable widower. Travis was an easy target, one so desperate for a wife he'd marry anyone. Josie would be safe here, depending on him to care for her child. And yet, that night she tried to seduce him made sense, too.

She wanted him to think the child was his, but he wouldn't have her.

Who was the father? Who truly was this Josephine Callahan? She fooled him, and now they were wed for life. His jaw hardened. Travis was married to a deceptive woman. If Josie hadn't mentioned the major detail about her being pregnant, how could Travis trust anything else she said? Was that speech about coming here to have a family real? She had pulled his heartstrings, telling him all about her family dying, leaving her alone. And he believed her.

Every word.

He rubbed his chin and glared at Aunt Polly. "Did you know about this?"

Aunt Polly's expression remained neutral. "I suspected. That's why I asked the doctor here."

Travis groaned, slamming the table with his fist. "She lied to me. She lied to us all. I let her care for my children! A deceiver lives under my roof!"

"Stop that," Aunt Polly snapped, pointing in his face. "You can't just assume things that you don't have the answers to. There's more to the story than what meets the eye."

"Doesn't this all make sense?" Travis gritted his teeth. "She's a young, attractive woman who threw away so many opportunities to come here. And *with child*?"

"I agree, it does make sense. However, you shouldn't judge her too harshly," Aunt Polly said. "The important thing is she came here to mother your children when no one else would."

Travis folded his arms. "And mistakenly forgot to mention she was expecting a baby?"

Aunt Polly gave him a blank stare. "And would you have married her?"

Travis grabbed his hat. He had to get out of the house. He had to be alone. No, he wouldn't have married her, but that wasn't the point. Josie wasn't honest with him, and he could never trust her again. He'd shared everything—his deepest, darkest demons that tormented him—and she'd deceived him. On their wedding night, she wasn't a confused young bride. She knew exactly what she was doing.

Travis stormed out the door. He could never look at Josie the same, ever again.

Travis's nails dug into the wooden fence as he steadied himself. He hadn't stepped one foot in that house since Dr. Gordon diagnosed Josie. He couldn't go in there. He couldn't bear being caught in any more of her deceitful webs. How could he not see this coming? How could he make her his children's mother?

Sophie would never do this. She would never defraud anyone. The woman couldn't lie, for her poker face was a sham. Travis always sensed when Sophie was hiding something. He'd cock a brow, and she'd burst into laughter. Then Travis would tickle the truth out of her in less than five seconds.

Travis could never do that to Josie. It took all the strength he had to stand close to her. But Josie would tense each time he touched her, like the time he taught her to use a scythe. Perhaps she was worried he'd see through her or her baby, but those brown eyes held something more prevalent, more serious than a hidden pregnancy.

Looking into the setting horizon, Travis sighed as he watched the orange sun rays hit the wheat. The stalks swayed gently, dancing with the breeze. His eyes settled on the gaps in the field where they recently harvested that week, now standing out among the sea of grain.

Travis had returned to the fields with Ivy and Jonas while Josie rested. Ivy helped guide the wheelbarrow, and Jonas loaded the cut stalks that fell to the ground. Travis looked down, studying the dirt that clung to his hands and shirt, and his skin itched from the sticky stalks. His blistered hands stung as sweat mixed with the grit, but he ignored it, drawing in deep breaths, anxiously awaiting morning to come.

He longed to work again, all day in the hot sun just as his papa raised him to do. No setbacks—especially from Josie—would stop Travis now. He'd let down his family once before with Pa's heart attack, and he'd never rest again. The harvest would be finished; there was another mouth to feed, and he'd make sure they had enough.

"I figured I'd find ya here."

Travis turned, seeing Aunt Polly standing behind him. Her silver hair was pulled back by a blue bandana.

"Why's that?" Travis asked.

"You didn't come in for supper."

Travis leaned his back into the fence, his palms flexing. "Wasn't hungry."

Aunt Polly stepped forward, her hand pressed against Travis's forehead. "You ain't warm, that's for sure. It doesn't sound like you've lost your appetite. You should eat and keep your strength up. We have a long day tomorrow."

Travis removed her hand and turned back to the field. "I can't."

"Why not?" Aunt Polly pressed.

"I just can't, all right!" Travis rubbed the crease between his eyes and sighed. "I'm sorry, Aunt Polly. It's been a day."

Aunt Polly joined his side, her hands folded over the fence. "It's been a difficult one for all of us."

"She lied to us, Aunt Polly. I just . . . I know how much the children love her, and I would never turn Josie away . . . but I don't know if I can ever trust her again." Travis's voice croaked, looking Aunt Polly in the eyes. "I can't trust my own wife."

Aunt Polly softly rubbed his sweat-coated back. "She's still the Josie you knew."

"Do you believe her? About her coming here for a family?"

Aunt Polly didn't blink or move a muscle. "Yes, I do. And I also believe there's another side to her story. You should ask her."

Travis shut his eyes, letting out a soft groan. "How can I? How can I look at her again, knowing she's a liar?"

"I'm not saying you have to trust her, but as I said this afternoon, think about her side of the story. You lost your papa at a young age. Could you blame her for wanting her child to grow up with a papa?"

Travis looked out over the horizon. Losing his father caused a large hole in his heart. Mama never married again and believed no one could replace Papa. That child Josie carried didn't have a father, and who was Travis to cast it aside? Whether he wanted another child or not, Josie's baby was innocent. Aunt Polly leaned in, resting her chin on his shoulder.

Travis needed to speak to Josie. He wouldn't rest until he had his answers, whether he was afraid of the truth or not.

Chapter Sixteen

Josie awoke to the soft orange light filtering through the window, her body wrapped in a fresh nightdress and covered by clean sheets. The red quilt had been replaced by a calming baby blue one, decorated with cheerful green and red flowers. She stared at the wooden ceiling, trying to process everything that had happened hours ago. Her limbs were too heavy to lift, and her stomach churned at every little movement. Pushing herself hadn't been a wise choice, but she had wanted to prove her strength, to show she was more than a spoiled Southern belle, Travis thought her to be.

That act was all a lie.

Weak-willed, she had allowed her father to talk her into marrying a man twice her age, naively believing he would be a romantic hero like the ones in her cherished novels. It was foolish to think Marcus would let her keep *Belle Vallée*; she had been ignorant to believe she could make a difference in the lives of the Negro children on the streets of Statesville with her practiced teaching skills. It was weakness to think Marcus wouldn't find out and beat her until she couldn't walk. It was stupid to believe that being bedridden would somehow shield her from her duties afterward. Weak. So weak.

Josie breathed in and out, trying to hold back her tears. *You're useless to me,* Marcus's gruff voice echoed in her mind. *You are worthless.*

Dr. Gordon's confirmation—that her affliction was simply a sign that her body needed rest—was a sudden miracle. *"It's going to be all right, Mrs. Blythe,"* he told her. *"It's normal for a woman in your state to experience pain. Get some rest. You shouldn't be working so hard."* Josie had been speechless, a wave of relief washing over her as she realized her baby was safe in her womb.

A heavy weight settled in her chest. Travis knew now, no doubt about it. What must he think of her now? Dr. Gordon was oblivious of the truth; he assumed Travis was a happy father. A chill ran down Josie's spine as she imagined Travis's clear blue eyes darkening into a glaring furnace, just as Marcus's had every time she hid secrets from him.

Josie was a liar. A deceiver. And above all, she was a murderess sleeping under Travis's roof and raising his children. She sat up in bed, her eyes falling on Ivy, who was curled up in the rocking chair next to Gideon's crib. Ivy looked up, revealing the tears glistening in her eyes.

"Ivy, dear, what's the matter?"

She watched as Ivy wiped her nose with her sleeve, her small voice trembling. "I was so s-scared. I thought you were going to die . . . like Ma."

Josie's eyes stung. It wasn't so long ago she lost her mama, too. Josie tried everything in her power to keep Mama and Susannah alive, and she failed. No wonder her father had been so eager to rid himself of her for the sake of his plantation. Josie didn't blame him one bit. She was willing then to do whatever it took to win his affection back. However, that situation was different entirely. Ivy had a father who loved her, and now she had a new mother, who loved her more than she loved herself.

Josie patted the mattress. "Come here, Ivy. I need to speak with you."

Ivy stood and walked over to Josie's bed. As she sat beside her, Josie took the girl's hands. "I know this is so hard for you. I lost my Ma, too."

Ivy's eyes widened. "You did?"

Josie nodded, consumed with memories. She could see her mother's face clear as day, thinking back to the days they had together. She remembered her smile and sweet voice. Mama was everything Josie wanted to be. She was a tough woman, hardly ever shedding a tear.

When Josie's three brothers died, her mother grieved in a way that Josie had never known possible. Instead of staying at home, wearing black and locking herself away, her mother dedicated her time to caring for the wounded and sick, pouring her heart into helping others. Josie had been right there beside her, assisting in the hospitals, doing everything they could to help the men make it back to their families since Zane, Trellis, and Oliver never would.

Then scarlet fever struck, and it spread through *Belle Vallée* like wildfire. Josie had been lucky, not having the worst case, but it didn't spare anyone else. Many of their slaves never saw freedom, succumbing to the terrible disease. Josie remembered how she nursed them until their last breaths, but in the end, it hadn't been enough to save them.

"My Ma died when I was sixteen. It still feels like yesterday."

"Do you miss her?"

Josie nodded. "Yes, but I remember she's still here with me, just like your ma is here with you."

"How?"

Josie smiled softly and pressed her hand against the child's beating heart. "In here. Your ma's memory will always be with you. Then when you leave this world, you will be reunited with her again. It will be in Heaven."

Ivy's thin pink lips curled in one corner. "I can't wait."

"Me too."

Ivy scooted closer to Josie and laid her head on her chest. "I'm sorry, Josie. I'm sorry I was so rude. I . . . I didn't mean it."

Josie kissed Ivy's forehead. "I know you didn't. I'm never going to replace your ma, but I want to help and care for you. I love you and your siblings, Ivy."

Ivy met her gaze. "You aren't going to leave us too, right?"

Ivy's question pierced Josie's heart. She couldn't lie to the child. She had yet to speak with Travis; it had been hours, and she couldn't shake the feeling that he was likely thinking of ways to be rid of her—just as Marcus had before his fall. The thought tightened in her chest like a vise. Surely he wouldn't, but anger could make a man do anything.

Before Josie could answer, Aunt Polly opened the door, carrying a tray of tea. She glanced over at Ivy, who was snuggled up against Josie, and a soft smile crossed her lips.

"It's nice to see you're both keeping each other company," Aunt Polly said gently. "How are you feeling, Josie?"

"Fine, thank you."

Aunt Polly set the tray down and extended a hand to Ivy. "Come, come child. I need you and the other mites to get ready for bed while I check on Josie."

Ivy jumped off the bed and headed for the door. "Bye, Josie. I hope you feel better soon."

The hairs on Josie's neck stood as Aunt Polly shut the door behind her. The woman crossed her arms and stared at the floor.

The silence caused bumps to rise on Josie's arms, especially when she couldn't see Aunt Polly's face. Was it wearing worry? Disappointment? Hatred?

"I assume you know," Josie said, her nails digging into her arm.

Aunt Polly nodded and stepped closer. She settled on the mattress, clasping her hands in front of her. "I do, and I can see from your standpoint why you did it."

"What does Travis think?"

Aunt Polly sighed. "He's been tending to the crops all day. I thought it best for him to be alone."

Josie envisioned the man slicing through the wheat, imagining he was striking her. He probably was planning her punishment, just as Marcus would have done for betrayal and lies. How would Travis make her suffer? Would he beat her? Lock her in her room? Starve her? Or worse, send her home?

"Tell me about the father," Aunt Polly said.

Josie closed her eyes, seeing Marcus suffocating her with his hands latched around her throat, blocking every airway. She wouldn't tell him about the baby—not for anything. Marcus falling down the stairs was nothing shorter than a miracle—one Josie would pay for eventually. She couldn't tell Aunt Polly or Travis the truth, but she could say part of it.

"He's dead . . . He was my husband."

"No inheritance?"

None that she could have control of now, especially with the law pursuing her. "No."

Aunt Polly folded her arms. "I understand why you wanted to come here, being a destitute widow, pregnant and alone. But it was still wrong. You should have told Travis the truth."

"I know," Josie whispered, gripping the quilt. "I tried, but . . . he told me about his wife and how she died. I couldn't . . . I couldn't bring myself to do it."

Aunt Polly shook her head, biting the inside of her cheek. "Watching Sophie go through that nearly broke him. He couldn't do anything but watch. Childbirth is supposed to be a beautiful thing, but it turned to horror quickly."

Josie sniffed, her eyes burning. "I can see why . . . I can see why he just wants a mother for those poor dears. I was selfish, though. So selfish. I should have confessed, but . . . I was frightened."

Aunt Polly placed her hand on Josie's as her tears fell. "Why did you keep your marriage a secret? Travis would have understood."

"Why would he believe a woman he barely knew?" Josie asked sharply, as though Aunt Tia was speaking through her. "Isn't that exactly what an unmarried woman would claim—I'm a *widow?*"

"You don't know Travis then," Aunt Polly said calmly, pulling back her hand. "He sent you nearly all his savings to bring you here after your first letter. He trusted you. I know he would have understood. The man has a soft heart."

Josie felt like a fool. She gained Travis's trust by being honest about her experiences and returning his money, but now that trust was broken. She was no longer an honest woman in his eyes. He would no longer view her as the sweet Josie—an answer to prayer who longed for a family, not romance or wealth.

"You need to explain yourself to him."

"I can't," Josie croaked, pulling her hair behind her ears. "I can't face him."

Aunt Polly rose from the bed. "Well, you can't stay in here, locked away forever." Aunt Polly shot her a friendly smile before walking out the door. "Think about it."

Josie hugged her knees to her chest, bringing the quilt up to her chin. *It wasn't supposed to be like this.* She needed to tell Travis everything. However, the reason why she couldn't go home would have to stay buried. He was better off knowing one secret, not the darkest one that would destroy everything they could build. She would shame Travis more than she already had, and being a murderess was beyond having a secret child.

Josie wrapped her shawl tightly around her cotton nightdress before stepping outside for fresh air. After hours of being cooped up in bed, she had indeed grown tired of being alone in that room. When she stepped out onto the porch, she jumped. There Travis was, sitting in his rocking chair, the moonlight reflecting on his stubbly face. She was tempted to bolt back inside, but as his eyes met hers, she knew she couldn't leave him without the truth. She needed to face him before their distance became as wide as the ocean. Josie swallowed, trying to moisten her dry mouth. *Dear God, please help me.*

His gaze shifted to her midsection and locked back on her eyes with an intensity that made her heart race. "You seem to be in better health."

Josie nodded while clinging hard to her shawl's loose tassels. "I am."

Travis looked down at his lap. His hands rested on the arms of the rocking chair, fingers gripping tightly as he rocked back and forth. The creaking of the wood seemed to echo in Josie's ears, each sound quickening her pulse. Her legs wobbled beneath her, and she feared she'd collapse at any moment. But if she did, would

Travis be there, ready to pick her up off the ground? To hold her close again like before, showing genuine tenderness and care?

"When were you planning to tell me about the baby?" His voice held no bitterness or anger; it was flat and almost mechanical, making it hard for Josie to decipher the emotions beneath.

She looked at her feet. "I don't know." She clutched her shawl tighter around her midsection. "But it's right for me to explain now."

She stepped closer to him, slow and careful. When she made it to the second rocker, she settled in, drawing in a deep breath. The words faltered in her throat. She couldn't say anything to justify herself, but she owed him the truth. At least, the pieces that were worth saying—the pieces that would protect her child.

"My husband wasn't a good man. He hurt and . . . humiliated me . . . more times than I could count." She swallowed a burn at the back of her throat, fighting back her tears. "Before I went to live with my aunt, he passed away." The half-truth nearly caused her to vomit. But she managed to continue her story. "This baby . . . was who I was thinking about during my actions, but I would never use my child to excuse my deceptive behavior. It is innocent in all of this."

Josie looked up at Travis, who rubbed his forehead in silence. She didn't know what else to say. What could redeem her in such a situation? She deserved to be cast aside, destitute in the dangerous world. The thought of being turned over to the authorities sent icy tingles skittering up her spine and across her skin. If Travis found out somehow, would he turn her in? Could she trust her own husband?

"I . . . I understand if you want me to go. I won't insist on staying," Josie croaked.

At that moment, Travis's tender eyes met hers. Neither anger nor disappointment lingered in them as she imagined. "There will be no need for that."

Travis rocked in his chair in a strict medium tempo while gazing ahead again. His fingers intertwined like a prayer position on his lap. "You are my wife, Josie, and knowing the truth now, I don't blame you. I am still disappointed you hid this from me, but I understand. My mother was a widow, as well as Aunt Polly." He swallowed, his Adam's apple bobbing up and down. "I know they'd do the same if they had no other choice."

Josie closed her eyes. Did she have another choice? She could have lived in Aunt Tia's attic, alone, waiting for her aunt to pass and have someone else take control of the place. And running away? It was a miracle she wasn't recognized on the train.

"It's difficult raising a child alone, but I do wish you could have been honest," Travis said softly.

Josie wiped a solo tear, streaming down her cheek. "I . . . I wanted to . . . believe me. I am beyond ashamed for my actions—"

"I understand, Josie," Travis interrupted, leaning forward. His once-roving gaze rested on her. "And that is why I am going to take full responsibility for you and your child."

"But . . . I-I can't have you do that," Josie said quickly. Her mind flooded with thoughts of the three older ladies who surrounded them the day after they married. They were already shocked that Travis married in secret, never mentioning a courtship beforehand. She couldn't imagine the shame that would come once the baby came early.

"The baby will come too soon. The timing will be off . . . I can't bring shame upon your family with this." Josie placed her hand on her abdomen. "I'm already showing."

"I'm prepared for that," Travis reassured. "I've thought this through. You might not have been honest with me and my family, but that baby is innocent. I know what it's like to grow up without a father, and I can't let another child go through with that if I can prevent it."

"The town will think less of you. They'll think we . . ." She could hardly stomach the rest of her words.

"I don't care." Travis placed his hand on his chest. "Let them think less of me. That child deserves a life with a family that will love him or her no matter what."

"You don't have to take responsibility for a child that's not yours."

"Josie," Travis breathed, extending a hand to her. He placed it on Josie's armrest, inches from her fingers. "You are my wife. Let me love your child like you love mine."

Josie placed her other hand on her stomach. She didn't deserve Travis, but her child did. She'd spend the rest of her days making it up to him and wouldn't let dishonesty cloud their future again. However, in the shadows of her mind lurked another skeleton—one she had buried deep, hoping it would fade away. She was better off forgetting it, nothing more than a bad dream. But this life she was living now wasn't a dream.

It was real.

CHAPTER SEVENTEEN

GENERAL GRIPPED THE BED sheets with his bare hands, causing a slight rip as he waited to hear Dr. Colson's report. Since he had woken two weeks ago, Dr. Colson had come three times to check on him, only to give the same results. *"Get some rest and you should be able to walk in a month or two,"* he'd say. *"Do your exercises for ten minutes a day."*

Those exercises were useless. That old, fat mammy of Josie's would massage his feet and stretch and pull in many different directions as Colson had taught her, and they didn't help a lick, because General still couldn't feel his feet. Sometimes he'd suffer a cramp, but each time he tried to stand and show the doctor he was strong enough to walk, he'd collapse to the floor.

Colson continued to write in that tiny notebook of his, recording every moment of his observation as though General was a circus animal. *Experimental surgery, my foot.* What was he—an experimental specimen? He went to West Point at the age of sixteen and was promoted to colonel during the Mexican-American War, earning his title as a war hero. Being reduced to a test subject was beneath him, an insult to his contributions to the Confederacy.

General pursed his lips as his rage bubbled to the surface, causing him to rip another hole in the sheet. The doctor was useless garbage who couldn't help him. What was a doctor good for if he couldn't heal a patient properly?

General would rather die than be labeled as a useless cripple. How could he live in this confined room? He was no prisoner—never had been, and never would be. That's because he was an invincible warrior. He may have had a scarred face, but he wasn't bedridden yet. No doctor would make him a laughingstock.

He survived it all—hardly a bullet in him except once, and that didn't put him down. He kept fighting, striking down every Mexican soldier in his path. Then, he made his way to the medical tent just in time before he could bleed to death. He didn't earn his title by sitting in bed and having his wife's Mammy bathe and spoon feed him. He earned it by toughening up and not letting any emotions cloud his judgment. He pushed through and guarded himself like a steel wall. He wouldn't be weak like his father, who chose to kill himself rather than face his problems.

Melancholia—that's what those physicians had diagnosed his old man with. General's father couldn't get off opium after his wife died. The grief destroyed him, but General pushed through his mother's death. West Point made him a man, a man his father couldn't be.

Doctor Colson put his notebook inside his coat pocket and retrieved his stethoscope. He placed it on General's chest like many times before. General breathed in and out.

"Again," Dr. Colson said.

General took a large gulp of air then exhaled. He was ready for his examination to be finished. It was time for business again. He needed to find that wife of his and later teach the doctor a lesson. No, he'd teach those surgeons a lesson first. What a joy it would be to shake them up a little! A tiny chuckle escaped his exhausted lungs. Revenge was sweet—General could taste it like honey straight from the comb. Oh, what a time that would be to see their agony and admit their faults. They'd pay a great price for tampering with America's finest hero.

Dr. Colson pulled out his notebook again and began writing. "Have you been taking the morphine I prescribed for you?"

"Every day," General answered. *How many more times do I have to repeat myself?*

"How about the exercises?"

"Ten minutes a day, as you prescribed."

Dr. Colson nodded. "Excellent. We shall double that to twenty. Your muscles should recover smoothly, and you'll walk by Christmas or so."

General wanted to huff aloud. No, he'd walk before then. He'd triple those silly exercises. Nothing would confine him any longer.

"Have you been drinking?"

Mammy kept her head down in the corner, looking at her feet. General chuckled.

Dr. Colson cocked a brow. "How much?"

General crossed his arms. "What does that have to do with anything?"

Dr. Colson closed his book. "General Wellington, the amount of alcohol you've been drinking can ruin your chance at a quick recovery. You suffered a severe brain bleed. You should be dead! Take a break from drinking and let your body rest."

"That is preposterous!" General exclaimed, his fists curled. "I've been drinking since I could lift a bottle to my mouth. If it is that severe, I would have died long ago."

"You have a life-threatening injury. That brain of yours has pieces missing. The surgeons had to drill open—"

General gritted his teeth as his anger heated. "Stop that! I don't want to hear it! How much longer do I have in this God-forsaken bed?"

Dr. Colson didn't look up from his supply bag. "We'll have to wait and see. If you quit drinking, maybe I can arrange a chair."

A chair? What was he, a cripple? He wouldn't be seen as a laughingstock. "Are you an idiot? I won't be confined to a bed or chair! I want to walk! Do your job and make me better. You're a physician for goodness sakes!"

Dr. Colson's lips pursed as his nostrils flared. He closed the bag in haste. "A tantrum won't help you recover faster either. I'll be back in three days to check on your progress."

"Don't even bother coming back!" General shouted through gritted teeth.

He removed the pillow behind him and pulled out a nearly finished bottle of whiskey. He downed it as fast as he could then wiped his mouth with his sleeve.

"Mammy!"

The plump woman peered up from her spot in the corner, her posture slumped and her eyes timid. General threw his bottle against the wall. The sound of shattering glass made Mammy jump out of her skin.

"Where is my wife? You better tell me she's returning now!"

He wouldn't be bathed by any servant. This was embarrassing enough having an absent wife who wasn't there to nurse him. What use was she being with someone else's family? He wouldn't dare send her away on her own.

Mammy's gaze remained at her feet. "Missus Wellington ain't sent word, General suh. I'm sorry."

General pointed his finger. "You better find out where she is and tell her to get her sorry little self over here now, or her torn-up hide will be on your hands."

Mammy nodded.

"Do you hear me? Answer me, you stupid woman!"

"Yes, suh."

General sat back against his headboard. "That's more like it. Be a good girl and get me another bottle of whiskey. We're going to show that Dr. Colson what a real tough man this general is."

CHAPTER EIGHTEEN

TRAVIS'S MUSCLES ACHED WITH each swing of his scythe after another week of harvesting. He looked back as Josie gathered the cut stalks, her hair falling out of her braid. She bent over, filling the wheelbarrow, and wiped the sweat from her brow. Travis had instructed her not to work so hard, and he hoped taking the scythe away would help her rest, but he was wrong.

Josie's midsection had grown over time. Earlier, Travis hardly took time to notice her form changing, mostly because of his distance and the shawl Josie would wear. When the harvest first started, he couldn't understand why she'd wear the garment outside with her, but now everything was clear. Travis shook his head, drowning out his thoughts. He almost repeated the same lines he always did in his mind: *Before she lied to me.*

Josie never lied to his face—she had only concealed a secret. He never asked her, "Were you married before?" or "Do you have any children?" There was no reason to ask; she had never given him cause for suspicion.

"Jonas, quit horsing around!"

Travis looked up, seeing the frustrated Ivy scolding Jonas, who was throwing the stalks into the air. The children were behind the fence posts, binding the sheaves after they dried over the past week. Josie alternated between helping them and gathering more stalks to dry in the barn. That part was Aunt Polly's job, until she remembered she had to pay Mrs. Scott a visit, three miles down the road. The woman struggled with rheumatic pains, and Aunt Polly had a cream she made from comfrey and juniper.

Travis swung the scythe in a steady swish. His shirt clung to his back, soaked with sweat, and his hands ached from gripping the worn wooden handle. Every muscle in his body screamed for rest, but he kept going, determined to finish just a little more before the light faded completely. Only three more hours or less before they would lose daylight.

He adjusted his grip on the scythe, not noticing how slick his hands had become with sweat. As he swung the blade in a wide arc, his hand slid too close to the sharp edge. The scythe caught at a bad angle, jerking out of his grasp. A sharp sting bit through his palm.

"Ah!" Travis gasped. He looked down, his breath catching as blood welled up from the deep gash across his hand. Warm and thick, it dripped down his wrist, staining the cuff of his shirt. "Fool," he muttered under his breath, wincing as he flexed his fingers, watching more blood drip. He pressed his palm against his shirt.

"Travis!" Josie appeared by his side, taking hold of his arm. Travis winced, pulling away.

"I'm fine."

Josie huffed, grasping his wrist with a tighter grip than he expected. "Hold on." She bent over, pulling up her dress hem then tearing a shred from her white petticoat. Travis's eyes squinted as he gritted his teeth. The sweat seeped into his wound, burning his open flesh. Josie pulled his arm towards her and began wrapping his hand.

"Ow!" He jerked slightly.

"Sorry," Josie said sheepishly, her teeth biting into her bottom lip. "We need to get you inside. I need to properly dress the wound."

Travis withdrew from her, wrapping the rest of his palm himself. "No need for that. I need to get this acre finished."

"Don't be stubborn," Josie snapped. "You'll get an infection."

Travis went to retrieve his scythe. "Nothing Aunt Polly can't make an ointment for." Travis groaned, trying to grip the scythe. He had another quarter of this field to go and five more acres after. His family depended on him. Why did he have to lose control like that?

Josie gripped his shoulder, tugging him forward. "Come on. We don't want to worry the children, do we?"

Travis huffed and dropped the scythe. "Fine."

Josie waved to the children, who seemed to be getting along again. Lillian waved back wearing a huge smile.

"I'm going to start supper. Ivy, watch Lillian and Jonas."

"Can we have fried chicken?" Jonas asked with wide eyes.

Josie chuckled. "Not tonight, but some flapjacks sound nice."

Travis hid his injured hand behind his back and pointed at his children with his spare hand. "Behave. Keep tying those sheaves."

Travis followed Josie inside, and immediately, she filled a pot with water using the indoor pump. "I'm going to boil some water, so we can clean it again later. I have some ointment in the pantry from Aunt Polly."

Travis settled himself at the dining table. He looked at his palm, studying the red stains bleeding through Josie's petticoat. As the water warmed atop the stove, Josie retrieved the ointment from the kitchen shelf then to her room, returning with a sewing kit. Just the thought of a needle made Travis's stomach churn.

"W-What are you doing with that?"

"The wound is too deep. You need stitches," Josie asserted. She settled in front of him, unwrapping his hand. Next she used a wet rag, wiping around the cut's edge. Travis's palm stung, causing him to pull back.

"It's whiskey," Josie explained. "It will clean the wound well enough."

Travis's cheeks warmed. He hoped she wouldn't get the wrong idea about stumbling upon the bottle. He had kept it for medical purposes like sore throats and colds. He had tasted it only once after Sophie's death—and never again. Grief might have changed him, but he refused to surrender and drown in darkness when his children needed him sober.

Josie opened her sewing kit, revealing a tiny pair of scissors, four rounds of thread, and a small wooden box of needles. Travis gulped. She reached out to take his hand, but Travis pulled back.

"Have you done this before?"

Josie sighed, a smile tugging at the corners of her lips. "Relax. It's not the first time I sewed up a wound."

"When was that?"

Josie threaded her needle. "Here and there. Remember, my home was a battleground for four years." Josie chuckled, dragging his wrist towards her. "I've sewn up bullet holes, cuts, stab wounds, and even amputated limbs."

Travis nearly jumped out of his skin. "Y-You what?"

Who was this woman? Yes, Travis knew about the war and Josie's location, but she was a Southern belle. This woman had to be joking. What kind of woman in her station would have this experience? Amputated limbs? Just the thought left Travis feeling faint.

Josie tightened her grip around his wrist. "Hold still. This will hurt, but it's better than amputating your hand."

She pushed the needle into his skin, and Travis gripped his thigh, fighting back the urge to scream. He was a tough man and could take anything, but the sight of a needle turned him into a squirmy child.

"I'm only joking about sewing up amputated limbs, but I did witness it more than once. If it comes down to removing your hand, we won't need a doctor." Josie winked, but her joke didn't lighten the mood. She may have a humorous side Travis never guessed, but this moment was *far* from funny.

"A healer and a nurse. Boy, I'm lucky," Travis muttered through gritted teeth.

Five minutes later, Josie reached for her scissors. She cut the loose thread and sat back with a sly smirk on her face. "All done. That wasn't so bad, was it?" Travis rolled his eyes. "Sure. You just sewed through my skin like a cross-stitch board, and it was easy as pie."

Josie opened a bottle of green ointment, rubbing it onto his palm. Tiny bits of herbs floated in the pulverized paste. After, she reached down, tearing another piece of her petticoat.

"Woah, woah, you don't have to do that. We have rags everywhere."

"I don't mind," Josie said, straightening the make-shift bandage onto the table. "I won't be using this petticoat much longer anyway."

Travis bit the inside of his cheek while Josie wrapped his hand. *Much longer.* December wasn't far away, and even then, their lives could change in an instant. He could very well lose Josie just like he did Sophie. What if Josie's past physicians told her not to get pregnant? What if the cruel husband of hers did something to her that would complicate the delivery? Just the thought made his core tighten into a knot.

"Did you tell the children . . . about the baby?" Josie asked.

Travis looked up, hardly able to meet her gaze. "No, I figured we'd tell them together."

Josie leaned forward, her eyes forcibly meeting his. "What will we tell them?"

Travis scratched the back of his neck. *Lie.* He was tired of it all; it seemed lying was all the family did since Josie came. She lied to him, he lied to the town, and now they'd lie to the children.

"We don't say anything. They're getting a baby sister or brother, and that's the end of it. If they ask one day, we'll explain, but for now, let them be innocent. We don't need to confuse them."

Josie nodded. "I agree."

"Knock, knock!" Aunt Polly entered through the front door with Lillian, Jonas, and Ivy following behind her.

"Where's the flapjacks?" Lillian asked, her nose wrinkling.

Josie stood, giggling softly. "I'll start on them now."

Aunt Polly studied the table, her forehead creased and her brows raised. She halted at Travis's side, yanking up his hand. "My goodness, son. What happened to you?"

"He cut himself," Josie explained, looking behind her as she pulled a small sack of flour from the chest beside the stove. "I stitched him up."

Aunt Polly nodded at Josie. "I'm impressed. Did you use the ointment in the pantry?"

"I did."

Lillian looked down at Travis's hand with sad eyes. "Did you get cut?"

Travis smiled, patting his knee for her to sit. "I did get a cut, and Josic made it all better."

Lillian settled in his lap, and Travis roved his gaze to Josie, who was mixing flour and milk into a wooden bowl. His throat tightened, words caught somewhere between what he needed to say and what he couldn't bear to admit. He didn't want it to be true. He longed for things to go back to how they were, when Josie's only role was caring for the children, and he kept his distance, acting solely as the devoted father. He didn't want to draw closer to Josie. He wanted his family to be together but not twisted and tangled. Having a child between the two would only complicate the matters—even if the child wasn't his. How could he respect her now with her lies?

Faith. Just like Aunt Polly said. He'd give Josie another chance and take this baby as a blessing. The child deserved a loving family, and he had no doubt in his mind the children would love him or her.

"Josie and I have news," Travis began, his voice steady, though his heart hammered against his ribs. "How would you three like to have another baby sister or brother?"

The children exchanged wide-eyed glances, their faces lighting up with a mix of shock and excitement.

"Pa, do you mean it?" Ivy asked, her lips parting into a smile.

"We do," Josie replied softly, placing a floured hand on Ivy's shoulder.

"Wow! Another brother!" Jonas exclaimed, his arms in the air. "I'm gonna have another brother!"

"No!" Lillian shouted from Travis's lap, turning to him with a frown. "Can it be a sister, Pa? I want a sister."

Travis chuckled, kissing the top of her head and patting her back. "That all depends on what God wants for us, sweetheart."

"Then I'm gonna pray real hard, Pa," Lillian declared, folding her hands and squeezing her eyes shut. "Please, God, gimme a baby sister."

Travis looked up at Josie, giving her a soft smile. She looked back at him, returning the same expression. He looked away, not allowing his glance to be a moment longer. Travis lifted Lillian off his knee. "Now go help Josie with the flapjacks."

Lillian squealed as she slid off his lap. She scurried to the stove and wrapped her arms around Josie's legs.

Aunt Polly joined Travis's side and patted his back. "I'm proud of you, Travis."

Travis nodded, the corners of his mouth lifting in what he hoped was reassurance. Maybe a baby would bring happiness back into their home. But despite the hopeful thought, doubts circled his mind like vultures, refusing to leave him in peace. Something in his gut felt amiss, but he couldn't decide what it was.

Was it his fear of being a father again? Or maybe it was Josie—what if he'd never learn to trust her again?

CHAPTER NINETEEN

Willow Grove, Montana; Early August 1872

THE FIREPLACE ACROSS THE room roared while Josie sat at the kitchen table with Ivy in her lap, her eyes scanning the child's needlework. The afternoons were nearly as hot as the flames, but when the sun hid behind the clouds, the nights grew chilly, especially in a drafty cabin. Josie carefully guided Ivy's hand as she stitched through a white piece of fabric. The child had found it in Aunt Polly's scrap pile in her cabin and rushed back, asking Josie to help her make a nightdress for the baby.

Josie had learned to sew at an early age, focusing mainly on cross-stitching and embroidery. She never mastered the art of creating dresses until after the war and her marriage. When exposed to the extreme poverty in the Negro community, Josie felt a strong urge to give away her old clothes and take on the task of making dresses for little girls. With Marcus controlling her finances, she found it more practical to work from home, always in secret, worried that he might discover her efforts.

It didn't take long for Marcus to discover that she was teaching and making clothes. In retaliation, he took everything she owned, ensuring she wouldn't receive a single penny, even in death. Stripped of her possessions, she was left with nothing but the name "Mrs. Wellington," after her father had already passed on, unable to help. Marcus sold *Belle Vallée,* wielding his authority as her husband to abuse her.

Josie looked down at Ivy. After an hour of Josie observing Ivy's hand, the child was doing well with keeping her stitches straight and even. She cherished this time spent with her stepdaughter, especially considering that a month ago, she had feared such moments would never come.

Ivy was almost nine years old, and Josie had been just seven years older than Ivy was now when she was given in marriage to Marcus. Josie ran her fingers through her stepdaughter's thin reddish-brown hair. She was so innocent, so oblivious to the cruel world around her. Josie longed for the days of her youth, wishing she could reclaim the innocence that shielded her from the world's wickedness and the true nature of men. The war had changed everything, stripping away her carefree existence and replacing it with pain and hardship. It took everything from her, leading her to a life she loathed—one filled with sorrow and struggle instead of the warmth and security she once knew.

Josie peered up to see Lillian enter the living area, clutching the scraps of fabric that were removed to shape Ivy's piece into a nightdress.

"Josie, can I try?"

Ivy rolled her eyes. "You can't make anything with that. It's scraps."

Lillian's head hung low and poked out her lip. "Oh."

Josie gently tapped Ivy to encourage her to sit up before approaching the disappointed Lillian. Crouching to meet the child at her level, Josie touched Lillian's hand, which still clutched the scraps of fabric.

Josie smiled, opening Lillian's palm. "I think we can make something out of this. Follow me."

Lillian trailed Josie to the room's left corner, where the scissors still laid next to the kitchen stove. Josie picked them up and carefully cut the sides of Lillian's scrap to create a ribbon-like piece. She placed it around Lillian's head, tying the ends together at her crown.

"Now you have a headband. You look very stylish if I say so myself."

Just then, the sound of the door closing interrupted their moment as Travis and Jonas walked in. They had been loading grain to take to the mill the next day. Josie and the children had been winnowing for weeks. It was one of the few things Josie felt she could manage without overexerting herself

"Pa, look!" Lillian exclaimed, spinning in her little blue calico dress.

Travis smiled and picked Lillian up. "My my, you look like a little princess."

Lillian pointed to her headband. "Josie made this for me."

Travis looked up at Josie, his head giving a little nod. He still hadn't fully adjusted to her true identity, despite it being two weeks since he learned the truth.

"Thank you, Josie," he said. He put Lillian down and Ivy approached him with her needlework in hand.

"Pa, look what Josie is helping me make." She held up the half-made gown.

Travis stiffened for a moment. Josie anxiously awaited his re-action, her fingers nestled tightly together. Travis's flattened lips curved. "It looks nice, Ivy." Travis leaned closer to Josie. "I thought I'd come in and tell the children goodnight."

Warmth flooded through Josie, swirling in her stomach. It was the first time since June Travis came inside at night, wanting to put the children to bed. He only came inside to eat, and even then, he rushed, hardly saying a word. The only time he interacted with the children was when they were outside and Josie wasn't around.

"Of course. The children would be delighted."

Travis roved his gaze from her to the children in the living area. He grinned and clapped. "Last one to the bedroom is a rotten egg."

Josie watched as the children bolted into the bedroom. Travis chuckled softly before turning back to her. Josie's cheeks flushed, and she longed to say something, something that would fight this distance away. "Thank you, Travis. I'm glad you're doing this."

Travis nodded, his thumbs resting around his suspenders. "I thought it was about time."

Josie watched as Travis walked down the hallway, disappearing into the children's room. A faint smile tugged at her lips; it was comforting to see him with his children under the same roof as her. Times were changing for them, but doubt crept into her mind. After the Founder's Day Dance, she had hoped they might grow closer, maybe even become one family, but now . . . she wasn't so sure.

Travis had been bold enough to remain in her presence, yet it didn't mean he would truly accept her. And, deep down, Josie wasn't sure if she wanted him to.

The cabin was cozy compared to the loft, nearly tempting Travis to remain inside. Despite it still being summer, the mountain air was something else at night. He wished to be back in his own bed again, but it wasn't his place anymore. He could survive another cold night in the loft. Travis strode towards the crackling fire, feeling warmth on his face. *Maybe a night by the fire wouldn't be too bad.*

Lost in thought, he heard a creak. He turned, seeing Josie asleep in the rocker near the stove. She looked so peaceful with her eyes closed, relaxed in the chair, her hands resting on her growing stomach. Travis retrieved a quilt from the basket beside the fireplace and carefully stepped towards Josie. As soon as he draped it over her legs, she jolted awake, her breath hitching and eyes twice their size. Travis touched her shoulder. "It's me. Sorry I startled you."

Josie sighed, rubbing her forehead. "Sorry. I'm a light sleeper, you could say."

For a moment, Travis could swear there had been terror in her eyes. He often thought about her previous life, how she said her late husband would hurt her. There could be multiple interpretations. Did he hit her? Lock her away? Was he drunk during these moments? Did he ever apologize? Just thinking about it made his blood boil. Those eyes of hers could only hide so much.

"Is the fire warm enough?" Travis asked, pointing behind him.

Josie pulled the covers to her chin. "I thought you were with the children."

Travis pulled a chair from the dining table and set it beside her. "I was," Travis explained, lowering himself. "They said their prayers and were almost out by the time I turned down their lamp."

"I'm not surprised. They are exhausted."

Travis leaned back. "At least we have the worst parts of the harvest behind us."

Despite not working in the fields, Josie still labored like a dog. Aunt Polly advised her to rest most of the time, but she pushed herself forward. She was indeed the worker she had said herself to be—that was no lie. Josie woke early, made breakfast, took care of Gideon who was already walking, dressed the children, and supervised them as she winnowed the seedlings.

Sophie was strong-willed and stubborn during her pregnancies. She never let her condition stand in her way as a wife, mother, and homemaker. But that took a toll on her during her pregnancies with Gideon and Lillian. She grew terribly ill yet remained determined—until her final weeks of life.

"You should be resting as well. You work too hard."

Josie shook her head. "I'm fine. It's normal to be a little tired. I'll just have to push through it."

Travis sighed, shaking his head. *Stubborn woman.* "You have such a heavy load, Josie. You care for this house, children, me, and the harvest. I want to bring Aunt Polly back in to help out."

Josie's eyes widened. "No, you don't have to bother her. I don't need you to lose an extra person in the fields."

Travis could manage on his own. He'd done it before when Aunt Polly was sick with a cold years ago. He thought about asking Ronan, but he had trouble with his own harvest and five children to feed. Mr. Scott, who was two miles east, had hired hands, unlike Travis, who could never afford it.

"I can manage. You and the baby are my priority now. You should take breaks."

"And what will I do in these breaks?" Josie asked, her features twisted in what Travis couldn't read as anger or frustration. "If you're asking me to stay in bed all day, I won't do it."

Travis folded his hand in front of him. "Josie, please listen to me. I can't have you . . . I can't have you at risk again."

Josie stared towards the fire, rocking back and forth. "If it's that important to you, Aunt Polly can come, but she won't order me around. I'll try to manage the best I can. I am not only a mother, but I am also your wife. I vowed to stand beside you as your helpmeet, and that's the least I can do, given what I put you through." Josie paused, pulling her loose hair behind her ear. "You shouldn't be staying in that barn. It's getting colder."

"It's not too bad."

"I . . . I can stay in here and you could have your room back. Or . . . I can stay with the children in their rooms."

Travis shook his head. "No, you need your space. It's getting closer to your time."

"I'm fine," Josie sternly insisted. "Don't you worry about me."

Travis looked into her brown eyes, studying them now that her fear had melted away, now holding her stubborn spirit. Josie's pale face glowed as the orange light from the flames illuminated the room. She was a sight, but a sight that was too complicated to admit was beautiful. She was unlike any woman he met before—mysterious and unpredictable. Even though she deceived him, he couldn't deny that she had a way of drawing him in, like a honeysuckle to bees, a fly to embers, a moth to flame.

He couldn't trust her, and he couldn't trust himself getting too close. Who knew what would happen if he held her in his arms . . . perhaps kissed her.

"Goodnight, Josie," he said, standing up from his seat.

Josie placed her hand on her swollen abdomen. "Good night, Travis."

Travis shut the door from behind him, buttoning his coat around him as the brisk wind hit his face. He was free of her now. He told her what was on his mind, just enough to keep her safe.

But what needed the most protection was his heart.

Chapter Twenty

Statesville, North Carolina; Early August **1872**

GENERAL WELLINGTON SAT UP against the headboard, taking small bites of ham and scrambled eggs. He chewed slowly, trying to pass the time by gathering his thoughts. One month of confinement. One month of stupid exercises that seemed to do him no good. One month since he sent word to his wife, only to receive no reply.

"I don't know why the missus won't write," Mammy had said in her soft, gentle voice early that morning. *"Guess she's just busy with those young'uns. Yuh know how they be, suh."*

General stabbed his fork into his ham. Something wasn't sitting right with him—even Mammy's innocent storytelling. She knew something, and she wasn't telling him. Why else wasn't his devoted wife coming home? Had she deserted him? Had she died in an accident?

Perhaps an accident would do. Josephine hadn't been any use to him for the past seven years. Maybe this was a sign it was time to take another wife, one that was young enough to bear children and mature enough to understand her duties. That frightened little brat had been a child, but he had no problem training her up. He chuckled to himself. *Fragile little thing.*

In order to move on to his next bride, he'd have to confirm her death. Maybe even make it happen himself if she were still alive. That was why he took matters into his own hands by hiring the best detective he could find, Detective Albert Dalton.

General wasn't a fool anymore. Josephine had been gone too long. The little wench up and left him. He doubted she had cousins in Wilmington. Why? Because he would have known. He knew everything about his wife, and she could never hide from him. The girl had nobody, so who was she fooling?

"Excuse me, General," Mammy said, cracking open the door. "Detective Dalton is here to see you."

General wiped his lips with a napkin. "Bring him in."

The lanky man dressed in a gray striped suit and top hat entered, carrying his black leather case at his side. He removed his hat and shook General's hand.

"It's good to see you, Detective Dalton," General said with a cunning smile. As he studied the man, his smile faded. He squinted. This detective looked no more than thirty. Even beneath his stubble beard, he couldn't be fooling anyone. General's money better be worth it, or God help the staff in this house once he took matters into his own hands.

"And you, too, General Wellington." Detective Dalton seated himself at the desk in the corner, placing his briefcase on top. He crossed one leg over the other, so proper-like. If he had been a soldier, General would've made a man out of him one way or another. "I confess I have been reading up on you. It has been an honor to work for you."

Yeah, yeah. General wanted to roll his eyes. Detective Dalton was like any other money-hungry man, kissing up to him. "I heard you were the best, now I must be the judge of that."

Detective Dalton chuckled softly, his cheeks reddening. "You put me in a big position, but I will try my best not to fail you. After all, your family seems to be very important. Two sons from West Point. You must have been proud."

General wanted to burst into laughter. A proud father he was, two sons who were nothing but great disappointments to the Wellington reputation General worked so hard to create. Jared and Loyd were both ideal heirs—excellent swordsmen and riflemen with yearning for war pumping through their veins. General didn't baby the sons like his late wife Martha did, and that was why he sent them to West Point when they both turned thirteen. He couldn't have been any prouder when they came out on top of their class.

He was determined for them to get high rankings as soon as they joined the Confederate Army, and their accomplishments would redeem the family line, tarnished by General's cowardly father. Instead they perished alongside two of Josephine's pathetic brothers in the Battle of Gettysburg.

General cursed his bloodline, for his sons had taken after their grandfather, too frail for the world. He was a general—one of the best—who had two sorry excuses for sons. What a great shame they brought!

"My condolences, General Wellington," he heard for two long years following the deaths. *"Your family will be in our prayers. Your sons were heroes, and we are grateful for their service."*

Heroes? General could spit. It was a title they hadn't earned, only fought in one battle. A war hero had a sharp mind for combat and invisible strength and courage. He wanted to wring Loyd and Jared's necks for embarrassing him. That's why General never mourned. He never mourned for anything or anyone. Even when Martha died.

"Since you remarried, have you had any other children?" Detective Dalton asked, pulling out a notebook.

General swallowed back a growl. His muscles tensed as his hands balled into a fist. The day he saw Josephine walking towards him in white, a smile had formed on his face. She was young and fresh with the body that could bear him ten sons. Martha was useless, and he was glad to be rid of her. General had struck a deal with Stephen Callahan: he would help restore Callahan's plantation with his inheritance of gold, but in return, Callahan's young daughter would be required to restore the Wellingtons' family line. The perfect exchange. However, he had been deceived.

"None," General answered.

Detective Dalton's brows furrowed in concentration. "How many years were you two married?"

General gritted his teeth. How many questions was this man going to ask? "Where is this going? Aren't you supposed to find my wife?"

Detective Dalton leaned forward. "I understand your frustration, but I must build a persona for Mrs. Wellington so I can have a better picture at finding her. Now, did the former Mrs. Wellington ever disappear like this?"

Never. Martha was an obedient wife, to an extent. After Jared and Loyd's death, Martha turned like General's father—depressed and nervous. Martha was confined to bed and prescribed laudanum. She drank that bottle like it was water.

Heirless after his sons' deaths and married to a pathetic wife, General had to get rid of Martha. One of the free slaves, Myra of fourteen years of age, couldn't read. General gave her a bottle of cyanide, and she never knew the difference. The sheriff strung the child up without a second thought, ignoring her cries and pleas of innocence.

"None at all. She was ill, confined to her bed."

Detective Dalton wrote in his notebook. "And Mrs. Josephine Wellington? Has she run off before?"

General leaned his neck to the side until he heard a satisfying pop then did the same to his knuckles. It took a whole year before Josephine got pregnant, and the reason why it took so long was because she was devoted more to helping impoverished Negros than to her own husband.

"Can we please move on to April tenth? What are you, a nosy journalist?" General hissed through his front teeth.

Detective Dalton's lips flattened. "Very well. But I'd still like to know you and Mrs. Wellington's domestic situation. Was she happy?"

"Happy?" General spat, giving a daggered glare. "What does that have to do with anything?"

"I mean, was she content here? Sometimes women just want time alone, to get away."

Fury boiled, fuming out General's nostril, hot like fire. This was none of Detective Dalton's business. Josephine was mad, mad enough that she blamed three failed pregnancies on him. She said it was because he beat her, but that made General beat her more. She was too frail to endure the pain from the blows of his fists and too stupid to learn from her mistakes. He wouldn't be surprised if she ran off, embarrassing him further.

"Happy as can be." One more stupid question, and General might break this man's neck, regardless if he could move his legs or not.

"I'm trying to get a sense of her traveling fare. Wilmington is a long and expensive trip. Did she have any assets of her own?"

General's mind thought back to one of his most favorite days, the day he put Josephine in her place. Her face was flushed with anger, cheeks burning red and eyes wide with anger, her features taut with resentment. She charged at him, fists flying, pounding against his chest the moment she learned he had sold her beloved plantation home. Since she didn't give him an heir like Stephen Callahan promised, General had sold off her land, the land he promised to save in exchange for an heir.

Stephen Callahan had been healthy, but the heart attack was sudden—perhaps too sudden. Maybe the grief overtook Stephen like it had General's own father, or possibly someone tampered with his brandy. Either way, it was a miracle for the timing.

"None. I sold her plantation years ago."

Detective Dalton took a moment to write in his notebook. "And you say she went to see cousins in Wilmington?"

"Distant," General corrected. "There's no record of any relatives there. Josephine has no one. Only an elderly aunt who is old and out of her mind."

Detective Dalton continued to write. "Did your wife take a cab or a carriage from here?"

"It would have to be a cab. We have only used our own drivers, but according to the staff, they were off duty."

Detective Dalton continued to write until he closed his briefcase along with his writings. He stood from the desk. "That would be all."

General's brows raised. "That's it? All you got was enough information to write a book."

"I told you, I needed to know as much information as I could about your wife in order to find her," Detective Dalton explained, his notebook secured under his arm. "We don't have much to go on, given that you claim she doesn't have relatives in Wilmington."

Hot breath exhaled out of General's mouth as he groaned. He pointed straight in the man's face. "You better come back with something good. Or else you won't see the light of day."

Detective Dalton's Adam's apple bobbed as he swallowed. He picked up his hat and took a bow, not bothering to try for a handshake. "Good day, General Wellington."

General watched as the man left the room. General was one step closer. One step to teaching Josephine a new lesson. She had broken too many rules, and she wouldn't get away with it. Perhaps this would be a warm-up until he got to the bottom of the second mystery—why he was in this bed.

CHAPTER TWENTY-ONE

Willow Grove, Montana; Early September 1872

JOSIE REMOVED THE KETTLE from the stove and poured Rose a cup of tea. The cabin smelled like coffee early in the morning and again in the evening, so a cup of tea was a nice change. Though Josie liked coffee well enough, there was something more comforting about a warm cup of tea. It reminded her of home—the way her mother used to set the table with fine china and serve tea to their house callers. Those days felt like a lifetime ago. Mama always took pride in welcoming company into their home, and for a brief moment, Josie could almost feel her presence again.

Taking a quick look out the window, Josie grinned, watching Paul and Andy play with the children in the front yard. Lillian, wearing a wool coat that was too large for her, struggled to keep up with the others. And little Gideon was now using those chubby legs of his to participate, waddling after them a circle. Josie's chest tightened with dread, exhaling a soft sigh. *If only they could play with other children their age every day.* That depended on whether the town ever reopened the school. It broke Josie's heart to know the neighboring children wouldn't have educational opportunities like Asheville did, but that was what separated the wild frontier from civilization.

Josie gathered the tea tray, setting it in front of Rose. The wooden serving tray wasn't fancy like the porcelain ones Josie was used to, but Rose didn't seem to mind. She took a tin cup with gratitude, grinning as though it were delicate china.

"This isn't one of Aunt Polly's *specialty* teas, is it?" Rose teased, retrieving a spoonful of sugar from the small bowl on the tray.

Josie picked up a cup and filled it with tea. "Goodness no. This is just plain black tea. It came from Mr. Lynde's store."

Rose chuckled, stirring the sugar into her cup. "I'm glad to hear so. I've had a run-in with her remedies before—let's just say, one experience was enough."

"What kind of remedy, if you don't mind me asking?" Josie asked, settling into her chair.

"Fertility," Rose answered bluntly. "She gave it to me as a house-warming gift when we arrived."

"A fertility tea? Is that really such a thing?"

"According to her, yes. Aunt Polly makes it for every newlywed couple. It's a tradition of hers." Rose took a sip of tea and closed her eyes. "Now that's what I like better than coffee."

"You don't like coffee?"

Rose shook her head. "I've tried, but I never could stomach it. The smell is the only thing pleasing to me. My husband enjoys it though."

Josie took another sip of tea, then placed the cup down. "Speaking of husbands, where is the reverend?"

"Caleb is taking a missionary journey to a new settlement about fifteen miles from here."

Josie's nose crinkled. "A mission? I thought he was just a preacher."

Rose folded her hands on the table. "He is, but he's felt led to share the gospel outside our town."

"Being a missionary too is very humble of him," Josie remarked. "I'm delighted he's doing the Lord's work."

"I'm assuming Travis is taking your grain to the mill right now?"

Josie nodded. "He is. I can't believe the harvest is almost over."

"Thank God for that." Rose paused for a moment and placed her cup down. "I almost forgot. I have something for you."

Josie's eyes widened as Rose pulled a small stack of baby clothes from the bag beside her. She gasped. She hadn't told anyone at church about the baby. For the past month, she'd hidden her growing belly under baggy clothes and shawls, doing everything she could to avoid attention. Travis had assured her he didn't care about the gossip, but it unsettled Josie. The thought of people whispering and asking questions made her anxious. Now, seeing these tiny garments made it clear the secret was out, and the idea of it being public knowledge sent a stir of fear through her.

"I know you and Travis have been keeping it a secret, but Lillian told me during Sunday school. She explained her drawing was for the baby. So, I thought you'd like some hand-me-downs from the boys."

A laugh slipped through Josie's mouth. *That Lillian.* She never knew when to hold her tongue. Josie was surprised the girl kept the baby a secret the past month and a half. Josie ran her fingers over the delicate embroidered collars on the tiny gowns. It almost didn't seem real—after everything, she was actually having a baby. For so long, she had dreamed of being a mother to her own child, and now that day was drawing near.

"I'm sure you're already calculating how far along I am, knowing Travis and I just married two months ago." Josie began folding the clothes, ready to put them away, but Rose's voice stopped her. "Please forgive me. I didn't mean to offend or make you think I am a gossiper. I never meant to cause you harm by these gifts."

Josie shook her head. "No, I didn't mean it like that, Rose. I apologize for my tone. I just... I'm just worried about what people will say. They'll know the baby's early—"

"Josie, stop," Rose interrupted. "It's not my place to judge—nor anyone else's. This is between you and Travis," Rose paused, her hands gripped around her cup. "I knew something was off with your timeline when you married Travis. I didn't ask, and my husband never told me your situation. I want you to know that I only want to be your friend. I don't care if the baby is early or late. I want to be there for you and help you in any way I can."

The word "friend" made Josie's heart skip. She hadn't had a true friend since before the war, and hearing it now stirred something deep within her. For the first time in what felt like forever, she felt loved and appreciated. Marcus had taken that from her, stripping her of any sense of belonging or connection. But now, with Rose, she realized she wanted it back. She craved the warmth of friendship, something that had been missing from her life for far too long.

Josie swallowed hard, holding back her tears. She reached for Rose's hand, gripping it tightly. "Thank you, Rose. Thank you."

"What are friends for?" Rose giggled. "Now let's talk about the cribs and quilting. What do you have planned? Are there any colors you favor particularly? For me, I found yellows and creams perfect for either a boy or girl."

"I'm not sure. Yellow seems nice for a quilt, but I haven't had the time to shop for fabric. As for cribs, we only have one that

Gideon is still using. The baby will stay in the bed with . . . near its parents." Josie bit back the words just in time before saying, "with me." Would Travis be near the baby when it was born? The thought of caring for him alone suddenly weighed on her.

"Well, don't look too solemn," Rose said with a smile. "I'm sure the baby will love to be near its mama and papa rather than alone in a strange crib. Trust me, they do better when they aren't confined in a lonely bed."

Josie looked down, noticing Rose's cup half empty. "Would you like more tea?"

"Please," Rose answered, holding out her cup.

As Josie filled Rose's tin cup, Rose continued their conversational visit.

"Would you consider a quilting bee for the baby? I know the ladies of the church would enjoy the fellowship, especially one honoring a new life coming into the world."

Josie nearly spilled the teapot. She quickly pushed Rose's cup to her, then forced a smile. However, Rose seemed to see through her facade as though she was transparent glass.

"Whenever you're comfortable. Take your time with the decision."

The thought of women coming into their home, dedicating their afternoon to make her a quilt with her belly twice the size it was supposed to be, nearly knocked the wind out of her. More lies. She'd have to lie again, making her turn back to her deceiving ways she wanted to avoid. Deceiving one family was different than deceiving the whole town, and even with Travis, she couldn't hide for too long.

"I'll think about it."

Rose reached out, touching Josie's hand. "Whatever you need, don't feel shy to ask."

Josie's chest flooded with warmth. "Thank you, Rose." Tears pricked in her corners. "You're a wonderful friend."

Statesville, North Carolina; Early September 1872

General smiled as he gripped the bedrail. Carefully, he used his strength to push one foot forward, then he tried the other. As he propped his weight against the wooden rail, his chest swelled with excitement.

"Take that, Colson," he muttered bitterly.

General had spent the last month doing the man's ridiculous exercises, and at night, when everyone was in bed, he had attempted his own. One foot after the other, trying to balance himself, and he'd done it. Next, he removed his grip from the bedrail and held his arms out to steady himself. A grin stretched across his face. He was standing. All on his own—no doctor, no mammy. He didn't need anyone's help.

He chuckled to himself. Invincible General—that was who he was. No more would he be the house's prisoner. No more would he be Colson's little experiment. He'd be free, free to do what he set out to do since he woke.

Steps echoed up the staircase, and General's veins pumped intensely with enthusiasm. *Let's show them.* The door opened, and Mammy entered, her mouth open in shock, and her breath hitched. She held her hands over her mouth, muffling her scream.

"General, yuh're standin'!"

General crossed his arms. "Go fetch Dr. Colson. It's time to begin our little game."

Chapter Twenty-Two

Willow Grove, Montana; Mid-September 1872

JOSIE COULD HARDLY CATCH her breath in the claustrophobic cabin as the church ladies surrounded her, watching her every move. The hair on her neck stood as Caroline brought another handmade gift from their quilting circle, smiling down on her. When Josie was told this would be a quilting bee, she expected the day to be about sewing, not gifting. Caroline's presence gave Josie a little ease, but as she looked out, the curious eyes caused her heart to race.

"That's from me," Mrs. Lynde, the shopkeeper's wife, said, seated next to her daughter who seemed to not be much older than Ivy. Josie smiled, trying to show her gratitude.

As she looked down, ready to open the gift, the ladies put down their needles, their eyes never leaving her. Josie covered her bump with the present, trying to avoid prying eyes, but she could only hide so much. Sitting while wearing a dress that was definitely too tight wasn't helping any. Thank goodness for Caroline's extra clothes, but the woman must had been half her size during those pregnancy days.

Josie removed the brown paper and string, revealing a red and green quilt. The ladies *oohed* and *aahed* at the sweet gift that would wrap around a sweet little babe.

"That is gorgeous, Mrs. Lynde," Mrs. Scott said, pulling a thread through her side of the yellow and white quilt. "Did you make that by hand?"

Mrs. Lynde smiled, patting her daughter's leg. "With a little help from my Dolly Anne."

"It's beautiful," Josie said with appreciation. "This will go to great use."

"I made it from a couple of Dolly Anne's old clothes and a few other items. I hope you don't mind the mis-match."

"I don't mind it at all."

Josie noticed a slight Southern accent in Mrs. Lynde's voice. Since it was never brought up in conversation, she wouldn't ask. But the thought of her having a Southern ally nearby made her feel more confident she would be just as welcomed, even though she hadn't had any issues regarding her heritage. The frontier was a blend of many different sides of the war—North and South, giving her hope that one day the prejudice would pass.

"Here's the next one," Caroline said.

Josie took the package with a smile and looked out towards the ladies. A woman with dark hair and a blue cotton dress raised her hand. "It's from our family."

With her normal look of gratitude, Josie opened the package, and to her surprise, there were knitted pieces of booties, hats, blankets, and gloves. She gasped and covered her mouth, trying not to cry. This gift was so precious, a handcrafted item she did not deserve. Rose was right about hosting a quilting bee. Just seeing how much people cared warmed her with delight, distracting her from every fear she had. For a little while, she could push her past behind her and focus on the tiny face that would show in three months.

"Oh, how lovely!" Mrs. Lynde said, her lips parted into a grin.

Rose stepped closer from her area in the corner and picked up one of the hats. Her lips curved into a smile as she held it against her chest. "So precious."

"Maybe it will be cool enough in the spring for the baby to wear it," Mrs. Kent said in the chair next to Josie.

Josie's heart stopped beating for a moment, and her cheeks flushed. She looked up at Rose, whose face had turned white. Now Josie was back to where she didn't want to be—a web of lies.

She couldn't bear to speak falsehoods to these ladies who spent their time sewing and knitting to give the baby the necessities it needed. So, Josie faked a smile and nodded, limiting herself to a silent nod. However, the moment was cut short as Caroline gave her another gift to open. She looked down at Josie and laid her hand on Josie's shoulder, offering a friendly comfort Josie needed to get through the uncomfortable scene.

Travis stayed at Ronan's place until after dark, putting up some new fence posts around the back of their barn since they were wanting to invest in more livestock. The air had grown chilly, but as they continued to work and visit, the cold was the least on their minds. However, coming home was another story. The orange light glowing through the window and the smoke blowing out the chimney invited him in.

He had only himself to blame for staying in the barn loft on cold nights, but perhaps he could set a spot by the fire and leave early before Josie woke. That way, they wouldn't have to bump into each other. Before he set his gloved hand on the door latch, he overheard soft sniffling. Travis peeked through the window, catching a glimpse of Josie, her face buried in her hands. His heart sank. He knew he should walk away, but seeing Josie in such distress, he couldn't bear to leave her be.

Travis opened the cabin door and removed his clothing layers, starting with his buffalo-fur coat.

"Travis?" Josie sniffed. "Is that you?"

Her reddened eyes locked with his. A lump formed in Travis's throat. Never had he seen Josie this upset. She looked down swiftly, holding a knitted baby hat.

"Are you all right?" Travis asked, taking slow steps forward.

Josie gave a faint shrug.

He observed the room, noticing the baskets of yarn and yellow scraps on the dining table. "Was the quilting bee to your liking?"

Josie nodded, wiping her eyes with her fingertips. "Yes, it was."

Travis settled in a rocking chair next to Josie, his knees facing her. "Then what is it? You're upset."

Josie folded her hands in her lap and closed her eyes, taking steady, calming breaths. "I'm going to be a terrible mother."

Travis frowned. He scooted his chair closer. "Why do you think that?"

Had someone said anything to her? If they did, he'd give them a piece of his mind. Josie had seemed nervous hours before the event, but he believed that to be because she wasn't used to the town's company. First impressions were everything, especially in an intimate setting.

Josie met his gaze. "I'm a liar. What positive example can I set?"

Travis's chest tightened, guilt rising in his chest. Josie had lied to him once, and he had yet to forgive her. He tried his best to be supportive, but when he thought about his fears, he couldn't help but blame himself for marrying a stranger. He didn't bother to take time to get to know her.

"You were scared. I understand why you kept the baby a secret."

Josie shook her head, pushing her loose hair behind her ears. "It's no excuse. Those ladies believe I'll give birth in the spring because of . . . our timeline. When winter comes—"

"Josie," Travis said gently. "Stop worrying."

Josie buried her face in her hands. "I'm tired, Travis. I'm tired of lying."

She continued to cry, and Travis could no longer bear those sobs—painful sobs he couldn't help but feel responsible for. He treated her poorly all these months, not bothering to comfort her while she suffered in silence.

Travis placed his hand on her back, rubbing in soft circles. He hadn't wanted to touch her when they first married, and dancing with her had been an act of gentlemanly courtesy, but now, Josie deserved to be shown tenderness and care. Just enough that she could know he was there for her. Travis wanted to start over, to trust his wife again.

"You're going to be a great mother. You want to know why?"

Josie peeked up at him, tears streaming down her fair cheeks. "Why?"

Travis smiled, warmth swimming through his chest. "Because of the way you treat my children. I have no doubt that you'll be wonderful."

"But what about safety?" Josie squeaked. "I couldn't save my mother and sister when they were sick. What if I can't protect the children?"

"That's what we have God for," Travis reminded. "I know this isn't what we both planned, but as the days pass, I can see what a beauty God has made in our lives. We're one family, all of us. And now, it's growing with our new child."

Our. The thought made Travis's heart swell.

Josie smiled, wiping her tears. "Ours?"

"Yes. Is that all right?"

"Perfect."

Travis looked towards the fire, his now thawed legs desiring never to move. "Do you mind if I stay by the fire tonight?"

"Please stay," Josie said swiftly. "You shouldn't be in that loft now, anyway. You'll catch a chill."

Travis chuckled, running his fingers through his hair. "I don't know how I survived the past few nights."

"You're stubborn, that's why."

Travis's brows raised. "Stubborn? Says the woman who never rests, even when I beg her."

Josie exhaled dramatically, shaking her head. "I'm a farmer's wife now. I have a duty."

"A duty to our child, too. Remember, it's all right to take a little rest."

Josie placed a hand over her stomach. "I'll consider it." She rubbed her bump then shut her eyes. Travis leaned back, closing his eyes and listening to the fire crackle. He liked this, sitting in silence. He glanced over at Josie, a smile gracing her lips as she laid her head against the chair's back. She gasped, her eyes snapping open. She sat straighter, placing her free hand on her back.

A jolt of terror rumbled through Travis. "What's wrong? Is the baby—"

"It kicked," Josie explained quickly. She giggled softly, her grin widening. Travis couldn't help but smile too. Never had he seen Josie behave like this—so happy.

She turned to him. "Would you like to feel?"

Travis's eyes widened. He cleared his throat. "Really?"

"Yes."

He reached out his hand, placing it on Josie's belly. She stiffened for a moment, her hands resting on the chair, then, she placed a hand beside his. As a soft thump hit Travis's palm, a chuckle bellowed out of him. "This is real."

Josie fixed her gaze on him, her eyes meeting his. "Yes."

"I remember these days with Sophie, before . . ." Travis could hardly stomach finishing his sentence. Just thinking back to her last pregnancy, watching Sophie lose her strength little by little flooded his mind.

"She loved you very much. I can see it all over you, in the children too."

"I will always love her," Travis said swiftly. He removed his hand and placed it on the arm of his chair. "That's why it's so hard for me to talk about her."

Josie reached out a hand to him, the tips of her fingers barely touching his. "Whenever you are ready, I'm here. I don't want you to bear this alone."

Travis pressed his lips together as he nodded. "Thank you, Josie."

Their gazes bounded, and Travis never wanted to waver or pull. His heart moved to his throat, thumping hard. Josie shriveled back from his gaze and rose to her feet. She placed her hand on her swollen belly.

"I think I'm going to take your advice and rest."

Travis's corners curved. "I'm glad to see you're finally listening to me."

Josie chuckled softly. "Goodnight, Travis."

"Goodnight, Jo."

Josie raised a brow. "Jo?"

Travis's cheeks warmed. Had he said that out loud? "Ugh, is that all right? Since the children call you Josie, I just thought I'd call you something else. You know . . . to add some distinction."

Josie hummed thoughtfully and rubbed her chin. "Jo." She nodded. "I like it."

As she stepped out the room, Travis took in a large gulp of air then exhaled, his hand behind his head. *What just happened?*

CHAPTER TWENTY-THREE

Statesville, North Carolina; October 1872

"I'M SORRY TO SAY, sir, but I have investigated every record of cab drivers, interviewed marshals, sheriffs, and hotel managers in Wilmington. I'm afraid there's been no trace of your wife there," Detective Dalton stated.

General's fingers curved into fists, pressing his fingernails deep into his palms. His face and ears burned like coal. "You are telling me, I spent all that money on the best-known Pinkerton in Raleigh, and I received no report? How does that work, Detective?"

Detective Dalton's youthful face turned ghostly pale. "I deeply apologize, General Wellington, but sometimes even I hit dead ends. Please know, I have tried everything in my power to obtain information. This case honestly doesn't make sense, and neither do the facts you tell."

Idiot woman, General thought to himself. *She really thinks she can cover her tracks.* "And what do you suggest as your next step?"

Detective Dalton leaned forward from his chair. His voice lowered and his eyes moved around his surroundings. "General, I may be wrong, but I believe your staff might have played a part of your wife's disappearance."

General gritted his teeth. His wife was always too soft. She was an embarrassment to him, trying to befriend the servants. It was his grace to allow Mammy to stay, despite having forbidden their time together. Mammy's duties were strictly to run the house, and she was only to speak to Josie when given permission.

"What are you saying?"

Detective Dalton cleared his throat. "I believe if you investigate each of your staff members, you might find valuable information . . . They know more than they are saying. I'm not buying what that mammy says about most of the staff being in bed. She *knows* something."

The general's jaw clenched as his glare burned into the man before him. In a flash of fury, he leapt from his bed, seizing the lanky man's thin neck in an iron grip. Detective Dalton's eyes widened in terror as he gasped for air, clawing desperately at the general's hands. Unrelenting, General slammed him against the wall, his thumbs pressing deeper into Dalton's throat. The man's struggles weakened, his face turning blue as his body grew limp.

"General Wellington!" Mammy screeched, bursting into the room.

The plump woman rushed forward and shoved at General with all her strength, but he remained rooted, his grip unyielding on Detective Dalton's throat.

"Stop it this instant!" she barked, her voice shaking with a mix of fury and desperation.

Despite the rage surging through him and his overwhelming urge to finish the man, the General relented. He released Detective Dalton, who collapsed to the floor like a discarded rag doll, gasping and sputtering as he clutched at his bruised throat. General stumbled back, holding onto his bed rail. He heaved as his lungs tightened like an iron vise.

Mammy knelt beside Detective Dalton, her hands steady as she rubbed his back in soothing circles. "Breathe, Detective," she urged, her tone softening, though her sharp eyes darted accusingly toward the general.

"You coulda killed 'em, suh. What was yuh thinkin'?"

General's cold eyes followed the woman's every move, his grip tightening around his bed rail. Oh, how he longed to rid the world of both of these wretched creatures with his own bare hands. Mammy was hiding something—he was certain of it. And he'd get the truth out of her, one way or another.

But first, he'd have to be patient. Quiet. He'd watch her every move. He'd catch her red-handed and make her pay.

"Escort him out, Mammy. I don't want to see his sorry face again."

Willow Grove, Montana; October 1872

At nightfall, Travis returned home with a letter tucked into his pocket. He had picked it up from the post office earlier, assuming another offer to buy his grain. In the past year, cities like Virginia

City, Helena, and Cheyenne had contacted him about selling. Before then, he had sold only to Bozeman.

Standing on the porch, he read the return address, holding it up to the faint moonlight. He squinted, bringing it closer to his face. *Charlotte, North Carolina,* it read. His eyes followed each curve of the penmanship, transcribing the sender's name as Victor Anderson. His brows arched high.

Josie had never received a letter before, not even from the aunt she had lived with. So why now? And why from a *man*? A deep unease settled in Travis's core. What business did this Victor Anderson have writing to her? What man thought he had the right to write to a married woman? Josie was his wife, and if any man was trying to woo her, he'd get to the bottom of this.

The children were in bed, since it was already dark out, so he closed the cabin door behind him as softly as possible. Travis removed his coat, and as his eyes searched across the room, his heart skipped. In the glowing candlelight, Josie stood at the iron stove, wearing her forest-green dress from earlier, hugging her hips. Travis's jaw dropped. When Sophie was expecting, she wore baggy dresses, but it seemed Josie had yet to find the time to make them. His pulse increased, imagining Josie in her cotton chemises since they would be the only loose-fitting items.

Don't think of her like that. He wanted to kick himself. But she had indeed looked good on their wedding night, those slim curves, her smooth, soft skin. Travis winced as he bit his tongue. *Stop that. You can't trust this woman. The letter in your pocket is another reminder. Victor Anderson, my foot.* He could be a crummy old man, but still, the fact remained a mystery. Travis, indeed, knew nothing about his wife, other than the short truth that had too many gray areas—a dead husband, no family, and a baby.

"I hope you're hungry," Josie said, turning away from the cast iron pot on the stove. "I'll heat your stew."

Travis shrugged off his extra jacket and settled into a chair at the table, the letter crunching softly in his pocket. The stew bubbled on the stovetop, the rich aroma filling the air as Josie stood behind him, busy with dinner preparations.

"How was your trip into town?" she asked.

"Just another trip. Got the first half of the payment for the harvest. Some mill workers are taking the grain out to Bozeman next week. Then maybe, we'll get some more."

Josie placed a bowl of stew in front of him. Traces of carrots, beans, and venison floated to the surface. Travis bowed his head in a silent reflection of prayer. After he took the first bite, he reached into his pocket and pulled out the letter. He handed it to Josie and watched as she examined it. Her brows arched as though she didn't recognize the name, but her eyes widened, her face paling. She ripped open the letter anxiously, her hand over her mouth.

"It's from Aunt Tia's lawyer. Why would he be writing to me?"

Lawyer—the word was like a breath of fresh air. Travis was foolish for allowing his imagination to run wild, fearing the worst when it was simply a matter of legal affairs. Perhaps it was fear that had clouded his judgment. Some days, he thought he knew Josie inside and out, but other days, she seemed like a stranger.

A shrill sob escaped Josie's mouth, and her eyes brimmed with tears. Travis stood swiftly. He pushed his stew aside, joining her on the other side of the table. He leaned over her, studying the letter, but he could hardly read it from Josie's shaking.

"Jo, is everything all right?"

Josie's eyes remained fixed on the letter. She shook her head slowly. "M-my aunt has died."

She dropped the letter onto the table and covered her face as she cried. Travis wasn't good at comforting people, especially women. He tried his best to comfort Ma when Pa passed, but he didn't know what to do. He couldn't bring the dead back to life and no words could soothe the pain. Travis had hugged Ma close at that moment and told her everything would be all right, but that was a lie. "All right" wasn't possible with a great loss. Travis felt the same way when everyone gave their condolences and left food at his door when Sophie died. Comfort didn't make it better; it made it worse. Neither food nor condolences could bring his loved ones back from the grave.

"What happened?"

Josie dried her tears with her hands. "She passed in her sleep. The doctors said she had a fragile heart, but she seemed fine when I was with her. How can someone be fine and all of a sudden *die?*"

Fragile heart—the cause made Travis tense. It had been the same with his father. The man had been healthy, but one laborious load took him down. All because Travis was too lazy to help. Travis shook the memory away. Everything was different now. Travis worked harder than anyone, and he'd never rest again.

"I'm sorry, Jo. I know how important she was to you."

Her teardrops hit the table as she rubbed the letter between her fingers. "That was the last of my family. I have nobody. I-I'm alone. I'm truly alone. I don't have a family anymore."

Her voice reeked with pain. Travis stood behind Josie, wrapping his arms around her, holding her close as he had during the Founder's Day celebration. But this wasn't dancing. His wife had suffered a great loss, and now, only he could help her, comfort her.

"We are your family now. You will always have us." Travis turned her chin towards him, seeing those doe eyes brimming with tears.

"You aren't just a mail-order bride to me. You are my wife and the mother to my children. We're family."

"Do you mean that?" Josie whispered, her breathing staggered.

Travis nodded. "Yes. I mean every word." She was his wife, and this woman was his family. Despite all she did in the past, he couldn't help but care for her. He made a vow to love, honor, and cherish her. And at that moment, this is what he was doing—or what he tried to do. "Whatever you need, Jo, I am here."

Josie turned, picking up the letter again. "She left everything to me—the house, money, everything she owned."

Travis's eyes widened. He held onto the chair rail, careful not to lose his balance. He knew Josie came from a wealthy family, but he never expected they'd face a great fortune in their marriage. With the house, Josie could be a respectable widow and raise her baby without him. But the thought of her leaving nearly left him sick.

Despite his words, telling her she was his family, he wasn't sure how money fit into it all. Would she leave them? She married him for security, and now, she didn't need him. The thought nearly tore him to shreds. Would she abandon it all, his children, the town—and him?

He gripped the wooden chair, his throat clenching. "Are you going to take it?"

Josie laid the letter down. "No." Her fingers quivered, folded atop the white paper.

Travis's jaw dropped. She couldn't go back? This woman must be mad. Money, an estate, and in a civilized area? How could she not leave Montana behind? North Carolina would be safer than the wild, uncivilized frontier. He wanted her to stay. The children needed her to stay. Yet, how could he hold her back?

"But the baby . . . it will have so much. You can give it a better life away from here."

Josie's eyes looked back at him, and to his surprise, he saw a fire raging in them. "I will never return there. Never." She threw the letter across the table. "Someone else can have her money."

Josie's words were a relief, but something wasn't sitting right with Travis. She was crazy not to accept the money. The fortune was more than Travis could ever imagine.

"But she left it to *you*. You can live as a comfortable widow, independent." Travis choked on a swelling lump in his throat. "Don't you want that?"

Josie looked down, rubbing her stomach. "I want to leave that life behind. North Carolina is full of the nightmares I try to forget. Being there will only remind me of the woman I used to be. Weak . . . pathetic . . . fragile."

Josie's words lit a fire within Travis's core. His jaw hardened; his teeth clenched. Who was this man? Who would brainwash such a lovely woman and treat her like scum? He was glad the man was dead; that way he could never lay a finger on his wife again.

"What did he do to you, Jo?" Travis settled in the chair next to her, ready to hold her if needed. He wanted to shield her with his body, to keep the darts of darkness away from her. He wanted to set her free from that horror she lived. Each time she flinched, it hurt Travis more than pain itself.

Josie stayed silent, rubbing her thumbs together. She closed her eyes. "Too much to even put into words. Marcus was a monster. Being free of his grasp after seven years is more valuable than any money I could receive."

Travis had so many questions he wanted to ask, but he was careful not to bring up memories Josie wanted to forget. *Seven years? She was so young.* Travis thought about Ivy. Josie wouldn't have been much older when she married the man.

"I can't imagine what you went through, but you won't have that here. Not with me. I can promise you that." Travis placed his hand over his wife's. "We don't have to talk about him anymore. Forget about him. It's you and me now, Jo. And no one will ever touch you again. My body is your armory to be your protection. My home is yours to manage and live in." He rubbed his thumb over her silk, smooth skin. "I vow, on my life and those before me, I'll never *ever* raise a hand to you. God as my witness."

Josie's lips curved into a small smile. "You're too good to me, Travis. I don't deserve you."

Travis leaned in closer, lifting her chin and peering into her tear clouded eyes. All he wanted to do was dry them and prove how safe she was, more than by words of honor. Looking down at her moist lips, he nearly lost his breath at the thought of kissing them. What would they taste like? Perhaps strawberries—just as they looked. Oh, what he'd give to press his lips to hers, just once, to satisfy this aching curiosity.

Before he could have his answer, Gideon's cry pierced the quiet of the cabin, pulling Travis back to reality. Josie immediately pushed her chair back, her attention shifting to the source of the sound.

"I should see to him."

Travis watched as Josie left the room, his heart thudding against his chest. He leaned forward, elbows on the table and hands threading through his hair. What was he doing? Why couldn't he stick to his plan?

For the first time, he began to understand his wife. Josie wasn't just a woman who used him to cover her child's paternity—she was a frightened woman seeking sanctuary from a past that constantly tore her apart. Deceiving him was her choice, but her morals were clouded by desperation.

Travis hoped that, in time, he could help mend those broken pieces of her life, but first, he knew he needed to confront his own wounds. And perhaps, if the Lord would allow it, he could push forward. He could no longer hear Sophie's voice. He'd tried for weeks to seek her presence, but each moment with Josie, she seemed to fade further and further away. Tears pricked in Travis's eyes.

Why, God? Why must you torture me now?

PART III

Chapter
Twenty-Four

Statesville, North Carolina; Mid-December 1872

Blasted exercises! Colson's rules would never work, even if he tried his best to keep General in bed with drugs. General wouldn't be told what to do, and that's why Colson would never step foot in the house again. General spent the last few months walking around his room, climbing stairs, and taking short strolls around the perimeter. The cane he used had helped him get on his feet, but now, it was time for action.

He made his way up the stairs to the floor where the servants dwelled—one being that lying Mammy. General strained as he climbed, though barely out of breath, but he continued on, no matter how much his muscles ached. And at last, he stood on the top floor. He smiled as the drafty breeze hit his face. Mammy wouldn't know what was coming to her.

He didn't have any evidence to prove Mammy's involvement, but he sensed it, like a man on a hunt. After months of confinement, he wouldn't rest until he had his answers. Mammy knew where Josephine was. She really thought she could fool him by saying his wife was in Wilmington?

No. That was a lie Mammy would suffer for.

General may have had a head injury that damaged his cognitive thinking when he accepted the news, but he was no longer a slave to oblivion. He couldn't wait until he saw Mammy's face when he brought the proof before her eyes. He'd played her game for five months, and he was done letting her win. Once he got his answers, she'd suffer worse than when she was enslaved. It'd be easy to kill her, just like Martha and sweet little Myra.

The floorboards creaked beneath General's weight as he proceeded down the attic hallway and stopped in front of Mammy's bedroom. He slowly pushed the door open, noticing her absence. *Perfect.* Mammy was downstairs working in the kitchen. Now he'd begin his search, then torture her more by attempting the same game she was playing.

He bent over with a groan as a sharp cramp clenched his calf, pain surging through the muscle. Colson gave strict orders when it came to climbing stairs, but what did that fool know? Josephine could have already been home if it wasn't for Colson prescribing that garbage. General didn't need rest; he needed to rise above himself. He was strong, stronger than ever the more he pushed himself. The last thing he'd be was weak.

All General knew was when he had his wife back in his possession, she'd have it worse than before. Mammy's room was impeccably tidy, with her clothes neatly folded in the drawers and her bed perfectly made. As General began his search, the orderliness vanished. He yanked back the covers, only to find nothing. Frustrated, he lifted the bed and hurled it against the wall with a crash. He tore through her dresser, scattering clothes across the room.

Nothing but ladies' things! His nostrils flared, exhaling hot, ragged breaths. He opened her closet door.

More dresses.

Nothing.

General's head burned with rage, as if steam might burst from his ears. He yanked open the nightstand drawer—empty. Frustration mounting, he stomped hard on the ground as he headed for the door. But before he could leave, his foot plunged between two weak floorboards. He let out a low groan, steadying himself as he stood. Tugging his boot free, he glanced down. Something had been dislodged.

An envelope.

He snatched it, growling softly as his eyes landed on the return address—Charlotte. If he wasn't mistaken, that was where Josephine's withering aunt lived. General tore open the envelope, his fingers trembling with anticipation. Inside, the letter unfolded, revealing neat, deliberate handwriting. He began reading, his eyes narrowing as he took in the words.

Dear Mammy,

If you are reading this, I want to inform you that my Josephine is safe.

Sincerely,

Tatiana Callahan

General crushed the letter in his hands. Mammy was a fool to think she could hide Josephine away forever. General's anger boiled, nearly tearing the letter in two. Mammy would pay; all of them would. He never thought Josephine would be so desperate to hide out with a mentally challenged aunt. That aunt was so sloppy that she exposed Josephine. *She really thought she could protect the wife of an honored general.* General let out a low, gutted laugh.

Back during the days of war, top officials would write in code in case information fell into the wrong hands. This proved how naive and foolish the delicate sex was. They had exposed themselves to the enemy—and made it so easy. Nowhere was safe—especially with General being miraculously healed.

His thoughts were abruptly cut off by the creak of footsteps, moving cautiously across the fragile attic floorboards. A slow smile spread across General's face. *She's right on time.*

Mammy's eyes widened, her face draining of color as she took in the sight of General standing in her room, her clothes and belongings strewn across the floor. Like always, she covered her mouth, stifling her gasps. She straightened her posture, cleared her throat, and clasped both hands in front of her. A strained smile spread across her face, but she couldn't fool anyone. Her trembling fingers and the quick flicker of her eyes gave her away, subtle signs General had seen countless times when confronting a traitor. *Always trying to look innocent. You can't fool me no more, Mammy.*

"Excuse me, suh. I heard a noise upstairs, and I came to check."

General relished the unease that washed over her. Mammy was trapped, and there was no escape. All the proof he needed was clutched in his hand, concealed behind his back.

General smiled, creeping towards her. "Mammy, dear, I was thinking about how long it's been since Josephine went to visit her relatives."

General watched as Mammy's fingernails trailed up and down her forearms as they quivered. "'Bout eight months, suh." Her eyes widened as General took another step forward. "But she came back from time to time when ya was asleep."

General rubbed his chin. "She did? I didn't hear that. You said she didn't know about my injury."

Mammy's hands tightened around her forearms as she continued to shiver. "Guess I forgot, suh. Forgive me."

General's grin grew. He loved interrogating the poor woman, seeing her all frightened and nearly shivering out of her clothes. Perhaps that was why he took pleasure in Josephine's occasional disobedience; it gave him an excuse to impose more rules, knowing she couldn't possibly follow them all. Now, with Mammy before him, he had a new subject to interrogate. His veins pulsed with excitement. It had been too long since he'd been in power to torment.

"Mammy, don't you think that's a little *too* long?"

Mammy shook her head. "No, suh. She's helpin' her cousin and baby. It takes a while for new mothers to heal and get used to motherin'."

"Aren't you a little worried why she hasn't sent word? You know, since I woke up," General pressed. "You, as her mammy, should be shaking out of your skin with worry, but each time I see you, you are humming a tune with a big smile on your face. Why is that?"

Mammy paused for a moment. She looked at her shoes. "Because, suh, I trust the Missus Wellington. I know she be fine."

As General stood just inches from Mammy, he could hear her breath quicken, each shallow gasp feeding his sense of authority. Oh, how he relished that sound. He imagined her heart pounding in her chest, beating harder and harder with every second he pressed for her answers. Maybe he'd spare her if she told the truth, but a part of him wanted this game to go further.

"And *why* do you think that? Is it because you know she is safe . . . perhaps away from me?" Mammy's eyes shot wide with fear as General thrust the letter into her face. "Or is it because you helped her escape?"

Tears brimmed in Mammy's eyes as she covered her mouth in horror. She could hardly stand, her body trembling uncontrollably. "Please, suh, I meant no harm. I-I just wanted to help the Missus Wellington."

General grabbed Mammy's arm. "Help her how? Hmm?"

"T-To escape . . . from yuh."

General cocked a brow. "Me? Why so?"

Mammy's eyes flashed defiantly at him. "Because yuh're a monster!"

General tried to calm himself and hold back his fist to continue his mind game, but it was too late. His fist met her face and Mammy crumbled to the ground. As General stepped back, the sight felt familiar. He'd hit Josephine more times than he could count, but this moment in particular reminded him of one he'd forgotten.

Josephine wheezed as General wrapped his hands around her scrawny little neck. Each tremor and gasp only intensified his sense of control. Oh, how he loved dominating Josephine, seeing her so helpless.

"Marcus, stop," she begged.

General took one last look in her eyes, seeing how pathetic she was. She was so fragile that he could snap her with his bare hands with no issue. Such a great temptation, looking at this delicate creature. That was precisely what he wanted more than anything. He yearned to rid himself of this woman who had betrayed their agreement. Her father had deceived him, and he would no longer tolerate the presence of Josephine in his life.

This was where it would end—here and now.

His thoughts shattered as a hard object smashed against his head. He let out a low growl, backing away slowly as his vision blurred and the room swayed around him. General reached out towards the stair rail to maintain his balance, but he moved too quickly. The world disappeared as he fell backwards, falling farther away from the top floor.

General's body grew hot, his fiery rage consuming him from the inside out. He had been lied to and manipulated, and that wife of his was more than just a runaway—she was an attempted murderess. He would find her, regardless of the cost, and when he did, he would crush her fragile body with his bare hands, no mercy, no matter how much she begged. This was not over; it was only the beginning of her reckoning.

He peered down at Mammy, who lay on the floor, crying and moaning in pain. With a surge of fury, General grabbed her by the hair, yanking her up until she was forced to face him.

"You thought you could fool me, huh?" he growled. "Now look who's the fool!"

General imagined Josephine's face as he wrapped his bare hands around Mammy's throat. The old, plump woman struggled against him, but it only made General's grip stronger. He was more powerful being free from that bedroom, free from Dr. Colson's orders. No one would manipulate or control him again. He was in full control now, draining the life from Mammy's body as her very own angel of death.

Mammy's eyes widened as she croaked, trying to take one more gulp of the air General stole from her. She kicked and squirmed beneath him, and General pressed and pressed until her body gave out. He smiled, looking down at her lifeless eyes. Then he walked away, his veins thrumming with more power than ever.

Revenge starts now.

CHAPTER TWENTY-FIVE

Willow Grove, Montana; Christmas Eve 1872

DESPITE SOPHIE HAVING BEEN gone a year, the pain worsened during the holiday season. She had passed three months before the previous Christmas, and that was next to the hardest day for them all. That morning, the children had gathered around in the living room, wailing, begging for the one gift they wanted—their mother.

The home had been bare of any festive decorations—no ornaments, mistletoe, or holly. Decorating had always been Sophie's job. She'd dry flowers throughout the warmer months, saving them for Christmas. The least Travis could manage was cutting down a large spruce, but they had no ornaments to hang. No popcorn to string. No paper snowflakes. Christmas dinner was nothing more than leftover rabbit stew Aunt Polly had prepared. Travis had managed to gather a few small gifts, but the children lacked cheerful faces when they unwrapped them.

Gideon was a newborn then, and Travis had gone days without sleeping. Raising a baby alone was hard—Gideon needed the mother's touch, something he couldn't give. He kept his distance, only holding him when it was absolutely necessary.

However, this year was different. On Christmas Eve, the home was alive again, filled with the warm scent of freshly baked cookies and the lingering aroma of popcorn, strung just hours ago by the children around the tree. Holly and mistletoe adorned the table and draped over the mantle above the fireplace, bringing a festive cheer to the room. The soft glow of candlelight flickered, brightening the once-dim house, making it feel like home again.

The children were fast asleep, nestled together in one bed, just as Travis had tucked them in minutes earlier. The night was bitterly cold, and all three huddled under thick blankets, with a hot pan warming the foot of their bed. Outside, the wind howled as the blizzard thickened, its fierce gusts rattling the windows. A storm or two around Christmas was nothing unusual—snow had already piled calf-deep and more made no difference. The Rockies were known for harsh winters, and spring felt a long way off.

Travis walked down the hallway, passing the living area, where he spotted Josie crouched at the foot of the tree, arranging the children's wrapped gifts. The stockings hung over the fireplace, stuffed to the brim with candy and small handmade goodies Josie had crafted. Travis paused, watching her work, and couldn't help but think how much he relied on her. She had a way of breathing life back into the family, something he hadn't realized he needed until she arrived. He often worried he leaned on her too much. She had only been asked to be a mother, but she went far beyond that—one of the many things he appreciated about her.

Josie glanced over her shoulder. "You're not supposed to peek at your gifts until tomorrow," she teased, a playful smile tugging at her lips.

Travis chuckled, crossing his arms. "I would do no such thing."

"Are the children in bed?"

"More like all in *one* bed."

Josie giggled. "It's that cold, huh?"

"The one time of the year they get along—when they are too cold and must depend on one another."

"I remember those days," Josie said with a sigh. "Being with my family feels like forever ago."

Travis stepped closer. "And you will have it again. Just wait and see."

His eyes drifted to Josie's swollen belly, barely hidden under her flannel nightdress. Just days ago, Dr. Gordon said the birth would be any day. The bitterness Travis once felt over Josie's dishonesty had long faded. In truth, he was happy for her—happy that she would have a child of her own, even if it wasn't his. She deserved the joy, since she had no biological family left.

Josie took a deep breath, bracing herself as she pressed the palm of her hand to the ground, preparing to push herself up. Seeing her struggle, Travis quickly stepped forward, gently grasping her arm and placing a steady hand on her back to help her rise. She leaned into his support as he guided her upright with ease.

"Thank you, Travis," she breathed. Josie placed one hand on her belly and the other on her back, taking slow, deep breaths in and out. She closed her eyes, wincing as she let out a soft groan. Travis recognized the familiar grimace—she was in pain. The way Josie arched her back and winced brought back memories of Sophie's struggles as she neared delivery.

Travis rubbed Josie's back. "Are you all right, Jo?"

Josie shook her head, her forehead creasing as her jaw tightened. "I'm sorry, Travis. I haven't been honest. These contractions have been going on since early this morning." She met his gaze shyly. "And my water broke an hour ago."

Travis's eyes widened, his pulse quickening. "W-Why wouldn't you say anything?"

She bent over slightly, breathing through clenched teeth. "I didn't want to ruin the day for the children," she managed, her voice strained. "And I felt fine. It can take hours before a baby is truly ready to be delivered." Josie sucked in another breath, her face pale—paler than Travis had ever seen it. She groaned again, her body bending forward even more. "Now, I believe I am nearly ready."

Without thinking twice, Travis scooped Josie into his arms. "We need to get you to bed," he said, his voice steady despite the rush of nerves inside him.

Travis swiftly carried Josie down the hallway and pushed open the bedroom door, laying her down gently on the bed. He pulled the sheets to her chin, making sure she was comfortable. As he watched her, a memory flashed in his mind—Josie, ill and in pain in the fields. But tonight, she looked even more fragile. Brushing a hand through his hair, Travis exhaled, trying to stay calm.

Another birth, in the same room. A blizzard stirring outside. The doctor miles away. *Sophie.* Travis's stomach tightened, hard as a rock. He had to do something. Josie couldn't die on his watch.

"How are you?" Travis asked, his breath nearly gone from his aching chest.

Josie's brows furrowed as another contraction pierced her, making her moan. "It hurts . . . so much."

Travis raked a hand through his hair, a pulse blaring in his ears like a bass drum from a war party. There would be a war today—getting Josie the help she needed, facing the deadly storm outside. He glanced out the window, watching as the snow flurries whipped through the air so fast he could barely see beyond them. His heart sank. He couldn't let Josie give birth alone in the middle of a snowstorm, and he had no idea what to do if he ended up having to help.

The doctor wasn't an option in weather like this. Travis looked back at Josie, who was clenching in discomfort, her face tense and pale. There was only one choice left—Aunt Polly.

Without wasting a second, he turned toward the door. "I'm getting Aunt Polly," he said, his voice firm, trying to mask the worry creeping in. "She'll know how to help."

Travis stepped out of the room and nearly bumped into Ivy, her eyes wide with concern.

"What's happening, Pa?"

Pressure hardened in Travis's chest. The last thing he wanted was for the children to be scared. Seeing their mother struggle during Gideon's birth had left an emotional scar on them all, and he couldn't bear to put them through that again.

Travis crouched to Ivy's level, speaking in a gentle whisper. "Ivy, I need you to go in there and keep an eye on Josie. Do as she says. I'm going to get Aunt Polly."

Ivy's eyes widened. "But, Pa, there's a blizzard. You can't see."

Travis looked at the ground. He hadn't considered how him going out into the storm could affect his children, especially Ivy. He couldn't let them worry more than they already were.

"That's why I need you to keep an eye out. Don't open the door unless you hear me, understand? I can't have you freezing everyone in this house. Whatever happens, do *not* go outside."

Ivy nodded. "Yes, Pa."

Travis kissed the top of his daughter's head. "Now, look after Josie."

Travis chose two coats to bundle with, along with a hat and scarf. He had four children, along with Josie and the baby to think of.

Lord, please let this be worth it. He opened the door and quickly pulled it shut behind him.

The wind immediately howled around him, its sharp whistle cutting through the night. The freeze bit at his skin the moment he stepped out, forcing him to wrap the scarf tighter around his face. The snow was already to his calves, slowing his steps as he pushed forward. Aunt Polly's place was just three hundred yards away, but in this weather, it felt like a world apart. Each step felt heavier than the last, but Travis knew he couldn't stop. He had to get to her—Josie was depending on him.

He could barely see through the swirling snow, but he knew the barn was only a few feet away. Travis pushed forward, his boots crunching through the thick drifts. He only had so many minutes until he froze, so he kept his focus on the barn ahead of him. At last, the flurries parted just enough for him to catch a clear glimpse of the wooden building. With a rush of relief, he grabbed the barn door and slipped inside, quickly shutting it behind him. The barn wasn't exactly warm, but it was a reprieve from the relentless ice and wind. His gloved hands still felt frozen, but at least the wind wasn't slashing at his face anymore.

Travis rummaged behind a box of tools and grabbed a long rope, quickly untangling it until it was long enough to stretch in the right direction. He estimated it couldn't be over a hundred feet, but it would have to do. After securing one end to the barn door, he took the other end with him, gripping it tight as he returned to the biting cold. He held the rope close, trying to shield his face from the flurries, but the wind whipped around him, making it difficult to see. Each step he took was a battle against the storm, each foot of snow slowing him down. He knew he had to keep moving; the rope was his lifeline. Each step was a step closer, but it wouldn't be enough until the rope ran out. Only so many feet were left.

The wind picked up, howling like a pack of wolves in the night. Panic crept in as Travis thought about Josie lying in bed, ready to welcome a baby with only nine-year-old Ivy by her side. Poor Ivy—he couldn't imagine the thoughts racing through her mind. He prayed this birth would be different with Josie, but as he took each step, knowing his life was on the line, doubts crept in—doubts he thought he put behind him for good. Would he really die for a child that wasn't even his? If he and Josie both survived, could he father a child that didn't belong to him alone?

The thought sickened Travis. He couldn't think like this. Now wasn't the time for doubts or confusion. No matter what happened, he'd be there for the child; it was his duty as Josie's husband and as a Follower of Christ. Just like Gideon. The frigid wind hit him square in the face, stinging his eyes and nose. He tugged his scarf higher, a rough cough escaping his throat as the icy air burned his lungs. Gideon needed a father. It wasn't fair for Travis to risk his life for Josie and her child alone. Like Josie's baby would have been, Gideon had been robbed of a father. The realization struck him like a knife to the gut.

"Lord," he whispered between staggered breaths. "I know I haven't been the best husband to Josie and father to my children, but Lord, I promise if you help me save her, I'll do anything you ask of me. I'll father Josie's child as if it was my flesh and blood. I will never think twice. I'll hold Gideon close and shower him with more affection than I owe him. Please, Lord, help me find Aunt Polly."

Travis's feet grew numb as the snow buried him to his knees, and the rope ended. He was on his own now. Without his vision, all he could do was walk ahead in faith. *Lord, please guide my footsteps. Josie needs me, Lord. I don't want to give up on her.*

In an instant, the storm began to ease. The thick flurries thinned to a gentle swirl, almost as if the heavens had granted him a reprieve. A miracle, a true miracle. Travis couldn't help but smile as he glanced up and spotted Aunt Polly's cabin in the distance, the small log structure barely visible through the mountain of snow surrounding it.

Without hesitation, Travis broke into a run, pushing through the deep drifts as fast as his legs could carry him. There was no telling how long this break in the storm would last. He couldn't afford to slow down, not now. Reaching the cabin, he knocked on the door, his fist pounding with urgency.

"Aunt Polly!" he screamed breathlessly. "Aunt Polly! Hurry!"

The cabin door flew open, and there stood Aunt Polly; her sharp eyes met his, concern etched into her face, glowing in front of the orange light from her lantern. She was in her red cotton nightdress, her long gray hair braided neatly down her back.

"Good heavens, boy. What is the meaning of this? Are you crazy?"

Travis struggled to catch his breath, his chest tightening with each beat of his heart, pounding so fiercely he feared his lungs might give out. "It's Josie," he gasped, his voice strained. "She's in labor, and we don't have time—or a doctor."

Aunt Polly's eyes widened in shock, a quick gasp slipping from her lips. Without a word, she hurried to grab her coat and gloves. She returned bundled and carrying her medicine bag. With no hesitation, Aunt Polly stepped outside into the snow.

"You walked all this way in a blizzard?"

Travis clung tightly to his coat, still catching his breath. "Yes, but it cleared as soon as I got close enough to see your house."

"You could've froze to death, you know? Me as well," she scolded, her voice sharp with worry. "Couldn't you have delivered the baby yourself? Goodness gracious, you've got four children. You should know how this works by now!"

Travis shook his head, pressing his lips together, trying to think of the right words to say. Truth was, he was frightened—so much that he had to get away and find help. He couldn't be in that room one more second, watching Josie like that, standing there helpless like he had with Sophie.

"I won't have her death on my hands. I can't do that to the children again."

Aunt Polly rubbed Travis back as they managed through the snow. "Travis, that wasn't your fault. You did what had to be done. Gideon wouldn't be here if not."

Travis stayed silent. Poor Josie was suffering in the same bed his wife passed in. If she passed, he didn't know how much more of this life he could take. He couldn't let his children down, leaving them without a mother. *Lord, help my wife. Give her strength.*

When Aunt Polly and Travis came inside, Ivy was seated beside Josie in the bedroom, dabbing her forehead with a cool wet towel from the wash basin.

"Aunt Polly," Josie whispered feebly, her body trembling. Her eyelids drooped heavily. "You're here."

Aunt Polly quickly moved to Josie's bedside, setting down her medicine bag. Without wasting time, she pressed gently on Josie's abdomen "Ivy, would you mind boiling some water?"

Ivy nodded and walked away. "Yes, ma'am."

Travis stepped closer to the bedside but quickly looked away as Aunt Polly lifted Josie's covers. "How is she?"

"We'll have a baby tonight. How about that, Josie? Everything looks good."

After hearing Aunt Polly pulling down the covers, Travis turned his head, seeing Josie's eyes half open. "Aunt Polly, do you mind leaving Travis and I alone for a minute?"

Aunt Polly nodded, patting Josie's shoulder. "Call for me if you need anything."

At last, Travis and Josie were alone. He took her hand in his, feeling the quickening pulse in her wrist. It was the sign of life, a sign he rejoiced to know.

"Travis," she said weakly, her voice barely above a whisper. "If I . . . if I don't make it . . . I need you to promise me you'll take care of the baby—not out of duty but out of *love*."

Josie's words sent a shiver up Travis's spine. After everything she hid from him, all the emotional distance he created, she trusted him. However, Travis didn't want to think about the worst. He couldn't bear the thought of a world without his Jo. Josie was the missing piece that brought his family together, the heart that filled their home with warmth. She couldn't go—not now, not ever.

"Don't talk like that, Jo. Aunt Polly says everything is fine," he replied, pressing a gentle kiss to her hand as he held it tightly. "Everything will be all right." He pressed his forehead against hers, brushing the side of her head softly with the back of his hand. "I promise."

Holding her close melted a part of his heart he hadn't realized was still frozen. Ironic that he had to venture out into a blizzard to experience this. Despite all the distance, she broke through to him, or maybe, he broke to her. *God, if you let my Jo live, I vow to You that I'll never push her away again.*

Tears rolled down Josie's cheeks as she pushed with every ounce of strength she had left. It had been over an hour, and despite Aunt Polly's reassurances that everything was progressing normally for a first-time mother, she couldn't help but worry. Thoughts of her second pregnancy flooded her mind, darkening the moment.

That baby had been too early, and the doctor told her there was little hope for survival. She had tried to be a better wife to Marcus, to obey him and make him proud, but every time she thought she was doing well, his anger would strike her down. There was no escaping his wrath, no sanctuary from the pain he inflicted.

He must have taken pleasure in hurting her, watching her shrink back whenever he raised his hand or raised his voice. Why else would a man want to inflict pain on his wife and unborn child? The memory of that night flooded back—the beating that sent her into pre-labor, leaving her alone in her suffering with nothing to help her pain. Each time she pushed, she felt as if it was a waste of time. She would never hear her baby's cry. Never look into its eyes. It was the son Marcus had always wanted, but it didn't matter—it was born lifeless.

"Keep pushing, Josie. The baby's nearly here."

Josie sucked in a breath and pushed harder. This time felt different from the last as Aunt Polly smiled, giving her hope in every source of pain. Within seconds, Aunt Polly caught the baby, and Josie sighed. For a moment or two, there was complete silence. *Lord, please let the baby be all right this time.* Her heart raced in anxiety. Each moment felt like an hour. Josie tried to sit up and reach for the babe, but she was too frail. She fell back like a heavy sack of stones.

Then a loud cry pierced the silence. Josie let out a breath of relief, closing her eyes in silent prayer. After, Aunt Polly looked up at

Josie with a huge grin on her face, her eyes sparkling with joy. She held the baby up so Josie could see it.

"It's a boy."

A smile spread across Josie's face as an overwhelming sense of joy rushed through her body. Tears filled her eyes as Aunt Polly carefully washed and wrapped the baby—her baby. This was the child she prayed for, and he was safe. Her son would never know his father's wrath.

"Here is your ma," Aunt Polly whispered in a soothing voice.

Josie reached out and cradled her newborn son. His tiny body was warm against her skin, and she marveled at the sensation. As she gazed down at him, the baby opened his blue eyes, looking back at her, making her heart skip a beat.

"My son," Josie whispered, her voice trembling. She pressed a gentle kiss to the baby's soft head, noticing that his hair was blonde, just like hers. Relief rippled through her; it wasn't brown like Marcus's. Yet in that moment, it hardly mattered. This was her son, a precious gift from God, and she was finally a mother—exactly what she had always longed for.

She rocked him gently in her arms, hardly able to tear her eyes away from his perfect little face. He was everything she had ever dreamed of, and the thought of letting him out of her sight was unimaginable. Biologically, her family was gone, and her son was the last of them, carrying on the genetics of Susannah, Trellis, Oliver, Zane, and their beloved Mama and Papa. Each of his breaths was a part of them all, as though they were there in that moment, watching her hold their legacy in her arms.

After half an hour of bonding and assistance with the afterbirth, Josie peered up at Aunt Polly, who was still by her side. "Aunt Polly, do you mind bringing the children and Travis in?"

Aunt Polly nodded with a warm smile. "Of course, dear. It will be just a moment." She turned to leave, leaving Josie to continue basking in the joy of her newborn son.

She couldn't help but wonder how different everything would be now that she had a child of her own, along with four others to raise. It would be challenging, but that thought didn't matter to her. It was now early Christmas morning, and she couldn't imagine a better gift.

The door swung open, and in came the children. Ivy held Gideon on her hip, who was almost as big as she was. It appeared he had just woken from a deep sleep, yawning and rubbing his eyes. The other three stood at a distance, their faces lit with smiles as they took in the sight of their new sibling.

"Come meet your little brother, children," Josie called, her heart swelling as they approached. Leaning forward, she positioned the baby so they could see him clearly.

"He's so little," Jonas gasped, his eyes wide with wonder.

Josie chuckled. "It won't be long until he's as big as Gideon."

Ivy gently rubbed the baby's head with her spare hand, a warm smile on her face. Lillian moved closer, her head just about level with the height of the bed. Josie glanced down at the baby, who turned his gaze toward Lillian, seemingly intrigued by the new faces surrounding him.

"He's looking at you, Lillian."

Lillian giggled, poking his tiny hand that was reaching for the sky. "He's so cute." She looked up at Josie. "I guess I love him more than if he were a sister."

Josie couldn't help but chuckle hard, despite the pain in her midsection. Grinning, she looked up to see Travis standing by the door, her heart fluttering like the wings of a butterfly. He was watching from a distance, wearing a beaming grin as the children met their brother. A rush of warmth and gratitude swam through her. She struggled to find the words to express how thankful she was. Travis was more than just an honest man; he was a man of his word. She didn't deserve his kindness, but he was merciful—far more than she felt worthy of.

"What shall we call him?" Aunt Polly asked, wrapping her arms around the children's backs.

Josie sighed softly, lightly tracing her fingers over the baby's face. "Nathan."

"What a wonderful name," Aunt Polly said.

Josie glanced up at Travis, and the look on his face told her he approved of the name as well with his open-mouth smile and twinkling blue eyes.

"It means 'gift of God'," Josie added.

She looked down at Nathan, who was already drifting off to sleep. *Thank you, Lord.* Josie watched as Travis stepped closer to them, settling onto the edge of the bed to look at the baby. There was silence between them, but it was a good silence.

"I want to give him your name too," Josie whispered. "Is that all right?"

Travis smiled softly and wrapped his fingers around Nathan's hand that was slipping out of his yellow quilt. "I would be honored."

"Would you like to hold him?" Josie asked, her pulse rising at his delight. In another path, Marcus would've most likely sent the baby away to be with a wet nurse, hardly paying attention to him. Yet here was Travis—neither flesh nor blood—overflowing with pride as Nathan's pa. Josie's core warmed at the sight of such affection in his eyes.

Travis nodded and gently cradled the baby in his arms. "Hello, Nathan Travis Blythe," he whispered.

Josie bit her trembling lip as tears threatened to spill from her eyes. She had never imagined her child would experience a father's love like this. Reflecting on her journey, she was grateful for the wait—the pain and heartbreak had all been worth it to find her way here. God was giving her a life she didn't deserve, yet she embraced it fully, knowing it was a blessing beyond measure.

CHAPTER TWENTY-SIX

Charlotte, North Carolina; Christmas Day 1872

VENGEANCE RUSHED THROUGH GENERAL'S veins as he stood in front of Tia Callahan's home. The taste of sweet revenge lingered on his tongue, his adrenaline rushing fiercely. Oh, how he had dreamed of this moment since his confinement—with nothing else to do but think. He couldn't wait to wrap his hands around Josephine and crush her with every fiber of muscle in his body. He could almost hear the sound of her whimpers and bones crunching beneath his strength. The foolish girl thought she was so smart, but she wasn't smart enough to cover her own tracks.

Crazy Tia's house stood tall in the middle of the city, standing out with its crimson brick and piercing white door, decorated with pathetic Christmas wreaths that made General want to rip it to shreds. Christmas had been his parents' favorite holiday, but General hated it. Christmas was just another day, one to spread stupid happiness across the globe. And the hope in happiness made a person soft.

The estate was guarded by a large iron gate; however, it wouldn't keep him out. Josephine's vacation was over, and her hideout had been exposed. He could sniff a deserter out like a bloodhound, his skin prickling with anxiousness. General reached up and rang the bell above the entrance. He folded his arms over his chest as he waited, his pulse growing stronger, almost violently. *Wait—the best comes to the ones who wait.* And it would be great. It would be worth the eight months of her absence.

At last, the groundskeeper approached and opened the gate, and the General stepped through after introducing himself. He always found it funny that if he mentioned his military status, no one asked questions. The groundskeeper looked frightened, his body shuddering and his face pale.

Josephine thought she could kill him, but General wasn't weak. His accident only made him stronger and hungry for the final beating he'd give her. She'd have what she deserved. He was invincible, hardly able to be killed, especially by a pathetic woman. General survived two wars. The only thing that came out was a scar running down his right cheek. It was a battle scar, a sign of his strength.

General walked down the cobblestone paths and through the tall oaks standing sentinel above him. He stopped in front of the front door, wearing his black suit. Instead of the bride coming forward to the groom, he was the groom coming to her with a special gift in mind. Oh, how he loved the irony of the situation. General knocked with a firm fist and waited.

He knocked again.

Nothing.

He groaned, tapping his foot in frustration, teetering on the edge of losing his patience. He had the power to convict his wife, but hanging at the gallows would be too merciful for her. She deserved worse. General pounded on the door with increasing force, ready to unleash his fury and break it down if necessary. To his surprise, a young maid opened the door instead of a butler, her expression a mix of confusion and concern.

"May help you, sir?" she asked shyly.

May I help you? General mocked internally. He cleared his throat, forcing his irritation down as he prepared to address her. He adjusted his ascot tie, presenting himself as a gentleman. "Good afternoon, young lady, I am looking for my wife, Mrs. Josephine Wellington."

The girl's eyes widened for a moment before returning to a neutral expression. Oh, how he relished the art of interrogation. It wasn't every day that a retired general with a scarred face showed up unannounced. General craved the fear radiating from her, eager to feed off the girl's apprehension and grow more dominant and powerful before her.

"You must have the wrong house, sir. There is no one by that name at this residence."

General's jaw tightened at the thought of that senile aunt of Josie's. She had taken his wife from him once, but he vowed she wouldn't hide her for long. He would hunt them down, relentless and unforgiving, until he reclaimed what was rightfully his.

"Where is Miss Tatiana Callahan then? I need to speak with her."

The girl's face turned ghostly white. "Sir, I apologize, but Miss Callahan has passed on."

Anger surged within General like a raging storm, and his facade crumbled. There was no "gentlemanly husband" anymore, only unbridled fury and strength that once turned him into the invincible general.

"What do you mean she's *dead*?" General snapped.

"She . . . She passed two months ago."

General sucked in a deep breath, forcing himself to steady his rage. He needed information, and this pathetic girl could supply it to him. He had to be patient. General grabbed a few gold coins and held them out in his hands, letting the glint of the gold catch her eye.

"Would you be willing to supply information regarding my wife for a reward? I know you know something. I can see it in your eyes."

The girl stared at the shimmering gold. She bit her lip, then shook her head. "I'm sorry, sir, but I know nothing. I swear it."

"That's a lie!"

The girl stepped back, her bottom lip quivering. "I-I'm sorry. I told you all I know."

General shoved the girl aside and pushed open the door with great force and stomped inside.

"Josephine!" he screamed, his jaw tight. "Josephine!" He stormed the great hallway and called again. "Josephine!"

He heard loud footsteps echoing from above—the butler and two footmen appeared on the staircase.

"Where is my wife?" General demanded, his feet stomping the marble floor like gunfire as he strode towards them.

"Sir, I must ask you to leave. You are trespassing," the butler said calmly, pointing at the door.

General pushed against him, but the man was equal to his size and held him back with the help of the footmen.

"Not until I find my wife!" General screamed.

The three men pushed him back until he fell back on the floor. General sucked in a gulp of air as pain shot through his skull, just like when he first woke with this stupid injury. He winced, a low growl rumbling out of him. Josephine was really going to pay.

General breathed fire, his anger boiling over and coursing through him like molten lava. He wanted to tear the men's heads off for the offense against him. He had the right to be here. He had a right to take his wife home!

"Sir, if you don't leave now, I will send for the police."

General dusted his coat. He glared at them with sharp eyes, his head pounding more. "This won't be the end of this. I'll tear this place apart until I find my wife."

General walked out of the house, but it wasn't over. It would be nightfall soon, and he would strike again. A dull ringing echoed in his ear, making him groan. He had a mission, but first, he'd stop at a saloon. He needed a drink.

CHAPTER
TWENTY-SEVEN

Willow Grove, Montana; Christmas Day 1872

AFTER A FEW HOURS of delightful sleep, Josie awoke to the soft sound of a low, melodic voice. She blinked her eyes open, adjusting to the sight of Travis seated in the rocking chair, baby Nathan cradled in his arms. The baby slept peacefully, without a sound, as Travis gently rocked back and forth, a soft smile on his face. His hand moved rhythmically, rubbing the baby's back while he sang. Josie had never heard Travis sing before; in church, his lips barely moved.

His singing stirred memories of her brother, Zane, who used to entertain her and Susannah with his guitar during the long winter months. Cooped up in the parlor for hours, unable to go for walks or into town, his music had been a refuge.

Josie stayed perfectly still, not wanting to disturb Travis. She closed her eyes again, letting out a soft, contented sigh. He sang the melody again, the second time as soothing as the first. She peeked through her lashes, unable to look away. Travis's smile grew, revealing his teeth as he lightly rubbed the baby's head. Sleep had been hard to adjust to before the birth, even after, with the constant feedings and the exhaustion that followed. Yet at this moment, Josie had no desire to retreat back into her subconscious.

Travis was nothing like the men Aunt Tia had warned her about. If anything, Josie was more like those men with her dishonesty. Aunt Tia's advice, which Josie had lived by these past few months, had gradually faded, replaced by a deep sense of trust. Travis proved himself to be a man of mercy and care. Since Nathan's birth, for the first time in her life, Josie felt truly safe and secure. No more nightmares, no more doubts. What lay before her now was her future with this family. This peace wasn't like the fragile calm she'd known before the war; it was real, born from faith and love. All the battles within her had ended, and at last, she had a truce.

Travis never wronged her. He never raised a hand to her, never abused her like Marcus had. He was everything Marcus wasn't. Even when she felt she deserved punishment, all Travis gave her was another chance. No harm would come to Nathan or her now. If the law ever took her away, she could find peace in knowing Nathan would be safe and cared for under Travis's protection. But she couldn't let the fear of that possibility rob her of the happiness she longed for. She deserved this joy, this security. It was time to let herself fully embrace it, without the haunting shadow of the past.

"Beautiful," Josie said, pushing herself against the headboard.

Travis's cheeks flushed as he looked up. Josie had yet to see a man act so gentle. Travis, who once seemed tough and serious, now cradled a babe in his arms with a tenderness she never expected.

"I didn't know you were awake," Travis whispered.

"I've never heard you sing before. You should sing a special for Sunday."

Travis chuckled as he stood. "Now, that would be something special." He leaned over Josie, passing Nathan into her arms.

Josie cradled him to her chest and kissed his warm cheek. She glanced up at Travis. "Where did you learn the song?"

Travis settled on the bed, folding his hands in his lap. "My mother sang it to me every night when I was little. I haven't sung it in years . . . not even to my own children."

A comfortable silence settled between them as Josie gazed down at her child. He was so deeply asleep that their quiet whispers did nothing to disturb him.

"I don't know how to thank you, Travis. I know about what you did to get Aunt Polly. I might have been delirious, but after I put the pieces together, I don't know what to say." Her throat clenched, barely managing to finish the sentence. "You didn't have to risk your life for me."

"I wanted to," Travis said, leaning forward, touching her hand that cradled Nathan's head. His thumb brushed against her skin, sending a delightful shiver through her. "You are my wife, and I'm responsible for your safety." Travis paused, looking towards the window. "While I was out there, I was frightened I wouldn't make it home to you and the children. Before all hope was lost and the storm worsened, I prayed. I vowed to God I'd claim your child as my flesh and blood and never think twice. I want you to know that I mean it."

Travis looked down at sleeping Nathan bundled in a quilt, a smile crossing his face. "I've thought of him as mine since I held him in my arms. Nathan Travis Blythe is my son and nothing less."

Josie pressed her lips together, trying to hold back the tears brimming in her eyes. Nonetheless, they fell anyway. Her cheeks heated, realizing how many times she cried in front of Travis during their marriage. With Marcus, she had never been allowed to cry—tears made her weak in his eyes. She had held those tears in for seven long years, and now that she was free, they wouldn't stop. She might appear pathetic, but Travis didn't seem to mind. His grip tightened around her hand, not with any trace of violence, but with compassion.

"I'm sorry. I don't mean to be such a baby," Josie whispered.

Travis grazed his thumb under her eye, gently wiping away each tear as it fell. Then, with his other hand, he did the same for her other eye. "It's all right to cry, Jo," he whispered, his voice soft and reassuring. "I cry too, and there's nothing to be ashamed of."

Marcus's face flashed in her mind, and Josie winced, instinctively holding Nathan tighter against her chest. "My husband . . . my late husband . . . never let me cry. He beat the emotions out of me until there was nothing left. There have only been a handful of times I cried in the past seven years. He . . . He said I was too weak . . . I was too weak to bear his children."

Travis lifted Josie's chin. "You are not a weak woman. You're anything but that. Who else would survive a trip here, take care of four children, work as hard as a man during the harvest, and deliver a baby in the middle of a blizzard? That's you, Jo. You are a precious woman, and I vow never to take you for granted."

As Josie looked into Travis's blue eyes, she finally let go of every doubt. She believed him completely. Just months ago, she would have doubted such words, but now she was convinced that Travis was different. No man would ever steal her worth again.

Travis reached forward, and to Josie's surprise, she didn't flinch as his face drew nearer. His lips brushed against her forehead, and she closed her eyes, surrendering to the moment. For the first time, it seemed as though the distance between them had dissolved, leaving them closer than ever before.

CHAPTER TWENTY-EIGHT

Charlotte, North Carolina; Christmas Day 1872

NIGHTFALL HAD COME AT last, and General Wellington kept a watchful eye on Tia's home from a distance. He observed who left, who entered, who cleaned the windows, and whoever walked past. General kept his notebook out, noting the activities and their times. From his observations, he studied how pathetic the old geezer's guards were. By three in the morning, they were asleep.

General chuckled to himself. If those guards were his men, he'd wring their necks. A lazy man's work was a crime in his book—especially one of a soldier. That was why his sons were well-respected. That was until they gave up on themselves and disgraced his dear name, fueling the rumors regarding his cursed bloodline.

Keeping his head down, General walked the sidewalk and to the gate where the sleeping men were. As he stood there, they didn't bother to stir as they snored away against the fence. While they continued to remain in deep sleep, General fought the urge to slit their throats. But that would be too easy. What would be the fun in this battle? The more difficult the better.

He reflected on his first kill and how addicting it was, watching the life slip from their eyes like Mammy's. He had been oblivious to how spectacular it was until he killed his first man in the Mexican-American War. Afterward, he became eager to take more lives into his hands. It gave him a sense of control. General liked being able to take lives anytime he wanted to; taking their souls was like fuel to him, giving him more power.

He grew sick of the men who cried like babies on the battlefield, whose bodies quivered after taking their first life. Finding enjoyment was what led to General's promotion. But tonight wasn't for killing as many people as he could—he was going to take one life, one that would give him the most satisfaction. The more he waited, the better revenge would be. Her death was so near that he could almost taste it. *I will squeeze your soul out of your body, Josephine Wellington, and it will be more satisfying than any soldier's death.*

General removed the keys from a guard's pockets and unlocked the gate. He pushed it open, careful not to make a creak. At last, he was in. He ran like a soldier on the battlefield as he approached the door and unlocked it while a blaring thud pulsed in his ear, not like earlier, but because he was more than ready, so ready to close this chapter.

As he stepped inside, everything was just like it was earlier that afternoon. General tiptoed down the marble hallways and up the staircase. From his memory, he recalled the estate having four floors. As he reached the second floor, he felt like a fool, realizing how many doors there were. It would take all night to look, and there wasn't enough time.

Soon the staff would be awake and tending to their duties. He couldn't have those lowlifes destroy his plan again—especially the butler. Then, it hit him. *The servants' sleeping quarters.* It was time to assert his dominance over the weaklings of the house. He'd begin with a little fun, some interrogation. Oh, how he missed it. He thoroughly enjoyed it with Mammy and the maid from earlier. *Maybe one more time.*

General chuckled to himself. Even though he was saving his strength for Josephine, it didn't mean he couldn't have any fun with someone else. General stepped down the staircase and onto the ground floor where the kitchen was. Below was the kitchen staff—the perfect targets. They would have prepared Josephine's meals, so who better to interrogate for the truth?

General walked down the staircase, then the hallway until he found a room of his choosing. Ten rooms to choose from and only one could play his game. He rubbed his chin thoughtfully, deciding who the lucky helper would be. He chose a room in the middle and opened the door. Two little beds, more like cots, nestled in the corner of the room, each occupied by a young boy, no more than fifteen, sound asleep. General retrieved his knife from his holster, pleasure surging through him as he looked down at the sharp blade. *Wait. You must wait.*

He bent at the first boy's bedside, holding the knife to his throat. As the boy jolted awake, the blade nicked him. Just the smell of blood made General's temptation grow. *Stupid lad.* The boy opened his mouth, letting out a small croak, but General held the knife closer. The boy silenced and shivered beneath General's firm control. General smiled.

"Now, you listen to me," General whispered. "You make a sound or try anything stupid, I will slice your throat and this boy next to you. Understand?"

The boy whimpered silently and nodded.

"Now you get up and do what I say." *Oh, how I missed this.*

The boy slowly stood in his striped, blue nightshirt. He tiptoed out the door, his bare feet making no sound on the floor as he slipped into the hallway. General kept the knife against the boy's throat and whispered in his ear. "Now, you are going to answer my questions."

The boy nodded.

"I am looking for my wife. She is the niece of your dead mistress. Her name is Josephine Wellington. Which room is she in?"

The boy swallowed. "Who?"

General pressed the blade harder. "Better think smart, boy."

The boy struggled to gain his breath. "I-I—" he stuttered.

General rolled his eyes and loosened his grip.

"I heard rumors. The kitchen staff . . . They were talking about a woman in the attic. N-Nobody saw her."

The crazy old lady locking her niece in the attic? It seems right, given she was mad.

"Who is your boss now?"

The boy gulped a large breath of air. "Mistress Callahan's lawyer. H-He has an office upstairs . . . in the study . . . on the second floor."

General pressed the knife harder. It was starting to draw blood, the smell tempting General. How he longed to watch one more person die from his hands. "Take me."

The boy went up two more floors, and General followed after him. They walked another hallway until they stopped at the third door on the left.

"Mr. Anderson has been working here until her estate is in order."

The boy tried to open the door, but the brass knob only jiggled slightly with a groan. General watched in pleasure as sweat drizzled down the boy's forehead. Even though General had the key from the guard's pocket, he enjoyed seeing the struggle before him. The boy's breathing became more rapid. General patted the boy on the back and chuckled.

"Steady, lad. I have the key."

General was hoping the boy would smart off to him so he'd have an excuse to torture him a little more, but the boy was smart, smart enough to know his place—unlike Josephine. He'd give the boy credit for that. The door opened, revealing a large library with a shiny mahogany desk in the corner, surrounded by mountains of book stacks and walls of bookcases.

"Where is his safe?" General asked.

"I-I don't know, sir," the boy whimpered. "I'm just a kitchen boy."

General rolled his eyes. He grabbed the boy's face and showed him the knife that was already stained by his blood around the edge.

"Don't even think about trying anything, boy."

The boy nodded, his legs quivering as he attempted to stand tall. Ignoring the boy's nervousness, General checked the desk and drawers, rifling through their contents. They were filled with pens, useless papers, candies, and personal items like photos.

At last, General opened a cabinet and discovered a large chest with a sturdy lock. With a determined glare, he grabbed his knife and picked at the keyhole. It took a few tries, but finally, he managed to pop it open with a satisfying click. He sorted through the documents until he found what he was looking for—a file with an enveloped letter inside. He snatched the letter, eager to know its contents.

I, Tatiana Marie Callahan, give my estate, assets, fortune, and personal belongings to my beautiful great-niece, Josephine Eleanor Callahan Blythe, as my sole heir.

General paused in shock. *Blythe?* There had to be a mistake. After all, the woman was senile. She couldn't have been in her right mind to mistake Wellington with Blythe. He read on.

I ask on my deathbed for my lawyer, Victor Anderson, to defend my niece and protect her child located in Willow Grove, Montana. As I close my eyes in death, this is my final wish. These two are my last living relatives and must be protected and cared for. As for General Marcus Wellington, if he ever wakes from his illness, protect my home. Guard it day and night.

General's nostrils burned with rising heat. Either the woman was completely out of her mind, or there was more to Josephine's story. She had a child? *That witch! How dare she take my child from me! She couldn't give me a proper heir, and now she takes what belongs to me. She will pay for her crime! I will watch her suffer! I will have that child of mine!*

His father's weakness drove General Marcus Wellington to become a strong-willed Southerner. His mission was to continue the family line and fortify it for generations. Jared and Loyd had failed, and Josie seemed too weak to bear him a worthy heir. But maybe he was wrong. General smirked to himself. He couldn't deny it—she had proven herself by taking him down.

Yet she was also naive and foolish. Josie thought she could go far away and escape him, but she was wrong. He'd take what was his and destroy the woman who tried to destroy his life.

CHAPTER TWENTY-NINE

TRAVIS GLANCED BACK AT Josie while he built a snowman with the children outside. She stood behind the window, holding Nathan against her shoulder. Josie was a natural mother, and he knew that the day she arrived in Willow Grove. The woman may not have had experience with children, but she had an undeniable gift. This marked the first time she had been out of bed in a week, and as usual, she fought against rest. That was the Josie he knew, and as many times as he wanted her to slow down, she refused.

Travis sighed with a smile, watching Josie pat Nathan's back. Josie looked up, her eyes meeting his. Sending him a wave, Travis couldn't help but wave back, natural warmth swimming through him in the biting cold. He couldn't fathom why her first husband would poison her mind and use his strength to overpower her instead of protecting her. Most of all, he couldn't understand how any man could hurt someone as lovely and beautiful as her.

When Travis called her a precious treasure days ago, he meant it. Josie was a rare woman, meant to be cherished and valued, and he swore he'd never cast her aside again. All these months, he should have listened, forgiven her, but instead, he only thought about himself—fearing she might come between the memory of what he and Sophie once had. But now that those walls had crumbled, he couldn't imagine why he'd built them in the first place.

The first time Travis held Nathan in his arms, he realized he could learn to treasure Josie more with each passing day. He wasn't just a new father; he was a husband, bound by a vow to honor and cherish Josie—and he was determined to do just that. Loving Nathan was the first step in keeping that promise.

However, he knew he had to be patient with Josie. He couldn't ignore the way his heart fluttered whenever he looked at her, but he would take things one day at a time. When his heart was ready, he would welcome any new feelings that came.

A burst of cold smacked the back of Travis's head, chilling the nape of his neck and snapping him out of his thoughts. He turned around to find the children giggling, their faces full of mischief. Shaking his head with a smirk, he placed his hands on his hips, narrowing his eyes playfully at them.

"Was that a challenge?" Travis scooped a large handful of snow, quickly shaping it into a ball. With a grin, he hurled it towards the children, who shrieked and scattered.

Another snowball came flying in Travis's direction, narrowly missing him. The kids darted toward a cluster of trees, ducking behind them for cover. Travis followed, launching more snowballs. The icy air burned his nostrils, but in that moment, none of it mattered.

For the first time in a long while, Travis experienced profound joy. His children's faces were lit with wide smiles, and their squeals and laughter echoed through the frosty air. He kept hurling snowballs until Jonas ran to him, arms raised in defeat.

"Don't throw, Pa! I surrender!"

Travis chuckled as his son reached his side, his nose and cheeks flushed red as tomatoes.

"I'm joinin' ya!"

Travis gave Jonas's back a pat. "We men-folk must stick together."

Despite the cold, the moment warmed him. Snow leaked through Travis's mittens, offering him little protection, but he hardly noticed. The children continued pelting him with snowballs, laughing wildly as they threw as many as they could.

"When Gideon and Nathan get big enough, we'll beat those girls," Jonas declared, his fist held high.

Travis admired Jonas's confidence, the way he threw himself into the game with so much energy. Gideon was napping now, but soon enough, he'd be old enough to join in with his siblings. Travis looked forward to the day when all his children would play together, but the thought of how quickly they were growing tugged at his heart. Nathan was already a week old and bigger than when he was born.

Time seemed to be slipping by faster than he could grasp, but he'd enjoyed every moment, for who knew what the next day would bring.

After nursing Nathan, Josie adjusted him in her arms as she heard the children racing towards the door. She shifted the baby against her shoulder and began burping him. Within seconds, the door burst open, and the children rushed in, their cheeks flushed from the cold.

"There's hot cocoa on the stove to warm you up."

The children squealed as they hurried to grab cups for hot cocoa behind her. Travis removed his snow-covered layers and moved closer to Josie. His lips curved into a small, genuine smile, one that sent warmth flooding through her. She cherished those times when he smiled, especially after months of seeing it so rarely. Now, more than ever, she wished to see it every second of the day.

"How is my son doing?" Travis said, reaching for the baby's fist. Nathan's hand latched around it like he wouldn't let go.

Son. The word nearly made her heart burst. Josie could hardly believe how much that simple title meant. Just then, she heard a tiny burp escape from Nathan, prompting her to adjust him so he could see his pa.

"He just finished his breakfast, but it won't last for long. Soon enough he'll be wanting his lunch, then snack, extra snack, then supper."

Travis chuckled as he looked down at Nathan. "Then second supper."

"That, too. I hope he hasn't been keeping you up at night. I know since you're sleeping by the fire, you are on the battle front."

Travis brushed his fingers across Nathan's chubby cheek. "Not at all. I wouldn't trade these moments for anything."

"Would you like to hold him?"

Travis's blue eyes sparkled with excitement. "Of course!"

Nathan squirmed and cooed as Josie carefully handed him to Travis. In his muscular arms, the baby looked so small and delicate. Travis supported Nathan's head and smiled down at him, whispering sweet baby talk while planting soft kisses on his cheek. Watching Travis embrace fatherhood with such tenderness made Josie inwardly sigh. She couldn't resist wondering what she had been so afraid of. The Lord had truly blessed her beyond measure.

Josie thought of Aunt Tia, who, despite her age and wavering mind, had always possessed a certain wisdom in her whimsical ideas. It was one of the many things Josie was thankful for. She missed the woman with all her heart, wishing their reunion hadn't been cut short. Yet somehow, she knew Aunt Tia was proud of her. Even if Aunt Tia had completed her journey on earth before witnessing all that Josie had achieved, Josie had a keen sense of comfort knowing that she was watching over her, along with Mama, Susannah, Trellis, Oliver, and Zane.

As for Papa, she wasn't sure. He had returned home filled with shame over losing the war and had blamed her for the deaths of Susannah and Mama. No matter what he thought, Josie blamed herself more than he did. For a long time, she believed she deserved the punishment he'd inflicted upon her, but now, she recognized that it wasn't her fault.

Though she never had the chance to say goodbye or forgive him, witnessing the precious gift that had come from her seven years of pain and suffering with Marcus—a beautiful baby boy—shifted her perspective. In the light of this new beginning with Travis, Nathan, and the children, she found the strength to forgive, truly and deeply.

The children giggled at the dining table behind them, sipping their hot cocoa while playing with their chalkboards. Hearing them converse about their drawings, Josie looked up at Travis, noticing they were alone with Nathan by the fireplace. Travis smiled, adjusting the sleeping babe in his arms as he pulled his chair closer. Josie looked down, watching Nathan's tiny chest rise and fall with each breath. He was snug in his blanket and warm against his father's chest.

"He's so peaceful," Travis whispered.

Josie exhaled, relaxing her chin on her fist as she leaned forward. "I wish I could have those days, peaceful with no troubles."

"Me too," Travis added. "Imagine eating and sleeping all day and nothing else."

Josie chuckled softly with a large grin on her face. "How did your snowball fight go?"

"It was cold."

"You should have stayed by the fire with Nathan and me."

"Maybe I should have. When Nathan and Gideon are big enough, the boys' team will be unstoppable."

Josie leaned back against her chair, folding her arms across her chest. "Is that so?"

"I'll have to get another wife to help you win," Travis teased.

Josie shook her head. "You are terrible, Mr. Blythe."

"Not as terrible as you, Mrs. Blythe. I bet you couldn't handle a snowball fight anyway."

"I can too," Josie chided slightly above a whisper. "You won't think about getting an extra wife when you see how good I am."

"I don't think I can get a wife that's as good as you. I was beyond lucky. I couldn't ask for any better."

A blush crept up Josie's cheeks as she rubbed her thumbs together. "I don't believe that."

"I do," Travis said firmly in a low, husky voice. He reached out a free hand, laying it over hers. Her heart skipped as warmth flushed through her veins. "I am beyond blessed knowing I have you by my side. You're more than an excellent mother. You are a wonderful wife, Jo."

Jo. Just the sound of her nickname made her stomach flutter. She intertwined her fingers through Travis's, smiling wider than ever before.

Then out of nowhere, flashes of that night on the staircase filled her mind, causing her breath to nearly hitch. Josie gripped Travis's hands, keeping her smile. She couldn't let him see through her facade. She may be able to forget about her past with Marcus, but she couldn't bury how it ended.

CHAPTER THIRTY

Cheyenne, Wyoming; Early January 1873

AFTER A MISERABLE WEEK, boarding trains and getting off at new stations, General huffed aloud, his breath visible in the cool Rocky Mountain breeze like smoke. The crisp air bit at his ears and neck, making him wish he had prepared better. But he had been too anxious, ready to venture out to the Montana Territory and take care of business. It didn't matter if it was the dead of winter; he'd fight to retrieve his flesh and blood his wife had stolen from him. Then he'd carry out justice.

After stepping off the train and looking out from the station, his eyes met the saloon's sign, like a beacon leading him to a lighthouse. He longed for a drink. What had it been, a day or two? The train's liquor didn't agree well with him. He hoped for something less fancy, more natural and real. None of that overpriced wine and brandy.

He crunched through the snow and opened the saloon's door. Upon entering, men from every corner locked eyes with him, studying him from head to toe. Their attire was more appropriate for the weather—coats made of different fur types like buffalo, grizzly, and moose. Very robust for General's taste, but he was desperate. He settled himself at the bar, turning his head from the harlots in the corner, preying on the men seated at their own tables, playing cards or fooling around.

Oh, how General longed to break those girls' necks. Their behavior was repulsive, and he admired the thought that no one would miss them if he just—

"What can I get ya, sir?" the bearded barkeeper asked, a puff of smoke coming from his cigar. His eyes roved as he studied General.

"Get me a bottle of whiskey."

The man nodded. "Done."

General looked ahead, studying each bottle of liquor stored—brandy, rum, beer, whiskey, and gin. He longed for them all, but he couldn't delay his journey. There would be more to celebrate when he came home with the heir that would be his legacy's salvation.

The man returned with General's bottle, and he immediately popped off the top, ready to drink the remarkable beverage.

"You ain't from around here, are ya?" the barkeeper asked.

General took a sip and swallowed. "What gives me away?"

The man laughed. "You really want that answer? You look prim, like you a city folk."

General chuckled as the whiskey flamed down his throat. "General Marcus Wellington."

"Zack Yancey." He put out his hand and Marcus shook it. "What ya doin' comin' 'round here durin' the winter, General?"

"You wouldn't guess."

Zack leaned forward, his elbows resting on the counter. "A man of mystery. I like that."

"Know where I can get a stagecoach from here?"

Zack stepped back, shaking his head as a loud chuckle bellowed out of him. "You're a funny one, General. We ain't got no stage-coaches out here, not in this weather. You must be crazy."

General's grip tightened around his bottle. What right did this man have to insult someone of his status? He wanted to take hold of that neck of his and squeeze every ounce of breath out of him. Perhaps a duel for the insult. Those were his favorite in the days, a game of cat and mouse. Only the strongest could win, like Darwin's theory. How long had it been since he participated in one? Well, planning one wasn't too long ago. However, he decided poison was easier on Stephen Callahan.

General reached into his pocket, pulling out a pouch of gold. He couldn't be distracted by every little insult. He had more important matters to deal with. *Save your strength.*

"I'll pay anyone willing to take me out."

Zack continued to laugh. "General, please. Don't show off ya money like that. You gonna call bad attention."

"I *need* to get to Montana."

Zack sighed, patting the counter. "Look, General. If ya really wanna get there, wait till spring. I got a nice room out back, and you can stay there. I'll even send you a nice lady to keep ya company. Just don't do somethin' stupid."

General's muscles tensed. He didn't want a woman. He didn't want a bed here, despite the lovely supply of liquor. He wanted what was rightfully his.

"I'm good," General snapped. "I'll find someone else to help."

Zack walked off, shaking his head as he continued to laugh. "Good luck with that." The barkeep turned away and tended to another customer on the other side of the counter.

General took another sip of whiskey and put his money away. Some business Zack had here, insulting his customers. Perhaps if

General taught him a lesson, he'd think of something else to say, perhaps even get him a stagecoach. Something told General the man was just frightened and lazy.

"You lookin' for someone to take ya to Montana?'

General turned around, facing a man standing tall before him. He had a thick, black beard, streaked with smoky gray, that added to his rugged appearance. He wore an oversized buffalo coat that draped heavily on his broad shoulders, making him appear twice as large as he likely was.

"What's it to you?"

The man settled himself in the stool next to General, putting out his hand. "Buck Hanson."

General took the man's hand, shaking it with a firm grip. "General Marcus Wellington."

"General?" Buck repeated, his brows raised and forehead creased. "Confederate?"

"Yes."

Buck nodded with a smile. "Ah, well it's an honor. We might've passed each other on the battlefield once. I fought for the Confederate States. I'm a Louisianan, born and raised."

General grinned. "Well, that makes me proud. It's nice to meet another true man of the cause."

"I came out west after the war. I trap and trade now."

General took a sip of his whiskey. "You trade with the Indians?"

"I do," Buck said. "I hope you don't mind that I overheard your conversation, but I'm headin' out to Montana myself to trade with some Cheyenne. I have a sled already set up with supplies that'll last another month." Buck leaned in closer. "I know that barkeep said you're crazy for goin' alone, and he's right. It's not just the freeze you should worry 'bout. There's Injuns, lots of 'em, and they're out for blood. You need someone with experience to escort you out."

General's brows raised. "I'd be obliged."

"Anythin' for my general. I respect ya, just like I did in the army. You and me are brothers from the same side."

General reached into his pocket. "How much?'

Buck shook his head. "None."

General grinned. He reached out, shaking Buck's hand. "What time we heading out?"

CHAPTER THIRTY-ONE

JOSIE SAT IN THE Blythe pew, clutching Nathan against her chest while her hands trembled violently. Here she was, holding a three-week-old baby who was healthy in size and far from early. He was full-term, weighing nearly eleven pounds by now. Nathan was no premature infant; his plump cheeks, tiny fingernails, and healthy complexion made that clear.

Josie's thoughts drifted back to the gossip circles of her childhood, where stories of early babies and perfect health were whispered with suspicion. If she was still part of that circle, she'd be the subject of every conversation, sticking out like a sore thumb, being the topic of gossip for years to come.

She shamed this family, no doubt of that. If it wasn't for Travis's gentlemanly heart, she would gladly step up and take the blame. Travis wanted Nathan to grow up with the same love and belonging as if he shared their blood. Telling town members Josie was from Bozeman was a lie, but it was his way of protecting her.

Reverend Levingston closed his Bible after delivering the message. The building fell into a hushed silence until he called upon a man in the front row to lead the closing prayer. Josie bowed her head, her eyes fluttering shut as she held Nathan close. Her heart raced with every growing second, awaiting the subtle "amen."

Come unto me, all ye that labour and are heavy laden, and I will give you rest, echoed in Josie's mind. The familiar scripture wrapped around her, and the peace within those words slowly soothed her restless spirit.

At last, the prayer ended, and the congregation rose to their feet. Josie carefully adjusted the sleeping Nathan as she moved closer to Travis. The warmth of his forearms against her eased the tremors still coursing through her. Travis balanced Gideon on his shoulders, the little boy happily waving at everyone around. Josie had rarely seen Travis hold Gideon, so it comforted her to watch him keep the squirmy boy in his lap throughout the service.

Before Josie could leave the pew, she was stopped by Mrs. Scott. Forcing a soft smile, Josie greeted her, steadying her breath to calm her hysteric heart.

"I heard the news last week, and I couldn't help myself," Mrs. Scott said with bright eyes, reaching forth to touch Nathan's covered head. The knitted hats had come in handy, despite him not being born in spring as Mrs. Scott and the ladies had predicted. The woman gasped in admiration. "My, my he is a fine young lad." Her gaze switched to Travis. "You two must be *so* proud."

Travis smiled, wrapping his free arm around Josie's shoulders. "We are."

Mrs. Scott turned to Josie. "Mrs. Blythe, I was wanting to invite you to the ladies' spring quilting circle at my home. The one hosted at your place was a wonderful blessing, so we are all eager for another."

A flame soared up Josie's cheeks. Kindness was the furthest thing she was expecting, and the look on the woman's face and the other people around them seemed to knock the breath out of her. Smiles were all around, and men came to Travis, patting his shoulder.

"I'd love that."

Mrs. Scott folded her hands together. "Well, goody. I will get back to them, and we shall discuss a date."

Before walking away, Mrs. Scott reached out and gently pinched Nathan's chubby cheek. He didn't stir, remaining fast asleep in Josie's arms. He was a good sleeper, rarely fussing, and sometimes Josie felt like she was carrying a rock, so heavy and still he was. Josie turned, noticing Caroline approaching.

Caroline gasped, covering her mouth. "Oh, Josie, he's an angel." Her arm came around Josie as Travis stepped away, greeting the men surrounding him to extend congratulations.

"He has Travis's eyes," Caroline cooed, her lips curving.

Josie's heart thundered against her chest. *If only she knew.* All babies supposedly had blue eyes according to Aunt Polly, and if Josie wasn't mistaken, they would either turn brown or green. She deeply hoped they'd turn brown like hers. If they turned green—*those* eyes—she knew she'd have to bury those haunting memories deep within and focus on the precious gift in her arms. Nathan was here, and he needed her, no matter what color his eyes became.

"I take it Mrs. Scott invited you to her quilting circle," Caroline said.

Josie nodded, rocking Nathan gently in her arms as he began to stir. "Yes, she did just now."

"I'm looking forward to having fellowship amongst us ladies again."

Fellowship. Josie never thought she'd see the days she'd appreciate one word so dearly. That day had been overwhelming, but seeing how much everyone cared, despite what they could assume, made her heart sing. A new beginning was just over the horizon, just like she hoped. *Thank you, Lord.*

"I can't wait," Josie said, smiling.

Nathan's face pinched. He let out a soft cry, and Caroline frowned. Josie bounced Nathan, making shushing noises. Heat crawled up her neck. How many people were watching now?

"Oh no," Caroline cooed. "Someone isn't happy."

"He's not used to strange places yet. This is his first time away from the homestead."

Travis looked back at her, pointing out the door, his brows raising. Josie nodded, giggling softly. She looked back at her friend. "I think Nathan wants to go home."

Caroline sighed. "Oh well. We'll have to stop by and see him so he won't think us strangers."

"Come by anytime," Josie said, pressing Nathan's face against her shoulder, hoping a new position would calm him. She made her way toward Travis, who stood by the door, struggling to keep hold of a squealing Gideon. The little boy wriggled in his arms, eager to break free and join his siblings playing outside.

"That was very nice of the ladies," Travis said, setting Gideon down and holding his hand. "I hope you don't mind, but I overheard your conversation with Mrs. Scott before I was pulled away."

"Being invited to something was the last thing I expected."

"I told you there was nothing to worry about. We like to see the good in people in this town. Everyone wants you to feel welcome."

The Lord had been good to her even though she felt unworthy. Being loved by the church was nothing she expected. She was welcomed, and for the first time since the war, she experienced unity and love—no lines between North and South, all united in the West.

Rose supervised the children up ahead under the church's willow tree, her arms folded over her body. She turned, noticed Josie, and immediately trudged through the thick snow to greet her.

Rose covered her mouth and gasped just like Caroline did inside the church building.

"Josie, he's a gift from God!"

Josie grinned, still bouncing the now-quieted Nathan as he pressed against her shoulder. "That's why I named him Nathan. It means 'gift of God,' and that is what he is to me."

Rose placed her hand on Nathan's back and studied his face. "Children are a heritage from the Lord. You have been exceedingly blessed."

"I'll be honest, the children are more of a handful now. However, I wouldn't have it any other way."

"How about their schooling?" Rose asked. "I know you mentioned you started teaching them at home."

Josie sighed, pulling Nathan's bear-fur quilt over his face. "I'm afraid their studies have been neglected these past weeks. I'm still trying to adjust to caring for Nathan and Gideon, but I hope to start again soon. I don't care if there isn't a school—they need to learn."

Rose nodded. "I agree with you. I understood how hard it would be to come here with two boys and teach them from home, but it isn't the same." Rose took a pause and observed the children playing. There had to be at least twenty-five children under the age of sixteen. "I've been wanting to talk to you for a while about something that has been on my heart, but I've been pulling back until the baby was born. Your children have said in my Sunday School class that you're a good teacher. It's not official yet, but I want to start the school again. I was hoping . . . that is when Nathan is a little older . . . if you'd like to teach."

Josie's eyes widened, her pulse drumming. Her? Teach? She had dreamed for years of becoming a schoolteacher, imagining the joy of shaping young minds. But now, as a wife and mother, that dream seemed distant, almost like it belonged to another version of herself. The thought of pursuing it as a career hadn't crossed her mind—until now. What would Travis think? On one hand, she could make a difference in children's lives, fulfilling the passion she once held so dearly. Yet on the other, it would mean neglecting her duties at home—the harvest, chores, the children.

"I . . . I don't know. I'd have to speak with Travis first."

"I knew you'd say that," Rose said. "You two should discuss it and pray over this decision. If it isn't the Lord's will, we'll work something else out."

"Josie!" Josie looked down to see Jonas tugging on the hem of her wool skirt. "Come on! Come on! Pa's leavin'!"

Josie let out a soft sigh, followed by a light giggle while Rose's lips curled into a grin. "I don't want to be left behind."

Rose reached out and embraced Josie. "Congratulations, Josie. He's a wonderful boy."

Josie pulled away and trailed after Jonas. Her heart soared with delight, unable to wipe away her grin. The Lord had been so good the past two weeks, but what laid on her heart was which path He'd allow her to take.

It seemed as though new chapters were unfolding at every corner. Would she remain at home, or would she help make a difference in the community—the community that accepted her and welcomed her despite everything they could hold against her?

The children were quiet, bundled in the back of the wagon. Josie couldn't tell if the rattles from the rocky road drowned out their whispers or if they were simply worn out from playing after the service. Travis drove slower than usual, mindful of Josie, the newborn in her arms, and the thick ice beneath them. So many changes were happening, but the one that Rose placed on her heart was another.

"You've been quiet," Travis said, his focus ahead.

"I have a lot on my mind."

"And *what* is that?"

A knot of nerves tightened in her stomach. Josie couldn't quite pinpoint the source of her apprehension—whether it was fear of rejection or doubt about the idea of teaching itself. But she knew she needed to inform Travis about this decision. It wasn't just about her; it concerned the town's future and the children who needed an education. Education would be the key to the children's future success. Every child needed to know history, science, arithmetic, and literature.

"I spoke to Rose after service."

Travis chuckled. "I noticed. We were already loaded up by the time you finished."

"Rose brought to my attention how many children lack proper schooling at home."

Travis sighed, rubbing his forehead. "It's hard finding someone willing to come out here, especially when you expect them to adjust to a whole new way of life without offering a decent wage. We kept the same teacher my whole life, but she passed away six years ago. She was a sweet lady."

Josie looked down at Nathan, who stirred in her arms. He drifted off to sleep after she changed him. "I wanted to ask . . . Would you let me fill in until a teacher can be found?"

Travis cocked his head sharply and faced her. "You? Teach?"

"Only when Nathan and Gideon are older," Josie added. "Our children are blessed with my skills, but I think about the others in the town. Do they have the same privilege at home? I think I can make a difference. I've always felt like my purpose was to be a teacher one day. That was until . . ."

"Until you married Marcus."

Josie nodded. "Yes."

Travis rubbed his pinkened face. "The council won't be able to pay a decent salary. There's no one here who has the money to invest."

"I'm fine with that," Josie answered. "I don't care if I don't get paid a cent. Helping these children in the valley have access to an education is all I need. If I can make a difference in even one child's life, then it will be worth it."

Travis's eyes sparkled. "I'm very proud of you, Jo. That's a very humble thing to say. Most people wouldn't dare work without pay."

"I don't mind."

"Well, you have my blessing. These children are counting on you, Josie."

Josie's eyes widened in disbelief. She couldn't believe Travis was willing to agree. Without pay? With the cost of abandoning her duties at home? He was too good to her, far too good.

"Are—Are you serious? You'll let me?"

Travis chuckled. "Why wouldn't I? My wife is going to be a teacher!"

Her heart nearly skipped a beat. She loved him saying those two words together. My wife.

CHAPTER THIRTY-TWO

AFTER MAKING PORRIDGE, THE next morning, Josie sat and nursed Nathan while it cooled. Managing two babies alongside three other children was a major adjustment, but she was determined to make it work. She had already served Travis his breakfast before he headed into town to unload cargo at the mercantile. He seemed happy to take a break from plowing and harvesting, yet she could sense his desire to feel useful in other ways. During the winter months, both he and Ronan worked at the mercantile. The ground was still frozen, the weather hardly bearable to go outside and play, so the children spent extra time doing schoolwork.

Following half an hour of nursing and changing Nathan's diaper, Josie carried him into her bedroom and laid him on her bed, nestled safely between two pillows. She glanced over at Gideon, fast asleep in his crib, his tiny thumb tucked into his mouth. Josie preferred Nathan to be in bed with her, and until she was ready to move him, Gideon would remain in the crib. With Nathan hardly stirring, Josie returned to the kitchen to set the table.

The front door creaked open, and in walked Aunt Polly, bundled from head to toe in her thick winter layers. With a quick movement, she began shedding her heavy clothing.

Josie giggled. "How was it outside?"

"Too cold to bother being out," Aunt Polly grumbled, rubbing her hands together. "I don't know how Ronan and Travis do it. I'd rather stay cooped up all day rather than work out there."

Josie placed four bowls on the table. "Take a seat. I have coffee brewing to warm you up."

Aunt Polly settled into her chair as Josie retrieved a tin cup. She poured the steaming liquid and placed it in front of her aunt-in-law.

"How are the children getting along with the baby?" Aunt Polly asked.

"They love having another sibling. However, Gideon doesn't know what to think about him."

Aunt Polly chuckled, reaching for the coffee. "Two under two. That is one tricky experience."

"Travis told me you used to have twins," Josie said, but she bit her tongue. The surprise on Aunt Polly's face made her immediately regret asking.

Aunt Polly's eyes shifted downward. "I had two boys, Samuel and Solomon. They were bright lads and loved school like yours do."

"What happened to them?" Josie asked. "If . . . you don't mind me asking."

Aunt Polly sighed, her hands gripping her cup. "There was an accident. My husband was taking the boys on a wagon ride and the horse got spooked somehow. The horse took off, and the wagon lost its balance, crushing my little boys. My husband didn't live long after that. He suffered from internal bleeding."

Josie's breath hitched, and she covered her mouth in horror. "I'm sorry. I-I couldn't imagine. That must have been extremely hard for you."

"It was," Aunt Polly answered. "But looking back, I can see the beauty of it all."

"What do you mean?"

"Travis's father died when he was ten, and his mother passed away when Ivy was just two. Travis has always been like a son to me. I have a use for myself with him, the children, and you. You are my family now, and I couldn't ask for anything better."

Josie smiled softly. "Thank you, Aunt Polly. I don't think I ever said it, but I don't know what I'd do without you. You and Travis, Rose, Caroline, and this town have shown me more kindness than I'll ever know."

Aunt Polly reached out and took Josie's hand. "We love you, Josie. Always remember that, sweetheart."

"I will."

Aunt Polly let go of Josie's hand and turned to the empty bowls. "Isn't it time for the children to wake up? It's a little past their wake up time."

Josie removed her apron. "We wouldn't like that, would we?"

"You have adjusted very well."

Josie tiptoed down the hallway and opened the door to the children's room. Lillian and Ivy were snuggled together while Jonas slept alone in his bed. With a soft smile, she approached the girls, carefully removing the covers from them.

"Time to wake up, sleepyheads," she whispered, gently shaking them awake.

Ivy stretched and let out a big yawn, her arms reaching high above her head. Lillian, still half-asleep, rubbed her eyes with tiny fists. They both sat up in their flannel nightgowns and matching nightcaps, looking like two little angels in the soft morning light that filtered through the window.

"There's porridge on the stove for you two."

The girls spoke little in the morning, but Jonas, on the other hand, was always full of energy. The girls left out the door and Josie walked over to Jonas's bed, where he laid sound asleep, the sunlight landing on his tousled hair. She carefully removed the covers.

"Jonas, time to get up. Breakfast is ready."

Jonas didn't respond, not even a stir. Josie placed her hands on his shoulders and shook him again. He groaned but still didn't sit up. Josie's pulse throbbed, each beat pounding in her throat.

"Jonas? Jonas, what's wrong?" She placed her hand on his forehead and gasped. He was warm, too warm. "No," Josie whispered.

She turned the boy on his side, noticing a red rash below his ear. She had seen the same rash before at *Belle Vallée*. Josie choked on a breath. *It can't be.* If her inference was right, this was scarlet fever, the same illness that killed Mama and Susannah.

Memories of their moans of agony and Josie's long nights nursing them flashed inside her mind. Doctors were scarce and Josie was on her own. She had a mild case and was over the illness fast, but the worst cases had taken over the bodies of her loved ones, and they were too weak to fight it. She couldn't live through that again. Not when she made a promise to care for and protect them when she married Travis.

"Aunt Polly!" Josie screamed. She fought to hold back her sobs, knowing she needed to be strong. Her son's life was at stake.

Aunt Polly came rushing in. "What is it, dear?"

Josie hurriedly showed Aunt Polly the rash spreading across Jonas's skin, and a gasp slipped from her lips. She turned to see Lillian and Ivy at the doorway, their faces pale with confusion and fear.

"Girls, get away from here! Don't come near Jonas!" Aunt Polly shouted as she bolted to the door, closing it behind her.

"Josie! Aunt Polly!" the girls screamed, beating on the door. In another situation, Josie would calmly open the door and comfort them, but she muffled them out, panicking for Jonas's life. *Not again, Lord. Don't let this disease take everyone I love away for the second time.*

Aunt Polly felt his temperature. "We haven't had an outbreak in twenty-five years."

"What do we do?" Josie asked, her voice trembling. Deep down, she knew what needed to be done, but the weight of her past failures loomed over her. How could she trust herself again with the children she had promised to protect?

"I'm going to get the doctor, Josie. Stay with him and make sure the children don't go near that door."

Josie sat on Jonas's bed and ran her fingers through his brown curls. "Jonas, you must fight through this. Please, my darling boy."

Aunt Polly left, and Josie turned to see the girls still standing at the doorway. Tears hung in their eyes as they embraced each other. Josie kept her distance, not going farther than the girls' bed. Despite being immune, she couldn't risk coming close.

"Girls, you must listen to me," she said calmly. Josie swallowed the fear lumped in her throat. "Lillian, I need you to go to get a bucket of snow and melt it on the stove."

Lillian wiped her tears with her sleeve. "Josie, is Jonas gonna die?"

Josie tried to erase every possibility in her mind. She blocked out the memory of digging her mother's and sister's grave in the pouring rain, the cold drops piercing her shivering skin. "No, Jonas is going to be fine. We just need to pray for him because he's very sick. Only God can heal him."

Lillian nodded, her folded hands under her chin. "I will pray for him now."

Josie's gaze shifted to Ivy's, and her heart sank. Ivy was white as a sheet, her wide eyes reflecting the terror, as if she were staring at the angel of death again. "Ivy, I need you to get Gideon dressed and tend to Nathan. You are the woman of the house now, and I need you to be strong. Can you do that for me?"

"I-I'll try," Ivy whimpered.

Josie planted her hands on her hips. "Good. This is going to be a difficult day, but we must work together."

Ivy went towards the master bedroom, and Lillian rushed outside to get a bucket of snow. Josie sat at Jonas's bedside, feeling helpless as she watched him moan and squirm beneath the covers. *Lord, I can't do this again. I need you to give me strength and help me keep the promise I made to this family. Let your will be done, oh Lord. Only you can heal my son.*

An hour later, Aunt Polly and Josie stood in the corner while Dr. Gordon examined Jonas. He was barely conscious. When his eyes fluttered open, they appeared glassy and distant. Each new symptom Josie saw made it worse for her to bear—high fever, shivering body, pale face, and a rash. Every moment that passed, her thoughts returned to Travis.

He should be here. He should know. Aunt Polly was in such a rush for the doctor that she didn't have time to stop at the mercantile. Josie dreaded the moment he'd hear the news. He already knew how Josie's sister and mother died. It wouldn't give him any hope to know there was a high chance a boy as young and delicate as Jonas wouldn't survive.

"Can you open your mouth for me?" Dr. Gordon asked.

Jonas opened his mouth halfway. Doctor Gordon looked down his throat and asked him to close. From the look on the doctor's face, Josie knew there wouldn't be any good news. If Jonas's throat was red and swollen, he was indeed suffering from the deadly disease. The doctor patted Jonas's thigh and stood.

"Get some rest, Jonas. It will help you get better faster."

Josie wrapped her arms around herself, her heart racing in her chest. When Doctor Gordon locked eyes with her, a sinking feeling settled in her stomach.

"Jonas has scarlet fever," he explained. "And he's not the only one in these parts. I just came back from a homestead across Walnut Creek dealing with the illness. I'm afraid it's spreading faster by the minute."

"Oh, Lord, hear our prayers!" Aunt Polly cried, her hand over her mouth.

Dr. Gordon turned to Josie. "Take the children and get them to safety, especially the babies. This disease is deadly and could kill them in hours."

Aunt Polly pressed her lips together and swallowed. Clinging to her collar, her gaze met Josie's. "You take the children to my place. I'll look after Jonas. I can have a medicine brewed in minutes."

The thought of leaving Jonas sickened Josie. She couldn't leave him, not now. Especially with Travis still in town. Despite her failure in the past, she was the best person to stay with her immunity and experience. Aunt Polly may be the healer, but she didn't make a vow to be Jonas's mother and care for him as her own. Josie wouldn't break that promise, not now, not ever.

"No, I'll take care of him. I had scarlet fever seven years ago. I know what to do, and I won't leave Jonas."

Aunt Polly touched Josie's shoulder, her eyes puffy. "Josie, you can't. You have a baby to care for. Nathan needs his mother."

Josie shook her head. "I can't leave Jonas. He may not be my flesh and blood, but I'm not going to leave him . . . He needs his mother, too."

"Mrs. Blythe," Dr. Gordon said calmly. "Please understand, once you expose yourself again, you must not nurse for a long while. Close contact will put your baby at risk."

"I understand," Josie answered swiftly, swallowing a lump in her throat. "I know what I must do."

"I can send him to Rose. They have a dairy cow. Nathan will be well looked after until you can nurse again," Aunt Polly said. "And I have some willow bark at home that I can brew into a tea."

"Good idea, Aunt Polly," Dr. Gordon said. He turned to Josie, seriousness in his eyes. "Keep Jonas warm and burn everything he has touched. I can't have you risk your entire household."

Josie nodded.

Before the doctor could say another word, the sound of the front door creaking open interrupted him. Josie's heart raced, pounding in her ears; Travis was finally home. The thought of him returning after a long day at work to face such tragic news made her stomach churn. As he entered the home, Ivy and Lillian rushed to greet him, but this time, their voices were filled with cries of sorrow.

Josie watched from the corner as the girls cried against his legs. Travis's face was stunned and confused. He blinked twice, trying to understand what they were saying. It wasn't until he met Dr. Gordon's gaze that his mind seemed to comprehend. His face grew pale, and his eyes widened with terror.

"Dr. Gordon? What are you doing here? Is everything all right?"

Josie stood frozen in place. She longed to rush to him and explain, but she couldn't bear to leave the room with Jonas suffering inside. She watched as Aunt Polly placed a gentle hand on Travis's arm, whispering the devastating news. Travis's expression twisted in horror.

"No!" he screamed. "It can't be!" Travis tried to run to the bedroom, but the doctor and Aunt Polly pushed him back and protested against it.

"Let me see my son! I need my son!" he bellowed, his voice filled with desperation. Travis eventually broke free, darting to the room. Josie blocked him at the doorway, her hands pressing against his chest.

"You shouldn't be back here. You can get infected," Josie warned. She hoped she could stop him at a distance, but she couldn't. Her selfish desires were to stop another person she cared for from being infected by the deadly disease, but what right did she have to separate a father from his son? At last, he broke through.

Josie turned, her heart aching as she watched Travis drop to his knees beside Jonas's bed. He leaned over, clutching Jonas's hand as he wept openly. It was the first time Josie had ever seen him cry, and she couldn't blame him; she had cried just as fiercely when she knelt beside her own infected sister and mother. After giving him a moment to grieve, she quietly sat next to him, her fingers gently brushing across his back.

"I've been exposed to the disease, so I'm going to help him. I'm going to have Aunt Polly take them to the Levingstons tonight," Josie explained gently. "You should go, too. I can't have you get sick."

Travis cocked his head and met her gaze. "I can't leave him. Your family died from this disease, so there's a chance this could be the end for him. If it is, I must be here by his side. I could never forgive myself for letting him die alone."

Josie pulled him into a tight embrace. He buried his face into her shoulder as he continued to cry.

"He won't die, Travis. Jonas is strong, and I have faith the Lord will heal him."

Josie glanced back, noticing Dr. Gordon and Aunt Polly standing in the doorway. She gently cradled the back of Travis's head, running her fingers through his dark locks. She knew what a risk it was to have him in her arms, exposing him to a deadly disease, but she couldn't push him away.

She would never separate her husband from his son. And she couldn't bear to be apart from him, either.

CHAPTER THIRTY-THREE

TRAVIS KNELT NEXT TO Jonas's bedside with swollen, heavy eyes. He was careful not to surrender to sleep, for fear his son would take his final breath. The longer he stayed awake, the longer he could hear his son breathing. The day before, Jonas looked so healthy as he and Gideon played with wooden farm animals. That day had been perfect, sitting in front of the fireplace as a full family.

But nothing could have prepared him for this agonizing moment.

Their life was no longer blissful and whole as they now were all separated, praying for dear life that Jonas could make it another day. Jonas's tiny chest moved up and down, his eyelids closed and glistening from the oil lamp. His sun-kissed skin had turned icy pale, his body appearing smaller, nearly swallowed by the layers of coverings draped over him. Travis touched his son's face. The fever was still present. Jonas had survived the night, but the worst was far from over.

Travis stared at the inflamed red rash beneath the boy's ear. As long as it remained, there was a possibility Jonas would succumb to the disease. Travis wrung out the rag that rested in the basin of cold water and pressed it against the boy's face. Jonas let out a soft moan.

"Lord, please heal my poor boy. Spare him, I beg you. He's just a child," Travis whispered with full desperation in his heart.

The agony of his son's suffering made him explode into tears. Travis wasn't sure how much more loss he could take. At ten, he lost his father, which marked the beginning. When Travis lost his uncle and cousins, it made him feel as though he'd be lonely for the rest of his life.

Until Sophie. They vowed until death parted them, but Travis never thought that death would be a decade later. The thought of almost losing Josie had pushed him to the brink, and now, he faced the terrifying possibility of losing his son. Jonas was too feeble and young to succumb to such a disease.

A knock at the door interrupted Travis's thoughts, followed by the soft sound of footsteps that he believed to be Josie's.

"His fever hasn't broken yet," Travis muttered, his hands folded in front of him.

Josie sat beside him and set down a tray of tea. "We can't give up hope yet. He made it through the night, and the least we can do is have faith." She poured a cup and handed it to Travis. "Aunt Polly just brewed this—willow bark tea. It'll help bring the fever down. Lift his head so we can have him sip."

Travis lifted Jonas's head. "Jonas, take a few sips of this tea. It will help you get better."

The boy cracked his eyes open just a quarter of the way and took a few sips. Travis gently rubbed the back of Jonas's head, feeling the sweat dampen his curls. After swallowing, Jonas coughed a few times before whimpering. As Travis prepared to lay him back down, Josie quickly fluffed the pillows. Although the child's breathing had returned to a more normal rhythm, he was still very much unwell.

"Travis, are you all right?" Josie asked, her hand on his back.

Travis sighed, rubbing his eyes. Exhaustion still took a toll over his body, his vision growing hazier by the minute. All he wanted was to rest, but he knew he had to remain by his son's side. Jonas needed his pa with him; it was essential for his recovery. Simply being there might give the boy the strength to fight.

"It's nothing. I'm just tired is all."

Josie sat on the bedside, cupping his face in her cold hands. Travis jolted as a shiver ran up his spine. She rested a hand over his forehead, rubbing it softly. "Are you sure? You don't look too well."

"W-What do you mean?" Travis pulled her hand away and folded his arms at his chest. "I'm fine. I'm just exhausted from sitting here, waiting for my son to heal."

"Your eyes just look a little glassy." Her expression darkened, the color draining from her face as her lips parted.

"What is it?" Travis asked anxiously, his pulse rising.

Josie swallowed, her gaze firm. She clasped his forearm. "Travis, you need to lie down. I'll look after Jonas."

Travis shook his head. "No, I'm staying here. I'm just exhausted. All will pass when Jonas's fever breaks."

"I need you to lie down now, please. I beg you to get some rest."

"I won't," Travis snapped. He hugged himself tighter to preserve warmth. His thoughts drifted back to the time he left his father laboring in the fields while he ran off to play with a stray dog. He'd grown weary of the endless harvesting and dismissed his father's sharp scolding to keep working.

"Your father's heart gave out," Mama explained when Travis came home to a crowded home and sorrowful cries. Travis bit into

his lower lip and shook his head. No more breaks. He would never rest again.

"How would you feel if this was Nathan, hm? Let me stay with my son." Travis leaned and buried his face into Jonas's feeble hand.

"I understand what you mean, but you are catching the fever." Josie paused, and Travis's mouth parted as he sat straight up. *Fever?* That couldn't be true. He was exhausted; that was all.

"You can stay here and worry about Jonas, but I won't risk the children not having a father." Josie's voice turned more serious than Travis had ever heard. "If you don't, I will drag you there myself."

Travis peered down at Jonas. He couldn't leave him. He'd give his own life if it meant he could live.

"I let my father die," Travis croaked. His eyes burned. "I ran off during harvest and never told my him goodbye. I can't abandon Jonas for rest—"

Josie stood and touched Travis's shoulder. "None of that was your fault, and Jonas is going to be fine. I have faith in it."

Travis's throat clenched. It had been his fault. All his fault.

Josie cupped his face in her hands, tuning him to her. She brushed her knuckles down his cheek. "I vow to you that I will never leave his side. You can stay in the bed next to him, too. You must rest, please. Do this for your other children who love you with their whole hearts."

Travis took Josie's hand and kissed her palm. Tears trickled down his cheek, glistening against her skin. Travis didn't feel too terrible, but he yearned for rest. He wasn't sure if fatigue had set in yet or if he was simply too preoccupied with worry over Jonas to notice. Perhaps he could lie down for a few hours and then tend to his son again. Sleep beckoned him, a siren call he found increasingly hard to resist.

"I'll rest for a few hours, but I'm coming back to his side. He needs me."

Josie nodded with softness in her eyes, her thumb brushing across his skin. "I know, and I will look after him the best I can."

She rose from the bed, pulled fresh sheets from the children's drawers, and made the empty bed. The girls' bed was small, but Travis was grateful it was close. As soon as he closed his eyes, a wave of relief washed over him.

Rest. Sweet rest.

The pain in Josie's breasts intensified as another hour went by without caring for Nathan. He was constantly on her mind, and she worried endlessly about his health. Was he sick? Was he overcome with worry? Was he missing her? There hadn't been any correspondence from Rose, but that had been their arrangement. They had strictly agreed not to make contact until Jonas was better, but now that Travis had contracted the fever, she was unsure when that would be.

Josie and Aunt Polly spent the day burning the blankets and clothes that had been used before and during the illness. Outside, Josie set a pot to boil for washing dishes and utensils. On top of that, she brewed willow bark tea while keeping a watchful eye on her husband and son. She and Aunt Polly tried to take turns, but Josie could hardly bring herself to leave their sides. Aunt Polly kept to the main room unless she was needed. She spent every hour cooking, cleaning, and keeping the fireplace going.

Exhaustion wore at Josie's limbs as she sat between the two beds, but she had to stay strong. She couldn't let history repeat itself—not when she had been a helpless sixteen-year-old who knew nothing but how to throw parties and socialize. It had been all her fault she couldn't care for her family properly. This time, she'd do everything in her power to heal her new family.

Josie filled a cup with cold water just as Travis stirred, his eyelids fluttering. He groaned softly, struggling to sit up. She moved beside him and gently lifted his head before pulling another pillow behind him to support his posture. Bringing the water to his lips, she set her hand behind his head to steady him. He winced as he swallowed, followed by a harsh cough. Josie remembered the day she had the fever and how hard it was for her to swallow. Her tonsils had felt like they were on fire, and her head had throbbed with pain. Her eyes had been so swollen that she could barely open them.

"Travis, are you all right? Are you in pain?"

Travis sank into the mattress and shook his head. "Just . . . sleep," he whispered weakly.

Josie gently pulled the covers to Travis's chin and froze. A rash had formed along the base of his neck. A gasp escaped her lips, and she covered her mouth, desperately trying to restrain her tears. All this time, she had clung to the possibility that it was merely exhaustion, but now reality sank in. There was a chance her husband might be taken from her.

Travis was too good for her; she should be lying in bed with a deadly disease instead. His once-tan complexion was turning paler by the minute, and he almost resembled a corpse. Josie fought against those dark thoughts. This couldn't happen.

She knelt beside Travis's bed as he drifted off into a deep sleep, a sleep Josie wasn't sure he'd wake from. Folding her shaking hands together, she closed her eyes, saying a prayer with the most faith she could muster.

"Lord, please forgive me for these sorrowful thoughts. I want to have all the faith I can in You, but the past of mine comes back to haunt me, tempting me to think the worst. I know You have the ability to heal."

Josie looked down at Travis's hand, intertwining her fingers in his. His pulse was slower than usual, but Josie tried to focus on the good. His chest rose and fell rhythmically with each breath. He was still alive, and there was still hope.

"Lord, I know I haven't been the best wife to this man through my deceptions, but I know you have forgiven me as Travis has. I ask you now, with the humbleness in my heart, that You'd heal the man and boy I love more than life itself. Whatever Your will is, let it be done."

In another situation, Josie would gasp at her sudden declaration. She looked down at Travis's pale face, plastered with sweat. She loved this man. She genuinely loved him. Josie shifted her gaze to Jonas across the room, still sleeping in his bed. He was alive, too. He had just enough of a chance as Travis did.

CHAPTER THIRTY-FOUR

Travis pulled the covers tighter around himself as chills coursed through his body. Weakness weighed him to the point he could barely lift his eyelids, feeling as if they were made of lead. Suddenly, warm fingertips brushed against his face.

"Travis? Travis, can you hear me?" a sweet voice asked.

Travis attempted to move his arms to grasp the woman's hand, seeking more warmth, but his limbs were heavy and unresponsive. He tried to open his mouth to speak, but a fiery pain stung his throat, rendering him mute. A cold rag laid upon his forehead, making his chills rise.

"I know it's cold, but your fever is too high. I need it to cool down."

The woman left the cold towel resting on his forehead before quietly slipping out of the room, her footsteps fading away. Travis lay on his back, utterly unable to move, his mind swirling with confusion. The more he thought, the dizzier he became. After a while, he sensed another blanket being draped over him, and with each layer, the shivers began to lessen.

Moments passed again, and heat rushed from the foot of his bed to his legs. Each time he moved his feet farther down, the heat grew stronger.

"Don't move too far down. They are hot bricks."

The space beside him sank as the woman's warm body settled close to him. She gently dabbed the cold cloth over his face, her touch soothing against his fevered skin.

After a few minutes, Travis summoned the strength to slowly open his eyes. As his vision cleared, he recognized his children's room. He turned his head toward the woman, a soft glow surrounding her. A smile crossed his face as he took her in. He never thought he would see the woman he loved more than life itself again.

"Sophie," he whispered.

She hesitated then smiled, taking hold of his hand in hers. "Yes, Travis?"

"I-I can't believe you're here."

Sophie continued dabbing the cool rag on his face. "I'm here, but you must rest. You must get better."

"B-But I-I want to be with you, Sophie. P-Please don't . . . go again."

Sophie's grip tightened on his arm. "I'll be here. Just rest."

Travis's eyes filled with tears, hot, stinging tears. He had so many things he wanted to say, but his voice was too hoarse. Still, it would be worth every word to endure the pain. He wanted to lift his arms and embrace her against him. He wanted to kiss her until his lips turned blue. *Oh, Sophie.* A year without her had been unbearable.

Sophie adjusted the covers to his neck and kissed his forehead. "Rest, Travis. The children need you. You must get better for them."

Travis closed his eyes. He had to rest and get better for the children, but he wanted to see Sophie one last time.

Hearing Travis's words brought Josie back into reality. After playing the caring and loving wife for the past two days, she was abruptly put back into her place. How foolish of her to think Travis could suddenly stop loving his late wife and love her instead. After Josie and Travis married, he made it clear he couldn't love her. The best thing he could do was provide for her and the children.

How could Travis throw away a decade of marriage and just start over with someone new? He barely knew Josie, and there was nothing to love about her. She was a damaged young widow who sought to deceive a poor farmer into marrying her and keeping her baby safe. She was a murderess who could be discovered any day and sent to the gallows, only to shame the sweet family and town. She was nothing like the Sophie he and everyone else in town described. That woman would never do what Josie did. Sophie was loveable, and Josie was a disease who was unworthy of it all.

Travis avoided her like the plague for months, and trying everything in her power to nourish him back to health wouldn't change a thing. Josie was just a mail order bride—nothing more. Even his delirium confirmed so.

Rising from the bedside, Josie stood tall and pulled her shoulders back. She wouldn't cry about this. More serious matters demanded attention. Jonas was in the bed next to Travis, still feverish. She needed to pull herself together and focus on others' problems rather than her own. Josie removed herself from Travis's presence and sat next to Jonas. He was sleeping soundly, but when she placed her hand on his forehead, she noticed he wasn't as hot as usual. Her thrumming pulse slowed to a normal pace. Jonas would be all right. This marked the first improvement she noticed.

"Thank you, Lord."

Josie kissed the top part of Jonas's head. His eyelids fluttered open, and his eyes weren't as cloudy as they had been.

"Josie?" he said, his voice hoarse.

Josie ran her fingers through Jonas's plastered curls. "I'm here. How are you feeling?"

"A little better."

Tears ambled down Josie's cheeks as she smiled. "Your fever broke."

Jonas's blue eyes widened. "It did?"

Josie grabbed some pillows to prop behind Jonas. "Can you sit up? I'm going to fix you some broth. Aunt Polly is here. She's been taking care of you, too."

Jonas's little body straightened against the pile of pillows. He had lost a few pounds the past few days since he hadn't eaten, but Josie was confident he'd gain it all back soon. Josie went to the kitchen, seeing Aunt Polly sweeping the floor. Josie smiled with delight, standing before her aunt-in-law. Aunt Polly turned, dropping the broom upon noticing Josie's expression.

"Jonas's fever has broken!"

Aunt Polly gasped, immediately embracing Josie. She trembled in her arms, her tears dampening Josie's dress. "Thank God! Thank our wonderful God!"

Josie stepped back, gathering her petticoat as she scurried towards the stove where a pot of broth rested. "I'm going to take him some broth. The boy must be famished."

Aunt Polly took off down the hallway, not bothering to respond. Such a joyous time. Their Lord had not abandoned them. If she could have faith He'd heal Jonas, then He could heal Travis too. That be, if it was God's will.

Josie poured the broth into a bowl, hardly able to wipe the smile from her face. Jonas's recovery had been the light of the day thus far. She sighed, pushing away the event from earlier. She had more pressing concerns than her husband loving a woman far too perfect for Josie to compete with. Josie brought the broth into the bedroom, where Aunt Polly sat at Jonas's bedside, brushing his hair with her hands. Jonas glanced over at Travis; fear etched across his brow and in his eyes.

"Is Pa gonna be all right?"

Josie didn't know how to answer. Jonas was never as bad as Travis. Travis's illness progressed rapidly, bringing different symptoms—delirium and dehydration. His swollen tonsils made it nearly impossible for him to drink.

Josie dipped Jonas's spoon into the bowl and gently blew over it. "I have faith God will take care of Pa like He did you."

Jonas opened his mouth, sipping some of the broth. Josie glanced over at Travis, who shivered and muttered Sophie's name. His head shifted from side to side as he wrestled with the covers. Aunt Polly rose from Jonas's bed and moved to Travis's side. She placed a hand on his forehead, then turned to Josie. Her bottom lip quivered as she slowly shook her head.

Josie pressed her lips together. She was right about one thing—only God could take care of Travis now. Her job was to surrender it to Him. There was only so much she could do.

Chapter Thirty-Five

Wildflowers brushed against Travis's legs, swaying with the wind. Sophie had always adored this meadow, cherishing each flower whether she knew its name or not. The snow had melted, welcoming spring once more. A cool mountain breeze wrapped around him, carrying the scent of fresh earth as grass and wildflowers danced in harmony. Everything here felt untouched, unspoiled—a haven of quiet perfection. This was Sophie's place, where her spirit seemed to linger, as beautiful and free as the wind.

Then his breath left his lungs. Sophie appeared before him, wearing her familiar white-and-blue calico dress, her copper-brown hair stopping at her waist. She looked as radiant as ever. The moment felt too real, blurring the line between dream and reality. Was this truly happening? Sophie turned to face him, a soft smile on her lips, holding a bouquet just as she always had. The setting sun bathed her in a warm glow as she stepped toward him.

Travis's heart raced, his legs trembling. He couldn't just stand there—he had to reach her. Without hesitation, he desperately broke into a run, afraid she might disappear before he could hold her again.

He didn't stop until she was in his arms, his hands sliding around her slender waist as he pulled her close, embracing her against him. He buried his face in her neck, inhaling the scent of honeysuckles. Travis sighed, closing his eyes as he laid a kiss against her temple. Tears blurred his vision while he cupped Sophie's face, studying every inch of her. *My wife, my darling wife.* Her green eyes met his, those innocent eyes he'd never forget.

"My sweet Sophie. Tell me this is real. I beg you."

Travis leaned in to kiss her lips. Her kisses were like a drug to him, and the year without them had been pure agony. Now, with her back in his arms, he had the chance he never thought he'd get again, and he wasn't about to let it slip away.

Before his lips could touch hers, Sophie pulled back. Travis's brows furrowed in confusion. This wasn't like her. They had been apart for so long—why would Sophie turn away from a moment they both craved?

"Travis, I can't let you kiss me. It's wrong."

Wrong? Sophie had always been a good teaser, but something in him said this wasn't one of her flirty tricks. Why would she torture him again when her lips were so close?

"How is this wrong? You're my wife, Sophie. I vowed till death do us part."

"Travis," Sophie said softly. "Death did us part."

Travis shook his head, his grip tightening around her back, holding her closer. "No, we're together again. You're here with me now. We can start again, you and me."

Sophie removed his arms, pulling them to her sides. "You can't join me . . . not yet. You must be there for the children. They need you now more than ever. You can't leave them without a father."

The children were everything to Travis. He couldn't leave them, but when he looked at Sophie, he couldn't help but think about his selfish desires. He had already moved on without her and was now starting a new beginning with Josie. He knew she carried secrets, ones she hadn't yet revealed, but her caring and selfless nature never wavered.

He remembered the first time he made Josie laugh—the way her eyes squinted and her laughter spilled out, soft and musical like a melody. His mind wandered to the day he braved a blizzard to fetch Aunt Polly to deliver Nathan. Holding the child in his arms for the first time, he felt a rush of warmth he hadn't understood then, but now he did. The day he found Josie ill in the fields was the moment he realized he'd risk everything for her—and he had, more than once.

Travis's soul ached as he gazed into Sophie's face. How could he betray her? How could he let these thoughts consume him while holding the woman he had loved all his life in his arms?

Sophie lifted Travis's chin. "It's all right to love her, Travis. I gave you my blessing long ago when I left this earth. I want you to be happy. You won't betray me because I want you to live on with the joy life brings. You need Josie, and she needs you. You must go home to her and the children."

Travis pressed his lips together and closed his eyes, fighting to restrain his tears. He had already made his decision, but he wanted to savor this moment with Sophie one last time. He wrapped his arms around her and ran his fingers through her soft hair, just as he had done thousands of times before.

"I'm sorry, Sophie. Everything was my fault. I should have known what having another baby would do."

Sophie dried his tears with her fingers. "And it was all worth it. Please know that, Travis. Know that when you look at our son every day. Without your sacrifice to let me go, he wouldn't be here." Sophie pressed a kiss to the top of his forehead.

"I love you, Sophie," Travis whispered.

"And I love you," Sophie said with a smile. "Now, go to them. Live life to the fullest and tell the children how much I love them."

"Travis? Can you hear me?"

Travis's eyes fluttered open to the sight of Josie's tear-streaked face, her brown eyes puffy and red. Glistening tears clung to her cheeks, and his heart tightened at the worry etched into her features.

"Jo," he whispered hoarsely.

Josie touched his forehead, her expression melting into a happy grin. "Your fever has broken."

Josie adjusted pillows behind him and assisted him up. Travis groaned as she guided his body upward like a bag of feed. She was infinitely stronger than he thought, or maybe he was the weak one. Then his heart drummed against his chest as Josie unexpectedly leaned into him, her arms wrapping around him. He paused for a moment, then carefully lifted a hand, resting it behind her head. He threaded his fingers through her soft hair while she sobbed against him.

"I thought I lost you. You were growing worse by the minute."

Travis caressed her neck, tracing the skin with his fingertips. Sophie was right; Josie was exactly who his family needed. Here she was, devoting her time to him and Jonas and now showing how much she cared for him as her tears hit his shirt. Seeing Sophie had to be delirium, but why did it feel so real? Whatever it was, he experienced a wave of peace, coming over him like a warm blanket. He missed having Sophie in his arms, but waking up to Josie, a woman who risked her life and motherhood to care for him and his son, made him respect her more.

She had risked everything to care for him and Jonas. Nathan needed his mother, but Josie was at their side, her eyes baggy and red from exhaustion.

"Thank you, Jo," he muttered, his eyelids heavy. "Thank you . . . for everything."

Josie wiped her tears and smiled. "Jonas's fever broke. Yesterday he sat up and started drinking broth. He's asleep now, but he's going to be all right."

Travis tilted his head, his gaze shifting to Jonas, who was sleeping soundly in the bed beside him. The boy's color had returned, giving Travis relief. With a deep exhalation, he closed his eyes and whispered a quiet prayer. "Thank you, Lord."

"The children are still at the parsonage. After I burn these blankets and get the extras from the barn storage, we can all live together again."

"Good." Travis cleared his throat and winced. "I'm ready to get out of this bed and put myself to use."

Josie chuckled softly, her hand resting on his chest. "You will in time, but first we must get your strength back up." She stood. "I'll fetch you some broth."

When Josie left the room, Travis closed his eyes. After waking with Josie there, new feelings swelled through him—more than gratitude and stronger than before. Was this love—or was he just trying too hard? Love was supposed to come naturally and unquestioned. If he genuinely loved her, wouldn't he have loved her from first sight like he did with Sophie? He had only loved one woman, so this was an entirely new experience.

But one thing bothered him—Josie had a hard life in the past, being married to a cruel man. Had she ever known love? Did she trust Travis enough to give him her heart?

CHAPTER THIRTY-SIX

Montana Territory; Early January 1873

GENERAL WATCHED AS THE fire crackled, pulling his newly bought buffalo coat tighter around his shoulders. The frigid cold was far worse than he had imagined, and he endured harsh winters during his military career. Yet this Rocky Mountain chill was something else entirely. Even though his anger simmered just beneath the surface, it wasn't enough to chase away the deep, aching cold that seeped into his bones.

If Josephine wanted revenge, she was getting it, all right. General had to admit her plan was clever—but not clever enough. Only a hundred miles separated him from the endgame. She would lose, and he would win. He could hardly wait for that prize.

Buck Hanson smacked and took another bite of canned beans. "Ya got any family, General?"

"Sadly."

Buck's eyebrows arched for a moment before he burst into chuckles. "That there's a good one. Sometimes they're blessin's, but other times, they're nightmares."

General huffed and looked up at the night sky, folding his arms over his body. One thing the newspapers got right was that Montana truly was the land of the big sky. However, with the many clouds above, he could hardly see the stars.

"You meetin' family out there?"

"Something like that."

Buck swirled his spoon around in his can. "Ya never told me much 'bout your mission. I just assumed it was family. Didn't know for sure. Ya seem mighty anxious to get there."

"I'm going to fetch my wife and my heir."

"Heir?" Buck snorted. "Guess that's what you bigwigs call 'em. Boy or gal?"

"Don't know."

"Hope it's a lad?"

"Wouldn't be any use for a girl."

Buck shrugged. "I'm sure you'd love it all the same."

General nearly vomited at the word. "Love is a weak emotion."

Buck leaned back against a tree, taking a spoonful of beans. "Why'd you say that?"

Frustration swelled through General, a hot wave burning beneath his skin. Why did this man have to ask so many questions? Buck had been a soldier once—he should've learned to bury those silly emotions long ago. The constant prying, the need for conversation; it was all unnecessary. They were both hardened men, or at least, they were supposed to be.

"Love makes a man weak."

"What does your wife say?"

"She'll get what's coming to her," General muttered.

Buck sat straighter, setting down his empty can. "What ya mean?"

General groaned, ripping a piece of bark from the log he was sitting on. "I married my wife because she was young. She was supposed to give me four sons by now, but she was too frail." General gritted his teeth. "She blamed me for every complication, saying it was because of my discipline. Now she stole my heir."

Buck's eyes widened, his forehead creased. "You beat her?"

General's jaw jutted. "I taught her a lesson. She was stubborn and pathetic. She needed to be put in her place for losing my heirs."

"She's a woman, General!" Buck's frown deepened. "Ya had no right to do that. She couldn't help losin' those babies!"

"You sound just like her!"

"Well, maybe ya should hear it from a man rather than a woman. Maybe you'd listen!"

General stood and pointed in Buck's face. "This is none of your concern!"

"It is when ya're headin' in their direction. Somethin' tells me ya have more than a beatin' on your mind." Buck's lips pressed to a thin line.

General groaned and pivoted on his feet, stomping forcefully through the snow. "We're a hundred miles away from Gallatin County. You don't *need* to escort me anymore." He untied the reins of his newly purchased horse and led it to the wagon to grab his supplies. As he retrieved his bedroll, he heard a click. He turned to see Buck pointing a revolver at him.

"Sorry it has to be this way. I respected ya, but now, I gotta protect that woman and babe."

"You're weak," General spat. "I wouldn't doubt you were a deserter."

Buck's face shook with fury, and before he could pull the trigger, General lunged forward, grabbing his arm and thrusting it to the side. A shot fired, and General wrestled the gun from Buck's grip, only for him to drop it on the icy ground. General's fist met Buck's face, causing him to grunt. Buck growled, his eyes wild, and grabbed General by the collar, slamming a punch into his gut. Pain flared through General's abdomen. With a roar, he charged into Buck's midsection, tackling him.

General gripped his hands around Buck's neck, but Buck overpowered him, pushing him over until General's back was on the ground. Buck's fist plunged into General's face. A metallic taste filled his mouth. With a replenishing rush of energy, he pushed Buck off him and grabbed a knife from his belt.

Without hesitation, he stabbed it into Buck's gut. Buck screamed, and General pushed harder and twisted. He smiled as Buck's eyes met his with intensity.

"Don't . . . you . . . touch her," Buck whispered, blood trickling out his mouth.

General stood, pride consuming him. He wiped the wet blood from his face and grinned. *The road to revenge only gets sweeter.*

CHAPTER
THIRTY-SEVEN

JOSIE BURNED THE FINAL quilt, its beautifully stitched patterns curling in the flames while she watched from the porch. The fire crackled and hissed, the bright fabric slowly turning to ash. She had no way of knowing how long it would take for Travis to mend, but with each passing hour, Jonas improved. He was already joking around and playing with his toys again, telling stories about his wooden animals.

After two days without fever or symptoms, Aunt Polly and Josie moved Travis to Josie's bedroom. He could hardly walk, but with both of their strength, they were able to assist him without any complications. Josie couldn't recall a time in the past seven years when she'd been more worried. The man she desperately cared for had been on the verge of death while Jonas was in the clear. The uncertainty had hung over them like a dark cloud, wondering if God would grant them another miracle, and He had. Josie felt so relieved that she was able to have faith again. The Lord delivered her and Nathan from the hands of Marcus, and now Jonas and Travis were healing.

However, the epidemic was still spreading through the valley like wildfire. According to Aunt Polly, not everyone was as lucky as them. Thankfully, the children were coming home because deep in her heart, she knew the Levingstons would be busy conducting funerals.

Josie had her share of funerals during the war, enough to last a lifetime. After the Battle of Shiloh, she had two funerals for Olivier and Trellis. Then a year later with Gettysburg, burying Zane. In February of 1865, she buried her mother and sister. Six months after marrying Marcus, her father died from a heart attack. She desperately hoped to never endure such a trial again.

"Josie!"

Josie lifted her gaze and spotted Aunt Polly holding Nathan in the wagon, while the other children rode in the back. Overwhelmed by longing, after a week and a half apart, she rushed towards them without a second thought. Aunt Polly halted the wagon, and Ivy—cradling Gideon—and Lillian climbed down. Josie knelt to their level, enveloping them in a warm embrace. The short separation felt like an eternity. She kissed the tops of their heads, wishing she could hold them forever.

"I missed y'all so much."

"Please don't send us away ever again," Lillian begged.

Josie ran her fingers along the brim of Lillian's snow cap. "I agree. I never want to be separated from the four of you another minute." Josie pinched Gideon's cheeks. "You've grown too much, little man."

Gideon giggled and squirmed in Ivy's arms. Josie hastily stood to see Nathan. She felt as if part of her soul had escaped her body, being separated from her flesh and blood. Aunt Polly laid him gently in Josie's arms. His blue eyes had a hint of brown. Josie's heart skipped a beat. *Brown eyes.* He was going to have brown eyes just like her. She drew him close against her chest, determined never to let him go again.

"I missed you, sweet boy." Josie looked up at Aunt Polly, who was bundled in her buffalo-hide. "Was he all right? Did he cause any problems for Rose and the reverend?"

Aunt Polly smiled and touched the top of Nathan's bundled head. "Not at all. He was so precious, and Rose hated to give him back. Andy and Paul enjoyed playing with him. They're already asking for a baby brother."

"Maybe you can make Rose a magic potion," Josie teased, bouncing her son up and down.

Aunt Polly chuckled, her hands resting on her hips. "I'll start today. The valley should be overrun with young'uns."

"Where's Pa and Jonas?" Lillian asked, tugging at Josie's wool skirt.

"Jonas is in his bed, and your pa is resting."

"Can we see them?" Ivy asked, struggling to keep her squirming brother from tugging at her hair.

"If you're quiet. They need time to recover, so don't tire them out."

Ivy put Gideon down, and he chased after them inside, his chubby legs hardly able to work in the snow. It made Josie's heart ache to see Gideon walking. She missed the day she'd carried him in her arms and cuddled him. It didn't matter if she was pregnant with Nathan or not—he was her first baby.

"We have five deaths so far—some settlers homesteading east of the Kents," Aunt Polly said as they slogged their way to the cabin door.

Josie's lips pressed to a solemn frown. "I know how it feels to lose family to an unexpected illness. When the fever started, I almost lost my mind with worry. Nearly losing Travis—" Josie paused. She wanted to say more—so much that she thought she'd burst. But she needed to keep those thoughts buried, just like her dark secret she tried to forget. "I-I was so frightened, Aunt Polly. I thought I was going to lose him days ago. I couldn't bear that."

"And does Travis know about this? Have you told him how you feel?"

Josie's breathing grew shallow as she held Nathan tighter, willing every ounce of her strength not to spill too much, but she loved Aunt Polly so dearly. The woman was the only person who knew a small piece of what Josie hid from the town. Josie closed her eyes, remembering the painful scene during Travis's delirium.

"I'd look like a fool and ruin everything. While he was sick, he was delirious for two days. He . . . kept calling out Sophie's name, and I know he'd never love me when she is still in his heart. It's ten years of marriage that can never be replaced." Josie sighed and looked at her feet. "I'll forever be his mail-order bride."

Aunt Polly placed her hand on Josie's shoulder. "I would say sit down because we need to talk this out slowly, but out here, there's snow past our ankles and inside is full of chaos. Sophie and Travis had been in love for over ten years. From being a widow myself, I can see how hard it is for him to love again, but you must be patient. He respects you, and I know in my heart, he will grow to love you because he would be crazy not to."

Josie cradled Nathan's face close to her chest, keeping him warm for a few extra moments. "All I know about marriage is pain and abuse. This marriage . . . It's different, and I want it to work. Travis is a good man, and him being a father to my son should be enough, but the feelings I have are complicated. I don't know how to control them. I've never—I've never loved anyone like this."

Aunt Polly smiled. "Love is a beautiful thing, isn't it?"

"It is."

"You and Travis will be in my prayers."

"Thank you, Aunt Polly."

Josie and Aunt Polly entered the warm cabin as little Jonas and the other children's laughter echoed from the next room. It was the kind of joy Jonas had desperately needed over the past week. Travis still rested in Josie's bedroom, and she couldn't resist wondering what he might be dreaming about. But that thought faded; it no longer mattered.

She had to trust that their marriage was in God's hands and that whatever happened was meant to be.

As the sun set and darkness settled into the cabin, Josie gently tucked the children into bed. For the first time, Gideon nestled beside his brother instead of sleeping in a crib, their small bodies close together under the warm blankets. Josie closed the bedroom door and went to check on Travis. He'd slept all afternoon and evening, so the children were unable to see him. Surviving the deadly disease was a miracle, and while his recovery would take longer, Josie had faith Travis would heal completely.

He was a tough man, eager to work again once his fever broke. Knowing Travis's stubbornness and need to provide, Josie knew in her heart it would be hard to keep him in bed. He would tend to the livestock then return to the mercantile for extra work. Josie had a feeling there would be more jobs to fill after the tragedies.

Josie opened the bedroom door and found Travis sound asleep. His chest rhythmically moved up and down as he breathed. His color had returned, and he didn't look like a corpse anymore. It was nice to see Travis as the man in her memory. She thought back to the day he greeted her at the stagecoach, clean-shaven and in a brown suit and loose necktie. Except now his face was stubbly and his hair long and tangled.

Josie peered at the crib, seeing the sleeping Nathan warmly swaddled in a bear-fur blanket. Josie settled into the rocker in the corner after retrieving a quilt from the wardrobe. She placed it over her legs, rocking gently as she closed her eyes. She considered making a pallet by the fireplace like Travis had since the cooler weather set in, but after nearly losing him, she couldn't bring herself to leave his side—just as she couldn't with Nathan.

Thankfully, her milk supply hadn't completely dried, so she was confident that within another week she'd be productive enough for him to have more than a meal a day. Nathan had slept beside her since birth, but after their separation, he had gotten used to life without her. The thought broke Josie's heart, but she knew the day had come.

Rocking in the chair made Josie think about her own mother. Mammy would care for Josie all day, and at night, Mama wanted all the time in the world with Josie. She'd dismiss Mammy early, just to rock Josie to sleep. Josie enjoyed being in her mother's arms, hearing her lullabies. Now, she was a mother herself, and she hoped to be the same type of mother to Nathan.

"Why are you sleeping over there?"

Josie opened her eyes. Travis sat upright against the headboard, wide awake. The moonlight reflected over him through the window like a halo.

"I thought you were asleep," Josie whispered.

"I was waiting on you . . . and resting my eyes," Travis confessed. "I thought you'd be here next to me."

The vessels in Josie's face burned hot like coal. She couldn't tell if Travis was teasing her or if he spoke with genuine seriousness.

"W-Why would you think that?"

"Because this is your bed."

Josie held the blanket close to her bosom, concealing her cotton nightdress, but it didn't matter because Travis had seen a much more revealing gown on their so-called wedding night.

"It was yours first. I thought I'd stay here with you in case you needed me . . . and because Nathan is in the crib. I'll need to be close by when he cries."

Travis patted the empty side of the bed. "Come on up. You can be close enough here."

Her breath hitched. Her heart pounded like a runaway horse. Was Travis being serious? Or . . . was this a test to see what her true feelings were? Had Aunt Polly told him what she said in confidence? *Surely she didn't.*

Josie swallowed a lump and crept slowly and carefully to Travis's side. Her legs wobbled with each step, and her hands shivered. She placed one hand over the other, trying to hide her fear. Was this fear? She trusted Travis. Surely he wasn't asking anything intimate, especially while still recovering. She settled on the end, waiting for him to speak his next wish.

"I think you'd be a better nurse if you were closer to me." Travis peeled back the covers.

Josie steadily stuck her bare legs under, drawn to the warmth radiating from Travis's body. She had never been so close to him. Not like this, under the same covers. Travis pressed his head against his pillow and faced her. Josie pulled the covers to her chin, but the rest of her body laid stiff as a board.

Josie held her breath. Why did she suddenly feel frightened lying next to her husband? She shut her eyes. *He's nothing like Marcus. Forget about him. This is Travis, and you trust him.*

"I wanted to confess something that I have yet to," Travis whispered. "I've told you I am grateful for you, but . . . I never told you how blessed I am that you found me. I don't know how life would be if Aunt Polly never suggested I'd find a wife."

Josie smiled and giggled softly. "I guess you can thank Aunt Tia for that."

"I wish I could've met her. She sounded like a remarkable woman, just like you."

Josie bit her lip. Aunt Tia was up in age, but her intelligence never faltered. Josie wished she could have gone back in time and thanked her personally for this new life. She had been so bitter when Aunt Tia suggested it, but the woman had been right all along.

"I don't know what I would've done without her."

Be at the gallows, that's what. A shiver crawled up Josie's spine. She tried to forget long enough, but it weighed her down, pulling her into the darkness every time she had a happy thought. Travis already forgave her for her deception, but could he forgive murder?

"Have you decided what you'd do with your inheritance?" Travis asked.

Josie hadn't thought about the inheritance for so long. What vexed her most was how her lawyer had managed to find her, yet no warrants had been issued for her arrest. None of it sat right. She had cut all ties with North Carolina, leaving that life behind as best she could.

"I don't know," she murmured. "So much has happened, and it slipped my mind."

"I've been pondering about it since I've been trapped in this bed. I think you should put it in Nathan's name since she was his aunt, too. Then when the timing is right, he can make a choice to either stay here or make something of himself."

The thought was almost too perfect to be true. Josie tried to forget North Carolina, but she didn't have a reason to shield Nathan from it. One day he'd ask questions about his father, and he had a right to make a choice. He could make more of himself in North Carolina than Montana.

"But . . . who would run the estate until then?"

"The lawyer seems to be running it well. Let him handle it."

Josie bit her inner cheek. "Are you sure? That's an awful load to carry for at least twenty years."

Travis placed his hand over Josie's. "God will take care of it all, just as He did this week. I trust our Heavenly Father more than before, and I will never be doubtful again."

Josie turned her head towards Travis. "Me too."

Travis's arm slowly came around her, bringing her closer to him. As the right side of her body pressed against his, warmth traveled from her chest all the way to her toes. Josie's heart skipped. She didn't know whether to speak or move. She stayed still, staring into his eyes. He caressed her cheek with the back of his hand.

"Jo," he whispered. "I want this to work between us."

Her lungs pinched. She tried to inhale a breath, but she didn't know what to do. Had she heard him correctly?

"Me too."

The words slipped out effortlessly, without thought or restraint. Josie's pulse raced in her throat as Travis leaned closer, his mouth inches from hers. She ached for his touch, she longed for his kisses, but fragments of her nightmares echoed in her mind, drowning out her desire. A cold shiver raced down Josie's spine, bumps rising on her skin.

Marcus's hand latched around her throat, his scarred eye glaring with intensity.

The sound of him hitting the floor, the pool of blood running down the marble tiles.

Josie ripped away and turned her back to Travis, clutching the sheets as her breath hitched unevenly. The law would come for her eventually—it was only a matter of time. How could Travis hold her so closely, so intimately, when he didn't know the whole truth? She couldn't bear the thought of hurting him again, not when he wanted so badly for this to work.

Lingering in his arms or treading another step forward in their marriage felt impossible. She wasn't quite free from her past, not when she could be arrested any day. Josie wasn't sure when that day would come, but she craved freedom more than anything.

"I'm sorry . . . I-I can't . . . Not now."

Travis scooted away until their bodies were no longer touching. "I'm sorry, Jo. I shouldn't have acted so forward."

Josie shook her head. "No . . . It's my fault. I desperately want to make this work but . . ."

Tell him, tell him now. Josie shut her eyes, fighting her urge to cry. Her efforts were in vain as a tear drizzled down her cheek. The truth would set her free, but why was freedom miles away? How could she put this family through another heartbreak? It was better to remain distant once again than to submit to her growing feelings. This was the best choice for both of them.

Travis rolled onto his side, facing her back. Just him looking at her was as comforting as his touch, but she couldn't bear to look at him.

"I think some rest would do us good," he whispered.

Josie laid still on her side, staring at the wall. After rejecting him, she couldn't bring herself to see the sadness she sensed in his voice. "Yes."

Silence returned as though it was their companion. Josie pulled the covers to her chin. She was so close to having a real marriage with Travis, but now she was at the very beginning. Every bit of healing she believed she had gained vanished. Josie had believed her darkness would fade the day Nathan was born, but each ounce of light she gained was replaced by a sliver of gloom.

Josie looked over her shoulder. She wanted the man more than anything, but her pain and secret pushed him further from her reach. Perhaps a life together was all a hopeless dream, even if she told him the truth.

CHAPTER
THIRTY-EIGHT

TRAVIS AWOKE THE NEXT morning with a rush of energy. After days of rest, he felt strong enough to shovel all the snow from his front yard. Though still recovering, he sensed his strength slowly returning. Rolling over, he spotted Josie sleeping beside him. She looked absolutely breathtaking, her blonde hair tousled and her eyes closed in peaceful slumber. Propping himself on his elbow, Travis rested his head on his hand and gazed at his wife. He had feared that inviting her into his bed might fill him with guilt or discomfort, but instead, all he felt was peace.

He was determined to make this marriage work. Not just for the children, but for each other. There couldn't be any more distance between them. Travis refused to miss another blessing from God, not after being given a second chance at life. He would dedicate the rest of his days to making Josie happy.

What troubled him was the way Josie had acted last night. Perhaps he went too far. After all, she was the one who rejected him. Perhaps an evening meal with candlelight could have been a better solution to bring them together. Josie wasn't ready for physical touch or intimacy. One moment, she looked happy; the next, fear flashed in her eyes. He must have misread her intentions.

The thought of her past life disgusted him. Travis wished he could turn back time and confront Marcus, take him down with his bare hands—but that was impossible. Fate had served justice the day Marcus was buried in the ground. Josie didn't deserve the treatment she endured, and Travis would spend each day proving she was safe. More than anything, he wanted to hold her, kiss her, and show her there was more to life than fear.

Travis raised his hand to caress Josie's cheek but caught himself just in time. His heart stopped as Josie's eyes fluttered open, and he quickly pulled back. He longed to offer her tenderness every morning, to show her how much he cared. But for now, he would rely on words of affirmation.

"Good morning, my beautiful wife."

He wasn't sure how she'd feel about his endearment, but it slipped out. He was relieved to finally express what he had been thinking since the day she arrived. His wife was a beautiful creation, shaped and formed by the same God who had saved their lives and brought them together.

A soft smile tugged at the corners of her strawberry lips. "Good morning."

Travis sat against the headboard. "How did you sleep?"

"All right. How about you? Are you feeling better?" Josie sat up too, pulling the covers to her chest. Travis fought back a smile—he loved seeing his wife's modesty. It reminded him of their wedding night. Her beauty was undeniably tempting, but he knew he had to wait until the timing was right. For now, he'd court Josie, cherishing every moment until the day they were ready to take this marriage further.

"I feel like I could chop some firewood later," Travis said with a wink.

Josie exhaled dramatically. "You need to rest or else you'll never get better in time."

"What's for breakfast?"

Josie stood and grabbed a gray shawl, pulling it around her shoulders. "Probably biscuits and gravy. We have plenty of flour left in the pantry, along with milk and butter on ice." She undid her braid and ran her fingers through her waist-length hair.

"The advantages of being a wheat farmer," Travis muttered. He pushed the covers aside and stood in his nightshirt. He couldn't resist enjoying the way Josie blushed when his bare legs emerged from the covers. She wiped the back of her neck and cleared her throat before turning her attention to Nathan. He seemed to be sound asleep because she didn't bother to pick him up.

"I'll be in the kitchen if you need me," she said, darting off towards the door.

Travis's heart sank when the door clicked shut. Spending their first night together was an adjustment to bring them closer. He already felt more connected to his wife than ever before, yet a barrier still remained between them. He couldn't tell if Josie was keeping him out or if fear held her back. Whatever it was, he prayed she would overcome it rather than pull away. He had cherished the warmth of her body pressed against his—it gave him hope that someday, they would leave the past behind them.

Travis grabbed a clean shirt and patched work pants. He'd worn the same night shirt for almost a week. He hadn't had the energy to change into it beforehand when he was sick, but it was far better than the feel of rough pants against the sheets. Travis still felt a little frail and dizzy but being excited about growing closer to Josie made him stronger. He was ready to spend each day with her, eager to learn everything about her while sorting through the whirlwind of emotions stirring inside him. Lying beside her at night stirred feelings he could barely contain, threatening to push him beyond his control.

After dressing, Travis walked out the door, finding Josie kneading the biscuit dough in a bowl atop the table. He wanted to embrace her from behind and kiss her cheek, but it would be too much for her. After seeing her panic when he leaned in to kiss her, he realized there were certain things he needed to approach with care. He needed patience. Everything would be worth the wait whenever the timing was right.

Travis pulled out a chair and settled himself at the table. It felt good to be in his kitchen instead of confined to the bedroom. Josie huffed and placed her flour-covered hands on her hips.

"You're supposed to be resting."

Travis chuckled. "You can't keep me there for much longer. It gets lonely."

Josie shook her head, focusing on her tasks as she rolled the dough into small balls, placing them neatly in the cast-iron pan. In just a minute or two, she put the biscuits in the oven. Josie wiped her hands on a rag, then sat in front of Travis.

"I thought we could talk about . . . last night," she said.

Travis nodded, his ears warming. "I thought you'd bring it up."

Josie closed her eyes, sucking in a breath then exhaling. "I am deeply sorry about what happened. I'm just . . ."

Travis leaned forward. "You don't have to explain. I know what you went through was unacceptable—"

"It's not just that . . ." Josie looked down at her clasped hands and released a slow breath. "Why now? Why do you want this to work?"

Travis opened his mouth, but his words were cut short by the sound of the door creaking open. Aunt Polly stepped in, bundled in her layered coats. The color had faded from her face, and she didn't seem as happy as she had the day before.

"What is it, Aunt Polly?" Travis asked.

She stepped forward, clutching her hat in her hand and looking down. "The Walshes came down with the fever when you and Jonas did . . . the twin boy, Brendon . . . he passed on."

Travis leaned back against the chair in shock, his jaw dropping open.

"My goodness," Josie whispered. She pressed her hand against her chest. "Poor Caroline."

Aunt Polly bit her lip. "He was only a year older than Gideon." She sniffed and wiped her nose. "There are so many others who aren't as lucky as we are . . . I just never thought it would hit this hard—especially for the Walshes."

"I—I can't believe it," Travis said, his voice catching as a lump formed in his throat. "The boy was in excellent health. How could this happen so fast?"

Josie moved her gaze to the biscuits baking in the oven. "I'll go over there to pay my respects. I must see Caroline. I'll bring the biscuits for the children."

"That is a wonderful thing to do," Aunt Polly whispered. "I'll make breakfast for the young'uns here and get them ready for the day."

"I'll go with you, Jo," Travis said. "I don't care if you want me to rest. Ronan is my friend—he was there for me when Sophie passed, and I need to be there for him now."

Josie nodded. "I won't protest. We'll go as soon as the biscuits are finished."

Travis bowed his head in prayer. The worst was over for his family, but there were so many battling this epidemic. The darkness had yet to lift.

Josie stood at the Walshes' cabin door, holding a basket of warm biscuits. Travis still looked pale and had a slight cough, but she would never discourage him from seeing his friends. Despite knowing Caroline for only a few months, she felt as if they had known each other much longer. Josie understood Caroline's grief. She, too, had lost children—except there had been no one to mourn with her.

Travis knocked at the door, and it wasn't long until Alice Walsh answered. Alice's long, red hair was puffy and tangled, appearing not to have been brushed in days. Her gray dress, worn and frayed, seemed too small for her lanky frame, barely reaching her calves.

"Good morning, Alice," Travis said, removing his hat. "We have come to pay our respects. Josie brought biscuits."

"Thank you both," she said, her eyes peering down. "We're very appreciative. Please, come in."

As soon as Josie stepped inside, she was taken aback by the cabin's cramped space and disorder. It had to be half the size of theirs. Dishes were piled beside the indoor water pump and clothes were hanging in every imaginable place to dry. Given that Caroline was part of the Boston upper class, Josie assumed the home to have damask-wallpapered walls, elegant lace tablecloths, fine china displayed in a cabinet, oil paintings, and delicate trinkets adorning the shelves, even above the fireplace mantel. But instead, it reminded her of the shacks where her father's slaves had dwelled.

The Walshes' floorboards creaked beneath Josie's weight, making her fear they might give way at any moment. She held her breath, fighting the urge to gag at the sharp stench of mildew. Despite the fire burning, a strong draft lingered in the rooms, sending a chill through her layers and making her shiver.

The other three children appeared, their pale faces streaked with tears. Nan, her hair in messy braids, looked like she hadn't bathed in days. Liam, the boy about Jonas's age, had a face smudged with soot, and his shoes were so worn they barely held together. Molly waddled behind them, her brows raised in confusion. Josie softened her expression and curved her lips into a gentle smile.

"I brought biscuits. Would you three like one?"

They nodded and reached into the basket.

"What do you say?" Alice asked, her hands on her hips.

"Thank you," the three of them muttered.

Alice appeared beside Josie. "They haven't spoken much . . . It's the same with Mama."

Josie observed as the children clutched the biscuits with their dirty hands, nibbling on them. In another life, Josie would be disgusted by the mannerisms and ask them to wash up, but there were more important things to pay attention to. Their baby brother had passed, putting a pause on the life they knew to be normal. This home looked like it hadn't felt a woman's touch in forever, which was understandable given what had happened.

"My father is in the barn, tending to livestock," Alice told Travis. "He'd love to see you."

Travis turned to Josie, touching her forearm. "I'll be back soon."

Josie's heart hung heavy as she watched Nan struggle to swallow through her grief. The sight reminded her of the weeks it took for her to eat again after the epidemic at *Belle Vallée*. She'd been paralyzed by sorrow until Mammy stepped in, coaxing her to take each bite, refusing to let her waste away. Josie glanced over at Alice, who kept a watchful eye on the children, her own sorrow etched in the lines of her face.

"I'd like to see your mother, if you don't mind."

Alice wrapped her arms around herself, her voice strained. "She'd appreciate your company, but she's not in a good state. She hasn't left the bed since last night. She won't say a word, just cries all the time. I'm really worried for her."

Josie touched the fourteen-year-old girl's shoulder. "I know this is going to be hard on your family for a while, but it will get better, I promise. God always heals the broken."

Alice's eyes, filled with concern, searched Josie's face. "But why? Why would he take such an innocent baby? Brendon did nothing wrong. The worst he did was spill flour all over the floor. I don't think God would punish anyone for that."

"I know how you're feeling. I wondered the same thing for many years after my family passed. I don't understand the Lord's will, but someday you will. God puts us through trials to test our faith, but He promises to never forsake His children. This trial is to bring you closer to Him, to show that you aren't alone."

Alice pulled Josie into a tight embrace. Alice sniffled, her face buried into Josie's shoulder. "Thank you, Mrs. Blythe. You have the kindest words."

Josie rubbed the girl's back with her fingertips. She could almost see her former self in Alice. Alice was young, now having to grow up so soon with young siblings to care for, along with an ailing mother. Josie prayed silently for Alice, hoping she would find the strength to grow through the trials ahead rather than be consumed by them, as Josie once had been.

Alice pulled away and dried the tears with her sleeve. "If you follow me, you can see my mother."

Josie followed Alice through a quilt divider and stepped into the cramped space where Caroline laid in a bed barely big enough for one person, let alone two. Around them were pallets scattered on the floor, where the children slept. Another divider stretched across the room, offering what little privacy could be afforded. Josie's stomach sank as she took in the sight of her friend. Caroline was pale as a sheet, her eyes red and swollen.

"Mama, Mrs. Blythe is here," Alice said.

Caroline studied Josie from head to toe, her eyes lingering as if measuring her, before swallowing. After a moment, she gave a slow nod.

Alice touched Josie's shoulder. "Take all the time you need."

Alice slipped through the quilt divider, and as Josie stepped forward, Caroline's grief enveloped her, stirring painful memories she longed to forget—clutching her abdomen in agony, screaming as she lost her babies. She remembered holding her first son in her arms, his tiny form still and cold, knowing he would never take his first breath. And Marcus—his cruel, unrelenting voice echoing in her mind—snatching her baby within minutes, declaring that it was all God's punishment for her failures as a wife.

Josie took a wobbly step, then settled on the bedside. She reached out, taking Caroline's cold hand. "Travis and I came to pay our respects to your family," Josie said softly, her voice steady despite the ache in her chest. "I asked Alice if I might see you, to be a comfort if you need me."

Caroline's expression reflected Josie's own past. Wide, vacant eyes that seemed to stare into nothingness, a face marked by denial, yet layered with consumed anger and bitterness. *Be a comfort and tell her.* Josie hadn't spoken aloud about her painful memory she wanted to keep buried, but in the presence of a woman who needed it, it came to the surface again for Josie to relive.

"I have been where you are, Caroline. I don't speak about it much, even with my own husband . . ." She paused, allowing the painful memory to rush back. Josie wanted to forget it and lie in bed like Caroline, angry at God, but she had to move on, to forgive God and let this memory go. "I had children before Nathan—three of them."

Caroline's gaze met Josie's, and though she remained silent, Josie could sense her attentiveness. Josie rubbed her thumbs together.

"I was married before Travis, and no one knows about it except him and Aunt Polly. My husband was an evil and brutal man, so evil he'd beat me, even when I was pregnant. He caused three miscarriages and blamed me for them . . . I had one child that I was able to deliver . . . a son, my husband's heir . . ." Josie blinked back her tears. "I like to think my son was better off because he wouldn't have to grow up and know the evil and vile ways of his father, but it was still painful because I wanted to be the mother to him. I wanted to save him . . ."

Josie paused, taking a moment to regain her breath, nearly jumping in surprise when a cold hand settled over hers. She looked at Caroline, noticing her lip quiver as tears fell down her cheeks.

"I barely had time to hold him. My husband took him from me and called me a failure. He said I didn't deserve to hold what was most precious to him. I never got to give my son a proper funeral or a name."

Josie shut her eyes, locking the memory away. It felt good to tell someone, but she didn't want to relive it ever again.

"I'm . . . so . . . sorry, Josie . . . You didn't deserve that," Caroline whispered hoarsely.

Josie gripped Caroline's hand while the woman broke into more sobs. "The one thing that gives me comfort during my days is knowing my children will never experience the vile, evilness of this world. Instead, all they will know is glory and peace." Josie swallowed hard, a tear running down her cheek. "And they'll be there waiting for me when it's my turn to go."

Caroline pressed her lips together, fighting back her tears. "Thank you, Josie. Those words . . . They are the most beautiful words I've ever heard." Josie leaned in and embraced her friend. "How wonderful it will be when we get to spend forever with the ones we love."

Josie's silence concerned Travis on the way home. It had been a horrible after what had been a celebration of God's miracles in their own household. He wished he could do something for Ronan, but the man kept Travis at a distance, focusing only on making a tiny casket for his son—something no father should ever do. Travis glanced over at Josie, who was gripping the basket in her lap, biting her lower lip while keeping her gaze lowered.

His wife remained a mystery to him, and each day, he learned something new about her. But this time, what Travis learned was something he never expected or would wish upon anyone. He had stepped into the cabin to grab Ronan's tools when he overheard Josie speaking to Caroline. She sounded like she was in distress, so as a caring and concerned husband, Travis stepped closer to the quilt divide, listening in. It was wrong for him to eavesdrop, but the story Josie told nearly tore him apart.

He knew her husband was evil, but killing her children while they were supposed to be safe and protected in their mother's womb made a fire rage in him. Travis wanted to travel to North Carolina, just to spit on Marcus's grave. That man didn't deserve a proper burial, just as he didn't allow one for his own child.

"How was Ronan?" Josie asked, pulling Travis from his thoughts. He loosened the reins in his hands, realizing he had gripped them too hard.

Travis sighed, wiping his forehead. "He's holding it all in, trying to stay strong. He was out there in the barn, making a small casket for his baby son. There should never be a casket that small for anyone." He chewed his lower lip. "Ronan is really worried for Caroline. He's not sure if she can make it to the funeral."

Funeral. Casket. Baby son. Travis's gut twisted. *How could you say that?* He couldn't bear to look at Josie now. Those eyes of hers focused on her lap, brimming with tears. She tightened her grip on the basket, her lips pressed into a thin line. He had upset her; he should have been more mindful of his words.

After all those months of ignoring her when she needed him most, she needed him again—and this time, he would be there for her, just as a husband should. Ignoring the piercing cold, he pulled back on the reins, bringing the wagon to a sudden stop. He turned to Josie, and to his surprise, she leaned into him. He drew her close as she sobbed softly. He patted her back then caressed it in soft circles. *Lord, please give me the right words to say. I know only You can comfort my wife. Let me be a vessel if You'll let me.*

Travis's throat tightened, forcing the words out, knowing they could shatter the trust they had built. *Eavesdropping? How could you, Travis?* He could see it all play out—downhill they would go. But this was something they couldn't hide from each other. Josie had secrets, and him keeping his eavesdropping secret too would be too much. Secrets had to end on one side.

"I have a confession to make, Jo—one I feel sorry about, but I can't keep from you." Travis sucked in a quick breath, then exhaled. "I overheard what you told Caroline. I was getting some tools for Ronan, and I-I don't know why I listened. I hope you can forgive me."

Josie froze, her sniffling stopped, and she laid there in his arms, not moving a muscle. Would she forgive him now? That was an intimate conversation, only meant for Caroline's ears. If Josie wanted Travis to know, she would have told him already.

"I'm sorry I never told you, Travis. It's just . . . too hard for me to talk about." Josie pulled away, wiping her tears with her mitten. Travis searched her gaze, his soul nearly breaking at the reflection of pain written all over her.

"The Lord kept pressing the memory on my heart when I heard about Brendon's death. That's why I had to see her," Josie confessed.

Travis swallowed a lump in the back of his throat. He reached out, holding her wrist. "It must have been difficult for you to remember that today. I had no idea how much going there would distress you."

"I wanted to tell you," Josie croaked. "But I tried to forget it. If I never spoke about my past, it never happened." Her lips curved slightly, hardly a smile, but it seemed as though it was what Josie was trying to do. "I want to change now. I'd like to remember my babies when they were alive in my womb. I want to remember the days I delighted in my motherhood and celebrate their lives."

Travis wiped her cheek with his gloved hand, brushing away those salt tears. "He was an evil man and deserved what he got."

Josie's lips parted slightly, and her eyes widened like a skittish doe, just like the day Travis joked about how she thought he was going to strangle her at the dance. Josie bit her bottom lip and looked at her lap. She gripped the basket in her hands, making Travis's pulse race. He grabbed the reins and signaled for the team to pull ahead. Josie stayed silent. Like last night, it seemed as though she was back to the beginning—a frightened, timid creature. Whatever this burden was, she'd tell him when she was ready.

Something in Travis told him he didn't know everything about Josephine Callahan, the sweet and gentle Southern belle.

Chapter Thirty-Nine

Josie hurried out of the kitchen, startled by the faint cry coming from her bedroom. She quickly removed her apron, her thoughts fixed solely on comforting her small son. She tied her hair back with a ribbon she fished from her pocket as she opened the bedroom door. But an unsettling sensation crept over her, sending chills up her arms. The room had fallen eerily silent—not even the slightest whimper from Nathan.

Her gaze locked on the empty crib, and a wave of shock crashed over her. Where was Nathan? Why wasn't he in his crib? Her heart pounded violently as the room spun around her. Stumbling back, she grasped the rocking chair for balance.

"Looking for this?"

The voice was familiar, making the hair at the back of her neck stand. She never thought she'd hear that voice again; it existed only in her mind and seemed almost impossible. Josie slowly lifted her chin, her breath catching as her gaze met Marcus's piercing eyes.

He stood in the corner of the room, holding Nathan in his arms. Her stomach twisted painfully. Nathan was so small, so fragile—one snap of Marcus's temper, and he could be hurt in an instant. Seeing him stand before her brought her back into a delicate and vulnerable state. She felt small, exposed, like the frightened girl she had once been. He towered over her like a giant, and those hands of his were like a grizzly's paws.

He had her son. She couldn't save him. Josie didn't have the strength to fight Marcus, just like before. Nathan was in the hands of the monster who haunted her soul.

"Y-You're dead," Josie croaked.

A smile spread across Marcus's face. "You think you could get rid of me that easily? You're too weak, Josie. You'll never see the last of me."

Josie's heart pounded violently against her ribs as she gasped for air. Her body remained frozen against the mattress, her limbs locked. A warm arm draped over her while she struggled to regain her breath. The mattress shifted beneath Travis's weight as he sat up beside her. *It was just a dream*, she reminded herself through shivers.

But it felt too real. Josie often had nightmares, but they were usually flashes from the past, locked in her memory. This time, it felt different, as though Marcus was in the room with her. Travis rubbed her chilled arms, murmuring soft, shushing noises.

"It's all right, Jo. I'm here. It was just a dream."

Josie tried to speak, but her voice was too weak, her throat clamped shut. Her damp nightdress clung to her form like glue. "W-Where's Nathan?"

Travis caressed her cheek. "He's here. He's in the room with us."

Josie nodded, blowing out a breath.

"What happened? What did you dream about?"

Josie tried to lock Marcus out of her mind, but as long as Travis didn't know the full truth, he'd only torture her more. She could never be free, and she would be locked away from everyone she loved if she confessed.

To her surprise, Travis pulled her against him. She pressed her head to his warm chest, hearing his heart pitter pat against her ear. The sound of life echoed, a life Josie loved more than her own. Travis's body made her feel safe and his touch made her whole. The thought terrified her—that a man's touch could be both comforting and painful. But with Travis, it was a beautiful solace she couldn't quite express in words. Josie longed to stay in his arms for as long as possible, savoring the warmth and safety they offered. She knew deep down that Travis was unlike any man she had known, and she could trust him. The worst he could do was turn her into the authorities.

But what would he think of her, knowing she wasn't the woman he thought her to be? Josie was a murderess. If she was capable of taking a life once, she could do it again. Yet it ached more to keep it hidden. The barrier she yearned to break with Travis could only collapse if she revealed the heavy truth she carried. The secret could destroy their lives, but Josie would rather be shunned by Travis, full of shame, than hold onto her past.

Josie hurried to wipe the tears streaming down her cheeks, but Travis was quicker. His thumb gently brushed across her skin, gathering her tears with a tenderness that made her heart ache.

"Travis . . . There's something you must know about me," Josie began. "I've been wrong to keep so many secrets from you, and . . . after this afternoon, I can't keep them any longer. The torture is too hard to bear . . ."

"You can tell me anything, Jo," Travis whispered in a low voice. "I'm your husband."

Josie pressed her lips together, fighting her tears. "I'm afraid you'll see me differently . . . I'm not the Josephine you know. I did something awful. I tried to deny it . . . but I know it happened, and I am to blame."

Josie hesitated, searching for the right words while Travis remained patient, giving her space to gather her thoughts. When she finally pulled away from his embrace, it wasn't because she couldn't bear his touch. Deep down, she knew he would push her away soon enough and sparing him the effort felt easier.

"I never told you how my husband died . . . He . . . He attacked me the night I escaped. I never told Marcus about Nathan because I didn't want him taken from me, raised by his father . . . or hurt by him. That night, Marcus wanted to kill me for dishonoring him with my lack of childbearing. I—I wanted to protect Nathan, so I let him beat me. But I wasn't going to let him kill me or my baby.

"I fought hard for Nathan, so I tried to defend myself by grabbing what I could find . . ." Josie brought her knees close to her chest and tightened her grip as she replayed the fearsome memory in her mind. "I hit Marcus as hard as I could before I almost blacked out. He . . . He lost his balance and fell down the stairwell and . . . that's how he died. I killed him."

Josie closed her eyes, preparing herself for Travis's fury. Not only did she trick him into marrying a pregnant widow, but she also tricked him into marrying a murderess. She was a criminal who was being hunted and would be punished by death. She would be an embarrassment to his family and a terrible influence on the children.

Instead, Travis wrapped his strong arms around her form, pulling her into the most tender embrace one could never imagine. He rested his chin on her shoulder, his breath hitting her neck.

"It wasn't your fault, Jo."

Josie shook her head, choking on her tears as she clung to his arms. "I'm a murderer, Travis. I'm a wanted felon in your house.

I'm raising your children. How can you justify that? You should kick me out and turn me in. You can collect an award or something."

Travis cupped her chin, turning her face towards him. "No, I won't do it. If they come for you, I'll take them down one by one with my bare hands. Nobody is going to *touch* my wife."

Josie's eyes poured tears. They were painful sobs, freeing her body of the aches she had nursed while harboring the secret for months. Now, secrets gone and bare with no burdens, she was free, so free.

"I wish you had told me sooner, but I'm grateful you've told me now. It means the world to me that you're starting to trust me."

Josie buried her face in Travis's chest. Her tears stained his night-shirt, but Travis seemed not to care. In the pitch dark, he rubbed her back in small circles.

"I will protect you, Jo. No harm will come to you now."

Josie wanted to believe Travis's words. She kept them locked inside her heart because they gave her warmth. She could trust Travis, but the promise to keep her safe was something he couldn't control. If the law came, she'd have to surrender. But for now, she wanted to cherish their embrace, for one day she might never experience the sweet taste of love again.

CHAPTER FORTY

GENERAL GROANED ALOUD AS his horse trotted through the old crummy so-called town. Yes, traveling with an ignorant and ill-mannered trapper had been a curse to his pride, but the solo ride had been more his taste. Fifteen miles behind him, he left the sled safe and secured within a cave. He brought enough food in his saddlebags to last the journey to Cheyenne. It would have been smarter to bring the sled with him, but he couldn't cause too much attention—it would spoil the surprise. His wagon would be there when he made his way back. If not, he had the money to buy another one from one of these crude towns on the way.

The townsfolk stared up at him with curious glances. A child bundled in fur pointed and laughed at him, and a mother pulled him away. *Ill-mannered brat. Ever seen a man with a scar before?* All these prudish people were the uneducated and worthless country folks who were inferior to him. They were nothing but paupers who struggled to pay their taxes, so they came out west to a place that was entirely dirt and rocks.

General hated wasting his money on an exhausting journey. All that time with Buck had been a pain in the behind—all his chatter about love and treating women folk gently. General was anxious to find his wife and take his heir—so he could be raised as a proper gentleman, not an ignorant cowboy.

The so-called "streets" were nothing but mud and ice. Where were the shovelers? This road was a hazard. General continued riding until he saw a small—what he assumed to be—church in a field up ahead. *Maybe some nice Christian folks won't hold back.* The horse maintained its steady pace until General reined him in before the building. He dismounted and shifted his weight onto the creaking porch steps, the old wood squeaking beneath him as he took his first step. *Rotten boards. Don't they have enough trees to make more equipped steps?*

Josephine was raised to be a proper woman, and he could only imagine the suffering she endured here with manual labor, but it wouldn't be anything like she'd experience soon.

General opened the church door and peered around, finding it to be vacant. He removed his hat and closed the door behind him.

"Hello?" he called out. "Hello?"

After a minute went by, General huffed and put his hat back on. *Josephine's wasting my time and money.*

"May I help you, sir?"

General looked up to see a man dressed in a brown shirt and suspenders. General cleared his throat and put on the friendliest smile he could fake. He couldn't let the gentleman think any less of him. To him, General would be a simple Christian man, looking for information. That's all. He wasn't a man hunting down his wife and child, only to save one and kill the other.

"Hello, sir, my name is . . ." *Think of a name. Make it believable.* "Frank Shelton."

The young gentleman gave a welcoming smile and put out his hand. "I am the town's pastor, Reverend Caleb Levingston. What can I do for you this cold morning?"

General gritted his teeth as he continued his friendly voice and grin. Josephine would get a good beating for making him appear a fool. "I'm looking for someone, and I need information." *Think of an excuse.* "She's my niece. I was passing through Bozeman on business and thought I could drop by and pay her a surprise visit. I heard she lives this way, but I never got the direct information."

The reverend folded his arms and nodded. "Well, welcome to Willow Grove. We're a small community, but we know everyone, so you won't have a problem finding your niece. What's her name?"

"Josephine," General answered.

"Ah, yes," the reverend said, holding up a finger. "You must mean Mr. and Mrs. Blythe. I recently married them about seven months ago. She came from North Carolina. You must be from there too?"

General's fists tightened behind his back. *Married?* Heat boiled in his core. Josephine was getting too far out of hand. She was an embarrassment to him, a dirty harlot. She thought she could kill him and slip away into another man's bed. *Keep up the act, General. Don't be weak.*

"Married, you say? I haven't heard."

"Yes," the reverend said. "I thought you might've known since you're her uncle and all. This must be quite a shock."

"Indeed," General muttered through his gritted teeth. He was ready to snap his wife like a twig and hear her bones break between his hands.

"Well, they live about three miles that-a-way," the reverend explained, pointing to the right of him. "They are in a scattered location, but once you get to a rock that is in the shape of an arrow, you aren't too far. You won't be able to miss them. If you do, I'm sure we can find someone to drive you there."

General performed another polite smile. "Thank you kindly, Reverend. You're a good man." General reached into his pocket and pulled out a gold coin. "For your help."

The reverend foolishly pushed General's generosity away. "No, I'm afraid I cannot take that."

The general aggressively put it in the reverend's hand against his will, closing his fingers around the coin with his strength. "Keep it for offering then."

General tipped his hat and walked out the door. *Where are you now, Josephine? Wherever you are, you can't hide.*

Chapter Forty-One

General's adrenaline pumped ferociously, lurking behind a tall pine tree. He found his wife at last. He restrained himself, gripping the tree bark instead of strangling her with his bare hands right then and there. Josephine, three children, and that so-called husband of hers were playing in the snow. The children's squeals made General cringe. Josephine giggled as she shielded her face from a snowball. General hated seeing the grin on her face. He wanted to knock it off, just as he had done before. She had no right to be happy after all she had put him through the past seven years.

Josephine Wellington was a felon and an adulteress, and she would pay for her crimes. He watched as Josephine and two little girls darted behind trees while the young boy and the "husband" threw snowballs. General wished to grab his wife then and there, but he'd have to wait. He'd think of a plan she wouldn't expect. He wanted to torture her, not only physically but emotionally. He'd continue this game just like he had with Mammy and that pathetic kitchen boy.

General's gaze shifted to the dirty farmer husband bundled in fur like the rest of them. That smirk on the man's face would disappear once General killed him. He'd kill him right in front of Josephine, so she could see what her actions caused. Maybe the guilt from causing the little brats to lose their father would consume her. Wouldn't that be fun to see?

A playful squeal slipped from Josephine's lips when the man snuck up from behind her. He lifted her from the ground, and the squeals turned to giggles. *He doesn't know how to handle her.* Josephine was having too much fun with the man, and she needed to be put in her place.

"Put me down!" she demanded.

Josephine broke free, but the man's arms came around her waist, turning her around to face him. Peering up at him with a grin, Josephine seemed to enjoy his touch. She never looked that way with General. The woman would never do anything for him willingly, unless he threatened her. General observed how easily she melted into the farmer's arms. The couple's eyes locked for a while, making General want to gag.

His fists tightened by his side when he fought the urge to destroy them right there with the revolver in his holster, but he had to wait. It wasn't the right moment. Three snowballs flew towards the couple, interrupting their little moment. Josephine and the farmer man separated and threw snowballs at the children. The tiny cabin in the distance made General chuckle inside. Josephine left a large home full of riches for an old shack.

The cabin door opened and an elderly woman stepped out, holding a crying, bundled infant. The blanket was blue, making General's core swell with pride. A son. This was the son he wanted for seven years. Now Josie could be easily disposed of like Martha. The baby's crying pierced General's ear, making him huff. *Little brat has some lungs.*

Josephine took the child and bounced him up and down. General rubbed his scruffy chin. Perhaps he could wait to kill Josephine. He didn't care much for babies anyways. All he cared about was the boy's later years, when he could send him off to a military academy and make him a real man.

Maybe he could bring Josephine along to stretch out the game, making it last even longer. A smile curved at his lips. She'd suffer as she watched her son turn into his real father, and she'd grow insane not having any control. Then General would strip her of everything—a social life, motherhood, and the outside world. He'd make a prison of his own, full of twisted games. To the world she would be dead, and no one would come looking. She'd be trapped, forced to endure the rest of her life confined in a dark room with no escape.

A grin spread across General's face. Oh, how he loved his new plan. It was getting better and better. Killing Josephine would be too easy when he could torture her for the rest of her life.

The farmer stood behind Josephine and grinned, his hand on her waist. Then, Josephine turned and handed him the little boy. He stopped crying in the man's arms. General kicked the tree trunk hard. That man had no right to touch the boy. The child wasn't his son! General's heir wouldn't grow up under the influence of a poor farmer.

The urge for revenge rushed within General, and he wasn't sure how much longer he could last before his rage exploded.

Chapter Forty-Two

Josie wrapped her arms around Travis's waist, just before he left for work later that afternoon. Harsh winter days could change their lives in an instant, so she savored every moment of this embrace. The deep snow outside worried her because North Carolina winters had never been as harsh as those in the Rockies. She knew she had to learn to release her fears and trust that God would guide them through every challenge. Travis had spent his entire life in Montana and knew how to handle the severe winters, but it didn't make letting go any easier for Josie.

Travis gently pulled away and planted a soft kiss on Josie's forehead. The warmth of his lips sent a flutter through her. She could see herself getting used to this new life, the simple comfort of being close to him. But deep down, she longed for more—for everything that came with being husband and wife. Still, they both knew they had to wait until the timing was right. The anticipation made Josie grow restless, but she knew everything would be worth the wait.

"I'll be back soon," Travis promised, looking deep into her eyes. "Make sure the children behave."

Josie gripped his suspenders, grinning up at him. "They should be fine. I'm thinking of having a painting afternoon with them."

Travis smiled. "You are wonderful, Jo. I wish I could stay, but I need to go."

Josie nodded, though she still didn't like the thought of his departure. She wanted to be with him every minute of the day, but with a working farm, that was nearly impossible. "Do you have to go now? It's freezing outside."

Travis let out a sigh and frowned. "You know I can't be idle." His lips curled. "I'll be back soon. Mr. Lynde needs me now that Ronan is in mourning."

Josie patted his chest. "The earlier you leave and faster you get back, the more time we can spend together later."

"That will be on my mind the rest of the day, trust me." Travis shot her a wink. He placed a hand on Josie's shoulder. "Please, be careful."

"I will."

Travis grabbed his hat and large buffalo-fur coat, then turned, stealing one last glance at Josie before stepping out the door. "Goodbye, Jo."

As he walked out, Josie gripped the back of the dining chair, shifting her weight as she steadied herself. She rubbed her neck, her grin deepening. If only she could hold out until later. Just the thought of spending more time with Travis made her body swell with excitement. She was no longer an outsider—she was part of his family. And now, she was *so* close to having a real marriage, something she had almost given up on. They would all be one family, bound together, forever.

Josie crouched beside the crib in front of the fireplace and picked up Nathan. His dark eyes were wide and alert, and his mouth opened, letting out a soft yawn. The sight of him never failed to brighten her day. She smiled softly, the warmth of his little body reminding her that she was finally a mother, with the son she had prayed for. Yet, deep inside, she dreaded the day when he would have to choose between being an heir to Aunt Tia's fortune and the simple life of a farmer. No matter what path he chose, Josie knew she would support him. But for now, all she wanted was for him to stay her baby forever.

She shifted Nathan to her shoulder and set the table for the children's paint day. She laid out the colors—blue, green, red, and yellow. There had been more colors a few months ago, but money was tight since the winter had come. The livestock feed was running low, so Travis promised to bring some back on his way home. Planting season would arrive soon enough, filling their days with even more work.

Josie still couldn't believe Travis had returned to work so soon. He liked to admit he was better, but Josie noticed when he had to pause for small rests. She admired his determination but silently worried, wishing he would slow down for just a little longer. He'd do anything to put his hands at use. Throwing snowballs wasn't enough.

"Children, paint time!"

Josie gently set Nathan back down in his crib just as the children came out of their bedroom. Their eyes immediately locked onto the table, now covered with painting tools. Gideon squealed in delight, breaking free from Ivy's hand and running straight towards the colors. Ivy gasped, and Jonas and Lillian jumped up and down.

"Is this all for us?" Lillian asked, clutching her rag doll.

Josie nodded. "Yes, it is, and we will have a full paint day instead of school."

"No school? Really?" Jonas shrieked, his hands on both his cheeks.

Josie scooped Gideon up when he pulled on her skirt. "I thought we could have a fun day instead."

"I like school," Ivy said, pulling a chair out from under the table. "I wish we could have it every day."

Jonas rolled his eyes and huffed. "It's 'cause you're learnin' the fun stuff. I'm still learnin' the borin' alphabet."

"The alphabet is important, too," Josie told Jonas, bouncing Gideon on her hip. "Once you're more familiar with the letters and sounds, then you can learn to read."

The children immediately started dipping their brushes in paint while Josie daydreamed. She could hardly wait for the day the school opened when she would have a classroom of her own. The thought was almost too good to be true. Soon, Josie would be helping each child in town develop the same opportunities to learn, grow, and discover their potential.

Josie sat Gideon down in his wooden high chair while she assisted the children with their painting.

"I'm thinkin' 'bout paintin' the meadow," Jonas said. "I miss seein' it 'cause the stupid snow. I wish it'd melt already."

"I like the snow," Lillian butted in. "I like doin' snowball fights like this mornin'. It's fun."

Jonas groaned, painting his paper blue. "I hate the cold."

Josie sat beside Jonas and kissed the top of his head. "We all like different things, Jonas. Not everyone has to enjoy the same things."

"What's your favorite season, Josie?" Jonas asked.

Josie's mind wandered to *Belle Vallée* when the apple blossoms bloomed, filling the air with a sweet aroma. As the memories returned, she could almost feel the sun streaming through her window every morning, bathing the room in soft light. She smiled, recalling the clear lake in the distance with the swans gliding gracefully over the surface. Every morning and every evening, she would stand on the balcony and watch as the sun reflected over the crystal waters.

Belle Vallée was never meant to be a hotel for guests of Asheville. During the war, when everything seemed to fall apart, she would wake each morning and witness God's faithfulness in the beauty of His creation. The apple blossoms, the lake, the swans—everything was still in motion, reminding her that God's presence remained steady and unwavering. The place had been a beacon of hope, and now it was nothing more than a hotel for wealthy strangers.

"Spring," Josie answered. "Spring has always been my favorite, and I look forward to my first spring here in the Rockies."

"I'll paint it for you, Josie," Lillian said with a cheeky smile.

A smile curved from Josie's lips. "I'd love that, Lillian."

While the children continued painting, Josie looked forward to Travis's return. She couldn't wait for him to come home to fresh sourdough bread and a roasted venison smothered with brown gravy and onions. She had been preparing the meal since the night before. Josie observed the children's pictures, her heart swelling with every stroke of their brushes. Travis would be so proud of their creative projects when he came home. It'd be the perfect evening—just the thought made Josie's pulse race with excitement.

A giggle slipped from Gideon's mouth, and he squirmed in his chair. Josie looked back at him and tickled his belly. Gideon squealed.

"What's so funny, Gideon? What's so funny?"

Gideon turned his head and pointed at the window. "Silly clown! Silly clown!"

"Clown?" Jonas repeated, his nose bunching. "There ain't no clown."

"There *isn't* a clown," Josie corrected. She pulled loose strands of hair behind her ears. "He has a wild imagination."

"I wonder what made him think of a clown," Jonas said. "The only clown he's seen is in Ivy's circus book."

Josie chuckled and dismissed the thought; it made sense for Gideon to learn the word from a storybook. She rose from her seat and made her way to the window, pulling her shawl close. She wiped the foggy glass and squinted, only to see nothing. Perhaps Travis had come home early and was making silly faces through the window. A smile crossed her face. He decided to stay after all.

"I'll be outside for a moment."

Josie grabbed her coat from the door hanger then buttoned it tight around her, her heart skipping. Afterwards, she grabbed her gloves, scarf, and hat. Stepping outside, she noticed how peaceful it was. No snow fell from the sky, and the wind wasn't as brisk as it had been that morning. But she dismissed the peaceful thoughts when her boots sank into the snow, making her shiver. *The weather here sure has a bite.*

Josie stepped towards the side of the cabin where Gideon had pointed, eager to see her husband. But her smile was wiped away quickly. She halted abruptly when she spotted footprints in the snow—footprints too large to be Travis's. Her breath quickened as she scanned the area; no one was in sight, yet her nerves frayed. Perhaps Travis had another pair of boots she didn't know about. That thought eased her a bit. Clutching her coat, Josie pivoted to head back inside.

When she neared the door, strong arms wrapped around her, yanking her backward. A terrified screech escaped her lips. The grip was far too forceful to be Travis's, yet there was something hauntingly familiar about it that she didn't want to acknowledge. The figure spun her around to face him, and Josie's stomach dropped, her eyes widening in shock. Standing before her was a ghost from her past—Marcus Wellington, with the same scar etched into the right side of his cheek and eyes that seemed to bore into her very soul, filled with malice.

"Y-You're dead."

Marcus chuckled, a sinister smile curving at his lips. "I thought you'd be happy to see your husband, my dear."

Josie's pulse drummed in her throat as she struggled against his hold, but with each attempt to escape, his grip only tightened. Her worst nightmare stood right in front of her.

Worse than a marshal coming to arrest her.

Worse than the gallows.

How was Marcus alive? Josie had seen him fall; there was no way he could have survived. Panic surged within her as the horrifying reality set in—Marcus Wellington had returned from the dead.

"How—How are you alive?"

Marcus wrenched her close, crushing her chest against his and stealing her breath. "You might've put me to sleep for several months, but I am stronger than you think. It will take more than a fall to get rid of me."

Josie bit back a scream, determined not to scare the children. "Just let me go, Marcus, please."

"Not until you give me my son," Marcus snarled through his yellow teeth.

Son. The words sliced through her like a knife. How did Marcus know about Nathan? Josie might have been able to protect Nathan in her womb, but it wasn't possible now.

"You stay away from him," Josie hissed. "You will *never* have him. I'll call the law for kidnapping. I can convince the town. They trust me."

Marcus shook his head and tsked. "Oh, Josephine, you're a fool to think any law would want to help a wild woman like you. You wouldn't dare to stop me because I have too much evidence to have you hanged, and you'll never see your precious son again. What law would grant a child to a violent, adulterous woman, married to two men? Hm? Please tell me, dear wife, how will you manage to fight against your *real* husband?"

Josie's limbs went numb. There was no hope for her or Nathan now. *Dear God, please help me. Deliver my son from the hands of this monster.*

Marcus pulled a revolver from his holster and pointed it under Josie's chin. Josie closed her eyes, praying louder in her mind. If she was going to meet her Maker, she wanted Nathan to be safe first. She couldn't allow his mind to be poisoned by his evil father.

"Now, I am going to release you and no harm will come to those little brats if you give him to me. Try anything stupid and their blood will be on your hands."

Marcus's grip released, leaving tender spots on Josie's body like before. With trembling hands, she let him inside, a silent prayer rising within her for the safety of the children. She'd rather be beaten into a bloody pulp than allow the children to be subjected to Marcus's wrath. If he chose to spare Travis, she knew Travis would never forgive her for failing to protect their family.

The children's eyes rounded, and Gideon kept screaming *clown* like before. Josie placed a hand over his mouth and handed him to Ivy.

"Be calm," Josie whispered to her. "Everything will be all right. I promise. Do as this man says."

Lillian and Jonas sat frozen, their lips trembling. Josie's eyes brimmed with tears as she reached into the crib and lifted Nathan into her quivering arms. He looked so peaceful, completely oblivious to the chaos surrounding them. Overwhelmed with love and protectiveness, she buried her face against him, kissing his soft cheeks, wishing to shield him from the horrors.

"I love you, Nathan Travis Blythe. I will always love you."

Josie's limbs wobbled as she walked to Marcus. He yanked the baby from her arms and peeled back the quilt swaddling underneath the bear-fur blanket. He took a long look at Nathan, then his mouth curved into a devious grin, like a venomous snake.

"He's a Wellington, of course," he said proudly. Marcus seized Josie's arm. "Let's go."

Josie took one last glance at the children as Marcus forced her away. She once vowed she'd never leave them, but she had no choice, just like when Travis promised no harm would come to her. He wasn't here, and perhaps the lack of goodbye would spare lives.

"I love all of you!" Josie shouted. "Please remember that!"

Marcus yanked her arm harder. "Shut up, will ya, woman! We have business to attend to."

They trudged with purpose through the thick snow, the ice crunching at their feet. Nathan began to wail, and Marcus groaned and handed Nathan over to Josie.

"Hold the brat and shut him up!"

Josie took Nathan, kissing his tear-soaked cheeks. Marcus grabbed his horse by the reins and hoisted Josie over the top. The wind grew colder, and she pressed Nathan's face against her chest to keep him warm. Surely they weren't going back to North Carolina—not in the middle of winter. *God, please spare us. Give us an open window, I beg you. Save my son, no matter what happens to me.*

Marcus situated himself in the saddle behind Josie. The closeness of their bodies made her shudder. She'd never feel safe again. No longer would she be in the arms of Travis Blythe. Josie had ruined everything for them both. Their union was more dangerous than ever—it was illegal.

"You'll have your punishment once we have the business settled," Marcus swore, his breath hitting her neck. "Don't think you've been acquitted."

Josie's heart throbbed violently against her ribs. "What business?"

Marcus snickered, clicking the reins. "Oh, you will see. Your punishment will be far more painful this time."

CHAPTER FORTY-THREE

JOSIE STAYED ON TRAVIS'S mind all afternoon, and when Mr. Lynde dismissed him early, he could hardly contain his excitement. As he hoisted the last sack of feed onto the wagon, barely winded, he couldn't help but have a quiet satisfaction. His strength had returned, far beyond Aunt Polly's predictions. Bed rest wouldn't fill his pockets the way a day's work did.

Stepping back from the wagon, he grinned widely beneath his scarf. In all the months he'd known Josie, Travis hadn't thought of her this much. He ached to be by her side, holding her close enough to feel her heartbeat against his chest like last night. Two reasons pulled him towards her—the strange longing within him and the growing concern for her well-being. He never imagined a woman like Josie could be in such danger.

Travis didn't blame her for what she had done to her husband. Killing Marcus was an accident—an act of self-defense and desperation. If she hadn't fought back, he might have hurt her or worse. However, without the situation, Josie would have never found her way to Travis. She found safety, and Travis never knew how much he needed her. She was like the air that he needed to survive.

Losing Sophie had left a deep hole in Travis's heart, but being with Josie mended it, little by little. Now, he knew he could move forward as long as she was by his side. He never wanted to fall back into the way he used to treat her, realizing how foolish he'd been to ignore her. Now, he couldn't resist thinking of her constantly. She had a hold on him—strong and unshakable—and he never wanted to break free from it.

The sun peeked from behind the clouds, nearly blinding Travis as he looked above. He had grown tired of the freezing weather, yearning for warmth again. The only part of winter he appreciated was Josie snuggling closer to him in her sleep. That was one thing about the season he'd always cherish. But now, standing ankle-deep in snow with the wind nipping at his face and burning his nostrils, he wished for spring.

Travis shut the back of the wagon and climbed up the ledge, pulling his scarf tighter while the sharp wind hit his ears. With a quick signal, he urged the horses forward, the reins held firm in his hands. The wagon creaked and ushered slowly, the wheels crunching through the icy ground. The streets were nearly empty with most folks choosing to stay indoors. Travis would've done the same if not for the supplies and work. The Lyndes were counting on his and Ronan's help, but with Ronan grieving, Mr. Lynde was left without anyone else to rely on. Travis couldn't let them down.

It was only a matter of time before another blizzard swept through. Mr. Lynde ordered a large shipment from Bozeman, and Travis was glad to help. He had no intention of being caught in a deadly blizzard ever again. He had a wife and five children to provide for, and risking his life in the cold wasn't an option anymore—unless it was to save one of them.

As Travis neared the edge of town, another wagon pulled up beside him. He waved when he recognized Reverend Levingston. It had been quite some time since they'd crossed paths because church services had been canceled due to the epidemic and the harsh winter weather.

"Good evening, Reverend," Travis said.

Reverend Levingston pulled his reins back, slowing his team to a stop. "Good evening, Travis. What brings you into town?"

Travis pointed behind him. "Just getting back from the mercantile and taking home some supplies. How about you?"

"I went to visit the Walshes, and I'm on my way home."

Travis sighed. "It's terrible what happened to them. Josie and I went yesterday to visit them."

"We had the burial today. They didn't want to risk the illness spreading more, so we went ahead since I was already there. It's not right to bury a coffin so small."

"You're right," Travis agreed. "I can only imagine how hard it is on the young'uns."

"They don't look good, but I believe all will be better in time. God is watching over them." Reverend Levingston laid his reins in his lap. "I hope your surprise visitation is going well."

Travis's eyes narrowed. "Pardon?"

"Josie's uncle. He came by the church this morning, looking for you. I hope Josie is enjoying time with her family."

Travis scratched his neck. Josie's last-known relative was her great aunt, and the idea of an uncle suddenly coming to visit was too peculiar. No one down south knew where Josie was except that lawyer. Travis's protective instincts flared instantly, his fists tightening around the reins. He should have stayed home, especially now that he knew the truth about Josie's past.

"Who was he? Where was he from?"

"His name's Frank Shelton. He has a Southern accent, so I assumed he must be from North Carolina. He tried to pay me in gold for my help, but I put it in the church offering."

Shelton? Josie had never mentioned anyone in her family by that name. A knot tightened in Travis's gut—something wasn't right.

"Thank you for your help, Reverend. I'd love to visit more, but I must get home before dark."

Reverend Levingston tipped his hat. "Be safe, Travis. Tell your family I said hello."

Travis snapped the reins, urging the two horses to trudge faster through the snow. What a fool he had been to let his past get the better of him. Josie was right when Travis was sick. For over a decade he blamed himself and consumed his time in providing, but he had no idea how much providing could put his family in danger.

When Travis made it to the farm, he quickly noticed how quiet it was. Without bothering to tie the team, he sprinted to the cabin and noticed a mix of small and large footprints leading away from the front door. Panic surged through him as he bolted open the door, his chest rigidifying.

"Jo! Children!"

No answer, not even a stir.

"Hello?" Then, from his right, he heard a small whimper.

"Pa?"

Travis rushed towards the soft voice. He flung open the pantry door to find all four of his children crammed together, hugging each other tightly, their wide eyes filled with fear and their cheeks stained with tears. Their lips quivered while trying to form words. Gideon immediately pulled away from Ivy's arms, and Travis scooped him up, relief flooding through him as he helped the others out. Then his heart stopped, stealing his breath the moment he realized Nathan was missing.

"What happened? Where are Josie and Nathan?"

Jonas's bottom lip quivered as he sobbed, and Travis bent down to meet his son's tear-filled gaze.

"Jonas, what happened? Tell me, please."

"B-Bad man . . ."

Travis's stomach dropped, and his jaw hardened. His head began to spin, and a rush of heat went through his ears and neck as anger surged like wildfire. *I should have been here. I promised to protect them.*

"Who was it? What did he do?"

The more Travis asked questions, the more the children cried. Travis wiped his face with his hands. "Everything is all right. We'll bring them home. But for me to do that, you must tell me everything."

Ivy's face twisted as she whimpered. "He . . . He took Josie and Nathan and left. He had a gun."

"He had gray and brown hair and a scary scar on his face," Lillian added.

"When was this?" Travis asked, his veins pulsing.

"It was after we started painting," Ivy answered.

Painting. That had to be around noon. Travis stood and grabbed his rifle hanging above the fireplace mantel. He yanked bullets from the kitchen shelf, loading as many rounds as he could into his pockets. There hadn't been any real threats in Willow Grove for years; the rifle was merely a precaution against wild beasts or intruders. But this time would be different. He was going to hunt down this man and save his wife and son.

"Children, you are going to listen to me. I need you to bundle yourself up as warm as you can and go to Aunt Polly's. She'll keep you safe until I return."

"But Pa . . ." Jonas whimpered. "What if you get hurt?"

Travis squatted to their level and hugged them as tightly as he could. He kissed the top of their heads as if it was their last time together.

"I love all of you so much. Please know that."

Travis slipped on an extra coat and grasped his rifle. He loathed the thought of leaving his children behind, but time was slipping away. Josie and Nathan were his family, too, and he'd risk everything for them. He saddled his beloved horse, Flash, and they galloped off into the woods. Travis's eyes followed the hoof tracks like a hawk tracking his prey. While Travis's horse sped through the forest, he couldn't predict what lay ahead, but he would keep his promise.

God help the man who laid a finger on his wife. Travis spent his entire life losing the ones he cared for one by one, but now that he was on the verge of losing Josie, too, he felt a flame burn within him—a flame that urged him to fight against the dangers and bring her home safe and sound.

CHAPTER FORTY-FOUR

JOSIE UNCOVERED NATHAN'S FACE and felt his cheeks while Marcus's horse trudged through the piles of snow. Nathan was still warm, unlike her own numb body. She wished she could have grabbed more layers, perhaps one of Travis's buffalo coats.

Nathan squirmed. It wasn't right for this journey to be taken so early in the winter. There were too many risks—blizzards, lack of warmth, and resources. *Did Marcus bring anything with him other than this horse?* She knew he was evil, but he wouldn't be foolish enough to bring them home during this time of year.

The sun set ahead, and judging from the two hours, they couldn't have traveled over ten miles. The wind seemed to grow stronger by the second. They couldn't go on like this. It was over three hundred miles to Cheyenne, where they would be safe enough to travel by railway. They'd have to camp eventually. Surely they wouldn't ride all night without a fire.

Nathan wailed, and Josie bounced him up and down, whispering shushing noises in his ear.

"Hush him up. My ears are bleeding here," Marcus growled.

Looking ahead, praying he wouldn't lose his temper, she spoke soft and meekly, just as she had been trained to do those seven years, "Marcus, the baby hasn't eaten in hours."

Marcus pulled the reins back to a sudden stop and huffed. He dismounted, and when Josie looked down, her veins went cold just looking in those eyes. She swallowed hard, lifting her chin. He took her by the waist and pulled her down. Just his touch brought her back in time to her weakest point. Gone was Josie Blythe, the strong, hardworking farmer's wife. She was living her nightmare again, and this time, he was standing before her.

"Well, get on with it," Marcus hissed.

Josie's face grew hot, pulling the fussing baby close. Surely Marcus wouldn't ask her to nurse in front of him. Nathan needed to relax, and he couldn't if he sensed his mother's discomfort. Josie's stomach knotted. The last few times she managed to argue with Marcus, she suffered painful consequences.

"Can you build a fire, please? Nursing will take half an hour or less. Your *son* needs to be in excellent health." The word *son* sickened Josie, but it was the only way to turn him away.

Marcus groaned. "Fine."

Josie brushed the snow off a rock beside a tree and began feeding Nathan. Marcus disappeared to gather firewood. Josie spent each moment relishing her time with her son, not knowing how much longer she'd have with him. Of course, Marcus knew nothing about caring for infants, he'd have to keep her alive until they arrived back in Statesville. What really concerned her was his plan. He mentioned more than once that he had another purpose for her. What would that be? A wet nurse? Wasn't that why he was letting her live now?

Josie peered down at Nathan. She wished there was some way they could be saved, but it didn't seem likely. All Josie knew was that she had to survive and fight for her son. But what would happen once they returned home? Just the thought sent a shiver down her spine.

When Marcus returned, she quickly pulled Nathan's bear-fur blanket to her neck. Marcus's eyes bore into hers, making her skin crawl.

"Don't get too comfortable there," Marcus scoffed. "This fire is a foolish idea. We'll leave soon as you finish feeding that boy."

"B-But what about camp? It'll be dark soon. Going now won't be good for Nathan's health."

"*Nathan?*" Marcus snorted in disgust. "A weak name."

A small flame flickered on top of the gathered wood, and Marcus stood.

"It's from the Bible."

Marcus turned, his abominable green eyes tight in the corners as he glared at Josie. He stepped forward, jabbing a finger inches from her face. "Don't you correct me, woman. Nathan was an adviser to a king, a mere pauper if you ask me. He wasn't anything more than a servant." Marcus straightened his posture like a soldier, his chest poking out. "His name shall be Abner, the name of my great-grandfather and a great commander in the Bible. My son won't be a pathetic, weak boy."

Josie cradled Nathan tighter against her chest as he continued to nurse. She tucked the blanket snugly around his small form, shielding his face not just from the cold, but from the gaze of the man who had no claim to him. This child was Nathan Travis Blythe, and no matter what Marcus said or did, he would never be his father. She didn't know how yet, but she'd see to it. Marcus was a blasphemer, a demon clothed in human form, and he would pay for his sins in time. God's judgment would see to that.

"And don't think you'll brainwash him with that *meekful kindness* garbage," Marcus sneered. "You'll have your punishment as soon as we get back. The only reason I haven't killed you yet is because Abner needs a wet nurse. Before I know it, he'll be a mommy's boy, delicate and pathetic, just like my first sons were."

His eyes darkened as he continued, bitterness creeping into every word. "Martha was nothing more than a mind poisoner, taking them for walks through the garden and reading them bedtime stories. None of that makes a man. But the military does, and that's where he'll be—a military school. He doesn't need a mother. Mothers make their sons weak."

Josie wanted to fight back, to tell him she wouldn't dare let her son become anything like him, but she had to be smart; he'd kill her in an instant, and she knew that better than anyone. Josie's stomach churned as she held Nathan closer. She wouldn't let him break her child.

"And don't forget," Marcus leaned in, his voice low and venomous, "we're not too far from that so-called husband of yours. You know, I don't have to just kill him. No, I can turn him over to the authorities. Let him hang for bigamy."

Josie's jaw ticked, her temples throbbing. "No. You leave him out of this. We were led to believe you were dead."

"So you decided to run from the law? My, my Miss Josephine, some outlaw you are." His lips curved. "You may have left me for dead, but I was very much alive. The doctors called me a miracle. Just before they could bury me, I took a breath, frightened them all."

Marcus grabbed Josie's chin, forcing her gaze to meet his. Josie's teeth clenched. She wanted to spit on his face, wanted to hurt him just like he hurt her.

"It takes more than a flower vase to kill me. *You're* the weak one. Remember, Josephine? I'm invincible."

Travis gripped his rifle, ready to shoot the monster who held Josie's face in his hands. Travis hid behind a large pine tree at least thirty feet back, but he could sense Josie's fear. Nathan let out a small whimper, and the man stepped back. Travis wanted to shoot this man, but he knew any mistake could get Nathan and Josie killed. He needed a plan, one that would save them both, not put them at more risk than they already were. He couldn't bear losing them, not when they meant the world to him.

Who was this monster? Just seeing him grip Josie like that made Travis want to strangle him. Was he a marshal? Perhaps another enemy from home? A bounty hunter collecting a reward?

The man gripped Josie by the arm, pulling her upward. "Come on, let's get going," he snarled.

Josie gasped, buttoning the top layer of her blouse while adjusting the blanket around Nathan. The man yanked her away from the rock and towards the black horse tied to a tree. Travis took a few steps forward behind another cluster of trees, watching with eagle eyes. He wouldn't let them get far.

The sun was already setting, and given what little supplies the man carried, Travis wouldn't allow Josie and Nathan to stay out longer than they had to. Maybe he'd ride ahead on Flash, confront them nice and easy.

But what about the man's gun? He could easily pull it on Josie. Travis's lips pressed to a thin line and his muscles tensed. This was hopeless.

Travis took another few steps, his foot crunching against a tree limb shallowly buried under the snow. The man ahead froze, pulling out his revolver and aiming forward, his grip holding Josie's forearm.

"Who's there?"

Travis didn't move a muscle, let alone blink. He held his rifle in his hands, ready to shoot if necessary.

"I know you're there, Blythe! Show yourself!" The man yanked Josie and Nathan in front of him. Josie shrieked and closed her eyes as he pointed the gun against her temple. "Come out now or she's dead."

Travis's heart violently pounded, constricting his lungs. The man had Josie, Travis's sweet Jo. That man had no right to take her and hold her like that! Travis's nostrils flared. He'd kill this man with his bare hands, no problem. The woman he loved and his child were in danger.

"Let her loose!" Travis shouted.

The man took a few steps forward. Nathan screamed bloody murder in Josie's arms, fueling Travis's fury.

"Step out now!" the man growled.

Travis moved out of the clearing, his rifle aimed at the man. "Let's talk about this! She's my wife and that's my son. You would really hurt an innocent woman and child?"

"Innocent?" The man sneered. "What kind of poison has she been feeding you? This woman is *my* wife, and the child is my heir."

Travis's breath caught. *Wife?* Josie's husband was dead. She killed him herself. She came to Montana to escape the law.

"Don't hurt him," Josie begged the man. "He had no part in this. It's me you want, Marcus."

How was Marcus alive? It didn't matter—not when Travis would kill him as soon as he got the chance.

"Put the gun down or I'll blow her brains out," Marcus commanded. "We can talk this out, just like you want. After all, we are her husbands. Shouldn't we come to an understanding?" A sinister smile crossed his face.

This man knew nothing about understanding. He had hurt Josie, and now he was evil enough to bring the child out in this weather. What was the man thinking? Marcus was purely insane. But Travis had no other choice, so he'd play this man's game. He couldn't bear that gun being so close to Josie's face.

"All right," Travis agreed. He lowered his rifle and put up his hands. "Let them go. Let's talk about this."

Marcus threw Josie to the ground, and Travis's breath hitched. "Josie!"

She fell onto her back with Nathan still pressed to her chest. Travis ran to her, his hand cradling her head. Her eyes sprung open as her cheeks deepened with a fearful red. Travis looked down at Nathan who continued to scream like before. Travis glared back at Marcus, temples throbbing. He wanted to rip the head from his shoulder and watch him die an excruciating death.

Before he could stand, Marcus pointed his revolver. "Get up."

Travis stood, his hands in the air. "Let her go. You can do with me what you will."

"No, Travis!" Josie argued.

Marcus opened his coat, revealing another revolver. He threw it at Travis's feet.

"Let's settle this like gentlemen and have some fun. We both are married to the same woman, and there can only be one husband."

A duel. Killing Marcus was at the top of Travis's list, and now he had the opportunity. However, only one could be the winner.

"Travis, please don't do this," Josie begged, her eyes brimming with tears, clutching a screaming Nathan.

Travis's soul ached, seeing the fear in Josie's eyes, full of worry and sorrow. There was a possibility this duel would fail, permitting Marcus to take Nathan and Josie back. But Travis had to take this chance. He needed to have faith, and if it was God's will for Marcus to take Josie back, then he prayed the Lord would take judgment into His hands and spare Josie and Nathan.

"I have to do this, Jo." Travis bent down, caressing Josie's frozen cheek. A lump formed in his throat. "For us."

"There has to be another way," Josie pleaded, gripping the hand resting on her cheek. "You don't know him like I do. He will kill you."

He will kill you. Travis's eyes stung. The children. Would he really sacrifice himself, leaving them alone? "I know."

"Enough!" Marcus growled. "Come on! Let's go!"

Travis kissed Josie's head and picked up the revolver. Before he could join Marcus, he swallowed hard, saying the words he longed to for weeks. Though he never expected it would be this way. "I love you, Jo."

He turned quickly, not bearing to see her face. Did she look shocked? Relieved? Disgusted? He wouldn't know. If he lost the duel, he'd die with weight off his shoulders. Travis took off after Marcus, carrying the gun in his holster that could either be his doom or deliverance.

Marcus cocked his gun and smiled. "Just up ahead. You wouldn't want to miss and hit our wife, hmm?"

Just the man's idea of humor made Travis sick. He gritted his teeth. "I'm going to kill you."

Marcus snickered, just the way Travis would imagine. His scarred eye squinted in delight. "We'll see about that. Don't get too ahead of yourself, *Travis.*"

A low growl bellowed out of Travis, and his hand flexed. He was going to kill this man. Travis inhaled deeply, stepping forward as Marcus counted aloud.

Five.

Travis's heart pounded.

Six.

He took an extra breath.

Seven.

Muscles tightened.

Eight.

Hand on his revolver.

Nine.

Gripped hard.

Ten.

Drew.

He faced his opponent, aiming right at his core. Without hesitation, he took his shot. Josie's scream pierced the air as the shot rang out. Travis flinched, jerking his head to the side. The acrid smell of smoke filled Travis's nostrils, burning his throat and making him cough. His earlobe stung like fire. He winced, touching the side of his face. Wet and hot. The metallic smell told him enough. Blood trickled down the side of his face. Marcus's shot grazed his ear.

A twisted grin crept across Marcus's lips. Travis missed his shot. "Well, looky there. Looks like you earned yourself a souvenir. Down South, men would call that an honor to have a scar from a war hero."

Travis huffed and pointed his gun, his finger on the trigger. Marcus didn't move, only smiled. Travis checked the hammer and found the slots empty. His core tightened, seeing Josie's wide eyes as she clutched Nathan.

Marcus's revolver slowly rose. "God's judgment is coming for the adulterer," he sneered. "Turn around and put your hands behind your head."

Travis growled and charged towards him, but the man cocked the gun. "It's over, Mr. Blythe. Checkmate."

"No! Please don't!" Josie cried, running to them. Nathan wailed in the distance, wrapped in her coat and lying in the snow. "Stop!"

She positioned herself between them, shielding Travis with her body. "Take me! If it's judgment you want, kill me. Let Travis go!"

"And why would I do that, huh?" Marcus pointed at Travis. "This is between us men."

"Get outta here, Jo. Take Nathan and go!" Travis scolded.

"I have this, Travis. Please. You don't know him like I do," she whispered, her body quivering as snowflakes fell. Josie faced Marcus with a straight posture, evident confidence brewing through her. "You can let Travis and his aunt care for Nathan until spring. No harm will come to you. Just don't hurt them."

Marcus grinned, pulling back his hammer with one thumb. "Sounds like a deal, but I can't let you two live. One for revenge and the other for taking my wife."

"No!" Travis screamed, shoving Josie out of the way just as a gunshot rang. He froze. For a moment, everything stood still. He looked down, seeing no harm to him. Josie's cry cut through the silence, and she rushed back to Travis's side. He pulled her close, shielding her with his body. Slowly, he looked up.

Marcus was no longer the menacing figure from moments ago. He clutched his side, blood seeping through his fingers, eyes wide with disbelief. His mouth hung open, a mix of shock and anger distorting his face. He muttered curses, and with a shaky step, Marcus dropped to his knees, glaring at them with venomous intensity.

Travis pulled Josie close as she sobbed into his chest, her body trembling against him. Gently, he ran his fingers through her hair. "It's over now."

But as he looked past her, he spotted movement up ahead. There, behind a tree, stood Aunt Polly, her familiar silver hair gleaming in the fading light. She held a rifle, the long barrel still smoking. Travis blinked in disbelief. "Aunt Polly?" Her silver hair and buffalo coat could be picked out anywhere.

Travis looked down at Josie, wiping her tears. "He's gone. He can't hurt us anymore."

Josie looked over his shoulder. She burst out into more tears and collapsed against Travis. He pulled her away from Marcus's body and towards the spot where Nathan screamed. Travis picked the baby up and kissed his cheeks. *Nathan, my son.* He turned to Josie and embraced them both.

Aunt Polly rode out and halted before them. After she dismounted, she turned to Marcus, whose blood stained the pure white snow.

"Devil," Aunt Polly muttered, spitting in his direction.

Aunt Polly reached out and hugged Travis and Josie, burying them in her embrace. She then took Nathan from Travis's arms, kissing his cheeks after he settled down.

"I followed the trail," Aunt Polly explained. "When the children told me what happened, I couldn't stand by and wait. They're with the Walshes. Alice is looking after them."

Josie shuddered in Travis's arms. She looked over at Aunt Polly, smiling feebly. "I owe you my life."

"You don't owe me anything," Aunt Polly said. She looked at Marcus again and shook her head. "No one will find him. I'll make sure of it."

Travis pulled Josie aside, wiping her tears with his thumb. "I thought I was going to lose you and Nathan."

Josie's lips pressed together as she choked. "I thought we were going to lose *you.* I knew he'd cheat."

Travis placed his hands on her shoulders, gazing into her reddened eyes. "And we won. God is on our side, remember?"

Josie smiled. "I love you, Travis."

Travis's heart stumbled over its next beat, nearly leaving him breathless. "I love you too, Jo. I meant it when I said it minutes ago. I didn't want to die with regrets. I had to tell you the truth. No more secrets."

Josie buried her face in his chest and wrapped her arms around his waist. "I don't know how I can repay you."

Travis cupped the back of her head. "Being my true wife and staying by my side forever would be enough."

"Yes," Josie whispered, peering up at him. "A million times yes."

Travis looked down at her lips. They called to him, like a fish to water, but her dead husband was only feet away. They wouldn't have their first kiss here. It would be special, just like the day they'd call each other their own.

Chapter Forty-Five

Josie kissed each of the children goodnight twice, for she never thought she'd have the chance again. When Marcus had had his gun pointed at Travis, Josie immediately thought about her children. They already lost too much, and they couldn't lose more because of her.

Travis loved her, absolutely loved her. He didn't have to confess aloud before the duel. His actions spoke enough. However, hearing it was what gave her the confidence and faith to stand up to Marcus. Nathan would be safe in Travis's care because he loved her—and Nathan as well.

General Marcus Wellington would never interfere in their lives again. The man would never be written in history, for he had an unmarked grave that no one would ever know about. His body would decay and rot beneath the earth. However, watching the life drain from him while he cursed them both made Josie pity him for the first time. If only he had sought redemption. If only he had recognized his sin and asked for forgiveness in his final moments. Josie despised who he was, but she could never wish eternal damnation on anyone.

Josie rubbed Gideon's soft head. He was asleep, unlike his brother, with whom he shared the bed. Josie pulled the covers to Jonas's chin, and he looked at her with sweet eyes and smiled. "Goodnight, Ma."

Josie's breath caught. "Ma?"

"Is that all right?" Jonas asked, concern etched in his creased forehead.

Josie's eyes burned as her tears brimmed. She placed her hand on his cheek and smiled. "Yes," she said in a breathless whisper.

"I love you," Jonas said, snuggling under the covers.

"I love you, too."

This was a miracle—being here with her children again, all under the same roof. She couldn't bear to imagine how things might have been if the day had turned out differently. In this moment, she was the happiest woman on earth.

Josie closed the bedroom door and inhaled a deep breath. Behind the door of the master bedroom was her husband, her real husband. He loved her, just as much as she loved him. She twisted a strand of her hair and giggled softly. She remembered earlier when Travis looked down at her bashfully, as though he was contemplating kissing her. And she respected that. Josie wanted their first kiss to be special, one that would stand the test of time. She wanted to think back on their first kiss and feel warm and giddy inside. How could she feel that way, knowing Marcus tried to kill him right before?

Josie straightened her spine, standing tall. She put a smile on her face and sighed. All was over, her once-tense muscles now at ease. Behind that bedroom door was her future. This would be different than their wedding night. That night was full of lies and deceit, not of love. This night would be full of honesty and no secrets. She would give him her all, never pulling back.

With a steady hand—definitely not a trembling one—Josie opened the door. There Nathan was, snug in his crib and sound asleep. She softly shut the door, trying not to disturb him or this moment. Josie looked up at Travis seated on the bed, still dressed in his clothes from earlier, his ear cleaned and stitched up. His eyes met hers with a tenderness that softened her heart, and a gentle smile curved his lips.

"The children are tucked in," Josie said.

Travis sighed. "It feels good to have us all together again."

Josie smiled, stepping forward. "I have a feeling it will all be different for us now. Like we're more connected than ever before."

Travis stood from the bed, and Josie found herself just below his chin. His hand rose to softly touch her face, and she instinctively closed her eyes. She had never thought he would touch her this gently again, not like this. No more threats and troubles existed to keep them apart.

The question was whether they should take a chance, and Josie never wanted it more. She'd welcome uncertainty with open arms, making it her new acquainted friend. No more would she shy away from Travis. She trusted him without any doubt in her mind.

"I love you, Jo," Travis whispered, making Josie's heart thump. "After today's events and thinking I'd lose you forever, I'll never let a day go by without telling you."

Josie pulled him closer, one arm wrapped around his back and the other resting behind his neck. "I love you, Travis Blythe," she said softly, her gaze locked with his.

Hardly a second passed before Josie's dream became reality. Travis gently pressed his lips to hers, sealing their future together as husband and wife. Her first kiss—her first real kiss. She could hardly contain herself, deepening the gesture, erasing the distance that had been their constant companion since they married. There were no more gaps. No more secrets.

At last, they pulled away breathless. Travis pulled a strand of hair behind Josie's ear. "My wife."

"My husband," she whispered back, her hand resting against his chest. Then her gaze drifted down to his shirt's buttons. Slowly, she undid one, feeling heat rise to her cheeks. She glanced up at Travis, catching the sparkle in his eyes.

"Is this what you want? Truly?"

Josie pressed her lips to his then pulled back, caressing his stubbled cheek. "Yes. I want to move forward as your wife in every way. More than anything."

Travis kissed her one last time and pulled her close, wrapping his arms firmly around her waist. Without warning, he swooped her into his strong arms, causing Josie to gasp in surprise. She instinctively wrapped her arms around his neck, soft laughter bubbling. Travis laid her gently onto the bed and looked down at her with a smile.

Josie had finally found a man like no other, a rare man that was hard to come by. If Aunt Tia was alive, she'd never doubt her again. Taking the journey to Montana was worth every mile for in the end, it led her to Travis, the man who would always be hers. Until she found him, there was only darkness and fear, and now she had what she always dreamed of—a family, love, and peace.

EPILOGUE

Willow Grove, Montana; May 1873

"ARE YOU CERTAIN YOU have everything you need?" Travis asked for the third time as he placed a new reader on each of the children's desks.

Josie opened a wooden crate resting on her desk and pulled out books for arithmetic, science, history, and literature. "I am."

Her school supplies had arrived a day late, leaving much to unpack and sort before the second day of school began. But having Travis there to help had been a blessing. She and her husband had woken before dawn to organize the schoolhouse, making up for the chaos of the first day when the lack of supplies had made everything more stressful. Now, as she unpacked the last crate, a sense of relief settled over her.

"You won't have to escort us to school tomorrow," Josie told Travis, glancing up as she stacked the books by subject. The day before, he had ridden behind them all the way to town. "There's planting to be done."

Travis set his empty crate on Josie's desk and smirked at her. "Planting can wait." Taking her hand, he brushed his thumb over her skin in a slow, tender motion. "I'm going to miss you."

Josie frowned. "I'm going to miss you too . . . and Gideon and Nathan." Her heart sank at the thought. Spending the day without them yesterday had been torture. But knowing Rose was at the parsonage next door, watching over them, had been a small comfort.

Rose had advised her to wait a year or two before teaching, but Josie wasn't one to sit idle when work needed to be done—just like her stubborn husband. The town needed a teacher, and she was determined to do her best, even if it meant coming home to a pile of chores at the end of the day.

Travis lifted Josie's chin. "Let me know if you need anything. I want to help in every way I can."

"I will." Josie smiled, straightening her shoulders. "Don't worry about me. I have everything under control."

Travis's upper lip twitched before splitting into a grin. "Want me to gather some switches outside?"

Josie slid her hand across the desk and picked up a twelve-inch ruler. "I have it covered," she said with a sigh, patting it against her palm. "I just hope I won't have to use it."

Travis threw his head back with a deep chuckle before setting his hat on his head. "Boy, I thought you knew enough about children."

Josie's lips pursed, and she popped his behind with the ruler. "Hey! I never lied about that in my letter. You knew about my experience."

Travis gently pulled her wrist, closing the space between them. He pressed a firm, lingering kiss to her lips. Josie let the ruler slip from her fingers and wrapped her arms around his neck, melting into his embrace.

Travis pulled back, brushing her cheek. "I love you, Jo."

"I love you too, Travis."

The clock on Josie's desk rang, startling her. She quickly reached down to silence it. Travis tipped his hat with a smirk. "Well, I'm off, Mrs. Blythe. The wheat ain't gonna plant itself."

Josie huffed and shook her head. "The wheat *is not* going to plant itself."

Travis beamed, shooting her a wink. "Have a good day, wife. You're going to bring a wonderful change to this town."

Josie's cheeks warmed as she fought back a grin. Oh, how she loved that man. But she hated to see him leave. What would it be like now to glance out the window and not see him plowing a field? She sighed, then picked up the cowbell Jonas had bought her with his hard-earned nickels from mucking out the stalls.

As soon as she rang, the children stopped their playing and flooded into the schoolhouse. Seeing them eagerly entering made her heart melt. During the weeks of preparation, she had pinched herself countless times just to be sure this was real. She was a teacher at last, providing every child in the town with an equal opportunity to learn. Josie had thought it would be years before she could step into this role, given the town's limited funds, but with the community's support, the school had finally been approved. Josie would make hardly a cent, but seeing the children run to their seats with an eagerness to learn was more valuable than precious jewels or gold.

While the children took their seats, Josie moved to the front of the classroom and began writing her daily agenda on the chalkboard. The students' voices softened to whispers, just as she had instructed the day before. They were to use their inside voices upon entering and remain quiet unless called upon. Being the early stages of the school year, Josie was certain they'd grow tired of etiquette and eventually challenge her authority, but she liked to think positive.

Josie turned to face the classroom and clapped. "Students, please turn to page three of the readers on your desk."

The sound of pages turning ruffled through the classroom, but when the door opened, their attention shifted. Two boys stepped inside. The first was tall and lanky compared to the other who was much shorter. They removed their hats, waiting patiently for Josie to acknowledge them.

"Good morning. My name is Mrs. Blythe, the teacher," Josie said with a welcoming smile as she approached them.

"Me name's Jeremy O'Leary," the taller one with dark curls said in a thick Irish accent, looking no older than sixteen. The other boy stood beside him, reserved and quiet. "And this here's me brother Francis."

"Nice to meet you boys," Josie said. "We are all glad to have you both."

Josie hadn't seen the boys before and assumed they must have been new settlers coming into Willow Grove. According to Travis, the spring and summer months always brought new settlers from the east, but all the way from Ireland was a different story. The only Irish settler was Ronan, and he came from Boston with Caroline.

"Francis, how about you sit in the front by my son, Jonas. Jeremy, you may sit by Miss Alice Walsh to the right of you."

"Andy," Josie called, looking at the reverend's son, who was seated on the front row with his brother, Paul. "Would you read the first sentence to us?"

Andy nodded, straightening in his seat, and prepared to read aloud. As he spoke, Josie's gaze drew to Alice and Jeremy. She noticed how Alice moved a bit closer to him than the other children did with their desk partners, giving him a bright, gleaming smile. Jeremy peeked back at her, mirroring the smile with a hint of shyness. Josie couldn't help but giggle inside as she watched the scene unfold. It seemed she would have more than just misbehaving children to deal with; a new romance was blooming in Willow Grove.

Aknowledgements

First and foremost, I'd like to say thank you to my Lord and Savior, Jesus Christ, who died on the cross so the world can be saved. I fall short of serving and obeying the Lord as I should, and I am undeserving of His grace and mercy. However, Jesus saw me as worth dying for. Thank You for allowing me to publish another book. I pray You will use me to encourage someone with uplifting fiction. Without You, there would be no story to tell. I give You full honor and glory, God.

To my husband, who believed in me when I spoke about my fears writing a gritty western. He has been there for me from the start of my career, cheering me on. I would also like to say thank you for helping me write my villain scenes. It's hard trying to write someone so complex and evil, and having you there to bounce ideas on was very helpful. I am thankful you are nothing like General Marcus Wellington, and you have shown me nothing but love and appreciation.

To my family, I'd like to say thank you for the love you show me. This past year has been a challenge with my life changing in many ways, and you have been the encouragement and help I needed.

I'd like to say thank you to the local bookstores and libraries who have taken time to host book events and stock inventory of my books. Your support has been a great blessing to me.

To my editor, Leah Taylor, thank you so much for your support, encouragement, and assistance. You have been an amazing help in my publishing journey, and I am thankful to call you my friend. Your advice, friendly gestures, and editing skills do not go unnoticed. Also, I'd like to say thank you to my mother-in-law, Devonna, who helped me proofread.

Lastly, I'd like to say a huge thank you to my street team and publishing team who have done awesome jobs with marketing and the publication process. They may not have put the words on the page, but they know how to make them come alive with their excitement and skills. You guys know how to make a writing day special.

To my beta readers, Wyeth, Fadia, Samantha, Parker Jane, Audrey, Eva, and Dory, thank you so much for your feedback and insight. This book has gone through many changes and revisions to better the plot because of you.

AUTHOR'S NOTE

Dear Reader,

I believe *What You Can't Lose* was the most challenging story I've written thus far. Not only had it been difficult to write, but it went through many stages and changes. About eight years ago, I had the idea to write a western story inspired by the classic *Sarah, Plain and Tall*. One of my favorite tropes is the blended family and marriage of convenience, especially when it comes to western literature.

I found the notes on my phone in the summer of 2023 and sought to bring the story to life. However, the ideas I originally found were cliché and overused—a woman escapes an arranged marriage, goes out west, and must marry for protection. I wanted something original, something unique with twists that readers didn't expect. I'm not a fan of predictable fiction, so I strive to create plot turns that readers do not see coming.

I prayed over the story, and God placed a topic on my heart that is sensitive—domestic violence. Though I have never been a victim of domestic abuse, there are many close to me who have walked that dark and painful path. Josie's story is inspired by survivors, and my hope was to create a narrative that speaks of courage, redemption, and the healing that only God can bring.

Domestic abuse in the 1800s was tragically common, and women had very few rights to protect themselves. Many suffered silently with no legal way of escape, relying only on the Lord for strength and deliverance. If the Lord had not been looking out for Josie, she would have been trapped in a lifetime of torment. I wanted to write about a woman who, despite fear and oppression, leaned on God to fight her battles. Josie's faith became her anchor, a reminder that even in the darkest nights, the Lord is a refuge and a defender of the oppressed. Through her story, I pray readers see that God still rescues, restores, and gives beauty for ashes.

The other topic I wanted to cover was grief. I have experienced loss in my life, but it wasn't until last year, when my family lost someone very dear to us, that I truly understood the depth of that pain. Loss and grief have a way of drawing us closer to one another and, more importantly, closer to God. Even though much of this book was written before that season, I found myself sympathizing with the characters in a deeper way. You never fully realize how precious something—or someone—is until you face the reality of losing it.

But thanks be to God, we have a hope that cannot be shaken. Through Christ, we are offered salvation and heavenly treasures far more precious than gold. One day we will reunite with our loved ones and worship our Savior forever. This world is not our home, and what we can never lose is the eternal life promised to all who believe.

As the Scriptures remind us:

> "The Lord is nigh unto them that are of a broken heart; and saveth such as be of a contrite spirit." (Psalm 34:18)

"Fear thou not; for I am with thee: be not dismayed; for I am thy God: I will strengthen thee; yea, I will help thee; yea, I will uphold thee with the right hand of my righteousness." (Isaiah 41:10)

"Come unto me, all ye that labour and are heavy laden, and I will give you rest." (Matthew 11:28)

"And God shall wipe away all tears from their eyes; and there shall be no more death, neither sorrow, nor crying, neither shall there be any more pain: for the former things are passed away." (Revelation 21:4)

May these promises be a reminder that no matter the suffering we endure on earth, God's love remains steadfast, His deliverance sure, and His eternal home waiting for those who trust in Him.

With Love,
Mikayla Robbins
Email: mikaylarobbinsauthor@gmail.com

For those who enjoy

Mystery & Suspense

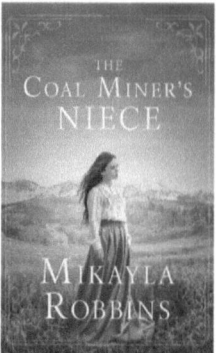

The Coal Miner's Niece
by: Mikayla Robbins

Some secrets are better off forgotten...

After surviving the devastation of the Great Chicago Fire, Mary Hawkins awakens to a world she no longer recognizes. Her memories are lost, stolen by the flames that engulfed her past. However, her confusion deepens when a mysterious mountain man claims to be her uncle, taking her on a journey to a secluded mining village in the wild Colorado frontier.

As Mary struggles to piece together her shattered identity, her uncle remains silent, withholding answers about her past. But as time goes by, she is tormented by vivid nightmares, shadows taunting and afflicting her, making her wonder if they are either dreams or memories.

When the opportunity arises for Mary to reclaim her place in Chicago society, she is torn between her desire for answers and the comfort of her newfound home—and the boy she has come to deeply care for. But as she delves deeper into the shadows of her past, she uncovers buried secrets, leading her to realize that the truth may be more sinister—and far more dangerous—than she ever imagined.

For those who enjoy

Civil War Fiction

Abide with Me
by: Mikayla Robbins

He left to join the war while she fought the one in her heart…

In 1863, the beautiful Southern belle, Christy Mayfield, wrestles with her heart as her once peaceful world is ravaged by bloodshed. Raised in a world of innocence and propriety, her life takes a turn with the arrival of Trenton McLain. While Trenton appears to be a Southern gentleman, he is tainted by the sins of his parents, but Christy chooses to accept him for who he is. As their romance blossoms, the borders become threatened, causing Trenton to enlist.

Levi McLain, Trenton's bashful and awkward cousin, has loved Christy since the days of their youth, though she only sees him as a friend. When Trenton rides off to battle, Levi sees an opportunity to win her heart. That is, if it's not too late.

As the war threatens to demolish Christy's world, she must reconcile her fading innocence with the harsh realities she now faces. Desperate to save her family's home, she is put into a position of pondering Levi's offer for a marriage of convenience. The echoes of war reach further than the battlefield, striking deep into the heart of love and loyalty.

For those who enjoy

The Victorian Era

MIKAYLA ROBBINS

the
CHOSEN

The Chosen
by: Mikayla Robbins

She was chosen for a life every woman desired but her.

After rescuing a wealthy family's young son, Anna Martin is favorably chosen to become his wife when she comes of age. As a decade passes, romance develops between Anna and a man below her station, complicating the arrangement. When she learns that despite her feelings, she must marry her betrothed in two weeks, her world crumbles.

Collin Nicholson is embarrassed that his father chose a wife for him. After years of hard work to take over the family business, he has no intention of settling down—until he reconnects with Anna. Captivated by the girl who once saved him, Collin grapples with his feelings, torn between his desire for Anna and the knowledge that she loves someone else.

Both Collin and Anna struggle with whether their marriage is God's will or merely their parents' design. Can they learn to love one another in an unwanted marriage and accept the destiny set before them, or will they abandon it altogether? *The Chosen* is a story of love, heartbreak, secrets, deception, betrayal, and the road to redemption.

For those who enjoy

The Roaring Twenties

The Favored
by: Mikayla Robbins

Her inheritance is guaranteed—if she can marry in time. As the clock ticks, the cost of wealth may be more than she's willing to pay.

Margaret Nicholson's life is turned upside down when her estranged grandfather names her heiress of his fortune. After years of hiding from society, Margaret must develop social skills and find a suitable husband before her twenty-first birthday or lose her inheritance. As she enters her grandfather's world, suitors line up to compete for her hand in marriage, but only a newly entitled British marquess catches her eye.

Roger McKinley, a former passionate poet, has suffered since he returned from The Great War. Feeling guilty and responsible for his brother's tragic death, he finds himself in a repetitive routine, working during the day as an accountant for the Nicholson Building & Loan and reliving his war trauma at night. When Margaret enters his life, defying the traditional roles he'd always expected women to play, she unsettles his routine, awakening feelings he thought were lost.

As time ticks by, Margaret finds herself torn between societal expectations and her own desires. While working as a secretary, her heart is captivated by a troubled accountant, yet she is also being wooed by a charming marquess. With her inheritance on the line and her birthday approaching, Margaret must unravel the mystery of her heart and decide which path to follow before it's too late.

Sign Up for Mikayla Robbins's Newsletter

Scan the QR code below to keep up to date with Mikayla's latest news on new book releases and events by signing up for her newsletter.